RUN FOR HOME

Sheila started work at fifteen as a presser in Hepworths, a tailoring factory. She married at eighteen and had three daughters: Dawn, Janine and Diane and a younger son, Michael. Recently divorced, she now has eight grandchildren, and every Saturday and Sunday can be found at a football match for the under tens and under fifteens.

Sheila has lived on the Homelands Estate (at present with her son and two dogs) at Houghton le Spring near Sunderland for thirty years.

Praise for *Run for Home*

'Quigley's gripping thriller, *Run for Home*, is a convincing portrayal of a violent underworld' *Independent*

'Fast-paced and overtly commercial, *Run for Home* is a modern version of Cookson's best-sellers' *Telegraph Magazine*

'A rattling good plot . . . it does't stop running until the final page by which tme you will be breathless' *Newcastle Upon Tyne Journal*

'A fast-mc

W

Run for Home

SHEILA QUIGLEY

arrow books

Published by Arrow Books in 2005

1 3 5 7 9 10 8 6 4 2

First published in the United Kingdom in 2004 by Century

Arrow Books
The Random House Group Limited
20 Vauxhall Bridge Road, London SW1V 2SA

Random House Australia (Pty) Limited
20 Alfred Street, Milsons Point, Sydney,
New South Wales 2061, Australia

Random House New Zealand Limited
18 Poland Road, Glenfield
Auckland 10, New Zealand

Random House (Pty) Limited
Endulini, 5a Jubilee Road, Parktown 2193, South Africa

The Random House Group Limited Reg. No. 954009

www.randomhouse.co.uk

A CIP catalogue record for this book is available
from the British Library

Papers used by Random House
are natural, recyclable products made from wood grown in
sustainable forests. The manufacturing processes conform to
the environmental regulations of the country of origin

ISBN 0 09 946574 4

Typeset by Palimpsest Book Production Limited,
Polmont, Stirlingshire
Printed and bound in Germany by
GGP Media GmbH, Poessneck

My thanks go first to my agent Darley Anderson; I sent it to the best and the best came through. Second, but second to no one, my publisher Susan Sandon. And thirdly, to Kate Elton who must be the hardest working editor in the business. And let's not forget the rest of Random House, fantastic every one of you. Also Julia and Lucie, of the Darley Anderson Literary Agency, two great girls.

Prologue

Sixteen Years Ago

78778877735.

Jack was running. A huge beast of a man, with an open friendly face and wild flowing black hair, his feet crushed everything they landed on. He felt no pain in his mad dash for life, even though he knew that he'd been shot. Blood flowed freely down his side, warm, wet and slippery.

He grimaced, biting into his lip. He'd give those bastards a right run for their money though, poxy-faced twats, the whole fucking bunch of them. And when they finally caught him – *cos let's be under no illusions here, Jack old son*, he told himself as he pounded on, *catch me they will, I'm a dead man – aye, why I'll spit right in the fucker's face.*

Pushing groping branches out of the way and dodging countless molehills, he seemed to gain a few yards. Not enough to stop, though . . . No way.

He bit down even harder, drawing blood as he forged on. He was far from an angel, he needed nobody and nobody's aunt to tell him that. For fuck's sake, Ma had been telling him that since for ever. But he had his limits. In his book there was things yer did, and things yer didn't. And offing women and kids was one of the latter.

He heard them gaining, and stretched his long legs

3

to the limit, but he had nothing left to give. His strength was going, oozing out of a hole in his body. He wondered vaguely where the little fucker of a bullet had lodged itself, and sighed. He could feel the blood pooling around his waistband now and felt a crazy urge to stop and scratch.

What would it be? His body in a shallow grave here in flaming Fatfield by the fucking River Wear, his head in The Man's trophy cabinet? *Cos make no bones about it, Jack, there's only one reason why The Man sends the Head Hunter, and that surely ain't to talk some sense into yer noggin.*

He'd well and truly blown it all right, when he'd refused to off the kid. He'd looked the curly-haired little bastard in the face, and what had he gone and done? Put the fucking gun back in his bastard pocket, that's what. A statement on its own. He'd watched the change come over The Man's face and had known it would only be a matter of time.

A duck, screeching and flapping out of the water, nearly stopped him in his tracks. 'Fucking hell, bastard bird,' he screamed, as his heart somersaulted right into his throat.

Managing to stop himself from falling by grabbing hold of a thick spiky branch, he went on, but each painful step was slower than the last.

Ten years he'd known The Man, and counted him a friend. He should have known better; the likes of The Man had no friends. For fuck's sake, it's not as if he hadn't seen the bastard off people for disagreeing with him before. But in all those years he'd never seen him become so obsessed with one woman. Not content with wasting the woman's husband, the mad fucker had wanted to waste the kid an' all. An A1 fucking psycho if ever there was one.

If Jack had possessed the strength to shake his head at the sheer stupidity of his coming death, he would have shaken it that hard the bastard would have fallen off.

He was flagging now, he knew it. His feet were beginning to weigh a fucking ton.

And he could hear them getting closer, could practically smell the sweaty bastards.

He'd got out of Houghton le Spring ten minutes after they'd dropped him off, all smiles and 'see yer later's. The fucking two-faced twats. If he hadn't took the time to kiss his ma, and grab a few clothes, he might have made it. The black-hearted bastard must have made his mind up to set the chase off as he was saying good night to her, telling her he'd be home later.

All of two miles he'd managed, two friggin' miles. Fucking Fatfield, of all the fucking places to die.

He'd spotted them following him just as the traffic lights over the bridge had turned red. He'd kept on going, but so had they. He'd taken the corner beside the Biddick pub fast, nigh on a two-wheel job. And if the fucking ugliest cat in creation hadn't decided to cross the fucking road, he might have made it. Swerving to miss it had cost him dearly; they'd caught up and tried to ram his car into the river.

If he ever got out of this . . .

Don't hold yer breath, son.

He stopped for a moment.

Only a short time.

Catch a breath.

'Ow, yer bastard!' he yelled, as a second bullet entered the top of his leg and exploded out the other side.

Looking down, he saw the mess of blood, flesh and bone, and at once felt sick, vomit sick. The kind of feeling that just drains the shit right out of yer.

That's it, I'm fairly fucked now. Can't run no more. He sank to the ground. *Ain't never gonna get up from here, mate. This is it.* He bit down hard on a sob.

For a moment he was out of it, only a glint in time really.

When he opened his eyes, the Head Hunter was grinning down at him, muddy fingers slowly rubbing up and down the cruel blade that had been used time and time again, the curved blade with the Chinese symbols embedded in the ivory handle. Up and down the fingers went, up and down.

Any moment now he would feel the bite.

He took a breath, nearly his last.

If he regretted anything in those last seconds, it was that Ma would sit for hours beside the fire, kettle on the boil, waiting for the fish and chips he brought her every Friday night.

When the Head Hunter bent down to take him, he found himself fascinated by the strands of hair that had somehow woven themselves into her long silver earrings. Her face came closer and her breath caressed his lips. For a moment he thought she was going to kiss him.

'Bitch,' he hissed.

She grinned, a satisfied leer that turned her into a spiteful parody of a woman.

Jack's only consolation, as he stared death in the face, was that he'd worked up enough spit to do just what he'd promised himself.

The Present Day

Monday

1

Kerry was running, her long legs a blur as she pounded up Newbottle Street, past the site of Houghton Pit which was now a reclaimed grassed-over area, and on towards Grasswell.

All of her papers were delivered now, and the two bottles of milk she'd nicked banged dangerously together every time the newspaper bag bounced off her hip.

She reached the garage at the top of the hill and headed downwards, into Grasswell. Turning at the fish-and-chip shop on the corner, she ran down the terraced street to her goal, the last house. Without breaking stride, she snatched the bottle from the step just as old Mrs Holland's groping fingers felt for it.

'Well, fuck-a-duck, Blackie,' Mrs Holland said. 'I could have sworn I heard the bloody milkman.'

Pulling her baggy green dressing gown around her thin frame, she squinted and looked blindly up and down the deserted street. The cat, a ginger stray which had taken the real Blackie's place two days after he'd been squashed flat by a double-decker bus, wrapped his body around her legs.

'For God's sake, Blackie, don't say me ears is going the same way as me eyes.'

The cat purred.

Shooing him in, Mrs Holland closed the door and felt her painful way down the hallway. She patted a piece of wallpaper that was coming loose. 'Have to tell our Jack to get this clagged back on, Blackie. Can't afford no new wallpaper, not on the measly pension the government expects us poor folks to live on. Anyhow,' she patted it again, 'this is pretty enough.' She had no idea that the once bright flowers had now faded to the depressing colour of late November leaves.

Around the corner, Kerry stood with her back against Mrs Holland's wall. She had already downed two thirds of the pint and was taking a breather before finishing the rest. Raising her leg and putting her foot against the bricks, she rested the hand holding the bottle on her bare leg, and with her other hand brushed her dark ponytail away from her shoulders. Her blue eyes peered out from beneath a fringe in dire need of cutting, and studied the Seahills Estate neatly laid out in front of her. It stood a field away from the rest of the town, as if the planners had left room for something else. Or more likely, as Kerry always thought from this viewpoint, so that the bloody place was quarantined from the rest of Houghton.

Kerry hated the Seahills, every bit as much as she hated her near breastless chest. She hated it as much as she hated her mother, who was having a long-term affair with the bottle – although it wasn't as if she was faithful to a certain kind. Oh no, not her; any bottle would do. Kerry hated her siblings – well perhaps not Robbie so much – and she certainly hated every bugger else who lived on the damn estate. In fact, at the moment Kerry hated everyone and everything she came into contact with. She especially hated anyone who had even the slightest hint of breasts. Jesus, Jason Smith had bigger breasts than she did and he was a bloke.

All she was interested in was her dream of one day running for England. God, then she would be miles away from the fucking Seahills.

From here she could see the rooftops of Tulip Crescent, where her used-to-be-friend Andrea lived. Kerry snorted. They'd been friends until Andrea decided she liked boys; Andrea and the rest of them in her class, like a bunch of bitches in heat. Thank God Kerry was now sixteen and would only have to put up with their blatant eyelash-fluttering and lip-licking for a few months longer.

She raised the bottle to her lips, and suddenly a voice she despised over all others said, 'Give us a drink then, Kerry.'

Turning her head, she glared at the pair standing there and curled her lip.

'In yer dreams, Pig Face,' she said, resisting the urge to spit the rest of the milk at them.

Stevie Masterton's face slowly turned a violent shade of red, which contrasted beautifully with his silver nose- and eyebrow-rings – two in one eyebrow, and one in the other. Not so long ago, Kerry had ripped the missing one out. Stevie had not forgotten.

Martin Raynor, whose face was permanently red anyhow because of the raging case of acne he was cursed with, grinned. At seventeen, he was a year older than Kerry and a year younger than Stevie.

Stevie moved closer. 'Just trying to be friendly, like. Got a fucking problem with that, have yer?'

'Fuck off, shit for brains. Yer wouldn't know friendly if it stood up and slapped yer right in yer ugly mug. And you, Fartin' Martin, on yer bike.'

Stevie sneered, while Martin ground his teeth together. A joke in assembly a few years ago had landed him with a nickname he hated.

Quickly, Kerry downed the rest of the milk. Then, menacingly, she raised the bottle over her head. She wasn't frightened of them. Like most bullies, they were cowards at heart. Anyhow, if push came to shove she could have another one of Stevie's rings out and be off before they knew it. Outrunning these two creeps would be easy.

Stevie took another step towards her then, remembering the pain he'd gone through the last time, said, 'Fuck you, bitch. Come on, Martin, she's not worth the hassle. Are yer, titless?'

Kerry raised the bottle higher. 'Fuck off before I stand on yer.'

Laughing, they broke into a trot and headed up towards Houghton.

Kerry was fuming; her breasts, or rather the lack of them, were a very definite sore point. These days it seemed that every girl she knew was, if not already fully formed, most definitely sprouting.

Sighing, she looked down at her chest. Her very flat chest. Not that she hadn't already checked this morning, but she lived in hope.

Nothing.

'Bastards,' she muttered.

With a face guaranteed to scare the hardiest of folks, she threw the empty bottle over Mrs Holland's wall. Gleaning a small shred of satisfaction from the sound of breaking glass – but fervently wishing it had been Stevie's head – she headed for home.

'Hope there's some of that left for me,' said Kerry's eighteen-year-old brother Robbie, as he walked into the kitchen yawning and scratching his bare armpit. It wasn't hard to see that he was Kerry's brother. With their brilliant blue eyes and black hair, and the same long legs and lean frame, both of them favoured their mother in looks and build.

Seven-year-old Suzy giggled; she too had the same build, but that was as far as the resemblance went. Robbie patted her fair head affectionately as he reached for the milk and she giggled some more. Eight-year-old Emma – small, chubby, and by everyone's account born anti-social – moved her head towards Robbie for the same pat, then pushed her red curls back into place. Meanwhile, eleven-year-old Darren threw his brother a don't-you-dare look. Darren was thick-set and football mad: if Kerry dreamed of running for England, Darren's own fantasy was to play for Sunderland. His black hair was gelled into a spike, and his eyes were even darker than his hair. His skin was also a shade or two darker than that of the rest of the Lumsdon tribe.

Thirteen-year-old Claire wafted in on a cloud of cheap perfume, immediately setting off Emma's asthma. Her almost-white hair was covered in pastel-coloured butterfly clips. She too had the family's long legs, but with more weight to her frame, and she looked and acted with the confidence of someone way beyond her age. Claire was strikingly beautiful, and she knew it. She'd been thrilled when she passed two of the Seahills' gossips the other day and heard them call her jailbait. She studied her wheezing sister with supreme indifference.

'For Christ's sake, Claire.' Kerry rummaged in the drawer for Emma's inhaler. 'You're stinking the whole bloody room out.'

Claire glared at Kerry with venom in her eyes before snapping, 'Well, if there was ever enough hot water in this shit-hole for a bath every day, I wouldn't have to cover meself in this cheap stuff, would I?'

Robbie cringed and looked away. Claire was seriously courting trouble, and lately she'd been pushing Kerry more and more. He knew it was only the fact that Kerry was out training most days for the county running championships that had stopped her from going for Claire by the throat.

He looked back at Claire when she threw a letter at him and said sarcastically, 'Giro day at last. I thought it would never come . . . I take it we'll have more than stinking tomatoes on dry toast today.'

Turning from Robbie, she picked up one of the remaining glasses from the bench and swallowed the milk. Then, with all the arrogance of a thirteen-year-old who knows it all, she left without a goodbye for any of them.

Robbie pulled a face at Kerry that raised a half

16

smile. 'Wow, was that a skirt, or was that a skirt?'

Kerry shrugged. 'I think the silly cow puts another hem in every week.'

Her eyes, however, had not been on her sister's hem, but on her chest, where she was sure she'd seen signs of growth. 'Damn.'

'What?' Darren said, as he passed her and reached for his glass.

'Nowt . . . Anyhow, who was talking to you, Nerd.' She slapped the back of his head.

'Ow.' Darren rubbed his head, and checked with his fingers that his hairstyle had not been messed. 'What was that for?'

'For being a horrible nosy little rat. That's what for.'

Darren pulled a face behind her back before downing his milk. He glared at Emma's grinning face, threatening her with a fate-worse-than-death look if she told Kerry on him. Emma sniffed loudly, and stuck her tongue out.

Kerry glanced quickly at the clock and realised they were all going to be late again. She turned to Robbie. 'Finish sorting this lot out, will yer? I'll go up and change. Make sure,' she pointed at Darren, 'our scruffy here gets washed. He seems to think that if he gels his hair nobody will notice his dirty little mug.'

Darren was just about to come back with a quick retort when he got a slap round the ear from Robbie. 'Ow, what was that for?' he asked indignantly. In his book, he hadn't done anything wrong. Not this time.

17

'Guess . . . Come on now, move it.'

Grumbling, Darren moved to the sink, where he washed his hands and face.

Five minutes later, Kerry had changed into her school uniform – which was becoming far too small, in all the wrong places. But with only a few months to go before she left, there was no point in buying a new one. *Like there's even a fat chance of that*, she thought, hurrying down the stairs.

Ushering Darren and her two sisters out the door, she slammed it hard enough to raise the whole street. Her sole intention, though, was to get the attention of her mother.

Robbie winced when the door slammed, knowing full well who it was aimed at. His mother and Kerry had not got on for a long time now. Sometimes, when he heard Kerry having a go at her, he thought she hated their mother, and more often than not lately he found himself unable to blame her.

He closed his eyes, then tore open the envelope he was still clutching. Holding it at arm's length he counted to ten, then opened his eyes. The usual amount, thirty-nine quid, mocked him. 'Once again you have not miraculously changed into a grand in the post,' he muttered, as he threw the Giro in disgust on to the brown, chipped coffee table.

The coffee table wasn't the only chipped item in the 4-by-3½ sitting room. Everything Robbie looked at seemed to have a chip in it somewhere, from the fake brown wood running up the sides of the green three-piece to the stained skirting boards and the window ledge, although the floor-length green and brown curtains hid most of those. The plastic red flowers in the mottled green vase in the window were a joke. He'd thrown them out once but Suzy had rescued them from the bin.

He shook his head; he tried to keep on top of things, but seven people constantly bumped off each other in the tiny council house, making it practically impossible to keep it even vaguely tidy.

Picking up the TV remote, he thought of Suzy's face when she'd squashed her feet into her shoes earlier; it seemed she was growing faster than any of them. *Looks like a job for the lifters*, he nodded to himself. With a bit of luck she might have a new pair to come home to. Red ones, Suzy loved red. *Have to see what's going on in the food department as well. It'll cheer them all up, even Madam Muck Claire, if there's something tasty for tea.*

The old TV set finally warmed up. Kilroy was on his soapbox again, and muggings seemed to be the order of the day. Robbie hated muggers, especially the cowards who picked on people who couldn't fight back. He was always amazed at the folks who bared all when appearing on these shows. The Americans were the worst. Last week, one cheeky slapper with half of her head shaved, and a face full of gold studs, openly admitted to the world that she'd slept with not one brother but three.

He listened as a young skinhead wearing the latest Nike gear casually admitted to mugging an old woman and shook his head in disgust, remembering a few months ago when he'd bought himself a whole load of trouble by stopping Stevie and his sidekick, Fartin' Martin, from mugging old Mrs Holland when she'd left Newbottle post office on pension day. Now that had been weird all right. Seeing what they'd been about to do, he'd stepped between them without thinking, and old Mrs Holland and her jam-jar glasses had sauntered on past, blissfully unaware that she'd very nearly been attacked. He'd faced up to the snarling pair, knowing full well that he was not, and probably never would be, the fighter that Kerry was. Kerry would have launched herself at them first, then asked questions later; she'd been doing the self same thing since she could walk.

Not really knowing what to do, he'd stood watching them advance on him and then, as if someone up there had finally answered one of his prayers, a huge black man with a glinting gold tooth had appeared out of nowhere, and yanked the pair of creeps right off their feet.

He smiled to himself. That had been good to see all right; the man had shaken them like a terrier shakes a rat, then after banging their heads together, he'd thrown them into the gutter as if they'd been less than shit on his fingers.

While they'd floundered around in the gutter the man had looked at him, smiled, and said, 'Go.'

He hadn't needed to be told twice; he'd legged it for home, and sworn when he'd got there that he'd beaten Kerry at her best. Stevie and Martin hadn't bothered him since, but he had a feeling it was coming sometime soon. Their very silence was threatening.

'Still an' all,' he murmured out loud as he focused back on the TV screen, 'I bet Kilroy can live on thirty-nine quid a week.' He sniggered. 'Why aye, in a pig's arse he could.'

'Who yer talking to?'

Robbie looked up as his mother dragged herself into the room.

'Kilroy,' he answered, his eyes scouring her from head to foot.

'Answered yer back yet, has he?'

He watched as she lit up a cigarette and immediately began coughing her lungs up. The white bathrobe which swamped her, a present he'd bought last Christmas via the shoplifters, was a dirty grey, full of thrown-up dinner medals. He loved his mother to bits, but looking at her today he had to agree with Kerry: Vanessa Lumsdon was one hell of a mess.

He sighed inwardly, but she sensed his disdain.

'What's the matter, sourpuss?' Vanessa pulled her robe tighter, then took another draw on the cigarette, this time managing to keep the coughing at bay. 'Well?' she demanded.

Robbie felt like ignoring her and tried for a moment, but he couldn't. 'What's the point, Mam? Yer keep asking, and we tell yer, but it makes no difference, does it? Whatever me or our Kerry say, yer dry out for a week tops, then yer back in the same mess yer in today.'

Then, feeling lousy when he saw the hurt look on her face, he rummaged for the remote which had worked its way into a pile of dirty washing on the seat next to him. Finding it, he held it like a gun and shot Kilroy, pleased to be rid of him. He didn't know who was doing his head in the most, Kilroy or his mother.

But she was a mess, and if she wasn't careful the drink would kill her. She had been beautiful once, his mam, but now . . . What the hell, he couldn't take her looking at him like that any longer. Jumping up, he ran upstairs and quickly washed, then shrugged into some semi-clean jeans and rubbed at a spot on his blue shirt until the stain could hardly be seen, before racing back down. Last time he'd left the Giro on the coffee table it had mysteriously gone missing, with no one in the room but his mother.

To his relief, the Giro was still where he'd left it, and so was she, idly blowing smoke rings.

'Er, son . . .'

Robbie frowned. He knew what was coming next, it was the same thing week-in week-out. He waited though, still feeling awful about what he'd said a few minutes earlier.

'I . . . I need some cash. Just till I get me money on Friday. There's not much left, and the kids need . . .' Her voice was wheedling now. He hated for her to be like this, he hated having to look after his mother as if she was the child and he the adult, but she did the same thing every time, as if it was just a one-off. And he would do the same as he always did too.

'Mam, yer know I'll get some grub in.' Walking over to her he patted her shoulder. Her hair, which was long and in desperate need of styling, felt lank and greasy under his hand. He could have cried at the state of her. The booze and the fags, which seemed to be a permanent extension of her fingers, had done this to her. She looked easily twenty years older than she was. The shame of it, though, was that if she made the effort, she still cleaned up real good.

'Look, Mam, I'll get yer tabs, and a half bottle from one of the smugglers. I think Dixie's lot just got back. But . . .'

She looked up, wondering what he was going to say, and knowing without a doubt that whatever it was, she was not going to like it.

Deciding that something drastic had to be done to stop the slide she was on, Robbie took a deep breath and tried to be stern. 'Mam, I . . . *we* want yer to clean yer act up.' He looked into her dark eyes and at the darker skin underneath them, skin that looked almost bruised. Then, as if someone else, someone like Kerry, was inside his head telling him what to say, he cried, 'For God's sake, Mam, have yer seen the bloody state of yerself? Yer couldn't blame anybody for thinking yer was a hundred and ten. Yer look like a bag lady, an old scruffy bag lady that hasn't got anybody. But you have, Mam, you've got us.' Desperate to make her understand, he left her staring up at him as he turned and ran upstairs to the bathroom, returning a moment later with a cracked mirror. 'Look!' He thrust the mirror into her hands.

His own hands were shaking as he took hold of Vanessa's chin and raised her face up to look at him. 'If yer don't sort yerself out, Mam, you're gonna die and leave us all. And how can me and our Kerry manage the kids, Mam? How can we? They'll take them away. Put them in different homes, and none of us will ever see each other again. Then we'll all be up shit creek. Can yer imagine our little Suzy with a bunch of strangers? Can yer, Mam? She'd never cope.' He shook his head in despair, as his voice rose higher. 'And what about Emma, eh? How long do yer think Emma would last? She aggravates the life out of *us*, for God's sake, let alone folk who aren't even family . . . And Darren, imagine him miles away in a new school, when he's already made his friends? Think about it, Mam.'

He wanted to shake her, anything to make her see sense. Unused to allowing himself such outbursts, but knowing that every word he'd said was true – they were words he'd wanted to say for a long time but hadn't had the heart, nor the courage – he practically whispered when he said, 'Do yer want that to happen, Mam? Do yer?'

'But, but—' Vanessa started to say.

'There is no buts, Mam!' Robbie slammed his fist down on the coffee table, then felt like a right bastard when his mother jumped in fright. But there was no going back, not when he'd gone this far. 'Bottom line, Mam. If yer don't start today, yer getting nowt from me. We can't go on like this any more. It's like us kids is watching yer kill yerself . . . Like it's suicide or something. This time I mean it, Mam. We've all just about fucking well had enough.'

Face burning, and blinking hard to stop the tears, he turned and walked out. He'd said what he had to say and it had been a long time coming, but that hadn't made it any easier, nor made him feel any better. He was tempted to slam the door on his way out of the house the way Kerry often did, but he'd never possessed Kerry's temper, nor the power to sustain it.

For a long time after Robbie had gone, Vanessa stared into the mirror.

He's right, she thought, as her features slowly swam into focus and she looked at the ravages the booze had caused. She tried to smooth the deep lines that ran from the inside corners of her eyes to her mouth. Her face was so thin. Jesus, she'd always had high cheekbones, but now they stood right out, and were horribly sharp. Her hands started to shake and she threw the mirror down. Its fall was cushioned by one of Suzy's cuddly toys, a red monkey that lived under the television.

She bit her lip to stop herself crying, but the tears came thick and fast anyhow. *He's right. For God's sake, he's right. Look at me, look at the fucking grey hair. Jesus Christ, I'm thirty-nine and I look more like fucking fifty-nine. How long have I binged this time? A week? A fortnight?*

The shakes got worse, and her thoughts more frantic. She knew she needed a drink.

Where the fuck did I hide the last bottle?

Did I finish it?

There's got to be some left somewhere. Got to be. Got to find it.

Trembling, Vanessa went upstairs. Frantically, she began to tear the few items of clothing she possessed out of the wardrobe in case she'd stashed something there, but found nothing. She yanked hard at the top drawer of her cheap dressing table, splitting a nail right to the quick but not feeling it as she desperately pulled the other drawers out, scattering their contents all over the place. Crawling on all fours to the old battered pink wicker chair in the corner, she practically tore the cushions off it, then crawled back to search under the bed.

Nothing.

Sitting on the edge of the bed, she began rocking back and forth as she hugged her arms around herself. God, if only she could blot out the pain. But whenever she was sober the floodgates opened and the hated memories poured back. She wanted to tear at her hair, and had to grip her elbows hard to stop herself, her fingernails biting into her flesh.

None of them knew. The things she'd seen, the memories she'd had to live with. The nights were the worst, always had been, that was partly the reason why she'd sought a little company now and then just to ease the nightmares. Someone to hold her when the bottle wasn't enough, just like she'd held Robbie and helped him through the bad years. It was a while since she'd heard Robbie cry out in the night and she was terrified to ask him if he too still had the nightmare. And the fear, always the fear. A tear dripped down the premature lines on her face; she left it, it was one of millions.

She would never stop crying. For her there were only two ways out: the bottle or death.

She sobbed and let go of her elbow to stuff her

hand into her mouth, because the next sound would be a scream, and if she once started screaming, she would never stop.

She was still rocking and biting into her fist ten minutes later when she heard a bang against the window. Gasping, she clutched her robe. Her heart was pounding, burning acid clawing its way up from her frightened stomach, her lungs snatching at air suddenly gone thin.

This was it. She'd waited long enough. For a brief moment she almost welcomed what was coming; it had been a long sixteen years.

The sound came again, and with an almost reluctant intake of breath it dawned on her that it was the window cleaner. As she came back to reality, she finally noticed her nail, which at once started to throb.

'For fuck's sake. The bastards already want a month's money. Fat fucking chance.' She glared at the nail.

Holding her hand to her chest to ease the throbbing, Vanessa rummaged through the pile of clothes on the floor until she found her black skirt and green blouse. She sighed. *I suppose it'll look to the kids like I'm at least trying if I get dressed.*

She ran a bath and stepped into it, then hesitated a moment. *Is it Monday?*

Gritting her teeth, she slowly eased her tired body down. *Course it's Monday, Robbie got his Giro.* She nodded as she sloshed tepid water over her head, then quickly ran a soapy sponge across her breasts, pretending to herself that she couldn't feel her ribs.

Shivering and covered in goosebumps, she got out

of the water. 'Damn,' she said out loud, reaching into the airing cupboard. 'The only friggin' clean towel in the house would have to be Kerry's.'

Does she have training tonight? Vanessa wondered, holding the towel up in front of her. Then she shrugged. *Gotta fucking use something.*

Drying as quickly as she could with one hand, she hung the towel over the radiator. Robbie will probably bring some coal in, she told herself. It'll dry in no time, and Kerry will be none the wiser.

Kerry, Kerry, Kerry. She flopped down on to the toilet. For a moment she'd actually felt a little better, but any thoughts of Kerry always drained her. It seemed that all they ever did was fight. Putting her elbows on her knees and resting her head in her hands she sighed, a deep end-of-the-road sigh.

Let's be honest, it isn't a teenage thing. Me and our Kerry's been fighting ever since the little cow could talk.

Why couldn't she be more like our Robbie?

Stupid question from a stupid drunk. How the fuck could she? Different dads. Like the rest of them, all by different dads.

'What a fucking mess,' she said to the once pink, now threadbare carpet. 'If me own mam could see me now, she'd turn in her friggin' grave.

'Everything's turned out the way that evil bastard planned. Poor Robbie, the same doors are as closed to you as they've always been to me. Every job, everything you've ever tried for. Poor bairn, the council wouldn't even set yer on as a road sweeper.' She swiped at more tears.

To feed two kids, I had another four, and if it wasn't for them, I'd have ended this stinking existence years ago. I might just do it now. Put meself out of this fucking misery.

'God,' she suddenly said through chattering teeth. 'Got to move now or they'll all come home to find me naked and frozen stiff on the loo. If I'm gonna do it it won't be where the bairns can find me. That would keep the Seahills in gossip for a month at least.'

Quickly she dressed, noting that the blouse could have done with an iron over it. She shrugged. *Who's gonna look at me now, anyhow?*

Downstairs, she collected the dirty clothes and put them in the washer. *Robbie will think I'm really trying.* She picked up the soap powder box but, finding it empty, threw it at the wall. 'Damn and blast, there's a fucking shock.'

Stomach churning with the need for a drink, and all thoughts of housework fast drifting away, she slouched into the sitting room, lit her last cigarette and flopped on to the settee. Teeth clenched until her mouth was nothing more than a grim line, so that the scream she felt building up inside of her couldn't escape, she turned the TV back on.

2

Claire hid in the alleyway at the bottom of the street, giddy with excitement. Getting to sleep had been a hard job. She'd been certain that Kerry the witch had sussed that something was up, what with all the tossing and turning she'd done, especially with the two of them in the same bed.

Lucky for me, she thought, *that the witch sleeps like a log. Close call this morning though. She certainly gave me the once-over – for a minute back there, I thought I'd grown a zit the size of a mountain. But I'm free now, and all I've got to do is wait here until Kerry and the brats are long gone.*

Her heart skipped into overdrive as Kerry, with the kids trailing behind her in single file, strode past. Claire bit down on a giggle. For God's sake! If Kerry was dressed in white and the brats in yellow, she'd look like a mother duck with her babies.

Another few minutes, that's all, make sure none of them's forgotten anything. Claire's skin tingled as a surge of adrenalin rushed through her young body.

Freedom loomed in front of her, and its scent was intoxicating.

A second later, though, she had to stifle a scream when she felt something on the back of her hand

and looked down to see a fat brown spider crawling towards her sleeve. If there was one thing Claire hated it was spiders, especially fat brown spiders that were heading for openings that would lead them to her body. She'd once had one trapped in her knickers when she was seven and had suffered nightmares for months.

'Oh Christ.' Shuddering, she shook her hand hard enough for the spider to drop off. Revolted, she tried to dance on it, but Mrs Spider had other ideas and scuttled away.

Face twisted into a grimace, she looked up the alley just in time to see fat Jason Smith and his black-and-white collie, Jess. Dogs Claire could take at any time, especially Jess, who just lived to be petted. It was her master Claire didn't like. She didn't like the way he looked at her either; even when she'd been smaller his eyes had seemed to single her out from the other kids. Creepy Jason Smith, he looked like he'd be more at home with a snake draped around his ugly fat sweaty neck than with a dog at his side.

Claire froze as Jess stopped and sniffed the air; if the dog sussed her out, so would the King of Creeps.

She took an exaggerated side-step which put her behind the fence and, once there, pulled her mobile phone – a present from the delectable Brad – out of her pocket to check the time. Still a few minutes left before the Sunderland bus arrived. The phone was on her top-secret list, and she kissed it before slipping it back into her pocket.

Deciding she had enough time for a make-up check, Claire drew her compact – another present from Brad and also on her top-secret list – from her other pocket. She covered her lips with a bright red lipstick, and her cheeks with a blusher only slightly paler. Satisfied with her appearance, she pocketed the compact then, fingers crossed, began a slow walk up the alley.

Ecstatic because her escape plan was working so well, she forgot herself and began humming the new Robbie Williams song, then nearly had a heart attack when she almost stepped out in front of her own Robbie Lumsdon.

Hastily, and with a pounding heart, she slipped back as Robbie, frowning at the ground and obviously angry with somebody, walked quickly past.

Damn. Bumping into Robbie had not been part of the plan.

Wonder which way he's going? If I miss the bus Brad will be in a huff all day.

Cautiously, Claire shuffled back out, unconsciously imitating the spider she'd tried so hard to squash a few minutes earlier. Good, he was heading up Tulip Crescent. Must be on his way to Houghton; if he turns right at the top he's cutting through the homelands.

When he did turn right, she punched the air and mouthed a great big *Yes!* Skipping across the road to the bus stop, she smiled sweetly at Dolly Smith, Jason's mother, and old Mr Skillings. Dolly looked down at her through thick brown-rimmed glasses – everything on Dolly's sixteen-stone frame was brown, from her head to her toes – and after giving Claire the once-over, she turned back to dapper Mr Skillings and continued her conversation.

Claire leaned forward to listen in on the gossip, which centred around last night's stabbing outside the Blue Lion pub. Mr Skillings gave Claire a smile before reminding Dolly that there had been more than one stabbing outside the Blue Lion, and plenty of beating-ups inside the place too. Dolly, defensive about the fact that her son worked at the pub with the worst reputation in Houghton, sniffed angrily at him.

Claire was relieved when the bus came a moment later; less risk now of the pair of them deciding to turn their attention to her. But even as she boarded it she realised that the previous night's drug raid in Daffodil Close was next on their agenda, and what she might be up to was way down on their list of topics.

The bus took ten minutes to reach Newbottle, and when Dolly and Mr Skillings got off at the post office, neither had missed a beat nor stopped for breath. Armed and ready with all the latest news, the pair joined the queue. What the folks of Newbottle had not already learned for themselves this morning, they were about to find out.

Each long minute of Claire's journey to Sunderland was filled with thoughts of Brad. She'd met him a little over a month ago, when she and her best friend Katy Jacks had been at Washington bowling alley. She'd had to run hundreds of errands to the shops for the neighbours to save up the money to go bowling even once a month, so her heart had fairly dropped when, after chatting to her and Katy for over an hour, Brad had left and said he would see them there again the next night.

'What we gonna do, Katy?' she'd wailed on the

way home. Katy had shrugged for, although both of Katy's parents worked, she'd often told Claire what a tight-fisted pair they were. Then she'd come up with a lifeline. 'We could stand outside, like. Get there real early, and pretend it's too hot inside and we don't feel like bowling tonight.'

Claire had thought this one over and decided that, short of robbing a bank, it was the only thing they could do.

The next night, excited to death but playing it really cool, they'd got there early and watched as Brad arrived. The bright red sports car he'd climbed out of had left them both with their mouths hanging open, and they'd nudged each other and tried hard not to giggle as he'd walked up to them.

Far from slow, Katy had realised almost at once that Brad's smile had been purely for Claire and, after nearly an hour of being ignored, she'd decided to go home, refusing to let them walk her to the bus. If Claire was honest, she hadn't behaved too well to Katy, not that she could help it; goosebumps had covered her from head to foot each time Brad had smiled at her, and he'd smiled a lot.

Once Katy had left, Brad had taken her for a ride in the sports car. They'd gone right along the coast to sit on the rocks at Roker Beach and watch the tide come in, then back again to Seaburn. It had been the best night of her life. And when he'd finally kissed her, she'd known that she was in love with him, and would be for ever and ever.

Katy had been quiet all the next day at school, and a bit standoffish. It had lasted another day, then she'd come round and now delighted in finding out each day what had gone on the night before.

Only nothing had ever really gone on. All they'd ever done was kiss, and then never enough for Claire. Every time she saw him, with his blond good looks and broad shoulders, her legs – as if possessing a brain of their own – went all weak, and begged her to lie down and open up.

She and Katy had been given detention last week for giggling at this confession. Neither girl could wait for the big day, and they had faithfully promised each other that, whichever one lost it first, every detail would be shared.

Claire had a feeling that today was the day, perhaps after the modelling job he had lined up for her. That's why she was playing the nick; some friends of his had seen them together and asked him why a looker like her wasn't already modelling for a living. When Brad told her she'd been thrilled to bits, and she'd harassed him to death to set up this photo shoot, as he called it. Of course she'd promised to do her best to get Katy in on the action, cos Katy was quite good-looking if yer ignored her too-long nose, then both of them would be rich and away from the Seahills.

The bus pulled into Park Lane bus station. Craning her neck, she spotted Brad standing across the road. Her body thrilled at the sight of him. Quickly she jumped off the bus and ran across the busy road.

He was smiling his special smile, and Claire's heart flipped. Then the smile faded slowly, like a dimmer on a light switch.

'What's that shite doing on yer face?' he demanded, in a very un-Brad voice.

Claire's fingertips went to her lips, and her heart, so happy a few moments earlier, plummeted. He had never spoken to her like this before; sometimes he'd acted as if he wasn't really there, and snapped at her a little for wanting to neck on a bit more, but never like this. Confused, she wondered what she'd done wrong.

'I thought you'd like it. It does say in all the mags that models have to wear strong make-up under the lights. I thought that's what yer bought me the compact for.'

'Yeah, well, them magazines is a pile of crap, they daresn't print what men really want. I like my women bare faced. Here.' He shoved a paper handkerchief at her. 'Spit on it, and wipe that friggin' mess off.'

Claire's face was now as red as her lipstick. Haltingly, she did as she was told.

'That's better.' He nodded when she'd finished. 'Come on then,' he hurried her, 'we've got people waiting.'

He smiled, and her face answered. Happy again, she slipped her arm through his then looked around. 'Where's the car?'

'It had to go in for a service. Anyhow, it's not too far.' He smiled, showing a predator's perfect white teeth and, like the lamb she was, Claire happily smiled back.

Leaving Park Lane they headed down past the museum, from where it was a ten-minute walk to the Hendon docks. They drew quite a few stares on the way and for some reason this seemed to put Brad on edge. 'Couldn't yer have changed out of that bloody uniform,' he snarled at her. 'It looks like I'm fucking cradle snatching.'

'But yer said yer were dying to see me in it!'

'I meant for yer to bring it, not parade around in it. Look at all the fucking nosy bastards staring at us.'

Claire shrugged, quite put out by his attitude; he wasn't usually like this. And he'd never sworn at her before. 'So?' she said, with a sway of her hips, pretending that she didn't care. 'Let them look.'

'So! Is that all yer can say? Yer stupid cow. Yer look like jailbait in that gear. Anyhow,' taking hold of her elbow, he hurried her onwards, 'gotta move. These people ain't gonna hang around for ever.'

'But I thought yer said they had a studio,' she said, struggling to keep up with him.

'They have, stupid. But cos it's such a nice day they thought some shots by the boats would be cool.'

'That's great.' She cuddled into his arm, as she pictured herself on the cover of *Hello!* magazine. In her mind's eye, Kerry was holding the magazine and her face was green, green, green.

Reaching the docks, and escorted by a squadron of kamikaze seagulls, Brad led Claire to a small fishing boat that rocked on its own, at least two hundred yards from the other boats. The whole place seemed to be deserted.

She tingled with excitement. How much would she get paid? And wouldn't Kerry just burn up with jealousy when she walked into the house and threw real spending money on the table.

They were nearly there now, and Claire could see two hefty-looking men standing by the boat, which was looking more and more like a wreck the closer they got. Both men wore navy-blue woollen hats, dark jeans and thick navy coats. She thought they looked more like fishermen than photographers. The smaller of the two was carrying a thick piece of rope that he twirled through his fingers.

'What took yer so fucking long?' the man holding the rope demanded when they reached them. Claire felt Brad's hand tighten on her arm. For a moment she felt a faint twinge of unease.

Brad had felt her muscles momentarily tense, but he could play his women well. He smiled at her as he gently squeezed the arm he held. Claire's fears fled. This was her man by her side; hadn't he sworn he would always love her and that they would be together for ever?

'It's all right, Claire, just get on the boat, there's a good 'un.'

Claire looked quickly around. 'But where's the cameras? You promised there would be cameras.'

The man holding the rope interrupted her with a huge belly laugh. 'Cameras, is it? Oh dearie me.'

There was something about him that Claire didn't like. The prickly feeling in the small of her back returned as he climbed on to the boat and held out his hand.

'Here, lovie, get yerself on here,' he sniggered, his top lip curling. 'Move it, the cameras are inside. Honestly.' The last word was said so sarcastically it practically threw itself out of his mouth.

Claire was nobody's fool, she knew a lie when she heard one. She began to back away, then she felt Brad's hand on her back. She froze, and sensed his breath on her neck as he whispered, 'Yer better do as yer told. I really don't want to see anything nasty happen to yer now.' As he pushed her towards the boat, the man leaned forward and grabbed her arm.

'No . . . no!' she yelled, throwing herself backwards. 'Brad!' She spun round so quickly she twisted her ankle, and falling hard she hit the concrete, taking tennis-ball-sized strips of skin off both knees.

The pain from her knees competed with the pain from her ankle then, when she looked and saw the blood, the knees won. Screaming, she was faster to her feet than any of the men had expected. Terrified, and suddenly feeling all of thirteen instead of the sixteen she'd pretended to be, she made a gallant bolt for freedom.

But the man with the sinister laugh was quicker than her. Jumping off the boat, he grabbed her round her waist, lifted her into the air and threw her on board. Frightened nearly to death, sobbing her heart out but determined not to give up, she reached up and grabbed the side of the boat to haul herself up. When she looked over the edge, the three men were standing together. Brad was holding his hand out and the taller man was busily filling it with fifty-pound notes.

'Brad! Brad!' she yelled. But he simply looked at her and smiled, before pocketing the money and walking away.

'Noooo!' she screamed in terror as the two men climbed into the boat.

But before she had time to scream again, she was yanked up and pushed into the small cabin.

Then she froze, the pain in her knees forgotten. For now it was the turn of her eyes, which were open so wide that they hurt.

Two other girls were already there.

Both of them were naked.

Both had their hands and feet tied with the same sort of rope that the man who had thrown her on to the boat still held in his hands.

Both of them were staring right back at her, wearing the same terrified expression.

Jade watched the new girl as she was pushed into the tiny cabin, and saw her own fear reflected in the girl's eyes. She had been on the boat since yesterday, conned into a modelling assignment by her new boyfriend. Some boyfriend.

Jade was sixteen years old and about as black as a person could get; she was also stunningly beautiful, with adopted parents who had adored her since she'd entered their barren lives at three months old. They'd listened to her dream of being trained as a model, simply telling her to be patient and trust that everything she wanted would eventually come to her.

Yeah, well, she hadn't been patient, had she? No, not her. She'd jumped like the idiot she was, at the first chance . . . only it had turned into a nightmare. The problem was, she didn't know where the nightmare was leading, but from the few words the pair of freaks who held her had let slip, she had a rough idea. It didn't look good for any of them.

She wished with all her heart that she'd listened to her parents.

Laughing Man, as Jade had nicknamed him, stepped into the cabin behind the new girl. Jade knew what was coming next and she cringed, pulling her knees into her stomach.

Claire had no idea he was there until he grabbed her shoulder and spun her round to face him. She tried to step back but there was nowhere to go. Suddenly he drew his right hand back and slapped her hard across her face. While she was in shock he savagely yanked her skirt with both hands. The button popped off and the zip burst; it was around her ankles in seconds. One meaty hand parted her thin white panties from her body.

'Yeah,' he laughed. 'A genuine blonde all right.' Reaching round with both hands, he squeezed her bottom.

She screamed and he slapped her again. 'Shut the fuck up, yer noisy friggin' bitch.'

The second slap had a different effect; it made her suddenly aware of the very real danger she was in.

She had to get away.

Get out and get help for these other girls.

Here he comes.

As he moved to take her jacket, shirt and bra off, she lunged forward, bringing her head up at the right time and catching him under his chin.

It was his turn to yell out in pain, and a moment later Claire regretted what she'd done as he attacked her in a frenzy, raining blows on her shoulders and chest and forcing her to the floor. The attack only lasted seconds, thank God, ending when the second man forced his way into the cabin and stopped his friend.

'What the fuck are yer doing? That's good merchandise and yer know better than to damage it, for fuck's sake!'

Tight-lipped, Laughing Man bent down and quickly tied Claire's wrists together. She lashed out with her left foot, catching him on his shin and at the same time finding her voice.

'Fuck off, yer dirty pervert! What do yer think yer doing? Let me go!' She pounded the floor with her feet. 'Brad, Brad!' she screamed, but Laughing Man, although there was no smile on his face now, quickly recovered, and with a snarl grabbed her ankles and had them tied in seconds.

'See what she's like,' he complained to his friend. 'Got to be the worst one yet . . . and there ain't no Brads around here, yer bitch, so just shut the fuck up.'

'Fuck off, yer ugly bastard.' She began hitting the floor with her heels again. 'I want to go home.'

The man grabbed her hair, knocking butterfly clips every which way. 'Listen, girlie,' he practically spat, as he yanked her face up to his. 'Believe me, I know lots of other ways to hurt yer, ways that won't make too much of a mess on that white fucking skin of yours.'

He put his left hand on the back of her neck, forcing her face even closer to his, then covered her lips with his own. Claire struggled as hard as she could, but he was much too strong for her. When he'd finished, he shoved her down next to the other two girls. 'Now learn a lesson and shut the fuck up, cos where you're going there'll be plenty of that.'

Laughing again, he left the cabin.

'Ohh, ohh!' Claire spat and spat. 'The filthy disgusting pervert. He stinks. And he stuck his tongue in me mouth, and his breath . . . argh!' She shuddered. 'The fucking creep. God, I want to be sick.' She went on spitting.

Tracy, a redhead with sparkling green eyes that became almost colourless when the light caught them in certain ways, let out the sob she'd held in as long as she could. Claire's outburst had finally penetrated her numbed brain and woken her up to the mess she was in.

'I want to go home,' she wailed. 'I want me mam! I want me dad!' She looked at the other two, her lovely eyes wide with despair, tears running down her pale face. 'His name was Billy. He told me he was gonna make me a singer. He said . . .' She bit down on a sob, was quiet for a moment, then went on. 'He said I sounded just like Tina Turner, and that the world was ready for another singer like her.'

Claire nodded. For the moment she was more interested in the pain she was feeling from her knees, ankle, shoulder and breasts. Her left knee was still bleeding and a slow trickle ran down her leg.

Jade looked at Tracy. Ever since she'd been thrown into the cabin last night and found another girl cowering in the corner, she'd tried to get her to talk.

But the girl had been in such a state of shock that Jade feared she'd lost it permanently.

It was what she said next that caused the prickles to rise on the back of Jade's neck. Tracy began to babble. 'I don't know what they've done to the other girl. I'm only fourteen, yer know . . . Oh God, me mam will kill me when the police find me with no clothes on.'

'What other girl?' Jade asked sharply.

'What?' Tracy looked at her.

'The other girl, you just said there was another girl.'

Tracy thought for a moment. 'Yes, she was here when I got here. They raped her. Over and over.' She started sobbing again.

'Oh Jesus.'

Claire had taken stock of her injuries and now she was able to take in what the other girls were saying. 'What do yer mean, another girl? Where is she now?'

Tracy ignored her and moaned, 'Billy said he loved me, said we'd be rich off me singing and we'd go all over the world.' She nodded her head in confirmation.

'Seems to me,' Jade said, 'that the three of us have let ourselves be taken for right mugs, and that we're in a big pile of shit.'

Claire nodded slowly, then banged her fists on the wall. 'I saw the other man give Brad a whole lot of money. The bastard's sold me. That's what he's done, he's fucking well sold me.' She began to beat the floor with her heels again, biting her lips to stop herself from screaming.

Tracy stared as Jade did her best to comfort her.

After a while Claire calmed down slightly, enough to beg Tracy to tell them exactly what had happened to the other girl.

'Don't know really. They just dragged her out and she never came back.'

Claire and Jade looked at each other. They were silent for a few minutes, each thinking of the horror stories they had heard about the strange men you must keep away from. Stories they had each learned at their mothers' knees. Stories that could never happen to them. Not in a million years.

Then Claire moaned, the long drawn-out sound a trapped animal makes when it realises its life is almost over.

3

Sandra Gilbride closed her gate behind her. 'Fucking joyriders,' she muttered as she looked up and down the street before stepping on to the road. 'Not safe crossing outside yer own fucking door these days.'

Sandra didn't care who she huffed or who she pleased, nor who heard her opinions. She'd been known to chase the pop man up the street on more than one occasion and give him a right tongue-lashing for driving too fast round the estate. Now he passed her gate with extreme caution, as did most of the people who owned cars on the Seahills.

She was a small dainty woman with a serious liking for very high heels, which she wore from getting out of bed in the morning to getting back into it at night. Her wavy brown hair was worn in a plait that hung halfway down her back, her eyes were light brown. She had been a pretty girl as a teenager, and at thirty-nine summers was a pretty woman.

As she crossed the road, the plastic bag she carried swung at her side. It was stuffed to bursting point with clothes that were now too small for her Clayton, but would fit Darren, one of her best friend Vanessa's kids, a treat. Clay, cute little bugger that he was, had also generously said that Darren could have his navy-blue Nike jacket, seeing as how his own lovely mam was buying him a new one for his birthday.

She smiled to herself. Guess he'll have to have one now.

Darren was two years younger than Clay, and although Sandra had four boys of her own, she'd always had a soft spot for Darren. Darren and little Suzy. And the rest weren't bad kids, actually they were quite good, considering some of the fucked-up spoilt brats around here. Claire was starting to get a cheeky head on her, swanning around as if her muck didn't stink, but Kerry would soon bring that little madam back down to earth.

Her own boys now, weren't they something to be proud of?

Her chest stuck out as she reached the kerb. Wasn't her oldest Grant doing just great for himself, learning to be a chef down in London and phoning home every night at eight on the dot? And her lads were never out on the streets after dark causing havoc on the estate, unlike a few others she could mention – and quite frequently did, whenever the opportunity arose. One minute late and she was out looking for her boys, and God help the little sod who didn't have a real good excuse.

Reaching Vanessa's gate, she prayed that her friend was sober – she'd realised that Vanessa had gone on another bender when she hadn't come over on Friday night. Sandra had done her best to keep her off the booze and had stuck by her all these years, but she knew that things sometimes became unbearable. And when reality closed in, as it did more often than not, Vanessa had to escape somewhere. Sandra knew more than most about her friend's problems. She knew they all stemmed from one cruel man, and what had happened all those years ago. What she didn't know, and didn't want to know, were names. Names were dangerous, and as much as she loved Vanessa and her brood, she had to protect her own.

Her own husband, a gem if ever there was one, had once asked her why she bothered; she'd given him one of the scathing looks she was famous for, and he'd never asked again.

She was halfway up the path when she heard the row coming from next door. *Christ, not again.* Stopping, she looked at the window and then, remembering the other week when in more or less the same situation she'd narrowly missed being beheaded by a flying chip pan, she moved hastily on to the porch.

The couple who lived there had only moved in a few months ago, shortly after old Mr and Mrs Ord had finally got the bungalow they'd been after for years. Strangers they were, and all anyone really knew about them was that they hailed from Silksworth. And cars came and went at all hours of the night. The speculation as to why was rife.

Also, when the place went up like it obviously was today, it was the lad who got the beatings, not the lass. His frequent black eyes were already a legend. The poor lad always smiled if he bumped into yer in the street or wherever, but Lady fucking Muck, with her bleached blonde hair gelled back like a lad's, wandered around with her nose in the air like she was a fucking heiress or something.

Shaking her head, Sandra opened Vanessa's front door and walked straight along the passageway to the kitchen, where she put the kettle on. Then, shouting loud enough for anyone in the loft to hear her, she called, 'It's only me, I'm making us a cuppa.'

Reaching into her carrier bag, she took out a small jar of coffee. Two for the price of one at Morrisons, so she'd treat Vanessa to the free one. Beside the coffee she put a small medicine bottle filled with milk and prayed there was some sugar in the house. After a bit of searching she found just a few spoonfuls, but enough for a couple of cuppas.

Coffee made, and the rich smell following her, she carried both cups through into the sitting room, not sure whether she'd find Vanessa there or have to go upstairs and drag her out of bed.

But she was there. Thank you, God. And dressed an' all. Always a good sign.

Smiling, Sandra put the coffees on the table and looked at Vanessa, then suddenly realised she was staring oddly at the television.

'What's the matter, mate?' she laughed. 'Yer look like you've won the lottery and lost the fucking ticket.'

Vanessa didn't answer. She just kept on staring, even when Sandra moved in front of the television. 'Come on, love.' She leaned over and gently touched Vanessa's shoulder. 'Yer freaking me out here, Vanny.'

It was several heartbeats later before Vanessa finally moved her head and tried to focus on Sandra.

Her face was paler than the milk her daughter had stolen an hour ago. She looked like she'd been dead for a week, as she muttered, 'Six toes. Fuck.' Then repeated twice more in rapid succession, 'Six toes. Six toes.'

'Six toes? What the hell are yer on about, pet?' Sandra turned and looked at the television, where the newsreader was just fading away to be replaced by the adverts. 'What's got six toes?'

Vanessa pointed at the television. Sandra looked at Vanessa's shaking hand, then back at her face. She watched as her friend wet her dry cracking lips with a tongue that looked absolutely dreadful, and shook her head. She'd seen Vanessa in some pitiful states, but never this bad. She'd gone so white she looked like she was in shock.

A moment later Vanessa fainted.

Robbie whistled as he walked down the street. He was on his way home and feeling quite pleased with himself; he'd had a good morning and there was still seventeen quid left in his pocket. His two carrier bags were overflowing with food, Suzy's shoes were paid for and delivery was imminent, and the big family tin of salmon for fifty pence was a bargain – so what if it wasn't the best brand, a bit of extra vinegar would flavour it up. Salmon sandwiches, tinned peaches and custard for tea would put a smile on even Claire's miserable face.

A new pair of running shoes, shorts and vest were ordered for Kerry, and guaranteed at less than half the original price, and if they came before next dole day – unlikely cos the lifters would have to find a specialist shop in Durham or somewhere – well, he could tick them on. No way was Kerry going to the Durham trials without the right gear. She'd look every bit as good as the kids from the posh schools. Robbie grinned to himself. Them posh kids wouldn't see Kerry's arse for dust, she'd burn the whole bloody lot of them off.

The Broadway, a large paved area with St Michael's Church on one side and the council offices and Houghton park on the other, had been buzzing with talk of a body found at Fatfield this morning. According to his best mate Mickey, who had sworn on his mother's life that it was true – seeing as how he'd heard it second hand from a friend of his who'd heard it right from the horse's mouth – the body had been there for God knew how many years and had all but rotted away. Nowt much left but a pile of bones. It had only been found cos all the rain had caused the riverbank to crumble.

The lad who'd found it had been out lampin' all night with his dog. Of course he hadn't told the coppers that, and he'd had a hell of a job to hide the three rabbits Duke had caught before he'd phoned the coppers on his mobile. But Mickey, always one to milk the drama out of any situation, his black curls bobbing and his dark brown eyes alight with news, had sworn again on his mother's life that the dead bloke had six toes on each foot.

Just as Mickey had said this, Dean, an old school-friend who carried seventeen stones on his short frame, had pounded into view, although they had actually heard him before seeing him. Nearly everyone stopped and watched, and moved quickly out of the way. He was being chased by a security man from Timpson's shoe shop and a beat copper. He'd winked at them as he'd passed, then run into the park.

A few minutes later, the copper and the security man, both red-faced, out of breath and narked to death, had come out of the park. A few steps behind them and wearing a bright red dress, had been a very fat girl with long blonde hair and Dean's face. The girl had strutted past them, fat stomach wobbling enough to burst the dress, and winked. He and Mickey had just about fell off the seat laughing. Both of them knew that Dean's Uncle Joe was head gardener for the council, and that Dean kept his disguise – unknown to his uncle – hidden in the back of the gardener's shed. A disguise that had come in handy more than once.

Still smiling at the memory, Robbie turned into his street. He said hello to Mr Skillings, who lived three doors down from them and kept the kids in sweets by sending them to the corner shop at least two or three times a day. But instead of his usual greeting of 'All right there, son,' he said, 'Everything OK at home?'

'Yeah . . .' Robbie was on his guard at once. 'Any reason why it shouldn't be, like?'

Mr Skillings shifted uncomfortably from foot to foot. 'It, er . . . it's just that when I passed earlier, Dr Mountjoy's car was outside of your house. Course, he could have been at them nutters next door to you. They were shouting their heads off again this morning.'

But Robbie didn't hear Mr Skillings' last words. Heart in his mouth, he was already racing home.

Stevie and Martin walked along Newbottle Street to the Blue Lion. Stevie had already popped a couple of pills this morning and the flush was showing on his face. Martin lagged behind, starting to regret ever getting involved with Stevie Masterton.

The Blue Lion had been a dump for years. Dirty windows, peeling paint, an overwhelming sense of decay – everyone knew it was the roughest pub around. If there was a scam going on, someone in the Blue Lion was sure to know about it. Martin curled his lip in distaste as they stood outside.

'What the fuck's the matter with you?' Stevie demanded, when Martin made no attempt to enter.

Martin shrugged and took a step back. He was frightened of Stevie, but when he weighed it up, he was more frightened of his father, plus he was fed up watching Stevie go off his head. It was every day now and he was getting deeper into shit to pay for his habit and dragging Martin along with him.

'Come on, we're gonna be quids in working for her. She sent for us, yer know.' Stevie puffed his chest out. 'Jason Smith said we had to be here by half-past eleven. And it's fucking well that now. This wife won't wait for nobody. She eats people like us, so fucking well hurry up, Fartin'.'

Martin shook his head as he backed even further away. 'I'm not coming in.'

'Yer better, or I'll fucking shove yer shoes right down yer gizzard.' Stevie was high and king of the hill. Grinning, he reached for Martin.

But Martin was fitter and faster and, his mind made up, he took off, leaving Stevie snarling at anyone who looked at him.

'Who fucking needs yer, yer useless prick?' he muttered and, turning, he pushed open the door of the Blue Lion.

Mrs Archer was standing behind the bar, her eyes taking in every movement as Stevie crossed the space between them. She was very tall for a woman and stick thin, her long red bottle-dyed hair rolled in a french pleat at the back of her head. She was decked out in masses of gold jewellery – heavy chains around her skinny neck, several large rings and dozens of bangles. Stevie looked at the bracelets weighing down her scrawny wrists: hadn't his stupid mother, the silly cow, nicked a couple when she'd cleaned here? His dad had got the clout for that, then he'd come home and kicked his mam all over the house. It had been hard to tell who had the biggest black eyes. The stupid bitch hadn't got a cleaning job anywhere in Houghton since.

He reached the bar. Silently, Mrs Archer looked him up and down, and for a moment he felt the way a woman feels when stripped by the eyes of an over-sexed creep. He shuddered, and the moment passed. Not meeting her eyes, he thought, *She doesn't have to open her mouth. Her ugly mug says it all. She thinks I'm a fucking dog turd.*

Then, earrings dancing from side to side, she

motioned with her head for him to follow her into the back room. Feeling as full of himself as if he'd passed some sort of secret initiation test, Stevie strutted after her.

Once in the room, Stevie looked around him. The place was full of dull browns and shadowy greys, the floor bare stone and carpet-less. A large desk took up most of the space, and the only chair sat behind it. On the wall behind the desk was a safe. On the wall to the right of him was a large mildew-stained mirror.

Mrs Archer sat on the chair, opened a drawer in the desk and took out a joint. She lit it up, held the smoke for a long time, then smiled as she exhaled through her nose.

Stevie stared, both frightened and excited. This woman's reputation had followed her from her origins, Hendon in Sunderland, all the way to Houghton.

For a moment his fright turned to fascination as she sucked the life out of the joint.

'Here.' She smiled again and offered him the joint which he took eagerly, thinking, *This is one woman who should never fucking smile.*

'Thanks.' He passed the joint back, nervous of touching her fingers.

She put the joint out and sat back in her chair, still staring at him. If she was trying to skitz him out she was doing a hell of a job.

Finally she spoke, and he jumped. 'So how's that fat thieving cow of a mother that birthed yer?'

Stevie dry swallowed, his confidence sinking fast.

He was in desperate need of a pick-me-up, and soon. 'She, er, she—'

'She's fatter than ever, so I hear. The ugly cow.'

Stevie held allegiance to no one, least of all his parents. But Mrs Archer managed to make his fucking bald dog of a mother look like a fucking beauty queen. *Jesus, does the woman never look in the fucking mirror?* Terrified of upsetting his future boss in any way, he gave her a weak smile and began to fidget.

'Hmm.'

Never once taking her eyes off him, she leaned forward and, making a steeple with her hands, rested her bony chin on her long fingers. Stevie froze.

'OK,' she said finally, her mind seemingly made up. She opened a drawer and took out a small clear plastic bag, the kind with a re-sealable top, and threw it on the desk. 'These are freebies.'

'Cool.' Stevie, eyes alight, reached eagerly for the bag.

His hand was swiped away. 'Not for you, yer stupid moron. Yer give them to the kids. Eleven- and twelve-year-olds. Got that?'

Unable to take his eyes off the bag, Stevie nodded enthusiastically.

'No younger than that, mind. There's something special coming for the babies.' For a moment she fell quiet as she smiled to herself. Then she looked at Stevie and smirked. 'And, moron, not the ones already hooked, OK? See if yer can fucking well remember that. It shouldn't be too hard to tell, you'll know exactly the ones to look for – the furtive ones, those with their hoods up, the ones that can't look yer in the eye unless they're already high.'

She paused again, this time running her tongue over her teeth. 'I want fresh meat, eager little beavers. By Friday I want their sticky little hands full of money and begging for more.'

'But—'

'But what, moron? You gonna tell me the schools is all fixed up, is that it?' Her eyes glittered, and her smile came again. 'It's your job to un-fix them. The Newcastle lot have had it their own way with our kids for too fucking long. Time the locals took over.' She stood up. 'Got that?'

She didn't wait to see if he had got it or not. Instead she walked past him and opened the door. 'From now on yer deal with Smith. He'll tell yer where and when.' She threw the bag at Stevie, who only just managed to catch it without fumbling.

'You'll notice these have an elephant stamped on them. A bigger kick, see?' She gave him a full-blown smile, and this time Stevie cringed visibly. 'Right then, fuck off, moron.'

His head practically scraping the floor as if she were old-time royalty, he backed out of the room.

4

Detective Inspector Lorraine Hunt of Houghton CID was blonde, beautiful and looked less like a police officer than should have been possible. She ran a tight ship at Houghton police station and was respected throughout the force, by male and female colleagues alike. Undercover, she was magnificent: the right clothes, a wad of chewing gum, some bright red lipstick, and she could be taken for a silly young woman out for what she could get. A bit more make-up, and she was the perfect pro. Smart suit, hair scraped back off her face, a pair of thick-rimmed glasses, and she was the perfect secretary.

She was also a karate black belt.

As Lorraine sat behind her desk eating her lunch, a sad lettuce-and-tomato sandwich, she worried alternately about the body found in Fatfield and the fact that her marriage was fast going down the toilet.

She was forced out of her ruminations by a heavy knock on the door. Before she could swallow, the door opened and PC Carter, a young man with ginger hair and innumerable freckles, stuck his head round. 'I think yer should know, boss, that they've searched the area thoroughly and there's still no sign of the head.'

Lorraine put her sandwich down and rubbed the bridge of her nose. 'That's just great, that is. And I suppose it's common knowledge by now about the six toes. I can't see the lad who found the body keeping that to himself, can you?'

'No, boss. It's . . . er—'

'What, Carter?'

'It's already been on the news.'

'For fuck's sake.' She swiped the desk with her arm, knocking a pile of paper clips on to the floor. 'And I bet it was all over the Broadway this morning seeing as it's Giro day. Any mention of the missing head?'

'No. It's a good job the lad didn't see the top half of the body.'

'Good, see that it's kept quiet. I can't believe it – that's the fourth this month. If Joe Public finds out that bodies with their most important parts missing are turning up just about everywhere, we'll have a full-scale panic on our hands, even though the last one's been dead at least fifteen years. Still, we might strike lucky with this one. Six toes isn't something you see every day.'

'You can say that again, boss.'

'It might just be our lucky break. A baby born with an extra toe on each foot would have been the talk of the town when it happened.' She thought for a moment. 'So get down to Sunderland hospital and get digging.'

'Sure thing, boss.' He left, and Lorraine picked up her sandwich. She looked with disgust at the soggy mess. 'Jesus Christ. A metal stomach couldn't digest this lot.'

Dropping it down on the desk, she sat back and laced her fingers together behind her head. Why were the bodies turning up now? After a moment she said to a brown stain that had been on the ceiling for ever, 'Got to be all the rain we've had lately, it's hardly let up for months.'

Frustrated, she brought her hands down and began tapping her nails on the desk. *But why no heads?*

Ritual killings?

Revenge?

Executions?

She was interrupted by the telephone and, guessing at once who it was, she answered it with a smile on her face for the first time that day. 'Hi, Mam. How was Canada?'

'Oh, getting psychic now, are we?' said the voice on the other end.

'No, Mam. Simple deduction. I am, after all, your favourite detective. In other words, I knew what time your plane was due in.'

'Clever girl. It was actually on time for once. And Canada was wonderful. Everything all right here?'

'Yes.' She paused. 'And no. I'll fill yer in later. I don't think I'll be able to make it over to yours tonight though, too much going on.'

'Oh what a shame! I was gonna make steak with all the trimmings. Mushrooms, tomatoes, chips, peas—'

'Mam, that's downright cruelty. You've got me mouth watering here, I can practically taste it.'

'Sorry, pet.'

'Maybe tomorrow or Wednesday.'

'OK, can't wait to see yer. Will what'sisname be coming?'

Lorraine took a deep breath and told herself to calm down. She knew her mother only 'forgot' her husband's name to get a rise out of her.

'I doubt it, he has classes nearly every night this week.'

They both said goodbye and Lorraine sighed as she replaced her receiver. When she'd first met John at the karate class he taught she'd fallen for him fast and hard. Already turned thirty, she'd felt the time was right for marriage. Her only flickers of doubt had come when, time and time again, Mavis had warned her away from him. She'd stated in no uncertain terms the very first time she'd met him that he was nothing but a useless poser, and that no good would ever come of Lorraine marrying him. But Lorraine had ignored her mother. John had hated Mavis equally, which was unusual, because just about everyone who met her mother took to her at once.

Mavis was a dyed-in-the-wool hippie who looked like she'd stepped through time. She lived in loose flowery dresses with lots of beads, her long blonde hair was curled to an inch of its life and, like her daughter, she looked at least ten years younger than she was. With a sigh, Lorraine put Mavis – and John – to the back of her mind and began sorting through some of the papers and photographs on her desk.

She was studying the photograph of a young girl that had landed on her desk an hour earlier, when there was a knock on the door. 'In,' she said, thinking it was Carter again, and looked up when a much deeper voice greeted her.

'Hello, boss,' Luke said as he entered.

Lorraine waited as he picked up the chair in front of her desk and placed it in his favourite spot, under the window and next to the radiator.

As usual, the chair was soon resting on its back legs, and Luke had his arms behind his head and one leg crossed over the other. Lorraine often had visions of the chair collapsing and Luke braining himself on the radiator, a thought which always made her smile. Not that she didn't like Luke, she'd just inherited her mother's weird sense of humour. He opened his mouth to speak, but Lorraine was faster.

'Looks like Newcastle's having it bad. They're missing a Tracy Scott, been gone two days.' She patted the photograph with her fingernail. 'Bonny kid. Only fourteen.'

'Yup . . .' He sighed, and looked at Lorraine. She recognised the sigh and took it as a sign of trouble.

'What?' she demanded.

'There's another one missing.'

'Oh Christ.' A knot started to form in Lorraine's stomach.

'A sixteen-year-old. Went missing yesterday. Name's Jade Somerby. Because she's sixteen she didn't go on the missing list until ten minutes ago.'

'Could there be a link?'

'Too soon to tell . . . Probably not though. No obvious geographical connection.' He shook his head.

'Are either of the girls streetwise?'

'Not in the case of Scott. We haven't got all the details of the Somerby girl yet.'

'Let me know as soon as yer find out.'

Luke nodded. 'Anything more on the latest body?'

It was Lorraine's turn to shake her head. 'It appears, wait for it, that this one has six toes. Which is just as well because it's been in the ground for such a long time that—'

'Six toes!' Luke shot forward so fast that Lorraine feared this was the day her vision was going to come true. 'Six toes!' he repeated. 'And how long has he been in the ground?'

Surprised at his excitement, she riffled through the papers. 'Scottie's preliminary report reckons about fifteen years. Why, what do yer know that I don't?'

'Jack Holland had six toes.'

'And you knew this Jack Holland?'

'Aye,' Luke nodded. 'Twenty years ago when I was fifteen and came here to live with my grandparents, I wasn't just the new kid on the block. I was the new black kid on the block. Up until then there was probably only a couple of other black people in the Houghton area. Anyhow, Jack Holland, bad lad that he was, was pretty good to me and a lot of the other kids. He sort of made things easier, know what I mean? Got us all playing football on a night. Treated us all to some sweets now and then, that kind of thing. Then he just disappeared – it must have been around the mid-eighties. We all thought he'd run off with someone. Sometimes I visit his old mam, take her some fish and chips. She's nearly as blind as a bat, and going senile. She thinks I'm her Jack.'

'And he's been missing all these years?' Lorraine felt her pulse start to race.

'Yep.' Luke nodded firmly.

'Well . . . We may have made some progress at last. Now all we need is a reason for someone to lop his head off. Can't come up with that an' all, can yer?' she asked hopefully.

Luke smiled. 'Sorry. All I can tell yer is that some pretty shifty characters used to visit him now and then.'

'OK. Let's have you on this one full time. See what yer can dig up. There's got to be a link somewhere between him and the others.'

Luke nodded, then grinned. 'That was a laugh though, the other three bodies turning up in Superintendent Clark's intended leek trench. Wish I'd been there to see the miserable git's face.'

'Aye.' Lorraine laughed out loud. 'He very nearly had a stroke an' all. Lucky for him he's only lived there a year. The house was unoccupied for years before he bought it to renovate.'

Still smiling, Luke rose and made his way to the door, where he turned. 'Is yer mam back yet?'

'Oh yes,' Lorraine rolled her eyes. 'She's truly back in town.'

'Give her me best then. I suppose Canada will never be the same again. Anyhow, tell her I'll drop that video around sometime Saturday.'

'What video's that then?'

'Oh, just some flower-power stuff me aunt had in her loft.'

'Go ahead, keep on encouraging her.'

'Me? Encourage Mavis? Never.'

Lorraine waved him away. When he'd gone, she picked Tracy's photograph up, then glanced quickly through the report. She noticed something she'd missed earlier: the girl had recently found herself a new boyfriend. 'Where are yer, girl?' she mumbled. 'Tucked up somewhere safe with this bloke? Or out on the streets working for him already?'

She shook her head. Time and time again she'd seen this happen. Women, girls . . . when would they ever learn? What was the attraction that the rogues of this world had for women? *Aye, if yer knew that, girl, yer wouldn't have fallen for one yourself.*

She brushed a few stray breadcrumbs off the desk into her hand and threw them into the bin. Then, taking a pencil out of the drawer, she began to chew the end so that she could think more clearly. The pencils were cigarette substitutes, and she needed something in her mouth to help her think. She wondered what that idiot Freud would have made of that.

'Fuck Freud,' she muttered out loud. 'Back to the matter in hand . . . One, I'm certain these girls are linked. They must be. I don't know why, but there's definitely something niggling.'

She was still sitting there an hour later, no further forward, when the light began to go. She glanced out the window. It was raining again. *For fuck's sake*, she thought, staring at the rain as it lashed at the window. *How much more rain can we take before we disappear into the flaming sea? And where the fuck's me husband?*

She was just reaching for her coat when the telephone rang. It was Scottie inviting her to an autopsy, making it sound like he was inviting her on a night out. Smiling, she agreed the time and place. Then, coat on and umbrella in her hand, she closed the door behind her. It was time to go shake one or two people up.

5

Darren had to take his two youngest sisters home. And didn't he just love that? Suzy forever grinning like an idiot at anything that moved, and that Emma . . . Darren cringed. Sniff, sniff, sniff, seemed like all she ever did was sniff. Sniff and spit. He could seriously live without her sniffing and spitting. And just being seen with her would totally ruin his street cred. That's if he had any, he thought gloomily.

Kerry was going straight from school to the Harriers for training, and Claire was rehearsing some stupid play and wouldn't be in till later. And, on top of all that, hadn't Ratchet the Hatchet caught him sticking his chut under the desk and given him two hundred lines. *I must not bring chewing gum into the class. I must not stick it under the table.* He mouthed silently, then stopped dead in his tracks.

'The bitch,' he burst out.

'Pardon, boy?' Mr Slater, the second-year head, asked from behind him.

'Nothing, sir . . . er, I was just singing.'

'Yes? Well sing quietly, boy.'

'Yes, sir,' Darren mumbled as he watched Mr Slater pass him and walk ahead. He sighed, and kept his thoughts inside. The sly bitch. That's really four hundred lines.

And who the hell gets lines these days anyhow?
The stupid bloody woman's lost the plot.
Any day now she'll be bringing the cane back.
Or making chewing gum a hanging offence.

Kicking a stone he'd spotted on his way to the gate, he added a further lament on his inability to get tickets to go to the Stadium of Light to see his hero Kevin Phillips and, intent on his woes, failed to see Stevie until he was almost on top of him. A well-placed hand on his chest brought him up short.

'Hey, what yer doing?' he squeaked.

'Come here, kid.' Stevie pulled him behind the gate's large stone pillars. 'Fancy a sweetie then?' He held one of the pills under Darren's nose.

Darren's heart beat a little faster. He'd heard of this creep and his side-kick before. Kerry and Robbie had told him all about them.

He looked around but couldn't see anybody else. He also knew just what sort of sweeties they were; his mother had drummed it into all of them, over and over. She'd shown them pictures of what happened to you. Had even, along with Sandra and her lot, hauled them all down to a place in Sunderland where kids went when they were hooked on drugs – or rather where the kids of rich people went, the council kids were mostly left to rot. The things he'd seen there had put him right off ever wanting to try some of this creep's sweeties. Besides he wanted to be a footballer, and drugs would put a sharp end to that dream. 'Er, no . . . Thank you.'

'No thank you? Well ain't you the polite little arse-hole. But see what it is, kid, I've only got two left and I've fucking well gotta shift them today, OK? So, seeing as most of the little shitfaces have already gone home, it looks like you're it.'

Darren looked quickly around. The road was deserted. Where was everyone when he needed help? He could do with the Terminator here, or at the very least a couple of aliens.

He was suddenly yanked back to reality when Stevie grabbed his tie and started shaking his head from side to side. 'Are yer ignoring me, yer little fucker?' Darren's face was so close to Stevie's that he could see the red veins in the corner of his eyes, could smell the bigger boy's stinking breath.

'No, no.' Darren pushed Stevie's chest as hard as he could, which did no good at all. His tormentor just laughed.

Darren knew now that he was, as his mam would say, up shit creek without a paddle. But no way was this creep gonna force him to do something he didn't want to do without a fight. Gathering his strength, and plucking up as much courage as he could, he kicked Stevie squarely on the shin, and was as surprised as his attacker when Stevie yelled out in pain and let go of him.

Elated, Darren hopped from foot to foot. Too late, he turned to run, and Stevie grabbed him from behind. 'Got yer, yer fucking little twat.'

Darren's heart hit an all-time low, he was well and truly dead now. Somewhere amongst the sound of his blood pounding in his ears, he could hear Stevie screaming and cursing. But then, suddenly, everything went silent as his tormentor froze.

'And what might be going on here, then?'

Thank you, God. Darren went weak at the knees with relief. He'd never dreamed he'd see the day when Ratchet the Hatchet's voice would sound so good. He would do her a thousand lines and willingly kiss her plates of meat in the morning.

'I do believe we have what is known as a classic case of bullying, don't we, boy?'

Stevie stared at her. The Hatchet was not the kind of teacher you ever forgot; for a year she had been the only authority he'd ever bowed down to, and it was obvious she still remembered him. Even tanked right up, you'd think twice before crossing her.

'Don't you have somewhere you should be, Darren?' She spoke as if he was one of her favourite pupils.

'Yes, Miss.' Darren almost snapped to attention.

'Well, go on then, be off.'

He needed no further bidding. The last thing he heard before he turned the corner was Stevie getting grief about bullying.

Reaching the junior school, he saw Suzy and Emma waiting by the wall.

'Where have you been?' Emma demanded, hands on her hips and staring accusingly at him, while Suzy gave him one of her dimpled smiles.

'Never mind. I'm here now, aren't I?' He was so relieved to be there in one piece, he actually patted Emma's back.

Shrugging him off with a growl, she sniffed, then

stuck her tongue out before yelling at the top of her shrill voice, 'I'm hungry and you're late. And I'm gonna tell our Kerry, and she'll clout yer.'

'Yeah, great. Make sure yer do that . . . Come on then, moan-a-lot, if yer that hungry, move it.' He resisted the urge to punch her as, sniffing, she bounded in front of him.

'Will Mam be better today?' Suzy asked, as she walked beside him.

Darren looked down at her. He could hear the hope in her voice and he wanted to say yes, wanted to say their mam would never be poorly again. He was old enough now to know that his mother drank and smoked too much, and that that's what was making her poorly and making her look really old. And sometimes she smelled terrible. He felt guilty for thinking these thoughts, he really loved his mam, but he worried that the tabs and the booze would really *make* her old instead of just making her *look* old. He didn't think Suzy would understand.

He shrugged, determined not to burden his little sister with his worries. 'Maybe. It's good when she's not poorly, isn't it?'

Suzy smiled. 'Yeah, she's really funny then.'

They headed for home, Emma in the lead wearing her usual scowl, Darren and Suzy holding hands behind her.

Kerry had finished her stamina training and was now cooling down by jogging around the track. Stan Mayfield, her coach, stopwatch in hand, followed her with his eyes. Stan had taken Houghton Harriers for the last ten years, and Houghton Kepier school allowed him to use the school facilities. He had a florid complexion and wore a grey tracksuit that had fitted well some seven years ago, but that was before his wife had dropped down dead one sunny Sunday morning. He drank too much now, and had the beer belly to prove it. He didn't do much physical exercise himself these days, but was still considered a first-class coach.

Standing next to him was a tall dark-haired man. He wore an expensive black overcoat, and his white shirt and gold tie complemented his tanned face, which had definitely not been acquired in this wet English spring. He held himself with total confidence, and his face would have been handsome if the set of it didn't scream arrogant. He had a cruel mouth and piercing blue eyes that followed Kerry as she ran.

'She looks good.' He nodded in Kerry's direction.

'She is,' Stan said with pride. He'd been coaching Kerry for the last three years and had known from the start that she had that elusive extra something that makes good athletes great. 'In fact, I'd go as far as to say she's the best I've seen in years.'

The man took a gold cigarette case and matching lighter from his pocket, and looked around at the rest of the hopefuls. 'Better than any of those?' He lit a cigarette, and blew smoke in Stan's direction.

'Why aye,' Stan bragged, before he started coughing. When he'd caught his breath he went on. 'I reckon she's about the best in the country. And she'll prove it an' all.' Stan couldn't resist puffing his chest out. 'Trained her meself. And, in a couple of weeks at the Durham trials, everybody will know Kerry Lumsdon.'

'Seems that you're very proud of her.'

'I am that. She's a good kid, Kerry, if a bit smart in the mouth. Like a lot of the kids round here, she just needs a chance.'

'The chance you never got, eh Stan?'

Stan was taken aback, although it was common knowledge that he could have had a fantastic career in the sport if he hadn't run into a few problems with amphetamines years ago. This man was a stranger. Or was he? Now that he thought about it, there was something vaguely familiar about him.

The man smiled at him, though the smile never touched his eyes, then turned and walked to his car, a chauffeur-driven BMW.

'Who was that?' Kerry asked, from behind Stan's back.

'Jesus kid!' Stan spun round. 'Fancy creeping up on people like that. Yer'll give me a heart attack if yer not careful.'

'No, Stan, the belly will do that . . . So, who was he? Cos I'm certain I've seen him somewhere before.'

'By, but yer a cheeky madam. I don't know who he was, but I've a strange feeling I should. He could be a scout.' He shrugged. 'Yer never know these things.'

'In me dreams,' Kerry mumbled, looking at the ground.

Stan sighed, a large exaggerated sigh. 'What do yer want me to tell you, kid? That yer the best thing since sliced bread? This yer already know. Why can't yer have the same confidence in yerself that I've got in yer? For God's sake, Kerry, yer've never been beaten yet!'

'I know, but—'

'No buts, kiddo. Look, I know things aren't as good as they should be at home, but yer better believe it, sunshine, there's kids out there who have it a hell of a lot worse than you do. Yer don't want to know how much worse. At least Vanessa tries.'

'Yeah, when she's sober. Which isn't a whole lot of the time, Stan.' She looked up at him and he remembered, with a pang of sympathy, how young she was and how much she had to deal with.

He patted her arm in a friendly gesture. 'Go shower, lass, then go home. I'll see yer again tomorrow. And remember, at least you've got a roof over yer head and food in yer belly.'

'Aye.' Kerry nodded. 'See yer tomorrow.'

Stan watched her walk away and smiled to himself. She couldn't bluff him with her false modesty. He knew she knew that she was the best. She just liked to be told now and again.

Hands in his pockets, he started to cross the field towards the changing rooms. Kerry had a rare talent, but Vanessa had been a superb athlete as well. He'd never quite figured out what had gone wrong: one minute she'd been a rising star, clinging to the same comet that he'd been, and although the whole damn world knew what his downfall had been, Vanessa had just sort of faded away. She'd married Big Robbie, fallen pregnant, given birth to Little Robbie, had herself a couple of years off and was just getting back into training when suddenly Big Robbie upped and disappeared. Nine months later Kerry arrived, without Vanessa telling anyone she was pregnant, and she'd been keeping her head down ever since.

Passing the hurdles, he shook his head in bewilderment. One thing he did know though: whatever he'd told Kerry, that bloke had been no high-flying sports agent, not unless he had the best footballers, plus some, on his books. The job just didn't pay that well.

He'd seen him somewhere before though. The crease in his forehead got deeper as he tried to remember where. No, it wouldn't come. But God knows, he'd be hard put to recognise anyone he'd hung out with back in the dark days of popping pills and addling his brain. One thing he did know was that he didn't like the bloke, and that was only after five minutes in his company.

Kerry reached the shower block, then remembered she'd forgotten her towel. 'Shit.' She threw her shorts and T-shirt into her bag, put her uniform back on, and headed for home. As she was crossing the road she saw the unknown man again. He was in a big car and stared at her as it went past.

Creepy bastard, she thought, as she broke into a slow jog.

By the time Kerry got home twenty minutes later, she was starving and dreaming up various concoctions of food. But she sensed something was wrong as soon as she opened the back door.

The table was practically groaning under the weight

of the plates of uneaten sandwiches. A tin of peaches and a tin of custard stood next to a pile of cracked, but clean, soup bowls. Food left untouched in this house meant serious business. Dropping her bag on the floor, she hurried through into the sitting room.

'What's the matter with you lot?' Kerry's heart was beating faster than after any three-mile stint at top speed. As she looked at the trio of miserable faces in front of her, Emma burst out crying and Suzy quickly followed.

'Darren? What the hell's the matter?' She'd never seen him looking so pale.

'It's our Mam, Kerry. She . . . she's in the hospital.'

Kerry flopped on to the nearest armchair. Hospital. The very word was terrifying. Christ, her and Mam hadn't been getting on for a long time, but to come home and be told she was in the hospital . . . Fuck. Suddenly, with a shock, Kerry realised how much she wanted her mam to be all right. All them nights lying in bed hating her and wishing she'd had a different mam . . . She felt as if a huge hammer with *guilt* written on it a thousand times was whacking her whole body over and over.

She looked at the younger ones. 'What happened?'

Darren fidgeted for a moment, not wanting to say the words in case it made it true. Then he blurted quickly, 'Robbie said something about her heart. He went to the hospital with her, then he came back to catch us out of school and said we had to sit here and not move until you got in. Him and Sandra's gone back to the hospital.'

Kerry shook her head. 'But she's too young to have

76

something wrong with her heart,' she said, desperately hoping that was true. 'It must be something else. Our Robbie must have got it wrong.'

For the first time in her young life, Emma was in agreement with a member of her family, and she nodded vigorously until Darren dashed their hopes.

'But what about the drink, Kerry? Remember? She drinks too much booze. And even I know it's not good for yer.'

Kerry looked at her younger brother, suddenly realising that her mother's drinking affected the others as much as it did her. She'd only ever really spoken about it to Robbie, forgetting at times that the ears in the walls of this house were huge.

Feeling her panic rising, she forced herself to breathe slowly and calm down. 'So what exactly did he say about her heart? And,' she could hardly ask the question, 'is she going to be all right?' *Please say yes, Darren, please.* She looked at him, willing the words she wanted to hear to come tumbling out of his mouth.

Darren shrugged. 'I've told yer what he said. Remember, you and our Robbie think I'm a little kid, and yer tell me nowt.'

Suzy, eyes already red from crying, sidled over and sat on Kerry's knee, where she cuddled into her neck. Watching them, Emma sniffed loudly then, wiping her nose on her sleeve, followed her sister.

'I want me mam to come home, our Kerry. Now,' she insisted as she climbed on to the arm of the chair and snuggled into her sister. 'Will she come home now, Kerry?'

Kerry tried to sound reassuring. 'We all want her home, pet, but we'll have to wait and see what our Robbie says when he gets back.'

And I wish to God he'd hurry up, she thought, watching Darren make his mind up whether he was too big now to join in the cuddle. One minute was all it took, then he was amongst them.

After a while, she persuaded them all to eat something. The sandwiches were curling at the corners, but the salmon inside was still fresh. They ate the treat as if they were eating cardboard.

Watching them, Kerry started to wonder where Claire was. *The selfish bitch is probably off with that Katy some bloody where, she couldn't give a fuck about what's going on here. Wait till she gets in.*

After they had eaten, and were back in a pile of arms and legs on the settee, Kerry switched on the television and caught the six o'clock news. They listened as the announcer told the nation that a body had been found in the North of England. When she said that the body had been found in Fatfield, only a couple of miles away from them, Emma started to scream.

Darren, who was sitting next to her, jumped. 'Emma!' he yelled.

'Don't shout at her, Darren,' Kerry said, even though she wanted to shout as loudly as he had. 'Shh, Emma, it's nothing to be frightened of.'

Suzy started to whimper, and Kerry felt like strangling the still-screaming Emma. She raised her voice to make herself heard over the racket. 'Emma, Emma, you've got to stop. Yer'll only make yerself bad if yer don't.' Emma just carried on screaming.

Kerry jumped up and stood over her. 'If yer don't fucking stop right now, I'll fucking well slap yer. You've set our Suzy off now.'

Emma buried her face in her hands and stopped screaming, but her sobs were nearly as loud. Darren sat with his hands over his ears.

Exasperated, Kerry sat back down and put her arm around Emma, then rocked her the way she'd seen their mother do when Emma lost it. Slowly Emma quietened down.

As Kerry held her, she glanced out the window and realised how dark it was becoming. 'Can anyone remember if our Claire said she would be late tonight?' She tried to keep her voice casual.

The girls shook their heads.

'Aye, I think she said something about seven o'clock,' Darren answered.

Kerry mulled this over for a moment, then said, 'I wish our Robbie was home. I can't stand this not knowing any longer. And our Claire should be in, never mind flaunting herself about. It's all starting to do me friggin' head in.'

'Aye, mine an' all . . . Kerry?'

'What?'

Darren stared at his feet for a long moment before saying, 'Nowt, it doesn't matter.'

But Kerry could see that something did matter. There was more troubling Darren than what was wrong with their mother. She was just about to question him when the door opened and Robbie, closely followed by Sandra, walked in. Both of them were smiling.

Kerry's heart lifted. 'Well?' she demanded.

'She's gonna be all right,' Robbie said, his smile broadening into a grin.

Kerry smiled back as relief flooded through her, and Sandra turned and gave Darren a quick hug. 'Put the kettle on, there's a pet.'

Darren jumped up. He would always do anything Sandra asked.

'So . . . what the hell happened, Robbie?'

Before Robbie could answer, Emma shouted up, 'Our Kerry's been swearing. And I want me mam!'

'Shut up, yer little bitch,' Kerry snarled, giving Emma a look of pure poison.

Robbie held his hands out for peace. 'OK, OK . . . It was a massive panic attack. Dr Mountjoy thought it was a heart attack. The doctor at the hospital says sometimes, until yer get the tests back, yer can hardly tell the difference. Anyhow, with all the drugs they gave her in case it was a heart attack, she's purely worn out, so they're keeping her in for a few days.'

'When can I go and see her?' Darren demanded from the kitchen doorway.

'And me,' Suzy added. Emma was still too busy sniffling to speak, but she nodded.

'Tomorrow,' Robbie replied, as he ruffled Suzy's hair. 'We'll take the troops in after school. So, has everyone eaten their tea?' He sat down and looked around and was answered with nods and smiles as Suzy climbed on to her favourite brother's knee.

'Jesus, Robbie,' Kerry said. 'I was really worried,

sitting here not knowing what was going on. And Bratty there didn't make things any easier.' She glared at Emma, who stuck her tongue out.

'I know, Kerry, sorry and all that, but I couldn't tell yer until I'd found out exactly what was going on. Yer would have rushed straight to the hospital, then we would have been stuck with finding somebody to watch these guys.' He took a bite of a sandwich and then looked back up at Kerry. 'And, guess what?'

Kerry was in no mood for guessing games, she gave Robbie the same look she'd flashed Emma earlier. Robbie laughed.

'She's actually talking about going to AA.'

'Mint, eh?' Sandra patted Kerry's knee. 'We'll have her right as rain in no time.'

'That I'll believe when I see it.'

Robbie sighed and squeezed Kerry's shoulder. 'Try to believe, eh, Kerry?'

She shrugged, and was on the verge of saying more, when Darren came in with the teas. Robbie reached for his, then stopped. Looking round, he asked, 'Where's our Claire?'

The shadows were growing in the tiny cabin, but there was enough light still for Claire to see Tracy's frozen stare. Gently she nudged the other girl. Tracy blinked once, twice, then slowly turned her head. Her smile, when it came after a long moment, was the smile of the damned and meant only as an acknowledgement of Claire's presence.

Claire shivered and turned her attention to the older girl.

'I don't think I can take this much longer.' She banged her heels on the floor in frustration, then winced as pain shot through her ankle and her left knee started to bleed again. She'd always looked down her nose at Kerry when she swore, thinking her sister was as common as muck, but at this moment in time a profanity seemed to be the only way she could express her feelings. 'Bastards.' She looked down at her legs. 'Look at the fucking state of me.'

Jade looked and nodded, as if sitting naked in a cabin and watching blood pour from another girl's leg was an everyday occurrence.

'Do they feed us, or what?' Claire asked.

'Yeah, they feed us all right.' Jade nodded.

'When? I'm starving.'

Jade shrugged. And Tracy found her voice. 'Me too.'

Claire swung back to Tracy. 'So, what do yer reckon happened to the other girl then?'

Tears welled up in Tracy's green eyes. 'She was here before me, and that night she started telling me what her and a boy she'd just met got up to on New Year's Eve. I think she was trying to keep me quiet, cos I was crying a lot and the . . . the man didn't like that.'

Claire thought for a moment, was about to say something else, when she felt a featherweight touch on the back of her hand. She screamed and flung her arm out, thinking, *Spider, Spider, Spider*. Whatever it was dropped on her knee and stuck to the blood.

'Oh, please, please get it off. Get it off!' She was becoming more frantic by the second.

'It's all right, it's only a flake of paint from the roof.' Jade moved closer so they were touching hip to hip. Her presence soothed Claire enough for her to glance quickly at the roof and see the peeling paint, then look down to her knee.

'Oh, thank God for that.'

'They found out she wasn't a virgin,' Tracy went on as if the last minute had not happened.

'What?' Claire said, trying to calm herself.

Tears were running freely down Tracy's face as she relived what had happened a few nights earlier.

'They must have been listening. The man who tied you up, the one who keeps laughing, he opened the door and grinned at her. He said she was worthless to them. He said the buyers only ever wanted virgins, and they were gonna have some fun with her before they tossed her overboard.' She sobbed into the suddenly silent cabin. 'Then he dragged her on to the deck. He propped the door open so I could see. He did it to her while the other man kept his hand over her mouth. I could hear her choking. I think she was trying to be sick . . .' She sobbed again, louder, harder. It took her a few moments to calm herself before she said, 'Then they changed places.'

'Ohh.' Claire shuddered. 'How horrible.' She was frightened to ask what happened to the girl, could visualise her being thrown overboard, could hear the splash her body would have made as it hit the cold dark water. She shuddered again, looked at Jade, and knew the other girl was thinking the same.

She turned back to Tracy. She wanted to know the girl's name, needed to know her as a person, but Tracy's head was down, and Claire had a feeling that they would be getting nothing else from her that night.

Then she heard footsteps on deck. Her skin tingled from her head to her feet, sharp pains of fear circled her chest until she could hardly breathe.

Please God, she silently prayed, as the darkness nearly became complete. *Please don't let them be coming for me.*

6

Scottie walked across to the other side of his stainless-steel domain. He stopped beside a wall filled to the ceiling with cupboards, and leaned back, letting the cupboards take his weight. He was a big man in every sense, except for his fingers which were long and slim and very, very quick. Dark hair poked out of his collar and from under his shirt cuffs. In fact, he had more hair on his body than on his head. His bald patch was getting bigger every day, but he refused himself the bald man's vanity of letting one side grow and brushing it over his head. He'd be damned if he'd do that. He was forty-three years old, but sometimes, like today, he felt a hundred and three. He sighed heavily.

Edna, his long-term assistant, glanced up from her microscope. 'What's the matter now?'

He shrugged and gestured with his hand to the table in the middle of the room. 'Well, what's not the matter?'

Edna, as small as he was large and as fair as he was dark, and two years past retiring age, looked at the table. She pulled a face then went back to her microscope.

'Thanks for that,' Scottie murmured. Edna ignored him.

He folded his arms across his chest and looked at the clock on the wall. 'Where the hell is she? It's nearly bedtime.' Edna looked at him with disdain.

'And since when did you go to bed at six o'clock? Learn some patience, she's a busy woman. She'll be here as soon as she can.'

Just then the door opened and the busy woman, followed by an obviously nervous Carter, walked in.

Scottie brightened up. 'Well hello there, pretty lady.'

Edna groaned and Lorraine laughed in unison. Carter followed Lorraine to the table as if he was frightened to be more than six inches away from her.

It was Carter's first autopsy. He'd promised himself he would not, under any circumstances, be sick or faint or do anything embarrassing. The lads at the station had had his life, filling him full of gory details. But this wasn't so bad. A near skeleton. Well he could cope with that, and the stink wasn't so bad either, more like an earthy smell than a fleshy one. He caught his boss looking at him and flashed her a smile. He got raised eyebrows in return.

He noticed that every bone was neatly labelled, but where the skull should have been there was an empty space.

'So,' Lorraine said, 'what have yer got for me, Scottie?'

Scottie picked up a large notepad that was attached to the table by a length of string. 'What we have here is the skeleton of a big male. He's been in the ground for at least fifteen, sixteen years. Damp ground, hence next to no flesh left. It'll have rotted away, and what didn't rot got eaten.'

Carter felt the bile begin to rise.

Lorraine nodded. 'Anything at all to go on?'

'Well, the head was sawn off using a large blade with the same distinctive serration we've seen on the others. Edna's made another cast of where the spine was severed and as I've said before, match it and yer've got the knife. But, more interestingly,' he moved to the bottom of the table, 'he did have six toes. Now that's not as unusual as it sounds, it just means that the small toe bone didn't fuse properly. I've seen it before, it can happen with fingers and easily be put right for cosmetic reasons. Believe me six toes is nothing compared to some of the mistakes Mother Nature makes. The good thing is, if he was born in a hospital there will be records.'

'Yeah, I've already got Luke on this. He thinks he might know who it is.'

'Good, this poor lad deserves a proper burial.'

'Do yer think it could all be part of some kind of ritual?' Lorraine asked. With four headless bodies now in the morgue, cult killings had to be at least a possibility.

Scottie thought for a moment. 'To tell yer the truth, with no flesh to work on, it's hard to tell. The body could have been ritually scarred, burned or anything.' He paused. 'We just don't know, but I wouldn't throw the idea away. As for the actual knife, with that kind of unusual serration it's quite possibly something more sophisticated than your common-or-garden knife. It's probably quite decorative, it could be very old, perhaps even valuable.' He shrugged, and when Scottie shrugged, his whole body moved.

'Up until now we've been assuming the heads were removed to prevent dental identification,' Lorraine mused. 'But leaving this one's deformed feet in place makes me wonder if we're not looking at something more sinister.'

'If yer ask me,' Edna put in, swinging round on her chair to face them, 'sixteen years ago we had a total nutter running around. And he – or I suppose she – is still on the loose.'

'Is it possible a woman could have the strength to do this?' Lorraine asked Scottie.

He gestured with his forefinger as he moved to the middle of the table. 'He'd been shot twice, once in the top of the leg, once in his chest. Here,' he pointed to the right-side ribs, 'then here.' He indicated the top of the leg. 'I reckon one bullet went right through the first and second ribs and that would have slowed him down some. Could even have taken a lung out or caused serious trauma to the heart, though between the decay and the animals it's hard to be exact. But the bullet in the leg would have brought him down. One way or another, he was dead or dying when his head was taken from his body. So a strong woman could easily have sawn her way through.'

'Oh God.'

Lorraine, Scottie and Edna looked at Carter.

'You all right?' Scottie asked, hiding a grin.

'Oh yes. Yes, I'm fine.' Carter coughed and straightened his uniform. The other three glanced knowingly at each other, then back down at the body.

Lorraine had noticed that the skin showing between Carter's freckles was considerably whiter than usual and decided to give him a break.

'Well, thanks for your usual in-depth explanations, Scottie.'

'Anything for you, gorgeous. By the way, when are we gonna take that trip to the sun?'

'Yer mean the trip you keep dreaming about, Scottie?'

'Yeah, that one will do.'

'Dream on.'

They both laughed, and Lorraine said good night to Edna while Scottie had a few words with Carter.

'Drop me at my mother's, Carter,' Lorraine said, when they got into the car. Then she looked at him and saw that the paleness had turned rather greenish. 'What's the matter? That wasn't a bad autopsy, there was hardly any smell at all. I thought yer did rather well, so?'

Carter looked at her as he started the engine. 'Scottie said not to forget to call at the chinky's on the way home for some spare ribs to suck on. How could he?'

Lorraine burst out laughing. 'Lighten up, Carter,' she said after a moment. 'Pathologists have a terrible job, so they deal with it the only way they can. Believe me, Scottie will have shown that body more respect in death than it probably ever got in life.'

An hour later, pleased that she'd decided in the end to call at her mam's on the way home, Lorraine pushed her plate away and patted her stomach. 'Thanks, Mam. That was just what I needed, a good juicy steak. I'll have to work out extra hard in the morning, but it'll be worth it.'

Mavis beamed her delight at her daughter's praise. 'Well, I must say I enjoyed it meself.'

Lorraine studied her mother for a moment. Sometimes it was like looking in the mirror. They were the same height and size – although she wouldn't be seen dead in anything out of Mavis's hippie wardrobe, long flowing dresses and waist-length curly perms were not for her. Tonight's dress was a psychedelic mix of green and lilac swirls. But she had to admit that although on anyone else the dress would be a total disaster, on Mavis it looked, at worst, interesting.

When Mavis talked, her hands fluttered in the air like a pair of nervous butterflies having an agitated conversation. How she managed to keep those long slender fingers still long enough to work the magic on the pottery she sold just about all over the North East was a mystery in itself.

'So, Lorry, how are things at work? Oh,' the hands fluttered, 'before I forget, please thank Luke for watering me plants, there's a good girl.' Her tone changed, turning uncharacteristically sharp. 'And how's what'sisname?'

'If yer mean my husband, yer know fine well his name's John,' Lorraine said, resigned to the fact that her mother would never use it but none the less upset by her antagonism.

'Yes, that one.'

'I've only ever had one,' Lorraine snapped.

'Aye, the wrong one.' Mavis had turned her head and spoken so low that Lorraine had to strain to hear her, but she guessed rightly what Mavis had said.

Lorraine groaned. 'OK. Let's just leave it for tonight, eh, Mam?' She just couldn't face the familiar argument after the day she'd had.

'Whatever, dear. So, what's new? Everybody in Houghton been behaving themselves while I've been away?'

'Far from it.' Lorraine put her head in her hands and her shoulders slumped. 'The drug problem is getting bigger by the day. We've got a bunch of party-goers that seem to think it's great fun to freak out the weakest amongst them – their latest trick is lopping off earlobes.'

'What?' Mavis looked at her daughter with disbelief. 'For God's sake, whatever happened to simple games like spin the bottle?'

'It's gone way past that, Mam. Way, way past. We've had six in hospital in the last five weeks. The last one was only fourteen. God knows what their drug-sodden brains will come up with next.'

'And I bet none of the kids talked, did they?'

Lorraine shook her head. 'Nope, they're far too frightened to say anything. We're watching a couple of houses though, we'll get the slimy bastards yet.' She sighed. If only drugged-up kids playing crazy party-games was all she had to think about.

Mavis had just opened her mouth to say something, when the doorbell rang. She looked at her

91

daughter, pulled a face, then said, 'Who on earth can that be?'

'There's one way to find out, Mam.'

'It could be what'sisname.'

The bell rang again. Lorraine was pretty damn sure it wasn't her husband. 'Are yer gonna answer it? Or should we sit here and play guessing games all night?'

'OK, OK, I'm going.' Mavis went to the door while Lorraine helped herself to a glass of white wine. A minute later, Mavis, face wreathed in smiles, was back. Behind her was Luke.

Lorraine, sensing trouble, nodded a greeting.

Luke wasted no time. 'Sorry, boss, but it looks like we've got another missing kid.'

Lorraine's heart sank.

'Shit, how old's this one?'

'Thirteen. She's also closer to home, the Seahills. She seems to have been missing since this morning. Her name's Claire Lumsdon and the family became worried when she failed to come home from a school play rehearsal. Apparently though, when the brother went looking for her, there was nothing on at the school tonight. Seeing as she's never done anything like this before, the lad got worried and called in to see one of her friends.' He checked his notebook. 'Katy Jacks. It took a while for the girl's parents to drag it out of her that Claire hasn't been to school all day.'

Lorraine frowned. 'Did this Katy Jacks say why, or give any hints that she knew and wasn't telling?'

Luke shrugged. 'Not that I know of.'

'I don't like the sound of this. We'll go see the family now.' Lorraine moved to get her coat.

'Cup of tea before yer go, Luke?' Mavis asked him.

'No thanks, Mavis.' He flashed her a quick smile before turning back to Lorraine. 'Oh, by the way, the mother is in hospital, some sort of panic attack this morning.'

'Not their day, is it?' Mavis said, shaking her head.

Lorraine kissed Mavis on her cheek. 'See yer soon, Mam.'

They arrived outside the Lumsdons' house ten minutes later. Lorraine stared at the red front door as her fingers rummaged in her pockets for a pencil, and finding none, she chewed the inside of her lip. She hated this part of her job, knowing full well that most of the time either she would return in the next forty-eight hours and look at the same front door, the bearer of bad news, or the kid would never turn up.

She walked up the path with Luke close behind. The sound of arguing reached them outside. She knocked on the door and it was opened by a small boy with the loveliest dark eyes Lorraine had ever seen.

She smiled down at him.

'Is anyone in, son?'

'Aye . . . Who are yer, like?'

Lorraine hid a smile as she showed him her badge. 'I'm Detective Inspector Lorraine Hunt, and this is Sergeant Luke Daniels.'

In a high-pitched voice the boy yelled, 'Robbie, Kerry, it's the coppers.'

A moment later a tall dark-haired youth appeared,

quickly followed by a chubby little red-headed girl, who stared at them and then stuck her tongue out behind the youth's back.

Charming, Lorraine thought, as she smiled at Robbie. 'Hello. Is it all right to come in for a moment?'

Robbie stepped back. 'Yeah, sure.'

Lorraine and Luke followed Robbie along the passageway and into the sitting room. A slim, dark-haired girl was sitting in a chair by the fire with the cutest little blonde girl on her knee. The older girl looked Lorraine up and down, then met her eyes with a worried frown. It was obvious that she was the central figure in the family.

'It's just a few questions about your sister. We need a clearer picture.'

'Sit down,' Robbie said from behind Lorraine.

She sat on the settee, while Luke chose to stand behind her. It was not the most comfortable settee in the world, she was certain she could feel a spring digging into her.

'So, you are?' She looked at Kerry.

'That's Kerry,' Robbie said, before Kerry had a chance to speak. 'I'm Robbie,' and he gave the names of the rest of them then said, 'And it's Claire who's –' he nearly choked on the word '– missing.'

'Right, son,' Lorraine said gently. 'Do yer have a recent photograph of Claire?'

Robbie looked embarrassed. The school photographer had taken photos just a few months ago, but they hadn't been able to afford them. The only picture they had of Claire was three years old. He

94

went to the drawer and withdrew a battered photo album, flicking through it until he pulled out a picture of Claire at ten years old.

'Here,' he gave it to Lorraine. 'She's only ten there, but she really hasn't changed that much.'

Kerry deposited Suzy on the floor, stood up and looked at the photo. 'Of course she's changed! Her cheeks are still fat there, and her hair is totally different now.'

Luke, seeing how upset she was, held his hand out for the photo and took a look at it. 'We can age it a bit by computer. It's not perfect, but if yer just tell us what her hair's like now, we should end up with a good likeness.'

'Oh.' Kerry sat back down.

Lorraine smiled at her. 'Clever now, eh?'

Kerry shrugged. 'So, how long will it take for yer to find her then?' The policewoman seemed OK, but Kerry was so worried she couldn't help snapping at her.

'She may not want to be found,' Lorraine said, trying to put it as tactfully as she could.

'What makes yer say that?' Kerry's voice rose in outrage. 'Our Claire's never gone missing like this before!'

'She did tell lies and say she was staying back at school, when there was nothing on.'

'She's with her boyfriend,' said a small voice.

Every eye in the room turned to Emma.

'What?' Kerry demanded.

'I heard her and Katy talking yesterday. She said she was getting shot.'

'Getting what?' Robbie said, while Kerry's eyes nearly popped out of her head.

'With photos.'

'A photo shoot?' Lorraine asked.

'Aye.' The little redhead nodded.

'How long has she had a boyfriend?' Robbie said, completely amazed.

'Years and years,' Emma announced proudly. Then, realising she was the only one to know that Claire was going out with a boy, she sniffed and pulled a know-it-all face at her siblings.

'If you're telling fibs, Emma, so help me I'll floor yer.' Kerry glared at her.

'Am not. I know what they call him an' all, so there.' Emma stuck her tongue out at Kerry, and sat down next to Lorraine.

'So,' Lorraine smiled at Emma, 'what do they call him?'

Relishing the attention, Emma actually smiled, before saying, 'Brad. His name's Brad.'

For the next fifteen minutes Lorraine questioned the family. When she was certain she'd gleaned as much information as she could, and that Robbie was of an age to take care of them with the mother in hospital, she and Luke left.

'Canny bunch of kids,' Luke said, as they set off for Lorraine's house, her shift long over.

'Aye. I hope the mother gets well soon. That Robbie's a godsend. And that oldest girl, Kerry, she's well able to cope for a few days. Seems a bit spiky, but obviously bright. Plus they have the neighbour, Sandra.'

Luke nodded, then said, 'Do yer think the girls are connected?'

Lorraine thought for a moment, then turned to him. 'I'm not quite sure. When you've dropped me off, will you pay a visit to this Katy, then phone me?'

'OK, boss.'

After Luke dropped her off he stopped for a moment to watch her walk up the path to a dark empty house. Lorraine was everything he wanted and could never have. She was his boss, and she was married. He sighed and drove off.

Mrs Archer slammed the door behind the barmaids. She shot the bolts, went to the bar and picked up a half bottle of whisky. Scowling to herself, she stomped her way upstairs.

It wasn't bad enough that the coppers had been called again to deal with a pair of crazed druggies threatening to kill themselves and half the fucking world. Oh no, a bastard that had disappeared sixteen years ago had only fucking well come back to haunt her.

The gossip had been rife all night. Each person that came in to the bar had their own version of what state the body found at Fatfield had been in. Even that moron Stevie had had his ten pence' worth. Still, he'd done good. Sold the lot – well, he'd handed the money over for the lot, but that glitter in his eyes was proof positive that more than one of the pills had found its way into his bloodstream. She'd have to do something about that. Druggies weren't to be trusted.

She went into her kitchen, took a glass from the

shelf, and filled it to the brim. Her hand shook slightly as she raised the glass to her mouth and took a good swallow. She felt the burn all the way to her stomach.

It was the other business that had her rattled.

Fancy that Jack Holland turning up after all these years. Fucking hell.

She banged her fist on the table before taking another drink.

'Got to do something,' she muttered, filling her glass up. 'Can't risk getting caught up in this, not with the plans I've got.'

A moment later there was a loud bang downstairs. She jumped and then, irritated, moved to the window and looked out.

For fuck's sake, just a bunch of kids kicking the door as they passed. She stared at them, she'd know them again all right, and when the fucking little twats got their comeuppance they'd learn not to mess with her door.

She finished what was in her glass and made her way to bed. She was alone tonight because she chose to be. She did her best thinking in bed. And boy, did she have some thinking to do.

Lorraine finished her coffee and took the cup through to the kitchen. She felt like throwing it into the tiny sink. She hated the cramped space, where everything was cold stainless steel; it reminded her of Scottie's place of work. She longed for a cottage like her mother's.

She looked at the video clock when she went back

into the sitting room, which was decorated in blue, blue and darker blue. His favourite colour. Eleven o'clock. 'Where the hell is he?' she muttered, going over to the window and looking out. She saw nothing but another wet night.

Tracing a raindrop with her finger as it made its slow journey down the pane, she thought angrily, *This makes it three nights out of five he's been late. I wonder what tonight's piddling excuse is gonna be. 'Sorry, love, got talking to this one or that one, and forgot the time.' Does the clown think I'm stupid or what?*

She threw herself on to the settee, then jumped back up a moment later when the phone rang. 'Hello, John,' she said, before she even had it to her ear.

There was a heartbeat's silence, then she heard, 'No, it's me. Luke.'

'Ohh, sorry, I thought . . . Never mind,' she murmured, embarrassed. 'Have yer got anything, then?'

'A bit. Apparently she's been seeing this Brad character for about a month. And, wait for it, he's hot.'

'Hot?'

'As in dead sexy. The mother nearly threw a fit when the kid slipped out with that one. But before she all but forced her upstairs with threats of eternal grounding, I managed to get out of her that he definitely was taking Claire on a photo shoot, and it was top secret. She wasn't even supposed to tell Katy.'

Lorraine was quiet for a moment, then she sighed and said, 'Looks like we've got ourselves some big trouble brewing, Luke.'

'Yeah, I was thinking the same.'

They both fell silent and she tapped her finger on the phone for a moment, then went on. 'OK, here's what yer do. Turn everything over to the boys in blue for the night, the beat coppers might come up with something. Tell them to get out of their cars and talk to the night people. I want them to pester the life out of anyone who looks even a little bit like they might know something. OK? Yer know how quickly the trail can disappear in these cases.' She paused, racking her brains for something else they could do tonight, but there honestly was nothing. 'Anyhow, if we're lucky the silly girl might even see sense and go home of her own accord. We both know that's happened before.'

'We can always pray, boss.' His tone told her that he didn't think it was any more likely to help than she did.

'Shame that's all we can do sometimes.' God, she had to pull herself together. Her tone became businesslike. 'Now you go home, get a good night's kip. I have a hunch we might all have to be on our toes in the morning.'

When Luke put his phone down, Lorraine held on to hers, not wanting to lose the contact of even a disembodied voice.

Where the hell are you, John?

She brooded for a while, staring out the window, alternately thinking of the missing girls and her wayward husband, before finally relinquishing her grip on the phone and heading for the bedroom.

She was still awake hours later, and still alone.

* * *

'Want to know something, Smithy?'

Jason Smith looked up from the back of the one-armed bandit, and watched as Stevie swirled his tongue around his newly acquired lip-ring, knowing full well that whatever Stevie wanted him to know would probably be the last thing he wanted to know.

'I'm gonna murder that little bastard in the morning.' He grinned at Jason. 'I'm gonna fill him that full of smack, the little rat won't know what the fuck's hit him.' He rubbed his shin. 'Me fucking leg's killing me, I've got a bruise the size of a friggin' orange.' He licked his lip again. 'I'll find out who the little fucker is and where he lives, and God help any bastard what tries to stop me. And her. Ohh, how I hate that fucking Lumsdon bitch. But see, Smithy, I know where she lives.' He nodded knowingly to himself. 'And one day soon I'm gonna burn the bitch out.' He laughed.

Jason nodded, he wasn't gonna disagree with no smack head. Best to let them dream on. He fastened the bandit back up before turning to the next one.

Annoyed that Jason wouldn't join in with his rant about Kerry, Stevie finally turned his attention to looking properly at what Jason was doing. And his eyes widened. 'So, how long have yer been creaming off Mrs Archer? I have to say, Smithy, yer've got more guts than I thought yer had.' Stevie laughed.

Jason shook his head wearily. 'Put yer head out the door and check the street, Stevie. We don't want her poking her nose in here, cos believe me, she'll take no prisoners if she decides to wander along and take a stock check. She's as sly as a bitch fox and she really does have eyes in the back of that ugly head of hers.'

Stevie went to the door and looked down the road. From the Golden Casino – a small gambling joint owned by Mrs Archer – you could see the whole street all the way along to the Blue Lion and White Lion pubs.

He thought he saw a movement near the White Lion, so he stepped outside. Although the calendar said spring, winter still had the North East of England firmly in its icy grasp, and Stevie shivered. But whatever he'd seen was gone now. He cupped his hands round his cigarette lighter and lit up a joint. He inhaled deeply, then felt something touch his leg, right on the bruise. 'Ow!' He glanced down and saw Jess looking up at him, her tail wagging. 'Fuck off, dog.' He kicked Jess hard in her side. She yelped and ran inside.

A moment later, Jason came out. 'Yer better not have hurt the dog, wanker, or I'll fucking strangle yer.'

'Aye, you and who else?' Stevie laughed. 'Fucking ugly mutt, anyhow.'

Jason snarled, 'Bastard, yer supposed to be watching the fucking street.'

'There's nowt happening, man,' Stevie complained. 'Everybody's gone home to fucking bed. Now can we get on with your fucking little scam? And I want me share, don't fucking forget. I need some money to spend tomorrow night.' He laughed. 'And by the way, I hope yer not fighting that mutt? Cos if yer are I'll borrow a grand and put it on the other dog.' He looked down at Jess who cowered between Jason's legs.

102

'Jess doesn't fight, yer useless piece of shit.'

Stevie laughed again and aimed a foot in Jess's direction. Her tail went even further between her legs. 'That's so obvious.' He took a deep drag on his joint. 'So get a fucking move on, will yer? I'm freezing me balls off out here.' He blew smoke in Jason's face.

Jason wafted the smoke away with his hand, counted to ten then went back inside. He knew he'd made a mistake asking a druggie with a smack problem to be a lookout. The bastard could blab at any time. But since his mate Chancy had got six months for fraud he'd been all on edge in case Mrs Archer walked in on him.

He finished with the last bandit, then bagged up around half the money he'd collected and deposited it in Mrs Archer's safe.

'Come in, creep.' Jason put twenty pound coins in an ashtray that was screwed to the floor. 'There yer go.'

Stevie slowly counted the coins. 'Twenty fucking quid, is that it? Yer expect me to put me life on the line for twenty fucking quid? Fuck off.'

Jason had had enough. He grabbed Stevie by his throat and pushed him against the wall.

That was all it took. Never naturally brave, and with his last fix wearing off, Stevie backed right down. 'OK, man, OK.' He held his hands up. 'Only joking.' But in that moment, Jason Smith became number three on Stevie's hit list.

He didn't know that numbers one and two were less than three hundred yards away.

*   *   *

Kerry and Robbie had searched Houghton town centre three times. Darren and Sandra's son Clayton had done all the side streets on the way up through the Burnside. It was past twelve.

Kerry sat on one of the benches facing the church and waited for Darren and Clay to put in an appearance, while Robbie had one more look behind the Britannia. Twice they had been stopped by patrol cars wanting to know their business, and both times the police had assured them that they knew about their missing sister and they were doing their best to find her.

Kerry swiped at a tear which had been promising to overflow for the last couple of hours. She dreaded the next morning. If Claire didn't turn up before then, they would have to tell Mam. They couldn't keep it from her for ever – it's not like she'd have to do a head count or something to miss Claire.

What if she never comes home? That gloomy thought sent waves of depression through her whole body.

And how come she never mentioned this fucking boyfriend before?

The tear finally gave up its tenacious grip and dropped on to her knee. *When was the last time our Claire mentioned anything?*

They used to be pretty good friends once, a year or two back, but didn't that just seem like for ever now.

Please come home, Claire, we'll be friends again. Just please, please come home. A sob escaped into the night, as her whole body ached for her sister to be in the house when she got back. She could even be as stroppy as she wanted – for a while that is.

Robbie had finished his circuit and crossed over to where Kerry was sitting. He found her staring at the frost which was fast materialising on the grass.

'Hi, sis. You OK?'

She looked up at him. 'What if we never see her again, Robbie? Have yer thought about that? What if our Claire never comes home?'

'She will, Kerry.' Robbie was adamant, and nothing anybody could say would shake him from his conviction. His sister was coming home. 'Didn't the coppers say that most of them turn up the next day, feeling sorry for themselves? Didn't they?'

'But face it, Robbie, for fuck's sake. Some of them *don't* turn up.' She clutched at his jacket. 'I bet there's hundreds of them what never come home again, ever.' Her voice rose steadily. 'Have yer thought about them, Robbie? Have yer . . . ? The ones who can't come home . . . because they . . . they . . .' She couldn't go on.

Robbie licked dry lips as he took hold of the hand clinging so tightly to his coat. 'She'll come home, Kerry, OK? I just know she will. So don't go talking like that when our Darren comes back with Clay, all right?'

Kerry looked back down at the grass. She registered that the frost was much thicker now, reminding her that Claire had left home wearing next to nothing that morning.

A moment later, the quiet was disturbed by a loud whistle and Robbie breathed a silent sigh of relief. 'That'll be our Darren and Clay.'

Kerry didn't answer, she just kept on staring at the ground.

Robbie whistled a reply, and a moment later the younger boys turned the corner and made their way towards them.

Clayton shook his head, and Robbie could see that Darren had been crying.

'We looked all over, Robbie,' Clayton said, 'but there wasn't hardly anybody about to even ask if they'd seen her.'

Darren shivered, and Robbie shook his head and said, 'Right, that's it. Time to go home, we'll start again in the morning.'

The boys stared at him, and Robbie raised his hands in a what-else-can-we-do? gesture.

Kerry stood up to object, but the sight of Darren's wretched face kept her tongue still.

Totally dejected, they set off for home: three kids missing a sister, facing the unknown, and a young boy missing the girl across the road he'd known for as long as he could remember.

Later that night, the bed seemed huge without Claire, and Kerry tossed and turned, trying for the sleep that seemed to be slipping ever further away. She couldn't get Claire out of her mind, conjuring up image after image, none of them good.

Emma started to snore, which made things even worse. Finally Kerry gave up and got out of bed to sit by the window.

She was still there when dawn cracked the sky open.

Tuesday

7

Kerry woke up to the sound of Emma and Darren squabbling. It took her a moment to realise where she was. Her arms hurt as she stretched to get the kinks out, and she was mid stretch when she remembered why she'd been at the window in the first place. Quickly she swung round and looked at the bed, but it was empty.

'Shit.'

Exhausted, she lay down on her bed for a moment. She could only have had a couple of hours' kip, and the last thing she remembered was hearing Robbie shouting and groaning in his sleep. He'd always had terrible nightmares – horrible recurring ones about men with guns pointed at his head, she could never understand how the rest of the kids slept through it – but she hadn't heard him in the night for a while now. It wasn't surprising that they'd started up again though, what with Claire and everything.

She stood and headed for the bathroom where Darren and Emma were battling it out for whose turn it was next.

Ignoring them, she banged on the door. 'Hurry up, Suzy.'

The chain flushed and Suzy, her usual smile not quite as sunny this morning, opened the door. Quickly Kerry grabbed Darren and Emma by their necks, pulled them back and ran into the bathroom.

'Not fair!' Emma screamed.

Scowling, Darren gave up and leaned against the wall, his arms folded across his chest.

Downstairs, Robbie, who hadn't slept much either, was busy making toast.

Suzy was down first, followed by Kerry, and then Emma, who had scratched Darren's face in her frenzy to get into the bathroom before him.

It was their quietest morning ever. They all chewed silently on their toast, then went upstairs one by one to dress. Robbie sat in front of a blank television screen, not daring to put it on in case Claire had already made the news by being missing. Or worse by being found.

He said goodbye to them all as Kerry hurried them out of the door to school, but she told them to wait by the gate and ran quickly back into the house.

'I'll be back when I've dropped them off, Robbie. I won't be going in today, not with our Claire missing and our Mam still in the hospital. OK?'

Robbie nodded. Kerry would do what she wanted to do, and there was no way he could force her to do otherwise. He'd tried it once a couple of years ago, and still had the scar to prove it.

Kerry and Darren dropped the girls off, amid strong protests from Emma, which were ignored.

'I'll go the rest of the way meself,' Darren said. 'They'll think yer babysitting me if yer take me up an' all.' Kerry nodded, but instead of moving off he stood looking at her.

'What?'

Darren shook his head. 'Nothing.' Then he turned and headed up the hill.

Puzzled, Kerry watched him. She sensed there was more bothering him than the trouble at home, and so she slowly began to follow. She'd come up with some excuse when she reached the school.

They were nearly at the gates when Darren glanced nervously across the road and stopped dead in his tracks. Kerry looked over, following his gaze. There stood Stevie and Martin, leaning against the wall and glaring at Darren.

Martin looked nervous, and with good reason. He didn't want to be there, but Stevie had banged on the door this morning and refused to go until he came out. The only thing keeping Martin going was the secret he was hiding from Stevie: the fact that he was leaving tonight, going to live with his dad in Newcastle. It was the only way, cos he knew that otherwise it was only a matter of time till he gave way to the pressure and ended up like Stevie.

'I don't fucking believe it,' Kerry said loudly.

Darren nearly fainted dead away. The very last thing he wanted was a confrontation with them. Cross as he was with Kerry for following him, he wasn't half relieved she was there.

Stevie straightened up, and out of the corner of his mouth, he muttered, 'Don't tell me them two bastards is related.'

Martin knew they were, but he didn't want to be

the bearer of bad news. He said instead, 'Ner, how can they be? He's too dark.'

'So, he's got a bit of black in him, that doesn't mean he can't be her brother, yer thick git.'

'Get into school, Darren.' Kerry gave him a gentle shove.

There was nothing Darren wanted more than to escape through those gates, unless a quick trip to the moon could be arranged. But he sighed, knowing he could never leave Kerry by herself, even though she didn't seem one bit frightened of Stevie or Martin.

'No,' he said, planting his feet and sticking his chin up. 'What if they come after you?'

'Huh?' She laughed. 'Like they're gonna catch me.' She looked across at them, then back at Darren. 'Have they been bothering yer?'

Darren put his head down. 'No.'

'You sure?'

Still looking at the ground, Darren nodded.

Kerry thought for a moment, then decided to leave it until he got home tonight. 'OK, then, get yerself in.'

'You'll not let them catch yer, will yer, Kerry?'

'They couldn't catch me in a million.' She smiled down at him.

Reassured, Darren returned her grin, then said, 'OK, but—'

'Just go in, Darren, yer starting to do me head in.'

'OK, I'm gone.' Darren hurried into school.

Kerry watched until he was safely through the doors, then turned to Stevie and Martin. Raising a fist at them, she yelled, 'Dare give him any grief, yer pair of pricks, and it'll be God help yer.'

'What yer gonna do about it, yer stupid bitch?' Stevie yelled back. 'Anyhow, one thing's for sure, yer can't fucking run for ever, yer titless twat.' He laughed, a high-pitched giggle that had Martin looking oddly at him.

Kerry gave them the finger, then set off back home in a slow mocking trot.

'What we gonna do now, Stevie?' Martin asked, as they watched Kerry becoming smaller and smaller, until she was the size of Martin's little finger when she reached the Seahills.

'What yer worrying about, Fartin'? I'll sort the bastards. If yer frightened of a tart, I'm not. And I'll get that little Mickey Mouse fucker hooked, if it's the last fucking thing I do. Him and the rest of them, however many little fuck-ups there are.'

'But what about Mrs Archer? Yer said—'

'Fuck her an' all.'

Martin paled. Stevie was on a fast track to destruction, and trying damned hard to drag him along for the ride. He couldn't wait for tonight, when he would be out of it for good.

Lorraine dressed quickly. She laddered her tights on a split nail and swore; looking at the offending nail, she swore again, as she thought, *That's not a split nail, kiddo, it's a chewed nail.*

'Where the hell are yer, John?' she muttered, looking at the side of the bed that had not been slept in. It had been nearly four o'clock before she'd finally drifted off, and as soon as her eyes opened at half-past eight, she'd known she'd slept alone.

It wasn't the first time in their two-year marriage that her husband had failed to come home – and the excuses, oh my, the fucking lame excuses. The best one was a dying uncle that didn't even exist, for Christ's sake. Last week's had been beaut an' all: his mother phoning him up because she couldn't sleep, a recurring nightmare of all things. And didn't Mammy's boy just have to run over and calm her down.

'I'll give the bastard nightmares this time, all right,' she said out loud as she put the black skirt back on its hanger and reached for her maroon trouser suit. She picked a white cotton blouse to go with it, then raked through her drawers for her new white bra.

Where the hell is it?

Jesus, why can't we have a normal sock-eater like other households? Why did theirs have to take a liking to her underwear as well as socks?

Eventually she found an old one and, making a mental list of all the washing to be done, she dressed, brushed her hair until it gleamed, and tied it up in a neat bun at the nape of her neck.

Downstairs she checked the answer phone. No messages. Some fucking answer phone. She glared at the machine as if it were to blame. Then, sighing, she went into the kitchen and had a hasty breakfast of toast and coffee before setting off for work.

She made it into her office by half-past nine, and as usual they were queuing up to see her.

Luke was first in, and the news was not good.

'So,' she said, after listening to his report, 'not one of the girls has turned up.'

Luke didn't answer; he knew it wasn't a question.

114

'Anything in yet to suggest they might be runaways?'

'Not really, none of them fits the regular pattern.'

'Has Claire Lumsdon's mother been informed yet?'

Luke moved over and leaned against the radiator, his back towards the window. 'No.' He shook his head. 'The oldest son's going in this afternoon.'

'I don't envy the poor lad. Send one of the uniforms down to the hospital later on, perhaps the mother might know more than the brothers and sisters.'

Lorraine sighed. If there was one thing she hated, it was missing kids. And what did she have here? Not one, but three. Strictly speaking, of course, two of them were out of her jurisdiction, but she sensed a link. And let's not forget the missing husband. Hell of a start to the day.

She threw the pencil she'd been chewing into a tray to join a pile of similarly destroyed ones. She could murder a cigarette.

'Start pulling the perves in. Every single one on the list. Grill them till they're ready to burst, then call me in.'

'They'll start screaming about their rights,' Luke warned.

'Who gives a shit? As far as I'm concerned, they have no rights. Never have and never will. And fuck the do-gooders. They should try doing our job one day, let them see what we have to scrape up off the streets.' Luke grinned as Lorraine went on. 'And the other business?'

'Carter has more on that. I'll let him tell yer himself.'

'OK, send him in.'

Before Luke was halfway out the door, Carter was easing himself in.

'OK, what yer got?'

Carter was giddy with information. 'Scottie phoned earlier, he's pretty sure the body is Jack Holland.'

Lorraine sighed, disappointed. 'Is that it? Nothing on the others yet?' She knew Scottie worked late and started early, very early.

Carter shook his head. 'Sorry, boss. But he's adamant, that knife's the key. Find the knife and we'll find the killer.'

Lorraine looked at her pencils as if they would suddenly stand to attention and start doing automatic writing, before saying, with a sigh, 'OK, Carter, send Luke back in please. He knows Mrs Holland, I'll send him round to talk to her.'

'Right, boss.' Determined to make a good impression, Carter swung smartly round, and went in search of Luke.

As Lorraine waited for Luke, she wondered again where the hell her husband was. *How in God's name do yer report a detective inspector's husband missing, without becoming the laughing stock of the whole bloody police station?*

She snapped a pencil in half and threw the remains at the wall. 'Where the hell are yer? Bastard.'

'Boss?' Lorraine hadn't heard Luke come in, and she jumped when he spoke. Moving over to stand in front of her desk, he looked down at her. 'You all right, Lorraine?'

'Of course I'm all right.' She spoke curtly, and Luke stepped back. 'Why wouldn't I be all right? And how many times have I told yer not to call me Lorraine in the office?' She glared up at him.

Luke was amazed. Lorraine was one of the calmest women he'd ever met, she rarely if ever snapped at anyone.

Realising she was near the edge, Lorraine apologised. 'Sorry, Luke, it's not your fault. Something personal.' She shrugged, her accompanying smile begging forgiveness; his answering smile, although a little cautious, gave it.

'Before yer start with the perves, could yer pop round and see Mrs Holland? I know she's senile, but she'll still have to be informed that her son, even though she doesn't realise he's missing, has turned up after a sixteen-year absence . . . I thought, seeing as you know her . . .'

'Yeah, no bother. She'll probably forget the minute I'm gone though.'

Lorraine thought for a moment. 'But don't these poor folk have good long-term memories?'

'So they reckon. She does waffle on a bit about the past sometimes.'

'Good, get her reminiscing. See what she comes up with.'

Luke left and Lorraine sat staring at the phone. After a few minutes, she picked it up and pressed the buttons; three rings and it was answered.

'Hi, is that you, Harry?'

'It sure is, and I'd recognise that voice anywhere. How yer doing, Lorry?'

As worried as she was, Lorraine couldn't stop the smile. 'I'm fine. I was just wondering if like, you'd, er . . . seen John lately?'

Harry didn't try to conceal his groan. 'Not since last week, pet. Thank God, I might add. I know Peter had to take his class last night, again. So what's the matter? The rat sick or something?'

When Lorraine was slow to answer, Harry jumped in. 'Don't tell me yer don't know where he is?'

'He didn't come home last night, Harry. And I don't know what to do.' Harry was her sensei – her mentor – and her mother's cousin; for a long time he'd been Lorraine's substitute dad and she trusted him as much as she trusted Mavis. It was because of him that she'd first got into karate and met John, one of Harry's fellow teachers, though the two of them couldn't have been more different.

She heard Harry grind his teeth before he said, 'I tried to tell yer the rat was no good before yer married him. But yer were head over heels. And I bet this isn't the first time he's gone AWOL, is it, pet?'

'No.' She hesitated, then decided to tell all. 'A couple of months ago he said his uncle had died and he was away for three days at the funeral. We were really busy here and I couldn't get the time off, not three days' worth, anyhow—'

'Where the hell was the funeral? Bloody Hong Kong?'

'Ireland.'

'Ireland, eh? Well, it doesn't take three days to get to bloody Ireland and back, it's just across the water.

And, as far as I know, the rat doesn't have any uncles. I sure as hell don't remember any at the wedding, do you?'

Lorraine shook her head, then remembered Harry couldn't see her. 'No, Harry. No uncles that I remember either.'

'Look, pet, find the rat then squash him, because if I find him first, I'll kill the bastard. And that's a promise.'

As Harry ranted down the phone for the next five minutes, Lorraine was left in no doubt as to what he would do with her two-timing bastard of a husband, if and when he found him.

After they said goodbye, Lorraine stared at the phone for a while. Then she looked at her watch. Eleven thirty already. Time for her briefing, but after that she was definitely going to get out of the station for a while to clear her mind. Perhaps getting a bit of distance from Luke, Carter, the paperwork and the phone would help things come together. She wanted to go and have another look at where Holland's body had been found, even though forensics had scoured the area. Scraping back her chair, she left for the incident room, pushing the troubling thought of her husband firmly to the back of her mind.

8

Robbie stood with Kerry, outside the ward doors. As Kerry looked up at her brother, it seemed to her that he looked a hell of a lot older than he had the day before. And she hadn't wanted to add Darren's troubles to his list, but she was certain that Stevie and Martin were after him for something. *Christ*, she thought, as she pushed the ward door open because it looked like Robbie was gonna stand in the same spot all night, *what the fuck is this? Get the Lumsdons week?*

Their mother was at the far end of the ward, and they could see from here that she looked much better, physically that was, though Kerry could tell that she was worried sick about something. *Oh God, she doesn't know the half of it yet.*

'Hi, Mam,' she said, as she reached the bed.

Vanessa looked up and managed a wan smile. She sighed, then said, 'I can go this afternoon. Would yer ask Trevor across the road if he'll come for me? He'll only take a couple of quid, where a taxi's gonna cost an arm and a leg.'

Although Vanessa was talking about coming home – babbling actually, Kerry thought – her tone of voice made it sound as if she didn't really want to come home at all. *What the hell is she gonna sound like when she finds out about our Claire?*

Kerry nudged her brother, she wasn't gonna pussy-foot around listening to both of them gabble on. She was about to kick his shin when Robbie took hold of his mother's hand.

'Mam, there's something you have to know.' He stopped and took a deep breath. 'I've racked me brains for a way to say this, but there is no way except to just tell you. Our Claire's gone missing.'

A long silence stretched between them, then Vanessa said, 'Missing?' in such a small voice that both her children had to strain to hear her.

'She didn't come home last night, Mam,' Robbie said in an equally small voice. 'And she wasn't at school all day yesterday.'

Kerry watched as her mother's face took on the same bleached white as the hospital sheets. Leaning over, Robbie put his arm around his mother's shoulders and the two of them rocked back and forth in silence. Kerry thought the tears that fell on to Vanessa's hands were hers, but no, her mother's eyes were bone dry, the tears were Robbie's.

Then, suddenly, Vanessa started screaming, high-pitched wails that drove into Kerry's bones. Screams the like of which she had never heard before. She put her hands over her ears, but they only dulled the noise. Her mother sounded like she was being tortured in hell. And in between the wails, Kerry could make out the same three words over and over. 'He's got her! He's got her!'

Terrified, Kerry pushed past Robbie and grabbed her mother, shaking her to try to calm her down.

'Stop it, Mam, please stop! What yer talking about? Who's got her? What d'yer mean?'

Trembling, Vanessa fell quiet for a moment and stared up at her eldest daughter. 'The Man,' she said, eyes open so wide she looked as though she'd lost it for good. 'The Man's got her!' And the terrible screaming started again.

Then, finally, a nurse came hurrying over. She drew a pink flowery curtain round the bed and shooed Kerry and Robbie into a side waiting room.

Kerry and Robbie sat down and stared at each other. Even with the door shut they could still hear their mother's screams.

'What the fuck's she goin' on about?' Kerry demanded. 'What the—'

'No idea.' Robbie shook his head slowly, still in shock at his mother's outburst.

'Do you think . . . ? Do you think she maybe knows something about who might have our Claire?' Kerry just couldn't get her head round it.

They sat in stunned silence until a few minutes later a doctor wearing the largest pair of glasses Kerry had ever seen walked into the waiting room.

'What on earth brought this on?' he demanded sternly, his glasses moving up and down with every word he said. Without waiting for an answer from either of them, he went on. 'You'd better have a damn good reason for whatever it is you just said to your mother, it's put her back days.'

Robbie looked ashen as he said, 'I'm sorry, Doctor,

I thought the cops . . . I mean the police . . . had told you.'

'Told me what?'

Robbie explained about Claire and what the police had told them to do, and when he'd finished the doctor's face softened. He put his hand on Robbie's shoulder. 'Look, I'm sorry, son, but no one informed us about your sister. Really, you should have told one of the nurses before you said anything.'

Robbie nodded. The doctor was right, he'd fucked up royally.

'The police will be coming in some time today, I suppose?' The doctor raised his eyebrows, waiting for an answer, and the glasses moved absurdly high up his brow.

'Yeah, some time this afternoon,' Kerry said. She knew that in different circumstances his glasses would have made her wet herself laughing, but nothing seemed funny any more.

'Well I'm afraid they'll be disappointed, I've given her enough to knock a horse out. She won't be fully coherent until some time tomorrow.'

'I'm sorry,' Robbie muttered miserably.

The doctor gave him a sympathetic smile. 'It's not really your fault, son. The police should have informed us themselves . . . Now, why don't the pair of you go home? I'm sure your sister will turn up eventually. Come back tomorrow with some good news, eh?' The glasses were in grave danger of disappearing in his hairline. 'And please, in future try to keep us informed of what's going on.'

Yeah, Kerry thought, staring at his glasses. *The*

trouble is half the time we haven't got a fucking clue what's going on ourselves. And after promising to see the ward sister in future with any news that might be upsetting to the patient, they left.

They reached the bus stop to discover they had just missed the bus. 'Well, that's fucking clever,' Kerry declared as she stood with her hands on her hips reading the noticeboard. 'It says here that it's another twenty-five fucking minutes before the next one.' She looked up at the sky. 'And I bet it's gonna piss down an' all.'

Robbie wasn't listening, he was busy counting his money.

With a grimace, he shoved it back in his pocket, looked at Kerry, and said, 'If we walk to the next bus stop, we can afford a bag of chips between us. What do yer reckon, hungry or what, mate?'

'Hungry?' Kerry stamped her foot, and her voice rose with every word. Suddenly all her worry about her mother, all her fear for her sister, and all her frustration about everything that went along with living on the Seahills, erupted. 'I'm bloody starving. Remember, I didn't do me papers this morning, did I? So, no nicked milk. Just a lousy bastard piece of toast. And that's the best you can come up with, a bag of fucking chips between us?

'What you fucking looking at?' she demanded of a hapless middle-aged couple who passed them and tutted, just as Kerry's stomach made a loud rumbling sound. She swung back to Robbie. 'I know, why don't we walk all the fucking way, eh? That'll be good, won't it? Then we might be able to afford a fucking fish as well as the bloody chips. That's a good idea, isn't it, eh? What do you reckon, man, good idea or what?'

Robbie held his hands up. 'I'm sorry, Kerry, it's the best I can do.'

For a moment Kerry was tempted to tell him what to do with his best – had it been anyone else she probably would have – but Robbie looked so hurt and defeated that her heart softened and she felt terrible for being so bitchy to him. After all, none of this was his fault.

She touched his arm, and with a watery smile said, 'I'm sorry, Robbie, honest. I know you do your best. You deal with stuff all the time while I mostly think about me running . . . But what the hell we gonna do? We can't go on like this. Every day for as long as I can remember has been fucking worse than the day before. Now our Mam's in the hospital and our Claire's out there . . .' She waved her arms in the air. Robbie, thinking for a moment that she was going to hit him, stepped hastily back, but that was the last thing on her mind. The wind out of her sails for the moment, she slumped against the bus stop.

But before Robbie could say anything to comfort her, she was off again. 'She could be any fucking where . . . Do yer know that? Any fucking where. What the fuck we gonna do, Robbie? What the fuck we gonna do?' The tears she'd held back splashed hot and quick. Robbie moved to put his arm around her but she pushed him away.

'The coppers couldn't give a fuck, do yer know that? What happened today wasn't your fault, that doctor with the stupid fucking glasses was right. The coppers should have told them long before we got there, but cos we haven't got a fancy fucking address they couldn't give a shit. Fucking bastards, that's all they fucking well are. Just cos we live in an old worn-down fucking estate that nobody, least of all the fucking council, gives a jot about, we're pushed to the bottom of the fucking list for everything. Well it isn't gonna happen, not with our Claire.' She looked at Robbie and he could see the steel in her eyes, the determination on her face.

'I'm gonna find her. And,' she waved her arm in the air, 'yer better believe me, Robbie Lumsdon, I'm gonna get to the bottom of what Mam was going on about in hospital an' all. There's more to this "Man" business than meets the eye. She's running scared in there, and I'm gonna find the fucker, whoever he is.'

Robbie stood with his hands in his pockets, watching her. After a moment, he shrugged, there was nothing he could say. He knew his sister; she would do what she said, whatever the cost.

Lorraine slipped into her mother's kitchen via the back door. Her visit to Fatfield hadn't got her any further with the Holland case and she was due back at the station in half an hour, but as she had to drive past Mavis's house anyway she'd decided to pop in. Mavis had lived here for ever, and would definitely remember any gossip about men like Holland disappearing fifteen or sixteen years ago.

She found her mother at the sink washing dishes,

and Mavis spun round when she heard Lorraine. Her hair hung in two plaits, one over each shoulder. She wore a skimpy top and black leggings, and two inches of tanned skin, a legacy from her recent trip abroad, showed in the middle.

Lorraine blinked and only just stopped herself from doing a double take. *No . . .* she thought. *That is not a belly button ring in my mother's navel. No way.* Mavis grinned at her as the ring caught the sun, which had for a time found a break in the clouds. 'Like it?' She thrust her stomach forward, and without waiting for Lorraine's approval, or disapproval, went on. 'I had it done on me last trip. Everyone's wearing them.' She flicked the ring with her finger.

Lorraine stared, more in wonder than anything else. Slowly she shook her head. 'You never fail to amaze me, Mother, I'll say that for yer.'

Mavis took the shake for a no. 'Yer don't like it? Never mind. Do yer want something to eat?'

'A cup of coffee will do, I've got to get back. I was on me way back to the station but I got to thinking and just ended up driving around.'

'Things getting to yer, are they? Now I've told yer before, it's a job that yer do the best yer can. But yer can't always solve everything and it's no good getting yer knickers in a twist. Now sit down and I'll make yer a ham sandwich, yer've got to eat something.'

Lorraine knew it was no good protesting. Mavis would follow her to the station, if needs be, to make sure she ate the sandwich.

'Right,' she said a few minutes later as she placed

the food in front of Lorraine, 'what's bothering yer?'

Lorraine looked at her mother. That they'd found a body with six toes on each foot was common knowledge; that there were three teenage girls missing was also common knowledge.

'Ever heard of a Jack Holland, Mam?'

'Yeah, old Mrs Holland's son. Bit of a rogue he was, but likeable. He never hurt anyone around here that I know of.' Suddenly her eyes widened. 'Wait a minute, that's him, isn't it? He had six toes, everybody knew that, it was the talk of the place when he was born. Must be over forty years ago now.'

Lorraine nodded. 'Luke knew him as well.'

'Nice lad, that Luke. Very nice.'

Ignoring Mavis's obvious hint, Lorraine went on. 'As to why he was killed, we haven't got a clue, nor do we have any idea who the other bodies might be.'

'What!' Mavis nearly choked. 'More bodies? No wonder yer sick as a chip.'

'Aye. They've all been dead for some time, so there's no need for panic. But actually, I'm clutching at straws here. I'm only telling you now, in case yer know some other local lads that haven't been around for a while. We're not making the others public yet so yer not to breathe a word. Not that yer would.' Lorraine knew that she could trust her mother.

Mavis thought for a moment. 'None that I can think of. And Jack Holland was supposed to have gone off with some woman. I can't believe he's dead.'

'Never mind, it was worth a shot.'

'I think they must have all been mixed up in something bad.'

Lorraine shook her head. 'Yer can't say that for sure. Especially as we haven't a clue who the other three are.'

'Ha'way, man. It stands to reason. Sounds like they've all been murdered, for God's sake, so don't go getting all politically correct on me. And I've already told yer, Jack Holland was no angel. Anyhow, what about this internet thing? I thought it was supposed to be a highway of information?'

'Yeah, well, between you and me, it's not all it's cracked up to be. Aye, yer can get a lot of stuff off it, but it's hardly likely to sit up and tell us who these bodies are, is it?'

Mavis shrugged. 'OK, so what's new on the girls?'

Lorraine blew air out of her cheeks. 'Not much happening there either.' She took a drink of coffee, and sighed. 'All we really know is that all three girls met new fellas in the last month or so . . . I'm hoping for a break later on this afternoon when we drag the perves in. The boyfriends seem to have gone to ground.'

'Don't yer think that's a bit strange? I mean, for all three to disappear? Are yer thinking they're linked?'

Lorraine shrugged. 'In this world it's getting increasingly hard to figure out what passes for strange, and what doesn't.'

'So what's their names?'

'Claire Lum—'

'No,' Mavis interrupted. 'The lads' names. Maybe I know them.'

'Oh . . . Well at the moment all we have from

various friends of the girls are the boyfriends' Christian names.' She frowned. 'A Brad, a Brent and a Billy.' Then she repeated each name twice more. Clapped her hands together, grabbed Mavis and kissed her. 'That's it, Mam, yer a genius.'

'What did I say?' Mavis looked confused.

'Most people who change their name, for whatever reason, choose a name with the same first letter. Easier to remember, see?'

'Right. So?'

'So, I'll bet yer anything yer like that our Brad, Brent and Billy are the same person.'

Lorraine reached for the drawer but Mavis's quick hands beat her to it; she pulled out a pencil and handed it to her daughter.

Lorraine smiled. 'Is there anything yer don't know about me, Mam?'

'No,' Mavis replied with a self-satisfied grin, then, 'oh yes, one thing. What the hell attracted yer to what'sisname in the first place?'

'Mother . . .' Lorraine said warningly, as she put the end of the pencil in her mouth and considered the boyfriends. Brad, Brent and Billy. Suppose they *were* the same man, a good-looking bloke preying on young girls. So what was he after? They could be looking at – her heart plummeted – a serial killer. But if he was killing the girls, why would he keep changing his name? The witnesses would be dead. He could be a pimp? But then some of the pimps Lorraine had on her books would have reported new girls on the scene. She frowned. 'I hope to hell we haven't got some sort of slave ring operating in the area.'

Mavis stared at her for a moment before saying, 'Had away . . . This is Houghton le Spring, man. Not some third-world country. Things like that don't happen here.'

'Oh but they do, Mam. Things like that can happen anywhere.'

'Then God help them poor bairns . . .' She glanced down. 'This doesn't seem so funny now.' She slipped her finger through her belly button ring and yanked hard.

'Ahh,' Lorraine yelled. 'What are yer doing?' She cringed, expecting blood – and lots of it – to spurt all over the breakfast bar. But when Mavis threw the ring on to the bar, she saw the flesh-coloured sticky tape.

Picking up the ring, Lorraine narrowed her eyes and glared at Mavis.

Mavis laughed at her daughter's face. 'Just a joke, darling. Yer sounded so depressed when yer rang to say you'd call in. I thought I might cheer yer up a bit.'

'And that's the best yer could do?'

'Short notice, pet. If you'd seen yer face when yer came in the door . . .' She laughed, and Lorraine had to smile.

'Actually, I'm pleased yer found out, these bloody leggings're killing me. I'm sure they've cut me circulation off.'

She disappeared into the bedroom and was back a few minutes later, dressed in her usual style. Lorraine noticed that today's dress was more subdued than usual – a plain brown with beige trim

131

– although every bit as soft and flowing as the others.

'Mam, I want you to know that what you just did was shocking. But I may have to forgive you.'

'Well, that's big of yer.' She sat down and, resting her hands on her elbows, stared into Lorraine's face. 'Right, now that the official business is out of the way, what else is troubling yer?'

'What do yer mean? There is nothing else,' Lorraine protested.

'Lorry, don't lie to me. I'm yer mam, and I know something's bothering yer, so spit it out.' Putting her head on one side, she pointed a scarlet-tipped finger at Lorraine. 'And I just bet it's got something to do with what'sisname.'

Lorraine sighed, and Mavis knew it came from the heart. 'Yer right, Mam. He didn't come home last night. I don't know where he is and I don't know where to start looking for him.'

'The bottom of the River Wear would be good.'

'Mam!'

'Well, it's not the first time, is it? I don't know why yer put up with it, I really don't. You being in the position yer in, yer could get any man yer want. I'm sure Luke—'

'Mother.' Lorraine gave Mavis a warning look.

'OK, OK. But yer have to admit, Luke is bloody gorgeous.'

Lorraine shook her head, then rested it on her hands. After a moment, she said, 'What the hell am I gonna do? If I report him missing, I'll be the laughing stock of the police station. Can yer just imagine what sort of jokes they'll come up with?'

132

Mavis rose, and in the sudden quiet the stool made a loud scraping noise on the floor. She stepped over to Lorraine and, taking her head in her hands, cradled it against her chest. 'There's not a lot yer can do, pet, he's a grown man.'

'But what if he's lying hurt somewhere?'

'Come off it. That one knows how to look after himself – in more ways than one, I'll bet. Now I know yer not gonna like this, but do yer think it could be another woman?'

Lorraine shook her head. 'I'm not sure. Sometimes, he goes all cold; it's as if I'm not there, not part of his life. It seems to start for no reason at all, and when it does we might as well be on different planets, for all the notice he takes of me.'

Mavis sniffed. 'Well, short of shooting the twat . . .'

'I can't very well do that, Mam. For one thing I can't find the bastard.'

'So . . . OK, here's what yer do. Move back home, and when the creep comes knocking, yer tell him to shove it.'

Lorraine laughed softly. 'You always make it sound so easy, Mam.'

'But it is, kiddo. It's never been so easy. Wake up! In case yer didn't know, women don't have to take that kind of shit any more. For Christ's sake, yer've dealt with plenty domestics.'

'I know, I know, but it's different when it happens to yourself.'

'Well, Harry says . . . Oh!' Mavis waved her hands in the air, and the right one fluttered to land over her mouth.

Lorraine jumped up. 'Yer already knew, didn't yer? Don't try to protect that big-mouth Harry by lying to me, Mother.'

'Well, er . . . Harry did phone, pet. After all, he is very close to us, and he was concerned.'

'Aye, he'll have phoned the minute I put the phone down.' She threw her arms up in the air. 'Between the pair of you, I swear . . .'

Her face was menacing as she moved towards Mavis, but she had to struggle to keep a smile inside as she grabbed her mother and cuddled her.

Claire was hot and sweaty; the air in the tiny cabin was stifling. Their ropes had been replaced by steel anklets, joined together by a heavy chain. There was no way to loosen them; Claire had tried as soon as their hands had been freed.

Jade was combing Claire's hair with her fingers, and Claire found it mildly soothing. She yawned, even though she'd dozed on and off through the day. She'd been terrified to sleep last night, terrified in case something with more than two legs crawled over her naked body. Terrified in case something with two legs came in in the darkest part of the night and raped her.

The only sound was the waves lapping at the side of the boat, and she'd just begun to drift again when Tracy lunged up from her seat and, screaming, made for the door. She'd moved so quickly that Claire and Jade were both yanked off the seat and Jade was deposited on the floor.

Claire, heart pounding, covered her ears with her hands. 'Jesus, Tracy.'

'Shut her up,' Jade said, from the floor. 'He'll be right in and start kicking the shit out of her.'

But Tracy kept throwing herself at the door, and with each thrust the chain yanked on Claire's bad ankle. Groaning with pain, she reached Tracy, knowing that she had to calm her down and dreading what would happen if she couldn't. She put her hands on the other girl's shoulders, intending to talk her back to the seat, but before she had a chance, the door opened and he stood there grinning at them.

'Now, now, girlie.' He stepped into the cabin, forcing them back without even touching them.

'NO, NO, NO!' Tracy screamed, as she threw herself at him.

For a moment he was surprised, but only for a moment. He grabbed her arm and slammed her into the cabin wall, brutally yanking Claire and Jade to the side. The anklets bit into Claire's flesh as, screaming, she lashed out at him. He spun round, and the fist meant for Tracy caught Claire on the side of her head. Just before she passed out she found herself looking at Jade's feet.

A few hours later Brad sauntered into the Blue Lion, a girl with long dark hair at his side, and winked at Mrs Archer, who nodded back at him. Tuesdays were always slack because it was karaoke night at the White Lion, so she manned the bar herself with a bit of help from Jason Smith.

Jason was pouring a pint for one of the regulars and watching Brad at the same time. He hated Brad, who loved himself far too much in Jason's eyes. He glanced at the girl; as usual she was a looker. *Where the hell does he get them from?* Jason shook his head as he handed the pint over.

'I'll have one of them, Jas.'

Jason cringed. He hated it when the smarmy bastard called him that.

Turning to the girl, who couldn't take her eyes off him, Brad said, 'What about you, love, what yer having?'

'Ohh, er, an orange please,' the girl replied, smiling and blinking her eyelids faster than the land speed record.

Obviously under age and never been in a pub before, Jason thought, as he put a pint on the bar. He'd be buggered if he'd carry the drinks to the table for the wanker.

'Gin it,' Mrs Archer said in his ear.

He reached for the gin and mixed a generous portion into the orange. He knew what was going on – they were one short of the quota. This poor kid must be the replacement and Brad, the bastard, was hurrying her along. Jesus, he wished he had the guts to do a spot of blackmail. Him and his mam would be set up for life. Aye, but it would be a damn short life an' all.

An hour and four gin and oranges later, the girl was nearly out of it. Mrs Archer bolted the door behind the last straggler and walked over to Brad and the girl.

She picked the girl's drink up. 'I'll just freshen this for yer, pet.'

'Thanks,' the girl slurred, as she slumped against Brad's shoulder.

Mrs Archer went behind the bar and took a pill out of her bag, then dropped it in the glass and stirred it up. Going back over to them, she handed it to the girl who took it with some difficulty.

'Get that down yer, pet, it's good stuff that.'

Obediently the girl took a large gulp. She wondered briefly why Brad and the woman were staring at her, before she blacked out.

'Right, that's it, get her out of here. And you,' she snarled at Brad, 'I've told yer before not to bring them here. For fuck's sake, are yer fucking daft or what?'

'I had to take her somewhere, they need her as soon as possible. Four were ordered, and yer know what this customer's like.'

'Aye, well don't make a habit of it.' She went to the back door. 'Come on then, the pair of yer. Ally will be waiting out the back. And make sure nobody clocks yer.'

She let them out then locked the door behind them.

'Bastard,' she muttered, as she went up the stairs. 'As if things aren't hairy enough, the prat has to bring them here.'

The walls seemed to be closing in on her when she walked into the kitchen, and feeling anxious she put the kettle on. As she waited for it to boil she sat looking down into the dark deserted street.

Wednesday

9

Claire blinked. It was daylight, and early by the look of it. For a moment, when she heard the soft snores of the other girls, she thought she was back home and that the last two days had been a nightmare. Then she remembered.

She turned over and moaned softly, aching in places she hadn't known existed, her head still throbbing from the heavy blow the night before. At least the other man – the one who wasn't Jade's Laughing Man – had removed the steel rings which had cut into her ankles. He'd obviously decided that after a couple of days of imprisonment and near starvation, they weren't strong enough to try and escape.

She blinked again, this time in surprise. There was a new girl crouched in the corner. Her arms were wrapped around her knees, hugging them to her chest, and her hair fell forwards over her face.

As Claire stared at her, the girl slowly lifted her head. She looked at Claire and started to cry. 'Where . . . ?'

Claire slowly shook her head, and pain lanced through her skull. 'Oh,' she gasped, holding her head.

'If youse two don't be quiet, he'll be on our backs.'

Jade had woken up and was staring at the new girl. 'All right?' she asked her.

But the girl suddenly started wailing, long loud shrieks that came from the depths of her terrified soul.

'Shh,' Claire and Jade said in unison, while Tracy, who had also woken up, stared unblinkingly at the wooden roof.

Then the new girl started vomiting. The smell was awful and the other three knew it was alcohol. Jade started to retch just as the door was yanked open, and he stood there laughing. In his hand there was a bucket full of cold water and he threw it over the new girl. 'Shut the fuck up, bitch, or I'll fucking kill yer.'

He slammed the door, and the girl sat gasping for breath. It was only then that she realised that she was naked. 'What's happening? Who are yer?' she cried, water dripping from her hair to run down and pool at Tracy's side.

'We don't know hardly anything ourselves,' Claire said quietly. She didn't want a bucket of water over her.

Jade, glancing at Claire, interrupted. 'What's yer name?'

'Donna,' the new girl replied, talking more softly now.

Jade nodded and started to tell her everything they knew.

'So what's the matter with her?' Donna said, pointing at Tracy, when Jade had finished.

Jade shrugged. 'I think she's losing it.'

'She's in a better place,' Claire added.

'Aye, well I'm going to a better place an' all.' Suddenly Donna jumped up, opened the door and ran out on to the deck.

Claire looked at Jade, her heart racing. She was terrified of moving, of getting caught, of making Laughing Man angry, but this might be her only chance. She couldn't afford to miss it. Jumping to her feet, she ran after Donna.

'Come back,' Jade whispered urgently. 'Please, Claire, don't do it. He'll kill yer.'

But Claire was going.

She burst through the door to find Laughing Man with one arm round Donna's throat and the other round her waist. His eyes opened with surprise when he saw her.

Claire blinked in the shock of daylight. Everything looked so disconcertingly normal, but the part of the dock where the boat was moored was still deserted – they'd chosen their location well. There was no one around, no one to call to for help.

Body pumping adrenalin, she jumped over the side of the boat and started to leg it. She tasted the fresh air, and loved it. She could hear Laughing Man still struggling with Donna, but she was going home. Home to her mam and the rest of them. When she got there she would send the police for the other girls, but at this moment in time all she could see in her mind's eye was her own sweet home.

She'd gone twenty steps along the quayside when she was brought down with a rugby tackle. Winded, she struggled nevertheless and fought her way round to see her attacker. The other man. The one who'd removed the chains. He must have been on his way back to the boat and seen what had happened. For a moment, even as she kicked and hit out at him, she felt a surge of hope. He had, after all, removed the anklets to make them more comfortable. But that hope disintegrated fast as, pinning her arms behind her back with one meaty hand, he fumbled in his pockets and brought out a knife. Holding it to her neck, he pushed her back towards the boat and Claire, feeling the cold, sharp steel against her pulse, gave up the fight.

He threw her back on board then climbed up after her and, grabbing some more tape from the deck, slapped some over her mouth. It tasted foul. The cut on her knee had opened up and was bleeding heavily.

Laughing Man, still holding on to Donna, took the tape from his friend and covered Donna's mouth. She tried to bite him, but he slapped her into submission.

'Bastards,' he said, when they were both trussed up. 'Let's sort the pair of them right here, then throw them overboard. Nowt but trouble.'

Claire felt herself begin to shake. She didn't want to die, not yet. She was only just learning to live. *Please God.*

Then the other man spoke. 'No, we've lost too much already. So far the marks are only surface, they'll heal and we should still get the asking price. Throw the pair of them back inside. Thank fuck we're moving them soon.'

Grabbing the girls by their hair he hauled them

into the cabin and, after giving both of them a kick for good measure, slammed the door.

Too terrified to cry, Donna stared wide-eyed at the others, while Claire helplessly watched the blood seep from her knee.

10

Lorraine, her problems locked deep inside of her, left her office and walked along the corridor to the interview room. They had spent all yesterday afternoon with the known perves and got nowhere, but it was standard procedure to call them all in when undersixteens were involved. This morning was the turn of the worst of the lot.

Clive Monroe, a forty-eight-year-old father of four girls, all of whom he'd abused before their third birthdays, sat with his back to the door. Lorraine had reread his file, which she gripped tightly in her hand, and knew the abuse would have continued if he hadn't become greedy and coveted his friends' daughters.

She noticed the black ring of dirt on the collar of his red shirt and pulled a face as she moved to her desk. Luke, who had been sitting in her chair, rose and moved to the window.

'Well,' she began, glaring at Monroe as she sat down. Sweat trickled over his greasy pockmarked face. His eyes, in between the heavy folds of flesh surrounding them, were like tiny black currants.

'It just keeps on saying it knows nothing, boss,' Luke said. 'Insists it's a good boy now.'

146

'Does it? Well, it better think of something more to say.' She smiled sweetly at Monroe, just before she kicked him in the shin.

He screamed and clutched his leg. 'Yer can't do that.'

'I just did. Yer on my patch, remember.'

Monroe started to shake, his hands came together and he began squeezing them in a nervous manner. He tucked his legs as far under the seat as he could, then said, 'Yer can still get wrong for what yer just did.'

Lorraine turned to Luke.

'Correct me if I'm wrong, Detective, but did it just threaten me?'

'It sounded that way to me, boss.'

'I have me rights, yer know.' Monroe's voice was thin and reedy; it had always got on Lorraine's nerves, but this morning it was driving her crazy.

Half standing, she leaned over her desk, her face inches away from Monroe's. 'Now let me tell yer something, yer pathetic piece of shit.' She poked him in his chest. 'You are just a thing to me and my good friend here, and all my other good friends out there. And, as a thing, yer have no rights at all. You gave yer rights up years ago, when yer assaulted them lovely bairns of yours. Where,' she poked him again and he winced, 'where were their rights then, eh, creep?'

'I . . . I . . .' he blustered.

'Did I say yer could open yer ugly yap, creep?'

Monroe knew when he was beaten. He'd been down this road with Lorraine before. He hung his head and stared at the floor.

147

'That's better. Now, we all know that yer had ambitions to carry on up the street with yer vile filthy ways, OK? So, what were yer planning next? Every little girl in Houghton? Don't ever hand me yer fucking rights again. Because as far as I'm concerned, creep, yer've fucking got none. And if I want to talk to yer as if yer a fucking leper, or even a damn Martian, tough shit. You will sit there and listen, and yer won't fucking well speak until I say so. And when I do tell yer to speak, make damn sure yer've got something to say. Has yer tiny pea brain got all that?'

Monroe sniffed.

Lorraine curled her lip. 'Oh, how fucking pathetic can it get? What do yer reckon, Luke, pathetic?'

'It is that, boss.'

Monroe started to cry.

'Oh, for fuck's sake.' Lorraine slammed his file on the table, making Monroe jump. Luke handed him some tissues. Lorraine watched as Monroe dabbed his eyes, then she said in a cold voice more threatening than any shout, 'What's the word on the street, creep?'

Monroe shook his head without looking up, and mumbled something incoherent.

'Speak up, arsehole. We can't hear yer.'

He cleared his throat nervously. 'I don't know nothing. I don't mix with those sort of people any more.'

Lorraine looked up at the ceiling. 'Pleeease, don't tell me yer've seen the fucking light.'

Monroe nodded his head vigorously. 'Yes, yes,' he

babbled as if his life depended on it. 'I've joined the Church.'

Lorraine snorted as Monroe went on. 'I converted five years ago when I was inside, but you lot still hound me whenever something happens. It's just not fair.'

'Not fair!' Lorraine exploded. 'Not fucking fair! Am I hearing right, Detective?'

'I guess yer heard the same as me, boss.'

Lorraine could feel her blood rising. This time she poked the top of his bony head with two fingers. 'Do yer think that for one fucking minute, just because yer a member of the Church, yer a fucking saint now? Saint Fucking Monroe? Do yer think that makes yer exempt from being a perve? Puts a veneer of respectability over yer, does it? The fucking Church?' Lorraine wanted to spit. 'All fucking goody-two-shoes there, aren't they?'

Sneering, she turned to Luke. 'Get it out of here, before I vomit all over it.'

'OK, boss.' Luke moved forward and took hold of Monroe's arm. As they reached the door, Lorraine spoke Monroe's name very softly. He turned slowly, barely able to look her in the eye.

'When this is all over, Monroe, if I hear the tiniest whisper that yer knew anything, anything at all, I'll come looking. And believe me, creep, the whole of the fucking Church won't be big enough to hide yer. Got that?'

He nodded, dropped his head, and Luke ushered him out the door.

After the door closed behind them with a soft click,

Lorraine rose and went to the window. She needed a shower, breathing the same air as perverts always made her feel dirty. She hated dealing with these men who betrayed the trust of their children, and when they broke down and cried – as many of them did, praying for forgiveness, saying that it was an illness and they couldn't help it – well, whoever heard of an illness that yer enjoyed?

Standing on her toes with her hands behind her back, she craned her neck and looked sideways out the window. From this angle you could see the court-room doors. People of all ages milled about the steps, smoking and talking.

She smiled when Ada Johnston, leaning heavily on a walking stick she certainly didn't need, limped to the front of the crowd and mounted the steps. At seventy-two years old, Ada was one of Houghton's most accomplished shoplifters. Usually, when caught, the goods were taken from her and she was escorted from the premises and told never to come back. A warning she repeatedly ignored. Obviously one of the shops had sickened of her antics and was prosecuting. Lorraine shook her head; Ada would most likely get a small fine, and be back in harness in the morning.

She looked down the row of regulation Nike or Adidas caps. Most would be up for possession, and probably not even a real dealer amongst them. *Yet the public complain daily that we do nothing.* She felt like banging her head against the wall. *Why can't they understand that if the dealers aren't pointed out, there's nothing we can do?*

A taxi came up the drive and stopped at the steps.

Lorraine tutted when Cal Black got out – now there was a thorn if ever there was one. He must have done hundreds of community hours, but she found it hard to stop a smile creeping over her face. The problem was, even when he did time in the community everyone he met ended up adoring the ground he walked on.

And she should know, didn't she used to babysit him when she was fifteen. Right little charmer he was then, and at eighteen he'd turned into a six-foot blond charmer. And a perfectly genuine one as well; half the time he didn't even realise just how charming he was. His downfall was his love of fast cars.

She watched as he grinned at two policewomen as he passed them going up the steps. Greeted by such an infectious smile, they could do nothing but smile back. She shook her head. What a waste; with his personality he could be anything he wanted, probably even be able to afford the high-priced cars he was addicted to stealing.

He's gonna have to start growing up though, the judge can't keep handing community hours out for ever. Pretty soon he's gonna get a sentence, and with those looks, God help the poor bastard when he gets inside. Although at least he always brings the cars back and leaves them where he's stolen them from. And mostly undamaged at that. Unbelievable. She shook her head again, then turned when Luke came back into the room. He was grinning.

'What's so funny?'

'Monroe. He reckons you are one fucking frightening bitch.'

'Huh. He doesn't know the half. But I'm certain he hasn't got a clue about what's going down.'

'Yeah, I think yer right. In fact, I don't think any of the perves we've seen so far are involved with anything at the moment.'

She sat down. 'It looks like it's gonna be a long hard slog, Luke. And for some reason, I've got a gut feeling this creep's gonna turn out to be an unknown.'

Luke nodded his agreement.

'Right then, send Carter in with the next one. He can watch one or two, see how we operate. It's time to let him loose, see what he can do. Can't hurt, can it?'

'No, and for what it's worth, I think he's a good man.'

Lorraine nodded. 'Yes, I do too. By the way, has anything come in from Scottie this morning?'

Luke shook his head. 'No, it seems like we're getting nowhere fast. The dig hasn't produced any more bodies.'

'Thank God for that. Superintendent Clark is gonna have to forget this year's leek competition at Houghton Feast though, seeing as his leek trench has been trashed.'

Luke saw the merriment in her eyes, and wanted nothing more than to grab hold of her and hold on tight. But he'd learned over the last three years to keep his feelings to himself.

By the end of the morning, Carter was as shell-shocked as the creeps that had cried and yelled in front of him.

He'd only been third string with the two detectives for the last three months, and he'd been thrilled when they had picked him to be on their main team. He'd always assumed, as anyone would, that the big black guy would be the aggressor. No way. To see the way his small beautiful boss worked was amazing. He'd actually learned a few new swear words. Pity they'd learned next to nothing about the girls.

He escorted the last one out of the building, then made his way back to the interview room. Luke was looking out the window and Lorraine was staring at a row of chewed pencils.

It quite broke his heart to see his boss looking so down. But, not quite part of the inner circle yet, he thought it best to say nowt and wait for them. Closing the door, he took a chair and placed it beside the bookshelf. He didn't see the amused smile that passed between Lorraine and Luke as he marked his spot.

Stevie walked around the outside of the empty house in Tulip Crescent. It had been boarded up for months, but he knew there was a way in; he'd been here before, he just couldn't remember where it was.

There would be kids inside, kids with vodka or pills, anything would do. The pills he'd had earlier – the ones that he was supposed to sell – were wearing off and he needed a fix, but if he couldn't get what he wanted, anything would do.

He kicked the door in frustration, and heard a noise inside. 'Where the fuck's the way in?' he demanded.

He was greeted with silence.

He kicked the door and started beating it with his fists. 'Open the fuck up, it's me! Stevie!'

He heard somebody fumbling about, then, 'Shh, some bastard'll hear you.' Then a flap on the door was pushed out. 'Come in and shut the fuck up.'

Grinning, Stevie climbed through the flap. 'I knew this was the way, I just fucking forgot, that's all. What yer got?'

'Lungs,' a twelve-year-old in his school uniform said, just before he dipped his head and took a good long suck of the cannabis.

'Good.' Stevie grabbed the cut-away bottle.

'Hey, it's my turn!' A fourteen-year-old girl with a black Gothic hairstyle screeched at him.

'Fuck you!' Stevie slammed his fist into her face. The girl fell back, and her black Goth lips blossomed crimson.

'There's no need to do that, yer nasty bastard. Look at her mouth!' mumbled another girl with the same hairstyle, about the same age.

Stevie ignored her as he used the lung. The hit was instantaneous. He settled back to enjoy it, and watched dispassionately as the second girl helped the first.

'You working for the Archer now, Stevie?' the twelve-year-old boy asked.

'Aye.'

'I saw yer up at the school the other day. Andrea Cole used to work for her, but she went missing. The word is the Archer had her killed, but I think she just took off for London. What do yer reckon?'

Stevie shrugged, he wasn't really interested. Andrea

Cole had been a right bitch. *But what if she wasn't in London?* A small voice niggled at the back of his mind. Andrea had been a smack head, and the word at the time was she'd been stealing off Mrs Archer.

Just like you're doing now, the voice said.

'Fuck off.'

'What?' the boy asked.

'Not you.' Stevie looked around at the two girls comforting each other in the corner. 'I'm off.' He jumped up and clumsily made his way to the door.

'Got to get to work,' he mumbled as he climbed out the door. In his hurry he caught his hand on a nail, tearing a diamond-shaped piece of flesh from his palm, but he felt nothing, and never noticed the steady drip of blood as he left a trail all the way up to Houghton.

Lorraine and Luke had called in at the Beehive pub for a quick lunch. They ordered hot beef sandwiches that Lorraine just picked at, and after a few minutes she pushed her plate away.

'Can't eat it. I'm worried sick for the girls. Each hour that passes puts them further and further out of our grasp.'

Luke nodded, his mouth full of sandwich. He took a sip of juice, then said, 'What else can we do? The trail is stone cold. Every inquiry meets a blank wall. We've pulled the perves, we've talked to the pros, leaned on the narks, but nothing. Not a thing. I've never seen everyone so silent.'

Lorraine mulled this over for a moment then, looking at Luke, said, 'Aye, it's like there's somebody pulling strings behind the scenes. I wonder. Can yer remember Colin Stone?'

'Not personally, but I've heard talk of him.' He didn't add that Lorraine had been likened to the legendary Colin Stone, a detective who had been cited for bravery many times in the early nineties.

'He came in once when I was first in the specials and gave us a talk.' She tapped her fingers on the table. 'From what I remember, he was after a gang-land boss that lorded over most of Sunderland and had his base in Houghton le Spring.'

'Stone died, didn't he?'

'Some say he died of natural causes, some say otherwise. Whatever, the gangster was never found. And hardly anything has ever been raked up about the bloke. Even the gobbiest nark gets tongue-tied if yer ever go there.'

'So he could be anybody.'

'Yup, and he could still be ruling the roost, for all we know.' Someone like that would be powerful enough to make everyone else shut the fuck up. Maybe it was worth pursuing, though chasing up leads on someone who no one would talk about – someone who most people insisted didn't exist – would be tricky.

Luke reached for his glass and accidentally touched the back of Lorraine's hand. She felt as if she'd been stung by an electric eel, and looked at him then quickly glanced away.

What gorgeous eyes he's got.

Oh Christ, I've been listening to Mam too much. She's finally getting to me.

She fumbled with her bag, pulling the zip shut, then she stood. 'Time we were getting back to work, Luke. Those poor kids could be waiting somewhere, praying to be rescued.'

11

Robbie picked the plates up. Beans on toast had not gone down well with Kerry. He was on his way into the kitchen when the front door opened and Mickey walked in.

'Hi, guys.' He greeted them with his slow smile, followed by his customary wink. 'Glad yer in, cos I lost me key again.'

Mickey didn't really have a key, but Vanessa was always threatening to give him one. He'd been a regular feature in the Lumsdon household since shortly after his tenth birthday, which was also the day his mother had married his stepfather.

'That's all we need,' Kerry said as she rose and walked past him. 'A morning full of worry,' she looked at Robbie's back, 'and a night full of dreams. And now you.'

'Now, Kerry, is that any way to greet a friend?'

'Hello, Mickey,' Robbie said.

'Things is not so good I hear, mate.'

'Then yer hear right,' Kerry said, returning from the kitchen with a glass of water.

Robbie brought Mickey up to date while Kerry, sipping from her glass, stared moodily out the window.

'Wow, that's some serious shit. I thought your Claire was always a bit stuck up like, yer know what I mean, not the sort to go off with just anybody. But if I'd known things were that bad I'd have come down last night. I was stuck at his stupid birthday party, and I couldn't escape the aunts and uncles until an hour ago.'

Robbie and Kerry knew without being told that the Him, was Mickey's stepfather.

'Weren't nothing you could have done,' Robbie said. 'By the time we got back from seeing our Mam at the hospital and collected the kids, all we could do was give them their teas and get them to bed. Not that any of us slept much.' He shook his head and looked bemused, as if the danger Claire might be in was only just sinking in.

'Well,' Mickey asked, 'has anybody ever seen this Brad person?'

Kerry snorted. 'We never even heard of him until Emma said our Claire had a boyfriend. And I'll tell yer this, just as I'll tell her to her face when I see her, our Claire's a sly bitch, and I just might punch her fucking lights out when I catch up with her.'

Mickey quickly nodded his agreement. He quite fancied Claire, with all that blonde hair, especially now she was starting to grow in the right places, but he'd always been in awe of Kerry, and the very last thing he dared to do was defend Claire in front of the female demon facing him. Not in the mood she was in, anyway.

Kerry spun round from the window. 'And I'll tell yer something else, an' all. As soon as that fucking school's out, I'll be waiting for that Katy Jacks and I'll shake the fucking truth out of her. She's got to know more than she's letting on. Our Claire wouldn't just go off like that. I know she wouldn't.'

'So, er, how's yer mam?' Mickey asked, hoping to change the subject for a while, knowing that once Kerry's batteries were warmed up, she had the power to go on for ever. But he was far from prepared for the next onslaught.

'There's something not right there either. She keeps babbling on about some fucking man. I'm gonna find out who he is an' all.'

Robbie stopped her in her tracks by heading back to the kitchen and asking over his shoulder, 'Fancy a cuppa? I think we can just about scrape up the makings.'

'Not for me, Robbie, I'm sick of the sight of tea,' Mickey replied. Kerry, facing the window again, shook her head.

Mickey followed Robbie into the kitchen. 'Youse all right for dosh?'

'Aye, well we'll manage till tomorrow, then I'll cash the book.'

'OK, it's just that if yer were short like, I know somebody who'll buy yer book. All yer have to do is go to the coppers like, say yer've lost it, then pay a visit to the social.'

'No way,' Kerry put in from right behind him. Mickey jumped. He hadn't realised she'd followed them into the kitchen.

'Mam and Sandra tried that one last year at Christmas, remember?'

'Oh, aye.' Mickey nodded.

'They only just got away with it. They even had a visit from the flaming fraud squad. Since then, having to tell all them lies, Mam says if she ever really lost her book, she'd never report it. The pair of them felt that crap. And they had to pay it back.'

'Right, so yer sure yer can manage till tomorrow?' Mickey pulled a ten-pound note out of his pocket. 'Cos, if yer pink lint, yer can lend this. Aunt Brenda gave it to me.'

Robbie was just about to say no, when Kerry neatly snatched the note out of Mickey's hand. 'Thanks, Mickey, you're a real friend.'

Mickey beamed at the praise. 'Right then, I'll be off. I was supposed to meet Cal at the court a couple of hours ago.'

'He up again?' Kerry asked, her eyebrows raised.

'Yep. Usual thing. And I'll tell yer something, I'm certain that judge has a share in that old folks' home on the hill, cos he keeps on sending him there. Cheap labour, see?'

Robbie laughed. 'Why aye, that'll be right.'

Robbie went to the door with Mickey; when he came back Kerry was putting her shoes on.

'Where yer going, Kerry?'

'Over the road to see Sandra. I saw her come in a few minutes ago. She's known our Mam for a long time so if anybody knows something, she will. There's a lot gone on in our Mam's life that we don't know about, and there's something bad. I can feel it. It's about time we were told just what the fuck it is. Nobody in the world can have all the bad luck we have without there being a reason, for fuck's sake.'

Robbie stepped back out of her way, as she headed for the door. When she reached it she turned. 'Yer know them nightmares yer used to have? They've started again, haven't they? I heard yer last night, and the night before.'

Robbie shook his head. 'I haven't had one for ages.' He hated to be reminded of the nightmares, because sometimes, in the middle of the night, when the rest of the house was asleep, he was half convinced that they weren't nightmares at all. They seemed just too real to be only dreams.

'Don't lie, Robbie, yer've never been very good at it.' Her voice softened. 'I think me first memory is of you screaming the house down in the middle of the night.'

Robbie looked at her, looked at the fire, looked out of the window, looked at the door; when he swung his eyes back to Kerry, she was still staring at him.

He swallowed hard, before admitting, 'They're getting worse, Kerry, and I'm not sure I can stand it much longer. Sometimes I wake up in the middle of the night soaked to the skin with sweat.'

'Jesus Christ, Robbie, why haven't yer let on?' She shook her head, hardly able to take in what he was saying. 'Once this is all over we've got to get you sorted.' She hugged him to her briefly before turning back to the door.

'Right, I'm going over there now, and I'm not coming back until I find out just what the fuck happened.'

After the door slammed behind her, Robbie went to the window and watched her march across the road. Kerry the Gladiator. He wished with all his heart he'd been born with her guts.

Kerry opened Sandra's door and walked right in. The house was bright, airy and impossibly clean and tidy. It was carpeted throughout in moss green, Sandra's favourite colour, and most of the furnishings were in a matching green, with buttermilk walls. Even the numerous plants that took up every available space had to be the proper shade of green. Sandra's husband Tom was a long-distance lorry driver, and he often said it was as if he was still behind the wheel and driving down a country road.

'It's me,' Kerry shouted, as she walked through the hallway and into the empty sitting room. Frowning, she turned to go into the kitchen when Sandra came through, wiping her hands on a green-checked tea towel.

'Hi, Kerry.' She greeted her with a smile. 'Everything all right?'

'No it bloody well isn't. And I think yer know some things that I want to know.'

Sandra flushed. 'What are yer talking about, Kerry?'

Kerry tried to calm down. She knew storming in and blurting out accusations wasn't the best way to persuade Sandra to tell her what she knew, but she was just so frustrated.

'Yer know . . . I know yer do. When we went up the hospital Mam was babbling about some man,

163

she seemed to know who might have taken Claire, and . . . and . . . and you've known Mam all these years. She's yer best friend, for Christ's sake, and I don't know who else to ask. I want to know who this "Man" is. And I want to know what happened, because it might have something to do with our Claire going missing.'

'Don't be daft, Kerry.' Sandra looked uncomfortable. 'How can something that happened years ago – that's supposing something did happen – have anything to do with Claire?'

Kerry sat down on the easy chair beside the fire. She made a big show of warming her hands before turning to face Sandra and saying in a calm cold voice, 'I'm not going out of here today until I find out just what the fuck did go on.'

Sandra looked at a suddenly grown-up Kerry, and knew there was no way she was going to be put off with excuses or lies. She answered in a quiet voice, 'I can't, Kerry, it's not for me to tell. What yer want to know must come from your mother.'

'They've knocked her out, haven't they? When she found out about our Claire, she blew a fucking fuse . . .' Kerry's voice broke, but she covered a sob, and went on. 'She was screaming all over the place, like a bloody mad woman. Something about a man. What fucking man?'

Sandra sat down in the matching chair facing Kerry, her hands wringing the tea cloth. She looked at the girl in front of her and couldn't meet her eyes. 'I'm sorry, Kerry, but it's more than me life's worth.' She shook her head. 'I can't tell yer nowt.'

Kerry stared unblinkingly at her. 'If yer don't tell me, I'll go to the coppers and tell them yer know something yer not letting on to. Me sister's gone missing, Sandra. For fuck's sake, she's only thirteen. She's never even slept out for one night before. Now you've always been like an auntie to us, yer have to tell me what yer know.'

Sandra sighed heavily as she looked at Kerry. So like Vanessa used to be, the same fire. Vanessa was broken now and had been for a long time, her fire burned out by that evil man, but Sandra had watched Kerry grow up, and knew there was pure steel beneath her fire; knew that Kerry would not give up until she found out just what she wanted to know. She made up her mind, knowing that really she had no choice.

'OK, I'll tell yer what I know, which, believe me, isn't all of it by a long way.'

'It'll do for starters.'

Sandra thought for a moment, then started to speak. 'Your mam looked very much like you do, Kerry, a real stunner. We met when she came here to live – a bit of a let-down from where she belonged, I can tell yer that. I went home with her once, before your grandparents were killed in that road crash, and they were right posh—'

'I know all about them,' Kerry cut in.

'OK. But I'll tell it as I can or not at all, right?' Sandra said sharply.

Kerry gritted her teeth and nodded.

'The way she looked she could have had any number of men, but Robbie was her choice. And they were really happy, Kerry, made for each other they were. Then Robbie lost his job – not his fault, the whole firm just went belly up.' She was quiet for a moment, thinking. A restless shuffling from Kerry brought her out of her reverie. 'He got into debt with some loan sharks, it happens to the best of us.'

'I don't understand. Who's this Robbie?' Kerry interrupted.

Sandra looked puzzled for a moment, then realised that Kerry was even more in the dark than she'd realised about her mother's past. 'He's your Robbie's dad. They were married. She used to have a wedding photo on the mantelpiece. One day she took it down so the rest of you wouldn't feel left out.'

'But I always thought that me and Robbie were—'

'Full brother and sister. For all I know yer might be. There's only yer mam can put yer right on that score.'

Kerry fell silent for a moment.

'She never speaks about our dads, none of them. Not even this Robbie. Whenever I've asked her she just shrugs it off and starts talking about something else.'

Sandra nodded, then smiled for a moment before going on. 'I know, Kerry, she's told me about your endless questions. Anyhow, I was there the night the loan shark people came for them. My Tom was away, the kids were tucked up, and I'd popped over for a couple of tabs until the morning. Then they turned up.

'It wasn't nice, believe me. There was nothing I could do as they dragged all three of them out of the house – Vanny, Robbie and the baby. One of them, a great big brick shithouse of a man, had Little Robbie under his arm. The bairn was screaming and kicking, terrified he was, but the big bastard didn't give a shit, he just threw Little Robbie into the car. I do remember one other man, even bigger than the bald bastard, he told him to go canny with the bairn, then they both jumped into the car and drove off. I got a black eye off a third man, and told to keep me gob shut, or else.'

'Didn't anybody hear the noise?'

'Oh, a few curtains twitched, but it was pitch black and pissing down, plus that night three of the street-lights didn't come on. The next day the council came round and put new bulbs in, but by then yer mam and Little Robbie were back. Only without Big Robbie.'

'Oh my God.' Kerry couldn't believe it. How could something like that have happened to her own family? It sounded like something from a film. 'So, who in hell is this "Man"? And what happened to Big Robbie?'

Sandra held her hands up. 'That I can't help yer with. And all I know about The Man is that he took a right shine to your mam. He wanted her to sleep with him on a regular basis. And if she did, it would settle the debt.'

For a moment Kerry sat with her mouth wide open. Then she said, 'Had away. That really is a bloody film script. Nobody, it doesn't matter who the bastard is, can make a person do things like that!'

Sandra shook her head sadly.

'Kerry pet, yer act so grown up at times that I forget yer still wet behind the ears. There's a lot of sickos in this world, and believe me, some of them help to run it. Anyhow, as far as I know The Man was completely obsessed with Vanessa. He would send flowers, chocs, fancy perfumes . . . if yer ask me it must have been fucking frightening, waking up every morning wondering what was gonna come next. Anyhow, she sent them all back.'

'But why didn't she just go to the coppers?'

'And say what? That a man was sending her presents, that he wanted to sleep with her? Kerry pet, didn't yer know that's what makes the world go round?'

'Aye, I'm not that daft. But not like that, for Christ's sake. It, it's sick.'

'Yer, I know. But by the time all this happened, Big Robbie, poor bastard, was practically going crackers. He'd been knocked back time and time again for whatever job he tried for. A few friends helped, on the quiet like, so they never starved.'

'And all this was before I was born?'

'Aye.'

'So why didn't they just move away? They could have gone and lived somewhere else. I would have, I'd have gone somewhere far enough away that the creep couldn't find me.'

'Trust me, pet, this man would have found yer mam wherever she went. Money talks, kiddo, don't ever forget that. For Christ's sake, this bastard can even reach into the post office. Giros often went missing, and when Robbie called in to the dole he was told he was a liar and not to bother them.'

'So what happened to him?'

Sandra sighed. This kid would dig right through to Australia to get what she wanted. 'All I know is that three of them were took out that night and only two came back. Yer Mam reported Big Robbie missing the next day, and that's about it. Except that from then on, whatever she tried to do with her life turned rotten. She just kept on getting kicked in the face. No one in Houghton would give her a job. If she did start one she was sacked within days.' Sandra folded the tea towel into a small neat square before meeting Kerry's eyes. 'Your mam is terrified of this man, pet. Always has been, always will be. So am I and I haven't even met the bastard.'

'But yer said yer were there that night?'

'His thugs came, Kerry. A man like that doesn't do his own dirty work. He sent big burly beast men, what glory in frightening ordinary folk.' She sighed before going on. 'And that's about all I know. Believe me, it's too much anyhow . . . apart from the fact that Vanny must know something about this body that's turned up, cos it certainly frightened the life out of her – it was seeing the report on the TV that put her in hospital. So now yer know as much as me.'

'But where does he live? What's his name?'

'Have yer been listening at all? I've told yer, I don't know his name and I don't want to. And neither do you.'

'Oh yes I do,' Kerry argued.

'Kerry, calm down. Listen, pet. He's bad, he's a posh bastard who ran the whole area. No one really knew who he was, some people still don't believe he ever existed. I remember a few years ago this copper was after him. He's dead now. The coppers couldn't even protect their own.'

Kerry sat for a while staring at the fire, and when she finally looked at Sandra her blue eyes were filled with sadness. 'How can one person ruin another person's life and get away with it? It's not right, is it? It shouldn't be allowed to happen.'

Sandra was examining the tea towel as if it were the crown jewels, nervously wondering if she'd said too much. At last she voiced her thoughts. 'What yer gonna do, Kerry?'

The sadness in Kerry's eyes melted and the steel took over. 'I'll tell yer what I'm gonna do. I'm gonna find our Claire, then I'm going looking for this bastard, and I couldn't give a fuck who he is. But first I'm going up the school and I'm gonna shake the shit out of Katy Jacks. I'm gonna shake her that hard she'll be fucking well pleased to tell me what she knows. Our Claire's life could depend on the stupid little bitch.'

'Kerry,' Sandra protested, 'you've got to promise me you'll be careful. Really, you're just a kid, and kids have a habit of going missing all the time.'

'Aye, tell me about it.'

Sandra bit her lip and wrapped the tea towel round her hands again. 'Sorry, Kerry, I didn't think.'

Kerry stood up. 'Right, I'm off.'

'Kerry, please promise me you'll be careful—'

The only answer Sandra got was the closing of the door.

* * *

Darren had handed the Hatchet her lines, every one neatly done, and damn if she hadn't gone and checked every last one of them. Then, as if his hand wasn't hurting enough, she'd only gone and set an essay on the flaming combustion engine. He'd whispered, actually he'd really only mouthed the words to his mate Kenny who sat next to him, that it was about time somebody told her that people had been on the moon for years now, and it was rocket engines they needed to learn about.

Of course she'd heard. Why wouldn't she? The woman could hear a silent fart. And that's why he'd been standing beside her desk five minutes after the dinner bell.

'Darren Lumsdon,' she'd said, in that big booming voice of hers which always made yer feel as if yer only just reached her bony knees, 'was that boy trying to sell you drugs last Monday, by any chance?'

He'd felt as if he'd been cut from his own engines and was floating somewhere in outer space. She'd poked him, none too gently, in his ribs.

'Er, what boy, miss?'

'You know fine well what boy,' she came right back at him. 'The boy with the face rings. There's generally two of them, the other has a pizza face.'

Pizza face! He'd nearly choked trying to keep his laugh in.

'Well?' she'd demanded.

'No, miss,' he'd denied, thinking that the woman had to be mentally challenged. Either that or a throwback from the combustion engine times. Had she any idea what would happen to him if he grassed?

'I think he was, Darren.'

'No, miss,' he'd denied again, as he'd tried really hard to keep his cool. His stomach had rumbled loudly. He'd known for certain that if she didn't hurry up with her third degree, there would be nowt left for dinner.

Then he'd had to stand through a ten-minute drug lecture, as if his mother hadn't already put the fear of God into him on that score, and he'd finally escaped to find that Milly, the dinner nanny who lived along his street, had kept him a plate of dinner, forewarned by Kenny. He'd downed the soggy cabbage, mashed potatoes, pretend steak and plastic carrots in seconds to get out to play footie. Hell of a game he'd had an' all, managed a hat trick pretending the ball was Stevie's head.

And now, getting on for home time, his stomach was talking again, but not only with hunger. His oh-so-nutritious dinner was rising right back up, along with the thoughts of what might be waiting for him out there.

As the large clock above the blackboard ticked the seconds away, he kept a wary eye on the Hatchet. The last thing he wanted was to be kept back again. He needed to be up and running the very second the bell rang. Alone on the streets, he didn't fancy his chances with Stevie.

Finally the bell went and he was free. Dodging past the other kids, he was first to the lockers, and in his haste to get the door open he dropped his key. With shaking hands he scrabbled about the floor, which was fast filling up with feet. Twice somebody trod on his fingers, then he had it.

'You all right, mate?' Kenny asked from behind him.

'Yeah, yeah.' He had the door open and his bag over his shoulder in moments. 'Got to go, OK? See if me mam's all right. See yer the morn.' Then he was off, leaving Kenny standing staring after him.

He was not the first out though, somebody had beaten him. And that somebody was pressed up against the wall with Kerry's hand around her throat. Quickly he looked round to see if there was any sign of the enemy. No. So, swinging back, he gave the scene in front of him his full attention; he felt safer anyhow with Kerry there.

Katy's face was fast changing colour.

'You gonna strangle her, Kerry?'

'I will an' all if she doesn't tell me right now what I fucking well want to know.'

'Er, I don't think she can, our Kerry. Not with yer choking her, like.'

Kerry thought about it, then relaxed her grip. Katy coughed as she rubbed her throat.

'Now, yer stupid little cow, tell me what the fuck his name is and where the bastard belongs. And what the fuck he looks like.'

'He's blond,' coughed Katy. 'Good-looking. Tall. He's er . . .' Her voice trailed off. 'He's called Brad. I don't . . . I don't know what else to tell yer.'

Kerry glared at her. That didn't give her much to go on. Then Darren piped up. 'She's a hell of a drawer,' he said, pointing at Katy.

Puzzled, Kerry looked at Darren. 'What yer gabbing on about now?'

'Katy, she can draw mint pictures.'

Katy, her eyes still bulging with fright, nodded her agreement.

'All them pictures on our Claire's wall? Katy drew them . . . so she can draw that lad.'

Kerry gave Darren an approving glance, then swung her head back to Katy, who flinched. 'So what yer waiting for? Draw the bastard.'

Quickly Katy rummaged in her bag, and pulled out an A4 drawing pad. Sitting down with her back against the wall, she began to draw in quick flourishes. Soon the paper was covered with Brad's face. She even wrote his name on the bottom.

'That's him.' She handed the drawing to Kerry. 'A dead ringer.'

Snatching the drawing out of her hand, Kerry studied it. After a minute she curled her lip and looked back at Katy, who was now standing up. 'Are you fucking daft or what? That's fucking what's-his-name out of *Titanic*.'

'I know, he's the spitting image. Why do yer think Claire fell for him? But honest, that's him.'

Kerry folded the drawing and put it in her pocket. 'If yer having me on . . .' She left the threat hanging, but Katy got her drift.

'Honestly.' She crossed her heart. 'That's him. Everybody was jealous when they saw Claire with him. He's bloody gorgeous.'

Kerry tutted, as if gorgeous boys were beneath her. 'So, what else do yer know?'

174

Katy shrugged. 'Not a lot really. He comes from South Shields, I definitely heard him say that. Don't know if he still lives there though. He sometimes mentioned his grandmother, but he didn't speak much to me after that first night.'

'Did our Claire ever say anything about running away with him?'

'No. She never said anything like that. Only . . .'

'Only what?' Kerry demanded, reaching for the other girl's throat when she hesitated.

'Just that he was taking her to get some model pictures taken. She was really excited about that. But I swear on me mam's life, she was never gonna run away with him.'

'OK. Draw another picture.' She turned to Darren. 'Go down and pick the girls up.'

The last thing Darren wanted to do was to leave the safe circle of his sister's protection, even though he'd glanced around a few times and seen no sign of his tormentor. He shuffled his feet, hesitating.

'Go on.' She glared at him. 'They'll be wondering where we are.'

Left with no choice, Darren went for his sisters, but was back in a few minutes after practically dragging the pair of them up the bank. Katy had finished the second drawing and Kerry had fished the first one out of her pocket and was comparing them. She could hardly find any difference.

'Right,' she said after a minute. 'You're certain this is him and not that bloody film star off the ship picture?'

Katy nodded. 'That's him all right.'

'Did yer give one of these to the coppers?'

'No, they never asked.'

'Typical.'

'What yer gonna do now, Kerry?' Darren asked, looking over her shoulder at the drawing. 'I told yer she was good, didn't I?'

'I'm taking this down the cop shop. You're taking the girls home.'

'Oh.' Darren looked quickly around. 'Can't you walk down with us, like?'

Before Kerry could answer, Emma sniffed, wiped her nose on her sleeve and said in a demanding voice, 'I'm starving.'

'It's OK, Emma, our Robbie's in, he's making tattie pot.'

'Yeah,' Suzy grinned. Tattie pot, a simple meal of corned beef, sliced potatoes and onions, was her favourite. 'Come on, Darren.' She took hold of his hand and tried to urge him on.

Faced with the wrath of Kerry, plus his two starving sisters, Darren wisely decided to do what Kerry said. He headed for home.

When they'd gone, Kerry turned back to Katy and did something foreign to her nature. She apologised. 'I'm sorry if I hurt yer, Katy, but when yer said yer knew nowt, I just saw red . . . I'm worried sick about our Claire and me mam.'

'So am I really, Kerry. It's just she's me best friend and I didn't want to drop her in it.'

Kerry nodded. 'It's OK. I'll go and give the coppers one of these. If they ask, yer only did one, right?'

'Sure thing, Kerry.' Katy was so pleased to be off Kerry's hit list, she would have agreed to anything.

Carter popped his head round the interview-room door just as Lorraine and Luke, after a busy afternoon, had taken time out to eat. He noticed that his boss had nearly finished her double cheeseburger and fries, and Luke was throwing the remains of his two Big Macs into the bin.

'Sorry, boss, but the sister of that missing kid from the Seahills insists on seeing yer. The kind of insistence that just won't go away.'

Lorraine wiped her mouth. 'It's OK, we're nearly finished here. Send her in.'

A few moments later Kerry walked in, and Lorraine smiled up at her as Luke stood and offered Kerry his seat.

She shook her head, and her words came out in a rush. 'I've come to find out just what it is yer doing to find me sister.'

'Straight to the point, eh, Kerry? I like that. But at the moment all I can say is we're doing the best we can.'

'Which is nowt,' Kerry said bluntly.

Lorraine took a breath and reminded herself what the younger girl must be going through.

'We start the second round of house-to-house inquiries at six tonight. We are doing our best, and we do take missing girls seriously. I promise you we won't let up until we've found her.'

'And when will that be?' Kerry's voice was rising

fast. 'When it's too late? When she's dead or some-thing?' The last word was shouted. Luke noticed her hands bunching into fists. He put his own hands on her shoulders, and gently pressed her into the chair. 'Come on, Kerry. Sit down, love.'

Kerry sat with a small whoosh, as if all the wind had gone out of her. She stared at Lorraine.

'Here.' She took the drawing out of her pocket and flung it across the desk. 'Feast yer eyes on that. Call yerselves coppers? Couldn't even get a picture of the bastard, could yer though?'

Lorraine picked it up, unfolded it, and frowned when she saw the handsome face staring up at her. For a moment she felt irritated. How had this kid got a picture of the person they were looking for? Then elation took over. If it *was* him, their job would be that much easier and they might find the girls in time.

'Who is this?' she asked, hoping Kerry would give her the answer she so badly wanted.

'It's him. Our Claire's boyfriend. Katy Jacks did it. She swears it's the living double of that Brad. She'd have drawn youse lot one an' all, if any of yers had had the sense to ask.'

Neither Lorraine nor Luke missed the sarcasm in Kerry's voice. Luke wondered briefly how long Lorraine would put up with the girl's attitude. Reaching for the drawing when Lorraine handed it over, he looked at it closely for a moment before whistling softly.

'Whoever drew this has one fantastic gift. We should set her on here, she makes the police artist's work look like a kid's drawing.'

Lorraine nodded. 'Get it faxed over to the other stations right now. That's as good as any picture.'

Luke left and Lorraine tapped her fingers together as she looked at Kerry with renewed respect. Misreading the look, Kerry glared fiercely back at her.

'Well,' Lorraine said after a minute, 'I don't intend getting into a staring competition with you, Kerry Lumsdon, so yer can come right down off yer fucking high horse now.'

For a moment Kerry was poleaxed, but only for a moment. The blonde bitch. Who does she think she is, swearing like that? Her a copper an' all.

'Yer can't talk to me like that!'

Lorraine leaned forward. 'You so disappoint me, Kerry. If only yer knew how many people have sat in that very spot and said the very same thing. I at least expected someone of your obvious mental capacity to come up with something original.'

'Oh yeah,' Kerry sneered again. 'How's this for fucking original? I bet yer don't know the wanker comes from South Shields? There now.' Feeling quite smug, Kerry folded her arms across her chest.

It was Lorraine's turn to look dumbfounded. 'Well,' she said, after a moment, 'yer have been busy. OK.' She spread her arms wide. 'Let's start again, shall we? How about we begin with whatever else yer've ferreted out, including how yer found out he was from South Shields.'

Kerry thought for a moment, debating whether or not to tell her about The Man. And that her mother seemed to know something about the body with six

179

toes. She decided against it. Her mother was too near the edge, and besides, she wanted to find out more about her mother's past for herself, before the coppers stuck their noses in. Lorraine seemed OK though – less sniffy than most police she'd come across. She decided to give them a little piece of information that couldn't hurt.

'Katy Jacks, who drew the picture, she said he was from South Shields.'

'Katy again, eh?' Lorraine made a mental note to pay Katy Jacks a visit. The threat of a charge of withholding information might get a bit more out of her.

Lorraine smiled at Kerry as she stood. 'Well then, I guess that's about it, Kerry.' She held out her hand. 'You've been very helpful. With a bit of luck, and many thanks to your efforts, we might find this Brad character a bit sooner than we thought.'

Kerry stared at the outstretched hand. She knew she was being dismissed, and didn't like it one little bit. But she'd done what she came to do, namely shake the bastards up. That would do for now.

She shook Lorraine's hand, and couldn't help but notice that the smile that came with the shake was warm and friendly and reached the policewoman's blue eyes.

Kerry smiled back, just a glimmer of a smile, but it was the first smile she'd attempted in over two days. Two days. It suddenly hit her that Claire had been gone for what was really quite a long time for a thirteen-year-old girl who had never even spent a night away from home before. Suddenly her knees went weak, and she slumped back in her chair.

Lorraine's heart went out to her and she was around the desk, placing a comforting arm over Kerry's shoulder, in seconds. As she watched Kerry struggle to compose herself, knowing she had to hold her family together, had to care for her brothers and sisters and protect them as much as possible from her worry about her mother, while doing everything in her power to help find the little sister who could be dead or worse, she knew she was looking at a girl of uncommon strength. *Please God, let it be enough to get her through what might be to come.*

'I promise yer, Kerry, we really are doing everything we can to find Claire,' she said gently.

Kerry knuckled a tear from her eye. 'Well why is it that yer not sending the coppers back out until six o'clock then?'

'Because that's when most people get home from work.'

'Work! On the Seahills? That's gotta be a joke.'

'Kerry, yer know as well as I do that a lot of people on the Seahills do have jobs, and even those who don't tend to go out through the day, shopping or whatever. And we're doing every estate in Houghton yer know, not just the Seahills. Now why don't yer go on home, I'm sure yer brother will need help with the kids. And I promise to keep yer informed about whatever turns up.'

Knowing that there was nothing else she could do here, that she'd had her say, and that in spite of herself found that she liked both of the coppers, Kerry nodded. She felt she could trust Lorraine. And there were places she wanted to visit, like South

Shields for one. She'd found this much out on her own, there must be more she could discover. Standing, she went to the door, but just as she got there it was opened from the other side.

A uniform with a thousand freckles nearly knocked her over in his eagerness to get into the room.

'Sorry, sorry,' Carter said, holding his arm out to steady her.

'It's all right,' Kerry muttered as she slipped past him.

He made sure she was out of the room and the door closed behind her, then he swung round to face Lorraine.

'Bright as a button, that one,' Lorraine told him. 'The drawing came from her efforts.'

'That's what I'm here about. Believe it or not, we've had results in already.' He was smiling all over his face.

'Right then. What's up?' Lorraine asked, hiding a grin at Carter's eagerness. He'd have wagged his tail if he'd had one.

'It seems the oldest girl, Jade, is friends with D.I. Watson's daughter over in Newcastle. And she only just happened to be visiting her dad when the fax landed on his desk. She swears it's the same bloke her friend Jade has been going out with for the last month.'

Lorraine's grin was as wide as Carter's. 'I knew it. Yer can guarantee that those three bastards are the same man. Find him and we'll find the girls.'

Carter, glad to be the bearer of good news, kept

on grinning. His smile slipped a moment later though when Lorraine said, 'But what's the game, Carter? Prostitution? Selling them on? What perverted creep has these kids? Cos I'd lay money this Brad, Billy or whatever his real name is, is not the boss here. He's just one of many small cogs. There's someone far far bigger than him. And that's the bastard I want. I wonder . . .'

'Sorry?' Carter asked.

She held her hand up, and walked to the window. Could it be the same man? The one who went to ground all those years ago. The one that Stone was after. Was that why no one was talking?

Lorraine looked out the window and watched as Kerry turned the corner up to Houghton. A big chauffeur-driven car passed a second later. There was no reason at all to connect it to Kerry.

12

The Queen's Head in South Shields was heaving with hopeful karaoke finalists and Debbie had to shove her way through the punters. Her aim was the far corner where she knew she'd find some friends who practically lived on the premises. Maggie, a petite girl with a blonde skinhead, saw her coming and raised a hand in greeting.

'What the fuck did yer have to wave her over here for? The ginger slapper.' This was from Lucy, who didn't much like anybody, least of all herself, and her own very wiry ginger hair. Both girls were in their late twenties and heavily made-up. They wore nearly identical short black dresses.

'Debbie's not ginger, yer blind bitch.' Maggie pulled a stray lock of Lucy's hair. 'That's fucking ginger. Hers is auburn and a lovely shade. And she's all right. Kinder than you are, anyhow.'

'Look, however yer dress it up with fancy fucking names, it's fucking ginger. And talking of dressing up, where the fuck does she work when she's not hanging here? Cos she's always got some fucking fancy high-priced threads on, that's for sure.'

Debbie gave them another wave before elbowing her way to the packed bar. She wore a skimpy red top with a silver embroidered dragon on each shoulder, and an even skimpier black skirt. Between the two garments, there was at least four inches of tanned skin.

She knew the barmaids and they knew her as a good tipper, which enabled her to get served quickly. Avoiding an argument with a thick-set skinhead by winking her sparkling green eyes and flashing a mouth full of teeth at him, then carrying her glass of lager at arm's length in case she spilt a drop, she made her way over to her friends in the corner.

'I don't fucking believe it,' Lucy groaned, as she watched Debbie come closer.

'What?' Maggie frowned at her.

'She's had her fucking belly button done. What, she thinks she's a fucking teenager now?'

Maggie shrugged. 'So, if it bothers yer that much, get yer own done. A nice silver ring in yer belly, yer don't know who yer might get in yer bed.'

'No fucking way. Ain't nobody poking holes in my body, it's not fucking healthy.'

Maggie laughed, a rich throaty sound that turned people's heads and made them smile. 'Yer know them punters that yer see every night? Well, they've been poking holes in yer body for years, yer daft cow.'

Lucy pulled a face. 'That's different though, that's a living. Sticking pins in people's bodies is sick.'

'For Christ's sake, stop fucking whinging, will yer? Just because yer haven't scored yet . . .'

'Hi, girls,' Debbie said as she reached their table.

Maggie pushed Lucy along the seat, making room for Debbie. Lucy glared at her before saying, 'Hello, Debbie. Long time no see.'

Debbie giggled. 'I've had meself a fella for the last few months. Big fancy flat up at the High Barnes in Sunderland, really really posh.'

'And . . . ?' Lucy asked, with a sarcastic air.

Debbie looked sad for a moment, and Maggie gave Lucy a dig in her ribs. Debbie took a sip of her lager, then said, 'His wife found out.'

'Tough . . . What she do, punch yer face in?' Lucy could scarcely keep the glee out of her voice.

'No, the sly bastard left and I had to find two fucking months' rent.'

Lucy found this hilarious. She laughed as she said, 'Come to make it up tonight, have yer?'

'Just ignore her, Debbie, she's got a right bitch's head on tonight.' Maggie gave Lucy a filthy look which the other girl just shrugged off, and turning back to Debbie she went on, 'I see you've had yer belly button done. Hurt much, did it?'

'It did at first, like the fucking devil. But it's all right now.' Raising her glass she took a long swallow, smacking her lips she put the glass back on the table. 'So, what's the score with you lot?'

'Same as ever,' Maggie replied. 'Me old man's still taking me money. I manage to put a bit away now and again.' She shrugged. 'Yer know how it is, the kids is wanting all the time. Our David threw a fit the other day cos I wouldn't give the little bastard the money to get his ear pierced, and him only fucking nine.'

'Nine going on twenty-nine,' Lucy put in.

'Aye, I'm dreading what the little twat will be wanting in a year or two. If I didn't make a bit on the game, like, we'd probably starve, cos what yer get off the fucking dole isn't enough to feed two fucking sparrows, never mind a house full of kids and a fucking eighteen-stone man.'

'Yeah.' Lucy grinned. 'If the money depended on the total weight of each family, you'd be worth a fucking fortune.'

Debbie shook her head. 'Why you put up with that lazy wanker, Maggie, I'll never know.'

'He's good with the kids. What else can I say? Without him I wouldn't be able to work at all.'

'But at the end of the day, they're his fucking kids. He should get off his fat fucking arse and support the lot of you.'

'I've been telling her that till I'm blue in the fucking face, Debbie. It's like water off a duck's back.' Lucy drained her glass and stood. 'I'm going to the bar, anybody want a drink?'

'Here.' Debbie rummaged in her handbag and came up with a fiver. 'Get them in, Lucy.'

'Sure thing, Debbie.' Lucy had the money out of Debbie's hand with practised ease.

Debbie watched Lucy push her way to the bar, then looked around. 'It's about time they did this place out. I mean, artex and black beams went out in the eighties, didn't it? The whole place is fucking depressing.'

'I guess so. But the posher places don't allow for the likes of us, do they?'

'Suppose not.'

They chatted for another hour, in which time Lucy happily trotted to the bar twice more with Debbie's money. It was half-past nine when Maggie nudged Debbie and said, 'It looks like you've scored.' Debbie and Lucy followed Maggie's eyes. A large black man was propping up the bar nearest them. He winked at Debbie.

'Christ,' Lucy said. 'I very nearly missed him there. With them black trousers and jumper all you can see is the whites of his fucking eyes.'

The three of them giggled, as the man who still hadn't taken his eyes off Debbie gestured to the door with his head.

'Looks like you've made your rent, Debbie love.' Maggie smiled at her.

Debbie winked at both of them as she rose to leave. 'See yer later then. I guess it's time to go to work.'

'Have fun.' Maggie waved her hand. 'Don't forget to keep in touch.'

'Aye, see yer,' Lucy sneered.

They watched as Debbie linked arms with the man and the pair of them walked out.

Maggie turned on Lucy. 'What the fuck do yer have to be so nasty for?'

'Who me?'

'No, that fat cow sitting next to yer.'

Lucy had the grace to look slightly ashamed, only slightly though, and then only for a moment, before she said, 'Aye, but when yer think about it, that punter might have been mine if she hadn't turned up tonight. I've got my fucking rent to pay an' all, yer know. Ugly ginger cow, that's all she is. I fucking hate her.'

Maggie sighed and patted Lucy's arm. 'Never mind, pet, something will turn up. One thing though, Lucy, Debbie's far from ugly. In fact, she leaves you fucking standing.'

'Oh yeah.' Lucy patted her wild locks. 'Well at least my hair's real, it doesn't come from a fucking bottle.'

'No, you just look like yer plug yerself in every night.'

'Cheeky bastard. Who the fuck do yer think yer talking to?'

Maggie softened. She thought the world of Lucy really, but sometimes she could be a royal bitch and get right on a person's tits. 'Never mind, Lucy pet, something will turn up. The night's still young yet.'

Mollified, Lucy smiled. 'Aye, yer right.'

Outside, Debbie and the huge black man walked over to a dark blue cavalier. She went to the passenger side as he got out his keys; he grinned over at her as he opened the door and the streetlight caught the glint of gold in his teeth.

When they were both strapped up, he turned to Debbie and watched as the startling green eyes were replaced by a beautiful summer blue.

'Thank God,' Lorraine said, as she put the contact lenses into a box and dropped them into her handbag. 'Those bloody things were irritating the hell out of me.' Taking off the auburn wig, she shook out her long blonde hair and ran her fingers through it.

Luke removed the skull cap and his wavy hair

sprang into place. 'Aye, and that thing irritates the life out of me an' all. Another five minutes and I would have tore it off in there. It really makes you sweat.' He scratched his head, then started the car. As he pulled out of the car park he asked, 'So, did yer learn anything?'

'Quite a bit.' Lorraine sounded excited as she went on. 'I gave them the usual line, yer know? Described this dreamboat I'd seen once or twice, gushed about how much I fancied him. When I said his name might be Brad or Brent Maggie's ears pricked up. She's certain she knows him. If it's the right guy, he hangs out in Sunderland. She reckons he's a right nasty. The type who would steal his grandmother's eyes and come back for the sockets.'

Luke nodded. They had both met the type often enough. 'OK, but where in Sunderland?'

'One of our own favourite haunts. The dog track. Maggie says every time she's seen him, he's had a different girl. Seems he prefers the blonde bimbo type.' Lorraine grimaced. 'Maggie knew him by the Brad alias, or perhaps that's his real moniker. Also, she doesn't know how he makes his bread, but he certainly throws plenty around. One of Maggie's regulars likes an odd night out at the dogs – apparently he thinks Maggie brings him luck – and it seems her regular knows him.'

'Great! So who's this bloke? He could save us a lot of time.'

'That's just it. No way was she giving names out. And the Debbie cover is just too good to blow on a name that might yield sweet F.A.'

Luke pulled a face. 'I guess you're right. Anyhow, I hope this is the lead we're looking for. Yer know the score. If we don't get this age group back by the second night, it's looking dodgy. And we're fast heading into night three.'

It was Lorraine's turn to sigh; she knew the score all right.

It only took Lorraine ten minutes to change into a pair of black silk trousers and a lace top, complete with gold waist chain. It stopped just short of the fake navel ring which she patted briefly, thinking that it had come to something for her to still be learning tricks from her mother. Putting on a silver-blonde Dolly Parton-style wig, she back-combed it a little higher, then thickened her lips with a bright pink lipstick. She had to pass her husband's wardrobe to get into the cupboard where she kept her various bags and shoes and, noticing that the door was slightly ajar, she opened it further.

It took her a good five minutes to get over the shock of finding it empty.

Luke watched her walk back to the car where he was still listening to his Eagles tape. He frowned at the slump of her shoulders, sensing at once that something was wrong.

As Lorraine got back into the car, Kerry stepped off the Shields bus. The bus pulled away and she crossed the busy street. Moving slowly, she studied the young faces passing by. Spotting three girls standing on the corner, she hurried up to them and showed them the picture Katy had drawn and an old snapshot of Claire. All three shook their heads, before moving on and leaving Kerry standing looking around her.

Noticing an amusement arcade further up the street, she decided to try there. *Can't just stop people off the street, they'll think I'm crackers. Them three idiots obviously thought I was . . .* On her way there she stopped another two girls. *Who gives a fuck if they think I'm fucking crackers? There's nowt else I can think of to help.*

The two girls had never seen anyone who looked like the drawing, but their reaction was different to the first lot, and they gave her enough encouragement to go on. She went into the arcade and the first thing she saw was a group of five boys playing a bandit beside the door.

'Excuse me,' she said, only to be ignored.

'Excuse me.' This time much louder.

One of the boys turned to her and frowned. He had a sharp pointy face with little piggy eyes. 'Piss off,' he said, before swinging his head back to the machine.

'You piss off, Rat Boy.'

This brought howls of laughter from the other boys, then the tallest of the group peeled away. He was dark haired, tanned, wearing the latest fashion, and very good-looking. He slowly looked Kerry over and seemed amused when he realised that she was doing the same to him.

'OK, chick, what do yer want?'

'First off, I am nobody's chick. Got that?'

The boy nodded. Yes, he had indeed got that.

'Second, I want you and your friends to look at these pictures and see if yer know any of them.'

'Who are you like, a midget copper, or what?' Rat Boy put in.

Kerry didn't think him worth an answer. Looking at the boy in front of her, she said, 'The girl is me sister, she's been missing since Monday. The last time anybody saw her' – she poked her finger at Brad's picture – 'she was with him.'

The boy frowned. 'Give us a look then.' He held his hand out. 'And you,' he looked at Rat Boy, 'just you remember you've got three sisters at home, and if they were missing for two days, you'd be bloody frantic an' all.'

Kerry prayed that Rat Boy's sisters looked nothing like him. The boys passed the pictures round, studying them carefully, and for a moment Kerry felt optimistic, but one by one they all shook their heads. The leader passed them back. 'Sorry, maybe you should try the pubs.'

'Our Claire wouldn't go into pubs. For fuck's sake, she's only thirteen.'

'Aye,' the boy pointed at Brad's picture, 'but he's not, is he?'

Kerry swept her ponytail off her shoulder, and looked again at the picture of Brad. The boy was right, Brad looked at least twenty years old. *He's got to be a fucking pervert,* she thought. *What decent twenty-year-old bothers with a fucking kid?* Suddenly the enormity of the task she'd set herself hit home. She leaned against a kids' musical helicopter ride.

'You all right?' the tall boy asked her. The others

had turned back to the one-armed bandit. She passed a hand over her face then slowly nodded.

'Here, do you want to sit down for a bit, like?' He pointed in the direction of a seated area with a small bar. Following his finger with her eyes, she pushed herself upright, made her way over, and slipped into one of the red plastic booths. The boy shrugged at his friends, then followed her over.

'Fancy a coffee?' he asked.

Kerry looked at him as if she was seeing him for the first time. At the mention of coffee, she realised that she was both hungry and thirsty. Her hand scrabbled in her pocket, counting her change, even though she knew she only had the exact bus fare to get home with. *Well*, she thought, *if he's buying*.

'Yes please.'

'OK, then.' And he went to the counter.

Kerry looked around. The garish lights and the loud noise seemed to hit her all at once; she could feel a headache coming on, and massaged her temples. *Where the hell are you, Claire?*

Suddenly she felt so alone. She should have waited for Robbie, but no, she had to run out of the police station like a flaming avenging angel. What did she expect, for Christ's sake? To come here and walk right into them?

A few minutes later he was back, and as well as the coffees he carried a plate with two doughnuts oozing strawberry jam. He put the food and drinks on the table, sat down and smiled. 'So, what's yer name then?'

'Kerry,' she replied, from a mouth full of jam.

'I'm Mark.'

'Yeah, OK. Oh, thanks, Mark.' The doughnut finished, she wiped her fingers and when Mark pushed his untouched doughnut towards her, she picked it up and it disappeared as fast as its predecessor.

He looked at the empty plate. 'Looks like you were a bit on the hungry side, like.'

'Actually, I was in such a hurry I missed me tea.' She stopped for a sip of coffee. 'Look, I'm sorry I snapped at your friends before. It's only that I'm so worried. Our Claire's never done nothing like this before, and . . . and when I find the little cow I'm gonna shake the shite out of her.'

'Can't say I blame yer. And me friend's nickname's Ferret anyhow, so yer were close enough.' Kerry laughed, and Mark went on. 'So what yer gonna do now?'

She shook her head. 'I don't know. I had this daft idea that I would more or less walk right into her and drag her home. Stupid or what?'

Mark shrugged. 'Not really. I'd probably think the same. That's if I had a sister, like. But there's only me.'

'Oh.' Kerry had often wondered what it would be like to be an only child. She'd quite often berated God for plonking her in the middle of her family, but now that one of them was missing . . . well, it changed everything.

Looking at the clock she was surprised how fast the time had gone; it was nearly half-past ten and the last bus was at eleven.

Standing up, she said, 'Thanks again, but I have to go now.'

'So what yer gonna do, look round the pubs?' Mark asked as he stood up beside her. 'Only if yer are it gets sort of hairy on a night sometimes, with all the drunks rolling around.'

'I'll be all right. I can stick up for meself, yer know.'

'I bet yer can an' all.'

'What's that supposed to mean?' Kerry snapped. After all, she'd been polite for long enough, she'd even said she was sorry twice, for Christ's sake.

Mark held his hands up in mock surrender. 'Hey, I didn't mean nowt nasty, it's just that I know me way around here, and you obviously don't. That's all.'

Kerry blushed, feeling a bit silly for overreacting. 'OK, but if yer want to help, we have to go now cos me bus won't be long.'

Mark grinned, and when he did he reminded Kerry of Robbie, who she'd always thought was one of a kind. 'I'll just tell the lads, then we'll be off. We'll do the pubs as we come to them, OK?'

'Yeah, whatever.'

A minute later they were back on the street. Mark stopped everyone he saw, and Kerry counted at least twenty people who shook their heads no. Then, just as they were going into the first pub, a girl Mark seemed to know quite well, with long blonde hair done up in at least a hundred tiny plaits, smiled at him and said the magic words, 'Yes, that's Brad.'

Kerry moved quickly forward to question her, then had to jump just as quickly back as a fight which had started in the bar spilled out on to the street. She was separated from Mark and the girl as the crowd grew bigger, and she felt a moment's panic. Not because of the fighting, Lord knows she'd seen plenty of that, but in case she lost Mark altogether – sometimes these things got right out of hand. She watched as a fat skinhead, covered in tattoos, quickly found out that the small blond lad with the bobbing ponytail was far from an easy victim. The sound of sirens growing closer quickly dispersed the mob, and when the street was nearly empty she saw Mark standing against the window of the pub. The girl had disappeared.

'Damn!' Kerry ran over to him. 'Where is she?'

'She's gone. But she says he used to live in her street a few years back. She thinks he moved to some-where in Sunderland.'

Kerry was disappointed. Even though she had no real concrete plan as to what she was going to do if she ever found this Brad – probably go storming off to his house and demand he produce her sister there and then – she wanted it over quickly. She wanted to go home tonight dragging Claire with her.

Mark saw the look of dejection on her face. 'Look, your bus will be pulling in any minute. Why don't you call it a night? I'll see if I can catch a few more people at the pizza place, and we'll meet back here tomorrow at,' he shrugged his shoulders, 'whatever time you like.'

What he said made sense, Kerry knew that, but it meant yet another night with Claire missing. She didn't know if she could bear that.

Her sigh was a heavy lonely sound that touched

something in Mark. He put a gentle hand on her shoulder. 'I'll do me best, honest. And I know it might sound stupid, but try not to worry too much. She'll probably turn up soon. She might even just have took the huff over something stupid, yer never know.' He paused, and looked down the street. 'Anyhow, here's yer bus coming. I'd go straight over if I was you, cos the last bus doesn't wait.'

Kerry looked at his deep brown eyes. Her instincts told her that he was like Robbie in a lot of ways, and that she should trust him. There was also a strange tingling feeling somewhere in the pit of her stomach, a nice feeling that she'd never had before. She made her mind up quickly. 'OK, then. I'll meet yer here at eleven tomorrow morning, if that's all right with you.'

Mark nodded. 'Yeah, that's cool. With a bit of luck I might have something to tell yer.'

'Right then.' Kerry went to cross the road then, turning back at the kerb, she smiled. 'Ta-ra.'

He smiled back and gave a little wave of his hand. 'Yeah, ta-ra.'

Kerry ran across the road and jumped on the bus just as it was revving up to go. 'Yer cut that fine,' the driver complained as he took her money.

'Yeah, whatever,' Kerry muttered under her breath as she moved to the back of the bus. She looked out the window with her hand half raised to wave, but Mark was already gone.

'Where the hell have yer been?' Robbie demanded as Kerry let herself in.

'Christ, Robbie, let me get me coat off.'

'I'm not joking, Kerry. I've been worried sick, man. You'd think it wasn't enough for yer that our Mam's in the hospital and our Claire's missing, then you have to go AWOL as fucking well.'

Kerry held her hand up. 'OK, Robbie, chill, will yer? I'm sorry, right? But nobody told me I needed a pass card to go looking for me sister, for fuck's sake.'

'So, where did yer look?'

'South Shields.'

'South fucking Shields!' Robbie's voice rose higher and higher. 'South fucking Shields!'

Kerry kicked her shoes off. The last thing she needed tonight was the third degree. 'Since when did yer turn into a parrot?'

'Kerry.' His voice held a warning note she'd never heard before.

Looking up at him, she saw the worry, the dark circles under his eyes that had not been there a few days earlier. The tight set of his jaw. And could have strangled him for making her feel so low.

'Look, I'm sorry, Robbie,' she said grudgingly, 'me crystal ball failed, OK? I should have guessed you'd be worried, but I got this lead and just sort of took off, OK?'

'Not good enough, Kerry. And what do you mean, a lead? What, yer setting up a detective agency now, are yer?'

Deep inside, Kerry knew she'd got it wrong, knew she should have told him. But he was seriously bugging her now. And so her voice was angry as she snapped, 'So what the fuck have you done since all this happened, eh? Nowt but sit on yer fucking arse, that's what.' She regretted the words the moment she said them. She bit her lip as Robbie sort of folded in on himself and sat down.

'Somebody has to stop with the kids, Kerry.'

She could hear the tears in his voice, hear her brother's heart breaking. It wasn't fair. Robbie was a good kid, he shouldn't have to shoulder all this shit. *He's just a teenager, for fuck's sake, he should be out with his mates having a good time.* And hadn't she just gone and made it worse? Roll up and watch, folks. Big-mouth Kerry does it again.

'Oh God.' She went over and put her arms around his shoulders. 'I'm sorry, Robbie, honest I am. I should have come home for yer. Sandra would have minded the kids. I goofed again.'

He patted her hand, only this made her feel worse. She'd said all those horrible things, and he'd forgiven her already. *I've got to be the biggest rat in history.* A hot tear fell on the hand that patted hers.

'Stop crying, Kerry. It's just that I was so worried when yer didn't come home, that's all.'

'No, yer right, I got it wrong again.'

Standing up, she went to the kitchen and splashed cold water on her face. She had to turn the towel round and round to find a clean place to dry it on. When she went back into the sitting room, Robbie smiled at her. 'So, Detective, what's new?'

She told him everything that had happened since she'd had Katy pressed up against the wall, and when she'd finished, he said in an admiring voice, 'Wow, our Kerry. It looks like yer've done more work in one night than the coppers have done in two days.'

She loved the praise and smiled when she said, 'Actually I think that woman copper's all right. She's different from most of them. So, are yer coming with me tomorrow, or what?'

'Try and stop me.'

'Right on. Now, I want to know who's been here tonight.'

Robbie managed a laugh. 'Really playing the detective now, aren't we? So how, Lady Sherlock, do yer know somebody's even been here?'

'Easy, I saw the fish-and-chip papers in the kitchen bin.'

Robbie laughed. 'Yeah, very good. Mickey and Cal called in. They brought fish and chips for all of us, but Mickey ate yours.'

'That'll be right. So, what happened with Cal? Community hours at the home again?'

'Aye, only this time there's an up-side. Seems the judge is gonna put him through his driving test, and then set him on proper like, when he's finished his hundred hours. Cool, eh?'

'I suppose. Only, what sort of car has this judge bloke got?'

'What for?'

'Cos you know as well as I do, if it's a nice little comfy thing it'll be perfectly safe. On the other hand, if it's a neat little mover . . .' She let the rest of the sentence trail off. Robbie knew exactly what she meant.

She yawned and was about to go upstairs when there was a loud crash from next door. They looked at each other in puzzlement, and a moment later there was an equally loud banging on the door.

'What the . . . ?' Robbie jumped up and hurried to the front door with Kerry trailing behind him. He opened it to find the big blonde girl from next door taking up that much space that she blocked the street-lights out.

'Please,' she gabbled, before the door was fully open. 'Phone an ambulance, will yer? It's Rick, he's gone and fell through the fucking ceiling. I think he's really hurt himself this time, cos there's blood all over the fucking place . . . I don't know what to do!'

As Robbie was telling her that they had no phone, but that he would run over to Trevor's and use his, Kerry was thinking, *This time? For God's sake, how many times has he been hurt?*

'OK,' the fat blonde said, then without even a thank you, she hurried back next door, her legs wobbling in the short skirt she wore. Kerry ran into the sitting room and slipped her shoes back on, then followed her neighbour.

The appalling smell was the first thing that hit her. Wrinkling her nose, she stepped over a mound of take-away cartons, which looked like they had been there for weeks. 'Jesus,' she muttered as she moved further into the house and looked around. The place was an absolute tip. *Christ.* She shook her head in disgust. *We've got nowt, and there's seven of us. The place gets untidy, but we don't live like this. A fucking pig would be disgusted.*

'In here.' The girl's voice came from the kitchen. Kerry walked along the passageway as if it were land-mined. God only knew what was waiting for her in the kitchen.

The girl was kneeling down and poor Rick, who to Kerry's untrained eyes looked quite dead, was lying in a pile of rubble. Kerry looked up at the gaping hole in the ceiling, then back down at the still form of Rick. She was not nurse material; the sight of blood had the same effect on her as vomit.

She was saved from having to do something – although she didn't have a clue what – by Robbie running in and pushing past her.

Robbie and Mickey had taken a first-aid course last winter, just for something to do with their time. Robbie had passed near the top of the class. Kerry suppressed a grin when she remembered why Mickey had failed. The reason the instructor had written on the sheet had been that if Mickey couldn't stop himself from showing amorous intentions to a rubber dummy, what would he do with a live woman who had fainted?

Swallowing a giggle she put her hand over her mouth. Jesus, she was losing control here. Pretty soon, if she didn't watch out, the men in white coats would be carting her away. She regained some control over her wayward mind and watched as Robbie set about staunching the flow of blood, and making Rick look more comfortable, even if the poor sod couldn't feel it.

'The ambulance won't be long, about five minutes. I think he's knocked himself out. It's a deep cut, prob-ably needs a few stitches, but I think he's gonna be all right.'

The fat girl stood up so fast she almost bounced.

'So,' she said indignantly, 'what the fuck yer saying? That there's fuck all wrong with the bastard? That I've worried for nowt? I don't fucking believe it, a few fucking stitches.'

While Robbie and Kerry looked on in amazement, she pulled her foot back and gave Rick a hard kick on the top of his leg.

'Useless bastard. I told him not to climb about in the fucking loft. Now look at the hole in the fucking ceiling. The council's gonna have me fucking guts for garters . . . Oh, and who's gonna do tonight's delivery, eh? Fucking bastard.' She moved her foot, ready to kick him again.

'How, give over. What sort of person are yer?' Robbie was shocked, and it showed. 'I'm only guessing, I'm not a doctor. All of his bones could be broken, for all I know.'

The girl backed away, sneering. 'Well if yer think I'm gonna be sitting in the hospital for fucking hours on end with him, yer can fucking think again. No fucking way. So you can sling yer hook.'

Kerry stared at the girl in total disbelief, and moved towards her. 'Are you for real or what? I've never heard nothing like it in me life. Look at him, yer stupid bitch. He's bleeding all over the fucking place. For Christ's sake, yer nothing but a big fat selfish cow.'

Robbie groaned. Kerry being Kerry, anything could happen now.

The fat girl snarled at her. 'What the fuck's it got to do with you, yer interfering skinny twat?'

'Me, interfering? You're the daft bastard that came knocking on our door, remember? Yer ignorant git.'

Robbie jumped up and tried to get between them, but Kerry was faster. She reached the girl and with one very stiff finger, poked her in the chest. Robbie knew it mattered little to Kerry that their neighbour could easily give her five stone and six inches; once Kerry's gander was up, she took no prisoners.

She went to poke her again but Robbie was quick enough this time and grabbed Kerry's wrist. 'Leave it, Kerry. She's not worth the bother. Come on, let's go. I've done what I can, the ambulance will be here in a bit.'

It wasn't easy moving Kerry. Her feet were planted solid and she was glaring nose to nose with the other girl. But at that moment they heard the sirens.

The fat girl stepped back. Sneering again, she said, 'Aye go on, fucking well get out. I don't need yer help any more. I'm sorry I asked for it in the first fucking place.'

Robbie lifted Kerry by her waist and spun her round. When he had her pointed in the general direction of the door, he turned back to the girl whose face was distorted into a mask of hate.

'Our Kerry's right, what she said about you. I just feel sorry for that poor bugger lying there.'

'Do yer now? Well fuck you.'

That did it. Kerry back-heeled Robbie in the shin, he let go of her, and she was past him in a second. All the frustration and worry of the last few days erupted, and she landed a right hook that guaranteed a spectacular black eye. While her opponent was still reeling, she grabbed her head and was about to knee her in the face when Robbie reached her again.

He dragged her off the girl who by now was staring at Kerry's knee and, knowing what was coming her way, screaming for mercy.

'Aye, yer just like all bullies,' Kerry yelled, as Robbie dragged her to the door. 'A fucking coward!'

The ambulance came to a stop as Robbie, still holding on to Kerry, got them to their own front door. 'In there,' he yelled at the driver, who nodded and quickly followed his partner up the path.

'What's the matter?' asked a sleepy Darren, coming down the stairs as Robbie slammed the door. 'I heard all the shouting. Is it her next door, the big fat one?' He realised that Robbie still had hold of Kerry. 'You all right, Kerry?'

'Course I'm all right. That bitch isn't though.' She shook Robbie off.

Robbie sighed, before saying, 'Put the kettle on, there's a good'un, Darren.'

Darren hurried in front of them, as Robbie guided Kerry into the kitchen. When she was seated at the table, she glared at Robbie. 'What the fuck did yer stop me for? I would have killed the fat bastard.'

'That's what for.' Robbie glared right back at her. 'Do yer think I want you inside on top of everything else?' He ran his fingers through his hair. 'For fuck's sake, just chill, will yer, Kerry?'

Kerry calmed down, probably the quickest calming she'd ever had in her life; it was the sheer dejected look on Robbie's face that did it. After a few deep breaths, she managed a small smile, and said, 'I bet she'll have a hell of a shiner in the morning.'

Robbie rubbed his shin. 'Aye, and I bet I'll have

a hell of a bruise an' all. Yer can't half kick, Kerry. I'll be limping for a year.'

Kerry laughed. 'That'll teach yer to interfere.'

Darren, pleased that everything sounded normal, made the teas and carried them over to his brother and sister.

As they sipped their tea, Robbie told Darren what had happened next door.

When he'd finished, Darren looked at Kerry and said with deadly seriousness, 'I reckon yer should have killed her, Kerry.'

Kerry grinned, as Robbie nearly choked on his tea. When he had his breath back, he looked at Darren and pointed to the stairs. 'Bed, brat.'

Darren held his hands up. 'OK, OK, only joking. But I forgot to tell yer what she did the other day.' He waited until he had their full attention, then went on. 'She knocked on the door with a cup in her hand, and guess what she asked for.'

'If yer gonna say milk, I'll throttle yer,' Kerry said.

'No, no, not milk. What she said was, "If yer give me a water sample I'll give yer a fiver."'

Robbie and Kerry looked at each other, then back at Darren. Kerry burst out laughing. 'I don't fucking believe it. I've heard of borrowing a cup of sugar, but a cup of piss!'

Robbie and Darren ended up laughing as loud as Kerry. When they'd calmed down, Darren asked, 'But what did she want it for, Robbie?'

'She's obviously on methadone. The doctors test a water sample, and if there's anything else in it, they won't give it out.'

'So she wanted my clean wee, so she could get the stuff off the doctor for free?'

'That's about it.'

Darren shook his head in disbelief and headed up to bed without being told. Kerry and Robbie followed him. He was still shaking his head when Robbie put the light out.

Lorraine slammed the car door and Luke winced. He loved his car.

'Waste of time. No, never seen him before. No, never seen him before,' Lorraine mimicked. 'You'd think the whole bloody lot were auditioning for the same stupid play. I felt like grabbing the mike off that bloody commentator and screaming to the whole lot of them that three bloody kids are missing.'

She slumped in her seat and Luke started the engine. 'Take me home, Luke. I'm fairly shattered and me brain's going round in circles.'

'And yer lost yer money again.'

'Did yer have to remind me?'

She looked at him, then hastily looked away. Mavis was right about him. *And that's all I need, a case of raving hormones when me bloody husband's missing. The bastard better be in when I get home, just so I can chuck the twat back out.*

They were passing Penshaw Monument, a folly in the form of a Greek temple about two miles out of Houghton, before she spoke again.

'We'll have to go there another night, cos I know he visits the place. Plus some of them had that look

208

in their eyes. That "I'm telling yer bare-faced lies" look.'

'Yeah, I got the same feeling.'

They reached her house, and as she went to get out of the car she was tempted to ask him in for coffee. *Just for coffee? Why aye. But what if John has come back? Unlikely. And what if Luke doesn't want to have anything to do with me? What if he runs away in shock, or disgust even? I'm gonna feel a right mug when I've got to work with him. Oh shit, who wants a man anyhow? Certainly not me!*

'See yer, Luke.' She slammed the door.

Luke winced again then, turning his head, he watched her walk up the path.

Jason Smith heard the phone ring just as he was about to turn the key and go home. For a moment he was tempted to ignore it, but if she heard it and knew he was still on the premises there would be hell to pay.

Quickly, he crossed the room and picked up the phone. For a few minutes he was silent, then he said, 'Right-oh, I'll go and tell her now. Ta-ra.' He put the phone down and went to the bottom of the stairs and was about to shout out when something touched his shoulder. Heart hammering, he spun round.

'Who was it?' Mrs Archer demanded.

'Jesus, yer frightened the life out of me.' He only just stopped himself from adding, *Yer ugly bastard.*

She couldn't have cared less if she'd caused Jason to have a heart attack. The size of the fat twat, it was just a matter of time anyhow.

'Who was it?' she asked again, and this time her tone was menacing.

Quickly, Jason said, 'Yer not gonna like this. There's some kid got hold of a picture of Brad and she's showing it around, asking questions like.'

'What!'

He nodded, not daring to repeat what he'd just said.

'Who the fuck is she?'

'Don't know, but she's been showing it around the arcades in Shields.'

'For fuck's sake. Phone the arcades and get the bitch warned off. If I didn't have enough on me plate with that bastard Stevie. The twat's helping himself to freebies, I know he is . . . Go on then.'

'Er . . .'

'What else?'

'The coppers have got a picture as well.'

'Oh, for fuck's sake.'

Jason phoned their contact back. When he put the phone down, Mrs Archer was standing at the door. He opened his mouth but she cut him off.

'I heard yer, now fuck off. And don't be late in the morning, there's some things need sorting out.'

'Aye, I'll be here.' Quickly he grabbed Jess's lead and left.

Mrs Archer slammed the door behind him. 'Fucking bastard,' she muttered, making her way upstairs. 'It's all gonna go pear-shaped, I swear to God. They're all getting too fucking careless. And that stupid blond fuck had to bring that girl in here last night. I'll tear his fucking head off when I see the twat.'

Thursday

Thursday

13

After another restless night, Lorraine dressed for work. She chose a smart navy-blue trouser suit with a crisp white blouse, did her hair in a neat plait and put tiny pearl studs in her ears. Then, remembering they were a present from her wayward husband, she took them out and replaced them with small gold hoops. All the time she was dressing, she avoided looking at the empty wardrobe.

Downstairs, she went through the motions of making breakfast even though her appetite was virtually non-existent. She drank her coffee with cream and two sugars, the only way she could drink it. Unaware that the girls she was seeking had lived on nothing but cornflakes for the last three days, she poured out a bowl and forced herself to eat two spoonfuls before pushing it away.

'Bastard,' she said to the soggy mess, then shoved the bowl even further away when the radio started playing Elvis's 'Jailhouse Rock'.

John had always been a big Elvis fan, and had the full collection of records and videos, which were played quite frequently. Actually, the more she thought about it, it wasn't just frequently it was constantly. Another reason why she couldn't stand the bastard.

She switched Elvis off with a savage swipe at the button and picked up her keys. Slamming the door behind her, she reminded herself to get the locks changed as soon as possible. *If that arsehole thinks he can swan back here whenever the fancy takes him, he can fucking well think again.*

Walking towards the car, she became more and more depressed with each step she took. Half a week gone and still no clue as to the whereabouts of the missing girls – or, for that matter, the bloody heads. *Jesus Christ, Clark is gonna go ape shit sometime soon.*

Hoping there would be some good news when she got to work, she pulled away from the kerb and joined the traffic. Swerving once to miss a black and tan mongrel, who had the bare-faced cheek to wag his tail when she beeped at him, she kept the car to the exact speed limit of each road she was on, and made it to the station with a few minutes to spare. But when she got there, she was in for a shock.

'Christ,' she muttered, as she drove through the gates to find the station besieged by reporters. 'What the hell's broke?'

Reversing the car she swung into a wide arc, and drove round to the back entrance. But, to her dismay, the ever-vigilant press were also there. 'Damn nosy bastards.' Knowing she had no choice, she prepared herself to run the gauntlet.

'Who knows?' she wondered as she picked her case up from the back seat. 'With a bit of luck they might think I'm just a secretary.'

No such luck though. She didn't even reach the

main building before they surrounded her like a flock of marauding crows.

'Detective Inspector Hunt.' One reporter's voice could be heard above the rest. Lorraine knew the voice and turned. She looked him up and down coldly, and he returned the look, an undisguised smirk on his mean-lipped face.

Of all the reporters in the whole friggin' world, it had to be him. Most of them were just doing their jobs and did them well, but there was always one. The last she'd heard he was in Bosnia, and according to Luke, who hated him every bit as much as she did, the bastard had probably started the war himself, just to make news.

He pushed his way through his colleagues, catching a blonde in a red jacket on her arm. The look the blonde gave him matched anything Lorraine could come up with.

Knowing he had Lorraine's full attention, he smiled slyly and asked, 'Is it true, Inspector Hunt, that the body found at Fatfield is actually missing its head?'

Shit. How had he found that out?

'That's Detective Inspector Hunt to you.' Her voice was still cold, but inside she was seething.

He placed his hand on her arm. Lorraine looked down at the offending hand as if it was contaminated with leprosy, then with eyes like winter ice she stared into his muddy brown pair.

Dropping his hand, he muttered a string of apologies. Ignoring him, she looked at the rest of them and, with as much distaste as she could muster –

and she could muster a lot – said, 'No comment.'

This was met with a chorus of complaints. Walking up the steps into the building, she stopped at the top, turned and faced them. 'As soon as we have anything concrete, you will all be told. Until then, please try not to delve into the realms of fiction.'

The door opened behind her and she turned, pleased to see Luke and Carter. Without looking back she entered the station.

'Nice one, boss,' Luke said, as she stepped past him. Nodding, she tried to keep as much distance as she could between them, then hurried down the corridor to the incident room. Luke shrugged as he closed the door, then he and Carter followed Lorraine.

'Right,' she said, walking into the room and throwing her bag on to the table. 'Where the fuck's the information leaking from?' She looked around at her officers. Including herself, Luke and Carter, there were ten altogether. All of them stopped what they were doing and stared at her. Rarely did she talk to them like that, but when she did they all knew it was an ill wind for someone.

Sara Jacobs, a petite dark-haired woman, raised her hand and said in a childish voice, 'They've been parked out there since seven o'clock, boss. I practically had to fight my way in.'

Lorraine gritted her teeth, and forced a thin smile. 'I didn't ask how long they've been camped out there. I asked where the fuck they've got their information from. How, for example, do they now know the body has no fucking head? Or is that question too much for a room full of fucking detectives?'

No one answered. Instead they looked at the ceiling, the floor, out the window, then at each other, as if trying to suss out where the leak had sprung from.

Lorraine sighed, which only made them more embarrassed. One of them had committed the prime sin. By accident or design. Tattled to a wife, a husband, or a friend . . . and this was something that had never happened before. They had been a good crew for years, and even the two newest members, Carter and Sara Jacobs, seemed to get on well with everyone. Although, if she was honest, Lorraine thought Sara was a bit of a simpering ninny and she suspected that the woman got on a few of the others' nerves as well as hers. The worst-case scenario, which really was unthinkable, was that one of them had held their greedy little mitts out to the press. She prayed that this wasn't the case. If it was, when she found the culprit he – or she – wouldn't get a job as a security guard in a jelly baby factory once Lorraine had finished with them.

She looked the team over once more, letting it sink in just how angry she really was, then walked to the board, her heels clicking in the silent room. On it were pictures of the three missing teenagers.

'Right. Travis, May and Jacobs' – she pointed at two men and Sara – 'I want the three of you to go over everything we've got on the dead bodies. And I mean everything, there has got to be something we're missing.'

Hearing a snigger she turned, her eyes seeking out James Dinwall. In every group there was always a comedian; in hers, it was Dinwall. She stared at him for a moment, then said drily, '*Besides* the heads.'

There was a smattering of soft laughter, which relieved the tension considerably, and Lorraine carried on. 'So far we only know the name of the body found at Fatfield. Not good enough. You three will go over what little evidence there is until you find something, no matter what it is. Whatever hunch you get, follow it up, and don't bother me until you have something concrete to show me. The rest of you,' picking up a long stick kept by the board, she tapped each girl's photo individually, 'I want these kids found. As you all know, we've so far been working on the theory that this is some sort of one-man Casanova. I now think otherwise. Also, I'm pretty sure he's no stranger to this game and that the whole show is very well organised.'

She paused a moment, letting this sink in while she looked at them all. 'OK, this is what I want. Get out on the streets of Sunderland with this Brad's picture. Talk to people. You all have your own contacts, so use them. He's got to have at least a couple of enemies that'll grass him for a few quid.' She shrugged. 'You never know, you could get lucky. If he flashes his money around – and most gamblers do when they've had a run – he could have a couple of jealous cohorts who might even give you a tip or two for free.'

Loud groans followed her speech and James Dinwall added in his gravelly voice, 'Why aye, boss, and pigs might fly.'

'Happen they might, James, but you better be

flying higher. I want answers and I want them yesterday, understand?'

She looked directly at Sanderson, a small wiry man with the look of a fox, which was emphasised by his sandy-coloured hair and moustache. 'We have some people coming in from Newcastle today. I want you to meet with them. Also, I'm putting you in charge of this lot, so don't let them give you any grief.'

Sanderson, who had been with Lorraine since she started at the station, looked as if he was going to salute. Instead he grinned and said, 'Sure thing, boss.'

'And,' she paused for emphasis, 'I want all of you to think long and hard about where this leak has come from.'

She put her stick down and headed for the door and then, her hand on the handle, she turned. Stressing each word, she said, 'It really isn't good enough, is it? Because of some stupid blabbermouth, we have to deal with the vultures out there. And you can just bet your sweet arses it will be in all the papers by tea time. Thank God they still don't know there's more than one body.'

She left to complete silence, and walked to her room. The door had barely shut behind her when Luke followed her in with two coffees.

'That told them, boss.' He put one of the coffees on her desk, then sat down in the chair opposite. Crossing his right leg over his left knee, he took a sip, then smiled at her.

Lorraine did not return the smile. Instead she sighed. 'What the fuck am I gonna do, Luke? If the papers find out the rest, and even guess that we tried a cover-up about a series of decapitations, Clark will go bananas.'

'Yes he will, but it was his idea to keep the lid on, not yours. You and I both said it was best out in the open. Anyhow, it's not as if they were recent murders, the newest body's been in the ground for at least seven years. The murderer's probably long gone by now, might even be bloody dead himself. It's not like we're dealing with an active serial killer.'

Leaning back in her seat, Lorraine studied the ceiling.

Watching her, Luke couldn't help but admire the smooth lines of her neck. 'Anyhow,' he went on, reluctantly snapping back to business, 'I don't know what you're worrying about. You've covered for Clark's cock-ups before . . .'

She dragged her eyes away from the ceiling and looked at him. 'It's the leak that's worrying me, Luke. I wouldn't have believed it, cos they're a damn good lot, but it's had to come from one of them.'

'It could have been a slip in a pub or somewhere,' he suggested.

'I hope so.' But as she spoke, her wayward and troubled mind was thinking, *What a beautiful man.*

Now where did that come from?

Whoa, slow down, girl, that's dangerous thinking. It's not as if you've been without a man for that bloody long.

It's Mam's fault, she's been singing his praises for too long.

She knew, though, that Mavis was right in just

about everything she said about Luke. Why couldn't John be more like Luke?

Then again, I bet he's got plenty of hidden faults an' all. When yer think about it, all of the bastards have. At the end of the day, all they really do is exchange one friggin' tit for another.

Mammy's boys, the whole bastard lot of them.

Luke was beginning to squirm under her scrutiny. 'Penny for them, Lorraine?'

'Sorry?'

'Your thoughts, you were miles away.'

Lorraine felt herself blush, a rare thing. Standing, she moved to the window and looked out. Having her back to him made her feel more in control. She shrugged, then said, 'Nothing really, Luke. Just thinking, that's all.'

Unaware that he'd been the subject of her thoughts, he drained his coffee, rose, and said, 'OK, then, I'll be off. I've to see Jade's parents again this afternoon and then first thing tomorrow I'm back at the hospital with Mrs Lumsdon. Hopefully she might fully understand what's going on now. Yer never know, she might be able to tell us something.' At the door, he turned. 'See yer later then.'

'Aye. By the way, you're being very good to the Lumsdons, Luke. It's kind of yer.'

'I feel sorry for them, they're a pretty decent lot that's been down on their luck for a long time.'

He had the door open when Travis appeared. 'Bad news, boss,' Travis said, walking past Luke who closed the door and moved back into the room.

Lorraine nodded for Travis to speak.

'A body's turned up.' Lorraine held her breath. Was it one of the girls or another body minus its head?

'That of a young girl,' a grim-faced Travis went on. 'Somewhere between the ages of thirteen and sixteen.'

Lorraine felt as if she'd been punched in the stomach. One dead. Where were the others – dead an' all? And which girl's family would she be visiting?

Before she could ask anything more, the telephone rang. Knowing it could only be Clark, she pulled a face at the two men and picked it up.

As Lorraine dealt with an irate Clark, Kerry and Robbie stepped off the bus at South Shields. Mark, figuring he needed a break from studying anyhow, had taken the day off and was waiting for them. Kerry felt the same tingle she had the night before as she introduced them. Mark gave Robbie a friendly smile and Robbie warmed to him at once.

'So have yer found out anything?' Kerry asked, fingers crossed in her pockets.

'Well, not a lot really. No one seems to have seen him for a week or two.' When he saw Kerry's disappointment, he hurried on. 'But I've found out where his grandmother lives. I thought, if we go there, she might just know where he's living now. Anyhow, it's a start.'

'Cool,' said Robbie. 'Can we go there now?'

'Sure thing,' Mark replied. 'It's not that far, just through the park.'

The park was across the road from the bus stop, and they passed through it to the accompaniment of at least fifty ducks and a dozen or so children.

'When we get there,' Kerry said above the noise, 'leave the talking to me, all right, guys?'

'No sweat, Kerry,' Mark said, while Robbie nodded at her. It was what he usually did anyhow.

They reached the house, a small Victorian type that had seen better days, although some attempt had been made to brighten the place up; spring bulbs were starting to flower in the peeling window boxes, showing hints of pink and blue.

A light rain started as Robbie knocked on the door, and Kerry turned up the collar of her black leather jacket – a bargain car-boot-sale item that Robbie had found just before Christmas.

'I hope she's in,' muttered Kerry. Then they heard someone moving about inside. It seemed to take for ever for the person to come to the door, but at last a thin reedy voice demanded to know who was there.

Kerry shrugged, bent forward and opened the letter box. 'Excuse me, but do yer have a grandson called Brad?'

The door slowly opened. A small woman, definitely a fully paid-up member of the blue-rinse brigade, snapped, 'Who wants to know, like?'

Kerry stepped back, the old woman's breath stank of tobacco. 'Hello,' she said politely. 'Me name's Kerry Lumsdon. A few weeks ago your grandson lent me some money. I'd missed the last bus home, see, so he lent me the money for a taxi. If yer could just tell me where he lives—'

She was cut short by the old woman's laugh. 'I doubt if it's our Brad yer after, pet. That one wouldn't throw a rope to a drowning man . . . Believe me, I should know.'

'Oh, it's him all right,' Kerry insisted earnestly. 'So if yer could just tell me where he lives, so I can pay him back . . .'

The old woman shook her head then, mean lips stretched tight, said, 'No, this doesn't quite ring true. The last time I had a lass at this door looking for our Brad, the stupid little cow was three months gone.' She looked Kerry up and down, her eyes settling on her flat chest. 'And to tell yer the truth, little girl, yer not his type at all. So what are yer really after?'

Kerry pulled her coat shut. *Old cow*, she thought, then decided she had no other option but to tell the truth. If the blue-haired witch wouldn't come through after that, well, they would just have to go back to the police.

'Please. I really need to see him. It's about me sister, see we haven't seen her for three days. And the last time anybody saw her she was with yer grandson. For Christ's sake, she's only thirteen and—'

The door was slammed in their faces.

'Why yer nasty old bitch!' Kerry banged the door with her fists. 'Come back out here, yer old cow!' She bent down and opened the letter box again. 'I know yer know where he is,' she shouted. 'I want me sister back, and I know she's with yer creep of a fucking grandson, yer smelly old twat.' Nearly crying with rage, she banged on the door again. 'Did

224

yer hear me? And I'm not yer fucking pet either.'
With that she kicked the door.

Robbie put his hand on her arm. 'Come on, Kerry,
it's a waste of time, she's not coming back out. And
if yer keep harassing her she'll have the coppers on
you.'

'Old cow,' Kerry snarled. But after giving the door
one more hefty kick, she followed Robbie and Mark
up the path.

'What we gonna do now?' Robbie asked, as they
headed in the direction of the park.

'We could try the arcades,' Mark suggested.

'Yeah, let's do that,' Kerry said, already heading
towards the sea front.

They searched the first arcade. Mark spoke to a
few people but no one had seen Brad. In the next
one they decided to split up to cover more ground.
Kerry questioned a few groups and then, disheart-
ened by their bored, blank looks as she showed them
her photocopy of Katy's drawing, she stopped to
watch a scruffy old man put pound after pound in
one of the fruit machines and win absolutely nothing.
Just as she was about to move on, someone grabbed
her arm and yanked her around to the back of the
machines.

A large hand gripped her chin and forced her head
up to look into a pair of steely grey eyes. The eyes
were bald, not an eyelash or eyebrow in sight, and
the effect up close was frightening. Kerry glanced
quickly at her attacker's head. *The bastard's got no
hair there either*, she thought, looking back at his
eyes. They were colder than drugged-up Stevie's,

colder than nasty Jason Smith's, and Kerry realised with a shock that she could be in real danger – the kind of danger she might not be able to talk her way out of.

'What's yer name?' the man demanded.

'Kerry Lumsdon,' she said without hesitation, though with a little difficulty. Her eyes darted left and right, desperately looking for Mark and Robbie.

'Well, Kerry Lumsdon, I hear yer've been asking about a friend of mine.'

It was on the tip of her tongue to deny it, when he gripped her chin even harder. 'And don't even think about spouting a load of fucking lies, yer nosy little bitch. I'm telling yer now, back off. If yer know what's best for yer.'

Suddenly he let go of her and pushed her against the one-armed bandit. Her head slammed back against the machine and he gave a grunt of satisfaction, then walked off without looking back. Kerry stared at the back of his bald head, badly shaken. But, more than that, she was more worried about Claire than ever. Her sister was in deep shit. She stared at the empty space the man had left as she rubbed her chin.

What do I do now?

Tell the coppers?

Now that would be really bright, first step to a wooden jacket.

Tell Robbie? She decided against it. If Robbie knew she'd been threatened he would call the search off right away, and Claire could end up being lost to them for ever. She would have to be careful, that's all, watch her back. She straightened her coat and pulled her shoulders back, regaining her confidence.

The cheeky bastard wasn't frightening her off. This was about her sister. Fuck him. Who did the bald bastard think he was, the fucking Mafia?

Brave words, but she was still shaking inside when she went to look for the boys, and she couldn't help but think, *What if they are the Mafia? Or somebody like them. Somebody even worse.*

What the hell are yer involved with, Claire?

'Ahh, there yer are,' Robbie said, spotting her.

Mark smiled at her, but she was in too much of a turmoil to respond.

Sensing something wrong, Robbie frowned as he said, 'Are yer all right, Kerry?'

The thought of telling them what had just happened flickered through Kerry's mind again, but she squashed it. They had to find Claire, that was all that mattered.

'Yeah, just thinking, that's all,' she mumbled.

'The way I see it,' Mark said, 'the only option yer have left is the police. At least you've found out where he comes from; they should be able to get that tough old nut to talk.'

'Huh, I doubt that,' Kerry grumbled as she turned and faced him. She wasn't really sure what to do now, but handing over to the police felt like giving up. And she couldn't do that. There didn't seem to be any point hanging round South Shields, though. 'I think we'd better go an' get the kids from school now. But, thanks for yer help.'

'It's OK. I, er,' he looked awkwardly down at the

ground for a moment, 'I'll walk back to the bus stop with yer . . . If that's all right, like.'

Kerry was already moving. Shrugging she replied, 'Yeah, no prob.'

A few yards in front of them, Robbie grinned to himself. He could see which way the wind was blowing even if his dumb sister couldn't. And he quite liked Mark, even though they had just met.

When they reached the bus stop Robbie stepped behind it and stood looking at the sea. Mark moved as close to Kerry as he could without actually standing on her. 'So,' he smiled the smile he'd practised in the bathroom mirror that morning, 'can I see yer again, Kerry?'

Heart skipping, Kerry played it cool. 'I don't know . . . I suppose so. That's if yer really want to. Only the problem is, yer live a canny bit away, and I haven't always got the money to waste on bus fares, like. And I've got me training for the county finals a week on Saturday, though fat chance of that if our Claire's still gone.'

'Oh, what's yer sport then?'

'Running . . . I'm a runner.'

'Cool. Look, it doesn't matter about bus fares, I can get a bus pass and come and see yer any time. That's if yer want. And me dad's got a couple of cars. I'm sure I can get someone to drop me off now and again.'

'A couple of cars! Can you drive?'

'I haven't passed me test, but me dad lets me drive round the estate.'

Kerry looked him up and down. His clothes were

good, and all the best labels. And sometimes his accent sounded a bit posh. His dad must have a hell of a job. 'So what yer saying? That if yer ran somebody over on your estate, you and yer dad wouldn't get wrong?'

Mark looked puzzled for a moment, then he smiled. 'Not a housing estate – me dad wouldn't let me drive round one of those. No, I mean where we live.'

It was Kerry's turn to be puzzled. 'Where yer live? What do yer mean?'

Mark blushed, slightly embarrassed, but he went on. 'We, er . . . We have a house with a fair bit of ground.'

'Fuck off.'

Mark burst out laughing. 'Honest, we have.'

Kerry was thrown. She liked Mark, but she hadn't reckoned on him being rich and having an estate of his own.

I wonder how many houses there is? And girls, there must be loads of good-looking girls living there. Girls with breasts. She looked down at her car-boot-sale jacket, which, granted, was still in good nick, but had been somebody else's first, it was just a cast-off. Probably from a girl as rich as Mark . . . *No, it'll never work.*

She felt a twinge of sadness, as she glanced at his top-of-the-range sports gear.

Where the hell's the bus? She looked to see if it was coming.

Anyhow, there's far too much going on at the minute for me to even think straight, never mind adding boys to me list of worries. Most of them turn out to be arseholes anyhow. Just need to look at me mam to know that.

Mind made up, she was about to tell him 'on yer bike', when he touched her arm.

'Don't yer want to see me again, Kerry?'

Before she could give him the curt 'no' that was on the tip of her tongue, Robbie came round to the front of the bus stop.

'Course she does. Here,' he thrust a piece of paper at Mark, who took it eagerly. 'That's our address. OK?'

The bus arrived and Kerry jumped on without looking at Mark. She ran up the stairs and moved to the back where she took a window seat.

'What the fuck did yer have to do that for?' she demanded, when Robbie, who had been paying the fares, joined her.

'What's the matter? I thought yer liked him. Anyhow, he's got the hots for you all right.'

'He's rich, yer idiot.'

'So? Just cos his dad's got a couple of cars doesn't mean he's filthy rich, they could be old bangers for all you know.'

'Huh, I doubt it. He's got his own house. And, wait for it, they even own an estate. There must be plenty of girls living there, so what does he want with me?'

'Estate?' Robbie frowned at her for a moment, then he started to laugh. 'Estate doesn't always mean a housing estate. It can sometimes mean a plot of land with a grand house on it, daft head.'

Kerry looked at him, to make sure he wasn't taking the piss, before saying, 'I knew that.'

'Like hell yer did.'

She shrugged. 'Anyhow, that makes it worse, he's right out of my league.'

'I wish you'd stop putting yerself down, Kerry.'

Kerry sighed, and it came from her heart. 'I am fucking down. Sometimes I feel so fucking down that I can't find the way up.' Looking out the window she blinked back a tear.

'Oh, Kerry.' Robbie squeezed her shoulder. 'Look, our Mam will be better before long. I'm sure she will. And I'll just bet that when we tell the coppers what we've found out, they'll find our Claire right away. Then you'll win the race and you'll be right back on top.'

Right back on top, eh? She thought. *No way.* The tear dissolved along with any memory that it had ever been there and she snarled, 'Do yer want to know something, Robbie?'

The tone of her voice told Robbie that no, whatever it was, he didn't want to know. 'I don't think so, sis, but I bet yer gonna tell me anyhow.'

'Too right I am. People like you make me really fucking sick, do yer know that? We're up to the eyeballs in shit here and all yer can do is look on the fucking bright side. Well I'm here to tell yer for once and for all – and get it through yer thick head – that for people like you and me, there ain't no bright side. Got it?'

Refusing to let her intimidate him, Robbie smiled. 'Course there is.'

'No, there fucking well isn't. Where Mark comes from they call the likes of you and me scumbags.'

'That's only cos they don't know us. They hear the worst about a few horrible druggies and they class us all the same. But I'm certain not all of them think like that. They're not all the same, just as the people that live beside us aren't the same.'

'Bollocks, Robbie.' She elbowed him in the ribs. 'Want to know something else, big brother? Yer getting right on me fucking tits. Why don't yer fuck off and become a priest? Now there's a way out.'

'Sorry, can't do that, Kerry. We aren't Catholics.'

'Well, a fucking vicar then. A monk even . . . For fuck's sake.'

Turning her back on him she stared out the window and spent the rest of the journey worrying about what had happened in the arcade, and how she was gonna deal with it. It was obvious Claire was in bigger trouble than any of them had imagined.

Kerry bit her lip. She knew she could take care of herself on the streets, better than most, but this was a grown-up world, and it was starting to become very very frightening.

Earlier that morning, as Kerry and Robbie set off to meet Mark, Darren had dropped the girls off at their school before slowly making his way up the bank to his own.

And none too soon, he swore to himself. *If our Emma had sniffed just once more . . .* He growled, his hands clenched in his pockets.

Kicking an empty lager can off the wall, he imagined it was Emma's head, then he jumped on it. The noise it made was supremely satisfying.

Why couldn't she be more like Suzy, and just chill?

'Hi, Daz.'

Darren went on kicking the now-flat can. There was no need to look, he knew the voice well enough, his ex-friend Kenny Jones. They'd rowed badly yesterday when Kenny had come round to practise football after school.

Kenny tagged along. He was small for his age, and his size was emphasised by the length of his school blazer. He looked like a kid playing dress-up in his older brother's clothes. 'You seen them lads any more, Daz?'

'What lads?' Darren asked, even though he knew exactly which lads Kenny was referring to.

'Him with all the spots, and the other one, Stevie somebody or other.'

'What yer asking me for? Yer told everybody we wasn't mates any more . . . Remember? And what do yer want them for, anyway?'

'I didn't mean it when I said we wasn't mates. How was I to know when yer shouted at me and called me broken brain that yer mam was in the hospital and your Claire was AWOL . . . ?' Desperate to be friends again, Kenny went on. 'Yer never told me, did yer? Best mates is supposed to tell each other everything.'

Darren shrugged, allowing for the fact that, no, he hadn't told Kenny about his mam and his sister. But only because he'd never had the time. In the name of friendship he let that fact go. 'So,' he said after a moment, aware that Kenny had avoided answering his previous question, 'what do yer want them two pricks for?'

'Nowt really.' Kenny kicked the ball he'd been carrying under his arm into the air and caught it on his knee. 'How many times do yer reckon I can keep this up?'

'Not as many as me.' Darren walked on, not interested in football for the first time in his life.

Kenny caught the ball and, putting it back under his arm, he hurried up to Darren. 'You all right, Daz?' Kenny had never known Darren to refuse a ball challenge.

'Aye, why shouldn't I be? I mean, apart from a poorly mam, and a missing sister, who could be on the friggin' moon for all I know, cos nobody tells me nowt – why wouldn't I be all right?'

'Sorry, Daz.'

Darren stopped, and with a sigh beyond his years, said, 'It's OK, Kenny, it's not really your fault.' He looked closely at Kenny as if what was going on in the smaller boy's mind would play across his forehead. 'Them lads, did they give yer something the other day? Is that why yer all fired up about wanting to know where they are? Did yer take drugs? Yer better not have, Kenny.'

Kenny studied his trainers as if he'd suddenly discovered he was wearing the boy next door's and they were ready for the dustbin.

'Kenny,' Darren prompted.

'All right, all right.' Knowing that Darren would

hound him until he told the truth, his words came out in a rush. 'He did. But our Stacy found it. Clouted me right in the face, she did, just after she flushed it down the friggin' loo. She never told me mam though, and I'm glad an' all, cos she would have friggin' well strangled me.'

'I bet she had to bend a long way to slap yer face.'

'Ha ha. Very funny, I think not.'

'What were yer gonna do with it if your Stacy hadn't snaffled it like?' Darren demanded.

'I just wanted to try it, that's all. See what all the fuss is about, yer know what I mean. I want to see what this buzz thingy is what they all bleat on about. That's all.'

Darren shook his head. 'That's all? That buzz can kill yer. Didn't yer listen to the talk the coppers gave us at school the other week? They said it only takes one, stupid.' He held up the forefinger of his right hand. 'Just one, that's all. And what did yer think, that they gave them away for ever? Dimwit. Only the first one's free. After that yer have to pay for them. That's why them druggies look all grey and greasy, and go around nicking stuff. It's a habit, see? Like you always picking your nose. Only with some of the drugs, like the kind yer sniff, yer friggin' nose falls off. Didn't yer listen at all? Do yer know something? Your Stacy's got fifty times more brains than you'll ever have.'

Darren walked on, angry now that Kenny should even want to try drugs after what he'd been told about them.

Kenny caught up with him. 'Aw. Come on, Darren.

I was only messin'. Probably wouldn't have even taken it.'

They heard the bell ring and they both broke into a run. 'Come on,' Darren yelled. 'The Hatchet's on yard duty today, and if we're not standing like friggin' tin soldiers before she rings the last bell, yer can forget footie practice.'

Kenny needed no urging, he'd had his own run-ins with the Hatchet.

At the mid-morning break, Darren looked for Kenny – not that he was hard to find; when he wasn't in the yard kicking his ball about, Darren knew where he'd be. He wandered over to smokers' corner, and there Kenny was, puffing away with the older boys looking like a cod out of water.

Kenny spotted him, and Darren gestured with his head for Kenny to come. Kenny nodded and passed his cigarette over to one of the others, who practically snatched it out of his hand in his eagerness.

'I thought yer wanted to be a bloody footballer?' Darren said when Kenny reached him.

'Yer know I do.'

'So what yer smoking for? The next thing, you'll be on the happy baccy.'

'No, that's behind the science lab.'

'Kenny man, it's not bloody funny,' Darren said angrily.

'OK, Mammy . . . So what is it yer want?'

'I thought we was mates again?'

'We are. Only . . .'

'Only what?'

Kenny looked behind him in the direction of

smoker's corner. 'Only they . . .' He looked up at Darren's serious face, sighed, then went on. 'Nowt, just forget it. What do yer want to do, kick the ball about for a bit?'

'No, not really.' Darren stuffed his hands in his pockets and shuffled towards the yard. Kenny, feeling a twinge of guilt, shuffled along beside him.

'I, er . . . I am sorry about yer mam, and Claire, Daz. Honest I am. I hate our Stacy, the cow. But if she was missing like your Claire I'd be shitting bricks. And, don't tell anybody though, I think I'd probably be crying a lot. Even though, honest to God,' he held two fingers up, 'I can't stand her friggin' guts.'

Darren nodded. He knew what it was like to have a sister or two that you truly couldn't stand. 'They never tell me nowt, yer know. That's what makes it so bad. They treat me as if I was a little kid or something, and it's not fair. It's my mam, and my sister an all, but them two—'

'What two?'

'Our Robbie and our Kerry. I heard them talking last night. They've only gone on a bloody mission to South Shields, looking for our Claire. They leave me out of everything.'

'Oh.'

'And the Hatchet's been on me case all bloody morning. She's fairly doing me head in, asking all sorts of stupid questions about Stevie Shite.'

'What's she asking, like?' Kenny kicked a ball that came his way, and for once his luck was in: if Miss Ratchet had not moved on when she did, it would probably have knocked her out. Kenny dry-swallowed, looked at Darren and whistled.

'Amazing,' Darren said, and they both looked back at the ball and watched as it bounced down the yard.

After a moment they walked on, and Kenny said again, 'So what is it she's asking, like?'

'About drugs. She caught him the other night trying to give me some, and since then she's been a right pain in the arse. As if I'd live to see tomorrow if I was daft enough to tell her where he gets them from . . . Hell, as if I even knew!'

'She needs some serious lessons in chilling, she does.'

Darren suddenly stopped, and turned to Kenny. 'What am I gonna do, Kenny? I'm starting to feel right fucked up.'

Kenny gave the yard a quick once-over in case there was a teacher within hearing distance, before saying with feeling, 'Aye, man, I'd feel right fucked up an' all.'

Then his face lightened and he said with a grin, 'I know, why don't yer come to my house for tea tonight? We can watch a video and Mam might let yer sleep over.'

Darren brightened slightly. 'Aye, we could watch *The Phantom Menace* again.' Then his face dropped. 'I can't.'

'What for?'

'I've got Suzy the drip and Emma the sniff to mind, in case Batman and Robin ain't back.'

'God, that's rough. Your Emma don't half sniff . . . Do yer reckon that's a habit?'

'Too right. An' a friggin' aggravating one an' all.'

'Tell yer what, I'll come down yours after tea, and see if the dynamic duo's back.'

They both stopped their shuffling, looked at each other and pictured the same thing. Kerry and Robbie running through the Seahills dressed as Batman and Robin.

'That's shocking, that is,' Darren said, as they both burst out laughing.

They were still giggling two minutes later when the bell went, but as they walked back into school Darren's mind flicked back to his missing sister. *Where are you, Claire?*

14

Claire was terrified, her heart pumping at twice its normal rate. An hour ago, Laughing Man had crashed into the cabin and bundled the new girl out. She'd gone quietly, and after a while he'd come back for Jade, who was a different story. When she'd refused to move he'd dragged her out by her hair. She'd screamed and kicked, and he'd slapped her hard, but it had only shut her up for a moment. Then she'd launched into full swing again. Claire and Tracy had heard the thuds as Jade's body had bounced along the deck. Then a deathly silence had fallen. The girls had looked at each other, their faces masks of fear, far too frightened to speculate out loud about where Donna and Jade had been taken.

Over the last three days they had been fed regularly, cornflakes for breakfast, dinner and tea – Jade had sworn she'd be perfectly happy if she never saw another cornflake in her life. Claire had kept her thoughts to herself; she didn't want to say out loud *how long is that life gonna be?* A bucket had been provided for their toilet, and was emptied immediately after use by Laughing Man – Jade swore the dirty bastard had to be watching them. Last night, after Jade had used the bucket and Laughing Man had appeared almost at once, Jade had called him a perverted creep and had received a resounding slap on her bottom. Shortly after that, what was left of their shattered dignity had been stripped from them as, one by one, they were taken on deck and hosed down with freezing cold water in the dark, with tape over their mouths again to stop them calling out.

And now Claire was on her own. Tracy had gone quietly, head down, tears washing the floor. None of them had come back.

Suddenly, Claire heard footsteps. He was coming for her now.

She moaned, then whispered in a small frightened voice, 'Please God . . . Please . . . Don't let him hurt me again . . . Please, somebody help.'

But there was no one to help her, just as there had been no one to help the others. Claire was alone, and the monster was coming for her.

The cabin door opened and he stood there, his bulk blocking out most of the light, his face in shadow. It could have been anybody's face – the man down the street, one of her teachers – but when he laughed she knew, as she'd known all along, that it was him. She wet herself.

'Come here,' he said.

Claire shook her head.

He laughed. Three strides and he had hold of her. Dragging her up from the crouch she hadn't even known she'd adopted, he said into her face, 'Better learn quick, little girl, if yer want to live a little. Where you're going yer can be killed on the fucking spot for disobeying an order . . . Or,' he grinned, 'just because they want to. Because where they live, they can do whatever they fucking well want.'

Where she got the nerve for what she did next she didn't know, but she spat right into his grinning face. She flinched at once, expecting at any moment to feel the sting of his hand, but instead, he laughed. 'Then again, some of them foreigners are wise, they like a bit of pluck, adds some spice.' And he grabbed her hair, then dragged her through the cabin door and on to the deck.

From what she could see, it was empty. She shook with terror, and her imagination went into overdrive wondering what had happened to her friends, wondering what was going to happen to her. She knew that their fate was hers.

Then she saw what was waiting on shore for her.

Laughing Man let go of her hair, and her legs gave way as she stared, eyes bulging, at the midnight-black hearse.

She collapsed into a pathetic little heap on the deck, then flinched as her eye caught a movement to her right. It was the other man, and he was standing in front of a coffin.

She screamed, a waste of time; the quay was deserted. She sounded just like one of the many seagulls that swooped and dived over her head. Then Laughing Man's hand clamped down hard on her mouth, and she watched in horror as the other man moved closer. In his hand he held a hypodermic needle.

'Another fighter, eh?' he said, taking hold of her arm. 'Now why couldn't yer have been like most of the others? Cowards, yes, but I just bet they'll live a lot longer than you and yer friend.'

He pushed Laughing Man's hand away from her breast, then plunged the needle into her arm. 'Such a shame,' she heard him say, before everything faded away.

15

Lorraine had been working out for over an hour, but she couldn't rid herself of the image of the young girl who had been fished out of the river. The kid was yet to be identified – she could be the Lumsdon girl, or just as easily one of the others. *One of the others, aye, and they are increasing by the day.* Not long after this morning's briefing, they'd had the news that yet another girl had gone missing. A Donna this time and yes, once again, last seen in the company of a bloke matching the description of this Brad.

Well, whoever the drowned girl was, the poor kid had suffered dreadfully. Scottie had phoned earlier and even he was shocked.

She gritted her teeth, trying to rid herself of the memory of the horrendous state of the girl's body. *And there's still tomorrow's autopsy to be got through.* Lorraine tried again to clear her thoughts: dwelling on it in advance wasn't going to help any. But her mind was being far from cooperative. It jumped straight from the girl to her missing husband. So much for thinking that an evening session at the club would help her wind down.

Finally deciding she'd had enough, she was

heading for the showers when Harry stepped in front of her.

'Harry,' she chided, 'yer fairly frightened the life out of me. How long have yer been here?'

'Long enough to know that at the end-of-the-year karate championships, you'll kill every opponent yer come in contact with, if yer fight like that.'

Unable to tell him about the girl, she blamed her missing husband for most of her anger, and punched out at a hanging bag.

'It's just so damn frustrating. Not knowing where the bastard is . . . Or why.'

Harry put his arm around her shoulder. 'It's not your fault, pet. Just you remember that. There's something not quite right about that bloke. I always thought he was a bit headstrong, and yer know, he's kind of . . . suppose what I'm trying to say, pet, is I'm not that surprised it's come to this.'

Lorraine looked him in the eye. 'Yer know something I don't. What?'

Harry looked anywhere but at Lorraine. 'It's only . . .' He gave a deep sigh. 'Look kid, I'm probably wrong.'

Lorraine was beside herself with impatience. 'For Christ's sake, Harry. I could do with a little help here, I'm going round the fucking bend not knowing. He's emptied his wardrobe, yer know. Gone, not a trace of the slimy bastard. It's as if the last couple of years never happened, for fuck's sake. Now if yer know anything, anything at all, I suggest yer tell me right now.'

Harry found it in himself to look at her. She was

his cousin's child. She was like one of his own. To tell her what he knew . . . he couldn't do it. He shook his head.

'Tell me, Harry,' she demanded. 'I don't care who she is, I have to know. For Christ's sake, Harry, I can't think straight any more! There're missing kids out there in very great danger, they need me full attention. For fuck's sake, I can't afford to be distracted like this.'

Harry fiddled with his car keys. Then, as if suddenly making up his mind, he cleared his throat and blurted out, 'I, er, . . . I don't think it's another woman yer have to be worried about, Lorraine.'

It took a moment or two for Harry's words to sink in, but when they did, Lorraine exploded. 'Yer what?'

Moving quicker than Harry could blink, she grabbed his lapels and stared into his eyes. 'What is it yer trying to tell me, Harry? That it's a fucking man? A fucking man? No, yer wrong, Harry, it can't be. I would have known.'

Harry's face turned red. 'I think it is, Lorraine.'

'Yer think so? Yer fucking think so?' She stepped back and started pacing angrily. 'Have yer any idea, Harry, what that means?'

Harry nodded. He looked so miserable that, despite her own shock and misery, she felt sorry for him. She stopped pacing and took hold of his arm. 'I'm sorry, Harry, but what yer said shocked me to death.'

'Yeah, I know. That's why I hate to be the messenger.'

'Why?'

'They always get shot.'

Lorraine sighed, then took a deep breath. 'Harry, I'm gonna get changed now. When I'm ready, I want to know everything, understand me? And that means every little thing that you know.'

Pleased to be away from her relentless gaze, even for a short time, Harry agreed. 'Sure, Lorraine pet. I'll be in the canteen.'

'Mine's a strong black coffee. I have a feeling I might need it.' All thoughts of sleep were gone from Lorraine's head.

'Yer can't begin to guess how much,' Harry muttered to himself as he walked away.

Lorraine watched him go. She had no reason to doubt Harry. Not for the world would he come up with something like this unless he was one hundred per cent certain of the facts.

Feet dragging, she made her way to the shower room. Just what exactly did Harry have to tell her? She bit her lip so hard that she drew blood.

A man!

No way.

She clenched her teeth and only just stopped herself from nutting the white tiles.

No way a fucking man.

Harry's wires must be crossed somewhere.

For fuck's sake . . . A fucking man!

She joined Harry fifteen minutes later. Her hair was still wet, and with it spread across her shoulders she reminded Harry of when she'd been fifteen years old. They had picnicked by the river and Lorraine had jumped in to save Topsy, their ten-year-old Jack Russell. Topsy had lived to a ripe old age thanks to Lorraine's bravery.

But bravery was something Harry knew Lorraine had always possessed. Yer either had it or yer didn't. And she was well and truly gonna need it today.

'Right, Harry.' Lorraine sat down and pulled the stool nearer to the table. 'Shoot, and don't miss anything out.'

Harry grimaced. 'OK, yer know I've known John for a while longer than you, about seven years or more. There was . . . there was something about him right off, that just didn't gel . . . Like, er . . . Like I was never too keen on the way he was with the young boys.'

Lorraine slapped her hand on the table, startling Harry even though he'd been prepared for an outburst. 'Don't . . . For fuck's sake, don't say he's a nonce . . . Jesus fucking Christ!'

'No, no,' Harry rushed on, 'nothing like that. It just seemed kind of strange that he showed absolutely no interest in any of the girls. I know that wasn't much to go on, but all the same, he was never a man's man, if yer know what I mean.'

'Which proves what?'

Lorraine was getting really angry now, and Harry knew it. He pressed on. 'That was just the first thing I noticed. Then one day, not long after you'd been married, I saw him with a bloke.' Harry could hear Lorraine's teeth grinding together and he hurried on, embarrassed. 'They were going into that gay bar in Sunderland.'

248

'I know the place. Carry on.' Lorraine's voice was ice cold.

'Lorraine, pet,' Harry took her hand and gently squeezed it, 'I'm not one of your suspects.'

'I'm sorry, Harry. It's just that . . .'

'I know, pet, I know . . . It's a lot to take in all at once. Anyhow, I saw them again a few months after that. When I was walking the dogs up by Penshaw Monument. It was the bloke I recognised first, but then I saw it was John too. They were holding hands, carrying on like people in love do. Lorraine, pet. I'm one hundred per cent certain it was John. I'm so sorry . . .'

'Jesus.' Lorraine sucked in a lungful of air, then blew it out through her teeth. 'Why the fuck didn't you tell me?'

'How could I, love? Back then you seemed so happy, and I kept wanting to think I was wrong, or that it was just a one-off. But as time's gone on I've been surer. And then one of the lads—'

'One of the lads, what, Harry?'

'John told one of the lads that he liked to dress up an' all.' Harry stopped, mortified.

'Well, well. That's our underwear monster caught. If nothing else at least that mystery's well and truly solved.' Lorraine gave a hollow laugh and then said from deep in her heart, 'I don't know how to deal with this, Harry. You've got to help me. It's all so new to me, and it's so fucking frightening.'

Harry's heart went out to her. He couldn't ever remember her looking so forlorn. It made him so angry, he had always loved her like a daughter, and he knew she looked up to him. He wanted to protect her, but the damage was done now.

'Listen, pet, just hold on to the fact that none of this is your doing. It's all that selfish bastard's fault. If he knew he was that way inclined he should never have become involved with a woman. If I had him in my sights, I swear to God, I'd shoot the bastard right between his ugly fucking eyes. Now I know people aren't supposed to be able to help what they are, but that bastard should have kept to his own kind and not used you as some sort of front. For God's sake, what if yer had got pregnant?'

He paused for a moment, tapped his fingers on the table, then went on. 'Wouldn't surprise me one little bit if that witch of a mother of his didn't put him up to it. Yer know what I mean, trying to make Mummy's little boy into a man? Cos she's capable of anything, that one. And she'll have known, trust me, there's nowt about that rotten son of hers that she doesn't know.'

Lorraine stared at the diamond pattern on the lemon tablecloth. Of all the things her mind had come up with over the last few days, this was the last thing she'd suspected. Another woman she could have dealt with, put it out of her mind for a time then sorted it later, but this! Jesus Christ, what the fuck was she gonna do? *I am*, she thought sadly, *at the very least, gobsmacked.*

'Does Mam know? Have you told her?'

'Do yer honestly think he'd be walking around today if I had?'

'What should I do, Harry? Help me here, cos I

haven't got a clue. I'm not stupid, I know that some people are bisexual – it's in the nature of the job, yer meet all sorts. And hopefully you put it all away when yer go home. But I never dreamed in a thousand years that I had married one . . . Jesus!'

Harry nodded, conveying a wealth of sympathy and understanding in the nod. He leaned forward over the table and took hold of her hand. 'First off, pet, I'd have a blood test.' When her face changed he hurried on, 'Just for peace of mind, like.'

'A blood test, a fucking blood test . . . Fucking hell.' She couldn't stop the tears then. Snatching her hand away, she banged on the table with both fists. 'Bastard.' The coffee cups jumped and Harry moved his legs out of the way just in time.

'Tell yer what, pet, why don't yer go over and see Mavis? I think yer need to be with somebody tonight.'

Lorraine nodded. Taking a paper handkerchief out of her bag, she dabbed at her eyes. Then, sounding a hundred years old, she said, 'I think you're right, Harry.' She stood up, collected her belongings and moved towards the door, with Harry close behind her.

When they reached her car, Harry opened the door and helped her in. 'I'll ring the hospital, see if there's any way our Jenny can get yer shoved in this evening.'

Lost in the world of wild imaginings and looking pale and deeply worried, Lorraine managed a weak smile as she drove off. Harry felt nearly as wretched as she did and, totally helpless, watched her go.

Before he phoned the hospital, Harry rang Mavis

and gave her a quick rundown, making her promise not to tell what she knew. He had never in the whole time he'd known her heard her swear but the language she used must have singed the wire all the way from her house to the sports complex.

An hour later, Harry walked into Mavis's house and found Lorraine and Mavis cuddled up together on the settee. Lorraine was fast asleep.

'How is she?' he whispered.

Before Mavis could reply, Lorraine opened her eyes. 'Hi, pet,' Harry said. 'Feeling any better?'

Lorraine gave him a grim smile as she said, 'A little.' Mavis, however, had a face that would frighten thunder.

Harry nodded before saying, 'Jenny says she can get you a blood test done if you can get straight down there. The only problem is, it's a week to ten days before we get the results.'

'How long!' Mavis demanded.

'That's really pushing it, Mave. It's usually three weeks.'

'Well that's a thorough disgrace. Fancy people having to suffer that long in this day and age.'

Harry shrugged his agreement. 'If you want, I'll run yer over to the hospital.'

'Thanks, Harry. Mam, I'll have a quick wash and get sorted before I go down there.'

'You do that, pet. And remember, stop worrying. What'sisname is far too healthy looking to have anything wrong with him.'

They watched as Lorraine walked through the

kitchen on her way to the bathroom. When she was out of sight, Mavis turned to Harry. 'I swear to God, if there's anything wrong with that girl, I'll slaughter the bastard.'

'Me too.'

'What did he do it for, Harry? Marry her, I mean. If he was that way inclined . . . Mind you,' she went on before Harry could answer, 'I never liked the smarmy so and so. As soon as I clapped eyes on him I didn't like him. Never trust a man whose eyebrows meet in the middle, that's what me mam used to say. And by God she got it right this time.'

'She's gonna be all right, Mave. She's a strong girl. She'll put all this behind her, just you watch.'

'Aye, but what if she is infected? That's her life ruined, her career down the drain, for that . . . that *thing*.'

Lorraine came back downstairs. She'd applied fresh make-up and tied her hair back.

'That's better, pet. You look smashing.' Mavis beamed at her, as she pulled a pale blue fleece on top of her grey tracksuit. Then all three of them left the house and got into Harry's car.

Lorraine had agreed to the blood test because it was the only sensible thing to do, but her mind was in a turmoil. She thanked God Harry had arranged it so soon. Ten days tops, he'd said.

She should by rights inform the department at once, but in the end she'd gone along with Mavis's advice. The cases she was on at the moment were far too important to hand over to anyone, four young girls depended on her professionalism. Plus she wouldn't be able to handle the pity and, yes, the disgust with which some people would look at her. She would just have to be careful.

Don't touch anyone. That's the first rule. Even though she knew that it couldn't really be transmitted just by touch, she would still feel guilty.

She choked back a silent sob as she stared out the window in front of her, praying that her mother was right and that John was far too healthy looking to have something wrong with him. And after all, it's not just a homosexual disease now, it's something everyone in the whole world has to worry about.

She would have to live in hope that John was clean, it was the only way she could function.

There is nothing wrong with me. This is just a precaution.

She said the mantra over and over, as they drove to the hospital.

When they finally pulled up outside the entrance, she almost believed it.

Friday

Friday

16

Jason Smith polished the bar again, aware that it had probably never, in its thirty-year existence, been polished so much. But he was nervous. Mrs Archer was well and truly on the warpath, and if the ugly bitch couldn't find the scalp she was hunting for, then she would have his instead.

He could hear her now, banging about in the back room, each bang accompanied by a scream of frustration. He gave the bar another rub as the loudest scream yet carried through the door. He cringed. 'Damn that fucker Stevie,' he muttered, polishing like mad. 'I hope his fucking dick falls off.'

'Yer hope whose dick falls off?' Stevie asked, from very close behind him.

Jason jumped. 'Yours, yer prick. And don't fucking creep up behind me like that again else I'll kick yer where the sun don't shine, bastard.'

'No need to be nasty now.'

Jason aimed a punch at Stevie's head, but Stevie grinned and neatly side-stepped past him. Gritting his teeth, Jason said, 'Open the fucking doors, moron, before I tear yer friggin' head off. It's past opening time already, and she's in a bad enough fucking mood to start with.'

'What's the matter like?'

'You are, yer bastard. She knows yer've been swallowing the shit instead of selling it.'

Stevie pondered the problem for all of two seconds then, with all the confidence of his latest high, shrugged and spread a line of white powder on the bar. He sniffed it up with a five-pound note.

'What the fuck? Yer dirty little creep. I've just polished the fucking thing, yer fucking smack head.' Jason rubbed the bar again. 'Fucking moron.'

Stevie shook his head, and sniffed. 'Aye, I can smell the fucking polish an' all.'

'It's a wonder yer can smell anything with that shit up yer nostril box. Just wait till it fucking falls off. Fucking broken brain, that's all yer are.' He pushed Stevie towards the door. 'Go on then, useless, open the fucker.'

'Aye, man.' But before he could reach it someone banged loudly on the other side. 'OK, OK, I'm fucking well coming.'

Jason shook his head. This wise guy was skating on seriously thin ice. If she heard him swearing at customers she'd have his guts for garters.

Stevie loosened the bolts and, just as he was about to step back, the door opened in his face and Lily, the daytime barmaid, swept in.

'How, man,' Stevie shouted. 'Watch me fucking face!'

'Oh dear, so sorry.' Lily, a forty-five-year-old bleached blonde with soft brown eyes and a huge bust that she never tired of showing off, grinned at him.

'I bet yer are an' all.' Stevie rubbed the side of his face, which threatened to bruise by evening.

Lily had nearly reached the bar, but she swung round on the high heels that brought her height to just over five foot, and headed back to Stevie. Reaching him, she stood with her hands on her hips and looked him up and down. 'OK, dick head. This is how it is. I didn't like yer fat-arsed thieving cabin-cat of a mother, and I like you even less. So my advice to you is to give me plenty of space. Got it?'

'Aye, aye.' Stevie backed away. 'No prob, just chill, OK?'

Jason laughed and Stevie curled his lip at him.

'Right then, I'm pleased we understand each other.'

She headed back to the bar where Arthur, one of the regulars, had slithered in unnoticed and taken up his favourite place. He touched his chequered cloth cap, a relic of the sixties which had belonged to his father and was never off his head. His father, Arthur the first, had never missed a shift down the pit. His working ability however had not rubbed off on Arthur the second, who at fifty years old had never held a steady job in his life.

'That's told the creep, girl. I'll have me usual, and get one for yerself.' He winked at her.

Unknown to any of them, Mrs Archer had been watching from the shadows at the far end of the bar. They all jumped when she shouted, 'Smith an' Co, in here now!' Jason and Stevie both cringed, then, without hesitation, did as they were told.

As soon as they were all in the back room, she slammed the door and, poking Stevie in his chest, stated, 'Never *ever* give Lily any of that lip again. She's the best barmaid around, worth ten of those two slappers from Hetton, and worth twenty of you. Understand?'

Stevie nodded vigorously.

'Right. You are going to get all that shit out of that wreck of a slimy body of yours, yer face is starting to erupt all over the fucking place. If yer want to work for me yer keep clean. And that starts now. At half three today you will be outside of that school with a handful of magic pills, and there better be some buyers.' She grabbed hold of his ear and gave it a savage twist. 'Or God fucking help yer. From here on in, yer do exactly as yer told or yer just might end up in the river. Believe me, yer won't be the first. The Wear's deep enough to keep a body hidden for years.'

Stevie groaned.

Mrs Archer turned to Smith. 'Watch him, do not let him out of the sight of them ugly little peepers of yours all morning. I want him clean. Later, after he's done his job at the school, yer bring him back and lock the bastard up. Don't disturb me unless the little toad starts foaming at the mouth.'

She turned back to Stevie. 'If I ever see yer pop as much as a fucking vitamin pill, I swear I'll chop yer fucking head off. Right?'

'Yeah, right, OK, whatever.'

She slapped him so hard it brought tears to his eyes. 'And I'll not be putting up with any of yer lip, not ever. Got that an' all?'

He was sullen, but he nodded. The prospect of

260

going cold turkey had suddenly slapped him harder than the bitch in front of him ever could. He knew what happens – he'd tried it once before, and hadn't made it past day one. He looked at her. *What the fuck was he gonna do now?*

Mrs Archer smiled, looking like something out of a fright magazine. He wanted to yell *please don't do that* but before he was overly tempted – because false courage still raged through his veins – the door opened and her smile faded.

A tall thin man, dressed in black and sporting a black goatee beard, walked unannounced into the room. Stevie watched with unabashed fascination as Mrs Archer's skin tone noticeably lightened by at least ten degrees. The room fell silent.

The man never spoke. Instead, he just beckoned with his finger. And it seemed that was enough. Turning, he walked back out.

Mrs Archer stared after him for a moment, in the nearest state to panic that Jason Smith had ever seen his boss, then she seemed to pull herself back to reality. She quickly grabbed her red coat and matching handbag, then hurried after the black-clad man. At the door she turned. 'Don't either of yer dare forget a word I've fucking said.' Then she was through the door and gone.

'Who the fuck was that?' Stevie said.

'That,' Jason said slowly, 'was The Man's man. When Archer speaks, we jump. When he speaks, she jumps.'

'Bloody damn high an' all, by the looks of it,' Stevie sniggered. 'And don't yer mean when he points his finger, cos I never heard him say a fucking word. Anyhow, I'm fucking pleased she's frightened of somebody.' His confidence rushed back. 'And, I'll tell yer this: no fucking way am I going cold turkey, mate. Been there, done that . . . So she can fuck off.'

'You gonna tell her that?'

Stevie bared his teeth.

'No, I fucking thought not. Look, get this once and for all: the people she knows are out of your fucking nightmares. So don't mess.'

Stevie shrugged. 'So, if she's so fucking clever and mates with all these big people, why the fuck are yer creaming off her?'

Jason moved fast for one so large; he had Stevie by his throat and pinned against the wall in seconds.

'Don't yer ever,' he banged Stevie's head off the wall, 'ever breathe a word of that. Just remember, you got some an' all. So if I go down the river, you'll be fucking following. OK?'

'Aye, man.' Stevie held his hands up. 'Just fucking chill, will yer?'

'You'll be that fucking chilled, you'll be stone fucking cold, yer wanker.' He let go and Stevie slid to the floor. 'Now fucking get up and get to the fish shop. Here.' He threw Jess's lead at him. 'Take Jess, and if she comes back by herself, God fucking help yer.'

Grumbling to himself, Stevie rose, picked up the lead, and went into the bar for Jess. She was lying in a pool of weak sunshine that just about filtered through the none-too-clean windows.

She wagged her tail when she saw her lead and

jumped up. Smith had followed Stevie out, and he bent to pat the dog's head.

'Go with the moron, girl. Get some dinner for Daddy.' Jess licked her master's hand, while Stevie watched this exchange with a look of total amazement.

After dropping the kids off at school, Kerry and Robbie set off for the hospital. When they reached Park Lane bus terminal both were starving; all they'd had in the house that morning was a few slices of dry bread, and Darren, Emma and Suzy had fast polished that off. Seeing a café opposite, they went in and Robbie ordered two meat pies and two teas, while Kerry sat in the window seat. When Robbie returned with the food Kerry said, 'Do yer think Mam'll be all right today, Robbie?'

'She should be, I think.'

'Good, cos I want to know who the fuck The Man is. And I want the full story, not the abridged version Sandra gave me the other night.'

Robbie put the remains of his pie back on the plate. 'Can't yer leave it, Kerry?'

'No.' She drank most of her tea, and stood up. 'Come on, we can finish the pies as we go.'

Fifteen minutes later they were entering the ward. The tall black detective was on his way out, and he winked at Kerry. 'Hi there. Everything all right?'

'No,' Kerry answered as she walked past him.

'Sorry about that,' Robbie apologised.

'It's OK, you're both under a lot of pressure,' said Luke.

'That's true. Can I talk to yer for a minute like?'

'Shoot.'

Robbie told him what they had found out on their trip to South Shields, and Luke was visibly impressed. 'Good going, kid. I'm on me way back to the station now and I promise yer we'll follow it right up.'

They shook hands and Robbie went in to see his mother, praying hard that Kerry hadn't started in with her brow-beating tactics. His prayers went unanswered.

'So, Mam,' Kerry was saying as Robbie reached the bed, 'I want to know who this Man is, and I want to know everything.'

Vanessa looked wearily at her daughter. 'Honestly, pet, it can't help. Raking the past up never did anybody any good.'

'But, Mam—'

'Kerry.' Robbie put his hand on his sister's shoulder. 'Not today, OK?'

He received a glare that would have sandblasted walls. Then Kerry looked at her mother and saw that, even though she still looked pretty poorly, she also looked a long way better than she had for some time. Her hair looked clean and her eyes didn't look as bloodshot as they had a few days earlier.

Robbie had also noticed. 'Yer look canny good, Mam.'

Vanessa took hold of his hand. 'I am . . . Well, I'm better than I was. I can come home tomorrow, and the hospital has arranged for me to attend the AA meetings. All I need now is for our Claire to turn up safe and well.' She held back a sob when she said

Claire's name, and Robbie squeezed her hand gently.

But to the surprise of both of them, it was Kerry who burst out crying. 'I'm sorry, Mam.'

'Sorry?' Vanessa looked puzzled and slightly wary as she asked, 'What have yer got to be sorry about?'

'For being such a bitch. I really do miss her, Mam.'

Vanessa felt a wave of relief as she patted Kerry's hand. With this one, yer never knew what to expect. 'It's all right girl, don't fret. The police seem confident they'll find her and the other girls pretty soon.'

'Oh yeah? Like that body they found with six toes and no fucking head? They can't bloody well find that, can they?'

'Kerry—' Vanessa said sharply.

Kerry thought she was getting wrong for swearing, but at this moment in time Vanessa was more anxious to find out just what her daughter knew about Jack Holland's body.

'What's this about the body having no head?' she asked.

'We saw Mickey on the way to the bus stop this morning, he reckons that the Broadway was buzzing with the news.'

'Well, that's it then. If Mickey's heard it, yer can guarantee it's law.' She lay back against the pillows and suddenly she looked exhausted.

Kerry stroked her mother's cheek, and Vanessa's eyes filled up. Kerry had never been a demonstrative child, not like Robbie or the others, but this simple gesture endeared her oldest girl to her and somehow gave her strength.

She smiled. A weary one, but nevertheless a smile.

'Our Claire will be coming home, kids. I promise. I can feel it, right here. Right inside.' She touched her heart, even though she hadn't mentioned the fear that was really there. The terror she'd lived with for years. All the things she'd kept from them, she was still going to keep to herself, for as long as she could. It was not for them to know. No matter how persistent Kerry became, she had to keep it quiet, keep the secret. They had it hard enough as it was.

Sighing, she opened her arms and her two oldest children fitted in.

17

Mrs Archer was finally shown into The Man's presence an hour and a half after she'd arrived. In all that time she had seen no one, not since she'd been led in by Jake, his butler-cum-chauffeur-cum-hard man. Never even been offered a cup of the disgusting foreign tea he was always so keen to shove down people's throats. Just left alone to fucking stew.

Not being completely one of the inner circle, she'd only been here two or three times before. She noticed as she walked in that the room hadn't changed much in all the time she'd known him. The furnishings were mostly different shades of red, the walls were light oak panelling, and expensive oil paintings covered them. Every one depicted naked men and women, all very tastefully done, and this somehow seemed to make them all the more sensuous.

She stood before The Man with her hands clasped and her eyes cast downwards to the woven carpet, but not before she'd risked a glance at his face. Not a glimmer of a smile below that daft skinny fucking moustache he'd just grown. *Somebody should tell the bastard that he doesn't suit it.*

Not her though, she hadn't come this far by being stupid. And above all certainly not when she'd been given the waiting treatment. Not so long ago she'd have been treated with more respect than this, even the fucker in front of her used to be wary whenever she was around. But that's what fucking semi-retirement does for yer. It was that fucking nosy bastard copper years back, he got too close and she'd had to keep a lower profile afterwards. Not that he'd frightened this posh bastard though. And the world thinks all the baddies come from the slums – well, it's time the world sat up and looked around at its privileged people. She sighed. She must be getting old; today she felt all of her forty-five years.

She tried a smile of her own, but it was not returned. Instead, he motioned with his head for her to sit down – well, that was something. She sat quickly and her earrings, the same colour as her coat, danced furiously.

He lit a cigar, never once taking his eyes off her. Then finally, in a deep, cultured voice, he spoke. 'It seems we have someone asking about Brad . . . Someone from Houghton.'

She breathed a silent sigh of relief. This she could deal with.

'It's sorted, I had her frightened off.'

The way he looked at her she could tell he was still not happy.

'Apparently she's just a kid,' Mrs Archer continued, 'and she even managed to find his fucking grandmother. There's been a woman looking for him at the dog track an' all. She could just be an old flame, but I've put someone on it. If she's there again tonight, she'll be questioned.'

He tapped ash into a blood-red ashtray and remained silent.

'But the kid, I have to say, was by all accounts a cocky little bastard. She took some scaring, but we're definitely rid of her. She was looking cos her sister's one of the ones waiting to be transported, Kerry Lumsdon I think her name is, but it's dealt with and—'

'What? What did you say her name was?'

The cultured drawl was gone, replaced by a sharp anger Mrs Archer didn't understand. This time her heart didn't just skip a beat, it plummeted right to her ankles. She felt physically sick as she repeated, 'Kerry. Kerry Lumsdon.'

The Man stared at her in silence, then looked down at the expensive pen in his hand. Tapped it irritably on the desk. Seconds passed and Mrs Archer shifted uncomfortably. Finally he looked up again and his eyes pierced her to her chair. 'I want you to find this girl. She is to be followed everywhere, but she is not to be touched. Understand?'

'But I tell yer it's all right, we've scared her off—'

The look The Man gave her stopped her. She understood all right. There were plenty of nutters out there who would do her old job – although not as good, mind you, nowhere near. They didn't take pride in their work these days.

She licked dry lips. 'So, what exactly do yer want me to do?'

'Nothing.'

'Nothing?'

'Please, do not add deafness to your many other faults. The major one being extreme ugliness.'

269

She felt her face go red. She'd known she was ugly since the very first day she'd started school; the other kids hadn't waited long to tell her, though all of them had had their pay-back before she'd left.

But this man was the only person in the world who frightened her. She dared do nothing against him but plan. And what plans she had.

He smiled at last, a thin cruel smile. 'I want her followed, but not touched in any way. I want everything she does written down and hand delivered to me every day. Do you understand?'

She nodded, already smelling the sweet air and relishing the moment she walked out of here.

'Right, you can go.'

Standing, she held out her hand. He ignored it. She turned and, silently gritting her teeth, made her way to the door. Just as she touched the handle, willing herself not to skip out of the place, his voice stopped her.

'Remember, keep your dirty depraved hands off her.'

Head down so that he couldn't see the blazing resentment in her eyes, she nodded and backed out of the room.

How dare the cheeky bastard call me depraved? she thought as she followed Jake to the car.

He's the depraved bastard, not me. If he's not the most fucking weird bastard in the world, then no fucker is. Time I was outta this fucking set-up. It's getting far too fucking dangerous.

She looked at Jake as he walked in front of her. Another weirdo if ever there was one.

And who does the bastard think he is? I walk behind no man. Least of all a fucking yes-man.

Lengthening her stride, she caught up with him. Ignoring her scowling face, Jake opened the door for her. Never a man of many words, he surpassed himself by not speaking at all on the way back to the Blue Lion.

Lorraine, her personal problems wrapped up tight, opened the autopsy-room door. Scottie was on his own and finishing off a ham and pease-pudding sandwich. His face lit up when he saw her. 'All right, kiddo?'

She looked at the table, saw the white sheet draped over the body and shook her head. 'Is that . . . ?'

'Sure is, poor kid.'

'Which one?' Lorraine was dreading his answer. Although she didn't know them well, she had become quite fond of the Lumsdon family – particularly Kerry, both her tears and her strength when she brought in the portrait of Brad had moved Lorraine in a way that surprised her. She did not want to have to break the news to Kerry that her sister was beyond hope.

'That's the rub, kiddo, it's none of the missing four.'

'What!'

'It's a faceless.' Faceless was Scottie's name for the unclaimed bodies that turned up on his slab. They had never been reported missing, and they came in all ages, from six hours to sixty years and older.

'She's in the thirteen-to-sixteen group, but precisely

271

what she looked like's practically impossible to tell. She's been in the water about four days and the fish have been at her. All I can really tell yer is that she doesn't match any of the existing descriptions. Too short for a start.' He put the remains of his meal in the waste basket then walked over to the slab.

'The internal damage is as bad as the external, and that wasn't caused by the fish. She's been repeatedly raped and beaten over and over. For her to turn up at Ryhope Beach, the coast guard thinks she must have been dumped somewhere near Hartlepool.' He gently uncovered the young body.

Lorraine looked, then turned away. Shaking her head, she sat down in the seat Scottie had had his tea on.

A faceless could have come from anywhere, or she could be connected. What the hell was she dealing with here? A single madman who gratified himself, then murdered them? Or an organised gang? Again, instinct told her the latter. Were the four girls she was looking for going to share the same fate as this poor kid? Worse, had it already happened to them?

She couldn't suppress a shudder as she stood back up. Looking at Scottie she said, 'There's not a lot we can do to trace her, is there?'

Scottie shook his head. 'Naked as the day she was born. No jewellery, no birth marks, no tattoos. We've run a fingerprint check, but no luck. And with her jaw so badly smashed, not a hope in hell of finding a dental match. We'll keep her on ice for the allotted time, then give her a decent burial. Nothing else we can do.'

Lorraine left after saying goodbye. On the way back to her car she pulled off the tiny round Elastoplast Jenny had put on her arm at the hospital the previous evening. She felt sad, not only for herself, but for the kid on the slab. She knew the 'decent burial' would consist of two people: the clergyman of course, plus Scottie, who went to the burials of all his faceless, and who sometimes cried.

Kerry and Robbie arrived home to find the street full of neighbours, and two police cars parked outside. Mickey and Cal were sitting on the garden wall, and with them were Sandra and Jason Smith's mother Dolly, who wasn't only the biggest gossip in the Seahills but also outshone anyone in the whole of Houghton le Spring, and the outlying districts. Although, as Sandra always said, it was a close contest with Mr Skillings.

'What's going on then?' Kerry asked.

'Hi, guys,' Mickey said, while Cal nodded hello.

'It's her next door,' Sandra put in. 'The coppers have been in there for over an hour, fairly ransacked the place. God only knows what they're looking for.'

'Hour and a half.' Dolly Smith said, nodding at each one in turn. 'And I bet it's got something to do with drugs. She's a bad one that; I never liked the look of her the first time I saw her. Ask Mr Skillings. As sure as God made little apples, that's what I said.'

'Whatever.' Sandra pulled a face behind Dolly's back. 'Anyhow, there's rumours going round that the poor lad what lived in there is stone-cold dead.'

'Never!' Kerry said. She glanced at Robbie who looked totally stunned.

'But he didn't look that bad the other night, honestly. I really thought it was just a couple of cuts and bruises.'

'Darren told us what happened,' Sandra said, 'but I've heard it wasn't the fall what killed him. They reckon that blonde bitch finished him off in the hospital.'

'Jesus Christ!' Kerry and Robbie echoed in unison.

'Smothered him like,' Dolly added, in her matter-of-fact voice.

'Wow.' Kerry looked at Robbie again. 'I told yer she was bloody crackers, didn't I?'

'Serious shit, eh man?' Cal said.

Just then the front door opened and every head in the street swung towards it. Two woman police officers, each carrying a black sack, walked down the path. They put the bags in the police car, got in and drove off. The crowd watched in silent speculation. A moment later all heads swivelled back as another two officers, this time men, dragged the blonde girl down the path. She screamed, spat and bit, but as big as she was the men were stronger, and they pushed her into the car. Face twisted into a snarl she glared out the window and, seeing Kerry, started to yell again.

'It looks like yer off her Christmas card list, Kerry. Been telling her a few home truths lately, girl?' Cal asked.

Kerry pulled a face at him as Robbie answered in a weary tone, 'Something like that, Cal, something like that.'

'Right.' Mickey jumped off the wall. 'The entertainment's over for today, let's be having the kettle on.'

'Want to know something?' Cal said as he pushed Mickey towards the path. 'You drink more tea than anyone I know.'

'Aye, and you nick more cars than anyone I know,' Mickey answered back. Robbie laughed, and the boys followed him down the path.

Slowly the street emptied. Dolly Smith wandered away in the general direction of her own house, stopping to gossip with everyone she bumped into, leaving Kerry and Sandra alone.

'How was she today then, pet?'

Kerry shrugged. 'Better, I suppose. She says she's joining AA.'

'Aye, pet. That's what she said to me an' all. It's great news.'

'Yeah, that's what Robbie said. Trouble is, he hasn't got the sense to see they've got her high on something. Of course she's all for it now, but wait till she gets home . . . Back to this shit.'

'For God's sake, Kerry, stop being so pessimistic! You have to have hope, else there's no point in going on, is there?'

'Hope.' Kerry spread her arms wide. 'Around here? Yer fucking kidding, aren't yer?'

'Now it's not that bad.'

'News flash, Sandra . . . it *is* that bad.'

'No, Kerry pet. This is home. It's my home, it's your home. It's where we belong.' She spread her own arms wide in imitation of Kerry. 'Where else

275

can yer get a cuppa free when yer need it, an ear when yer need it? These people won't walk past yer in the gutter, they'll pick yer up.'

'Aye, maybes, but they'll pick yer pocket while they do it.'

'No they won't. No one ever gets mugged or burgled on the Seahills.'

Kerry folded her arms across her chest. 'Have you flipped yer fucking lid? Nobody's burgled around here, Sandra, cos this is where the fucking burglars live. And the muggers, and the fucking car thieves. There's one just gone in my house, for fuck's sake.'

'Cal! He's a nice lad.'

'Tell that to the people whose cars he nicks. Anyhow, the Seahills you're thinking of died ten years ago. It's not the same any more. The place is full of fucking strangers that would cut yer throat for a fucking penny.'

'Aye why,' Sandra bristled, 'think what yer want but I know there are still a lot of decent people living round here. People that care. People, by the way, that are betting on you winning that race next week, Miss High and Fucking Mighty, so put that in yer pipe and smoke it. And another thing,' she pointed at Kerry's mouth, 'cut the fucking lingo or so help me God I'll wash yer fucking mouth out with soap and fucking water.'

Sandra turned and stormed off, leaving a slightly bemused Kerry staring at her stiff back. It was rare to see Sandra's cage rattled. *Must have been something I said*. She shrugged. She'd think about it later, for now she needed food and drink.

Mickey was pouring out tea when Kerry walked in. 'Cuppa?' he asked.

'Might as well.' Kerry took her coat off and hung it on a hook on the back door. 'Did Sandra seem a bit put out about something before we got back?'

Mickey scratched his head, pretending to think, 'No . . . Why?'

'Nothing really, it's probably me.'

Mickey turned away and grinned to himself. He knew that if Sandra and Kerry had had words the blame would be at Kerry's door and there would be no *probably* about it. Picking up a lime-green tray that Cal had borrowed from the home, he carried the teas through to the sitting room.

Kerry followed him in, grabbed the first cup and drank it down quickly as she gobbled a couple of chocolate biscuits which Mickey had bought via the shoplifters. Then she ran upstairs and changed into her running gear.

She would run. That's when she did her best thinking, that's when her mind was as free as her feet. As she tied her laces she caught sight of a family photograph taken a few years ago. It was lying on the floor and she guessed that either Suzy or Emma had been looking through the album and it had fallen out. Looking at Claire's smile, she sighed. Then muttered out loud, 'If Mam, Robbie and that bloody Sandra think I'm giving up on this Man thing they can bloody well think again. I know he's somehow responsible for every damn thing that's happened to us, and I'm gonna find out why if it bloody well kills me.' She picked the photo up, looked at it one more time, then put it on the bedside cabinet.

The bell went at last, and Darren heaved a sigh of relief; the last fifteen minutes had felt like ten hours. He was first out of his seat and first through the door, deliberately not looking at Ratchet the Hatchet, cos if she once caught yer eye, that was it, she homed in like a rocket.

Although Darren had been first out the door Kenny flew past him and was running out the cloakroom, coat on and zipped up, while Darren was still struggling into the dark blue Nike jacket that had come his way the other day. He yelled for Kenny to wait because he desperately needed the loo – in fact, it was getting damn hard not to dance – and he frowned when he saw Kenny's feet disappear out the door.

He made it to the toilet just in time, then hurried into the yard, but Kenny was long gone. Praising Sandra for the jacket because it looked like it might rain again he pulled the collar up and made for the gate. Where, to his horror, he clocked Kenny in deep conversation with Stevie.

Two girls and a boy were walking away, all three stuffing something into their backpacks. The only one of the trio he really knew was Jilly Belmont: she lived round the corner from him and was a mean sledger when it snowed, and better than any of the lads in a snowball fight. In fact, she was better than a lot of the lads at a lot of things; she could certainly climb Mrs Rogerson's apple tree better than he could. She had pretty red hair an' all.

He put Jilly's pretty red hair out of his head as he reached the gate and, hidden by its tall stone pillars, watched Kenny hand money over to Stevie and receive a small packet in return. His heart sank. He knew without a doubt what was in the packet.

Without thinking it through, Darren ran out and knocked the packet from Kenny's hand, yelling at Stevie, 'He doesn't want it!'

'Yes I do!' Kenny yelled back from the ground, where he was scrabbling for the all-important package as it inched its way to the drain.

'Yer fucking little bastard!' Stevie drew his hand back and punched Darren hard enough to send him sprawling.

Quickly picking himself up, Darren squared up to Stevie. 'Dirty stinking drug dealer,' he spat at him.

Stevie was livid, red and purple veins standing out on his neck. Looking around he saw no one to stop him and, grinning menacingly, he walked towards Darren. Kenny, precious packet in hand, hopped nervously from foot to foot as Stevie poked Darren in his chest.

'Who the fuck do yer think yer messing with, yer little piece of shit?'

Darren knocked Stevie's hand away as he came in for a second poke. 'You're the piece of shit, yer creep. Stinking Stevie Shite.'

Stevie, eyes wide and bulging, jumped at Darren, but Darren managed a neat side-step and grabbed the packet out of Kenny's unsuspecting hand. Spinning round, he dropped it down the drain. Kenny, mouth hanging open, looked at his empty hand, then at the drain.

'Oh, man,' he groaned. 'That bloody well cost me three pounds.' He moved over to the drain where the packet had already been swallowed and swirled down to the stinking depths of the sewage pipe. Shaking his head in disbelief, he said, 'I only wanted to try it, for God's sake.'

'I've told yer what happens,' Darren snapped at him as he backed away from Stevie who, murder glinting in his drug-bright eyes, was moving in for the kill.

A car pulled up and the driver pounded the horn. To Darren's immense relief, Stevie glanced round, then stepped back. Grinding his teeth in frustration, he yelled, 'One day, yer little fucker!' He wagged his dirty nail-chewed finger at Darren. 'Believe me, I'm gonna fucking slaughter yer.'

Darren had a quick retort on his lips but, feeling as if luck was on his side for once, decided against using it. He and Kenny watched as Stevie got into Jason Smith's car.

After they had driven off, Darren turned to Kenny his voice full of hurt, and said, 'Yer told me yer wasn't gonna try it, Kenny.'

Kenny shrugged. 'I can't now, can I?'

They stared at each other for a moment, then Darren turned and walked away.

Ten minutes later he entered the house, with Emma and Suzy trailing behind him.

'And where have you been, little mate?' Cal asked.

'We're all bloody starving. Here,' he tossed a five-pound note at him, 'be a good'un and get down to the fishy – chips all round, yeah?'

Darren shook his head, threw the five-pound note on to the settee, and went quickly upstairs to the room he shared with Robbie.

'What's the matter with him?' Cal asked in genuine puzzlement. Usually Darren was a pretty amiable guy.

'Take no notice, he's been funny ever since our Claire disappeared.'

Mickey stood up, stretched his lanky frame, and said, 'Yer can't really blame him, he's still just a bairn. Give us the money and I'll go.' Robbie picked the fiver up and handed it over.

'Yer know what though,' Mickey said, taking the money, 'we should have given it to your Kerry, she could have called in on the way back from her run.'

'I can see that happening in a million.' Cal laughed as he turned to Suzy and Emma. The pair of them were stood in front of the television and he waved his fingers at them. 'Hi, girls, I bet youse two want some chips.'

Suzy smiled shyly while Emma sniffed and stuck her tongue out.

'Nice,' Cal said.

'Just ignore her.' Robbie frowned at Emma. 'I swear the lot of yer are doing me friggin' head in. Get upstairs and change, and make sure yer hang those clothes up for school on Monday. The washer's packed in again.'

Emma tutted, pushed past Suzy, and made her way to the door. Suzy smiled at everybody as she followed her sister.

'Want me to take a look at the washer?' Cal asked.

'Thanks, but no thanks. A washing-machine engine's a canny bit different from a car engine. Anyways, Trevor from across the road says he'll pop over later and have a look, he got it going the last time.'

Cal shrugged. 'Whatever. So, what's the latest on your Claire?'

Robbie's face fell.

'That's just it, there is no latest. We still don't even know for definite if she's run away or if someone's picked her up. She's been gone since Monday and there's nothing.'

'God, that's rough. Amazing, isn't it though?' He shook his head. 'I mean, the coppers can't find a missing kid, yet they seem to be able to find me all right, whenever they want to.'

Robbie smiled, grateful for Cal's attempt to lighten things. 'That's cos you leave a trail a mile wide, simpleton.'

Cal laughed. 'Can't seem to help it, mate. Whenever I get behind the wheel of one of those sweet sporty types, that's it. I can't think of nothing else but the road in front.' He shrugged. 'Gotta start settling down now though. Me dad says this is definitely me last chance, any more trouble and I'm out. And to top that, me mam keeps crying, and that really does me head in.' He leaned forward in his seat. 'This time it's for real, Robbie. The bloke's giving me a chance and I'm gonna take it.'

Robbie studied Cal for a moment, and decided that his friend seemed on the level. 'That's cool, Cal. Go for it.'

Cal nodded again, then his handsome face lit up with sudden inspiration. 'Say, Robbie, why don't I ask up at the home, see if they need an odd-job man for the gardens or something, eh?'

Robbie shrugged. 'What's the point, mate? Every time I think I'm in with a chance they give the job to somebody else.'

'I can still ask, yer never know.'

Robbie thought for a moment.

'I er, I wouldn't have to nursemaid none of them old biddies, would I?'

'No, nowt like that. That's my job.'

'Oh, I couldn't do a job like that, man.' Robbie grimaced.

'Had away, they're great. Actually most of the time they're downright hilarious. I mean, this morning there was a scrap on between two eighty-year-olds.'

'No way!'

'Aye, straight up.' Cal burst out laughing at the memory. 'Betty said Flo had nicked her false teeth, and Flo – who's only one of the littlest people around – went and clocked her one.'

'Piss off.'

'Honest, you've no idea what goes on. Sneaking about in the middle of the night. Accidentally on purpose climbing into the wrong bed. Some of them's got more energy than you and me will ever have.'

'The dirty old sods.' Robbie laughed.

'Oh, aye. I've seen them fall out for months over

a game of dominoes, and they even cheat at bingo. Yer should be there then, man, all hell breaks loose.' The pair of them were still laughing when they heard a knock on the door.

Robbie went to the window, lifted the net curtain and looked out. He turned back to Cal. 'It's that black copper.'

'Straight up, man, on me mam's life, I haven't touched a car for months.'

'Chill out, he's probably here about our Claire. He was up at the hospital this morning and I told him some stuff, even though our Kerry was dead against it.' He went to open the door, but Emma had beaten him to it.

Luke smiled down at her and she gave him a toothy grin before turning and skipping back up the stairs.

'Hi, Robbie.' Luke held out his hand and Robbie shook it with a smile. 'Little Miss Happy, eh?'

'You must have something nobody else has. She usually spits or sticks her tongue out.'

Smiling, Luke followed Robbie into the sitting room, where he spotted Cal.

'Well hello there, Cal. No wheels?'

Cal spread his arms wide. 'Like I'm gonna be sitting in somebody's house in a car?'

'I suppose even you aren't that daft.'

'I'll take that as a compliment then, shall I?'

Luke gave a little smile, he knew he wasn't one of Cal's favourite people, having arrested him three times already. He had to say though, the lad always gave up gracefully and there was never any cheek from him.

He nodded at Robbie. 'I've just called round to keep yer informed. We've found the body of a young girl.' He heard Cal's sharp intake of breath as Robbie's face went a deathly white. He hurried on to reassure him. 'It's all right, it's not Claire. We don't even know if there's any connection.' He left the rest of the sentence up in the air, but Robbie got the gist.

Thank Christ. Not Claire. But some poor kid. Robbie's fear for his sister returned stronger than ever and he glared angrily at Luke.

'Have yer been to this Brad bloke's grand-mother's?'

'Of course. In a case like this all leads are followed up. Unfortunately she wasn't in. But we have a man parked outside and he'll stay there until she comes back. The next-door neighbour said she went out shortly after some young people came calling, and she hasn't seen her since.'

'And . . . ?' Robbie prompted. 'What happens next?'

'If she's not back by eight, a search and find will be put on her. Believe me, by tonight, one way or another, we'll get the information we want from her.'

'By tonight might be too late though, have yer ever thought of that?' Robbie's voice had more edge to it than Cal, who had known him a long time, had ever heard.

'Calm down, son,' Luke replied. 'We're doing our best. There are other leads being followed.' He put his hand on Robbie's shoulder, but Robbie shrugged him off. 'What else can I say, son?'

A sharp voice on the verge of tears interrupted them. 'Yer can bloody well say yer've found me sister, that's what yer can say.'

They all swung their heads round to find Darren standing in the doorway.

'And now Kenny's gonna die as well!' And he left them standing with their mouths open as he turned and ran out the door, bumping into Mickey who was on his way in, and sending bags of chips flying every which way.

'Is this house for real?' Mickey muttered, as he set about trying to rescue their tea. Half the bags had fallen inside the door and half outside on the garden.

Robbie went to run after Darren, but Luke stopped him. 'Leave him, son. He's been holding up too well . . . probably needs to be alone for a while. If he's not back in a couple of hours, give me a ring and I'll help look for him.' He started to leave, but then turned back. 'By the way, who's Kenny?'

'His best mate,' Robbie answered, watching Mickey trying to pick up as many chips as he could. He looked at Luke. 'But I haven't a clue what he's on about. Last I heard, Kenny was as fit as a fiddle.'

'Bit of a runt though,' Mickey said, passing them on his way into the kitchen. He'd managed to salvage most of the bags, and he set about putting them on plates. When he went back into the sitting room, carrying his own plate plus six slices of bread and butter, Robbie was seeing Luke to the door and Cal sat on the settee shaking his head.

'What?' Mickey asked.

286

'It's better than watching the telly, sitting here. The whole family's bloody crackers.'

Mickey, just about to take a bite out of his chip sandwich, laughed. 'Aye, they are, mate, but they're good crackerjacks.'

Robbie came back in. 'I heard that, guys. And I suppose youse two are reasonably sane?'

It was Cal's turn to laugh. 'Tell yer what though, I'm bloody pleased I've only got one sister, and she's long gone, married, no hassle.'

'Yeah, I wish . . .' Robbie said, on his way into the kitchen.

Coming back, he handed Cal his chips and snaffled a slice of bread from Mickey. 'I wonder what he meant about Kenny, though?'

Mickey shrugged. 'God knows. Kenny's sister now,' he held his hands in front of his chest as if cupping a pair of breasts, 'she's a bit of all right. I wouldn't mind fu—'

'Mickey,' Robbie stopped him and gestured with his head towards the doorway, where Emma stood watching them with her usual sullen expression.

'Hi, Emma.' Mickey waved his fingers at her. 'Chips are in the kitchen, lovey.'

She sniffed loudly, then turned her back on them. When Mickey turned back to his friends, it was to see Cal doubled up with laughter and Robbie well on the way to joining him.

It was Kerry that found Darren. She had run through Houghton, doubled back through Newbottle, crossed the top of the Seahills, and entered Russell

Woods. The woods had only been planted three years earlier, but the saplings were already tall and starting to show buds.

It was quiet, as the young trees weren't strong enough yet to encourage nesting birds, and she suddenly thought she heard a child sobbing and slowed down. Leaving the path, she moved towards a large rock with carving on it, and as she got closer she saw that the rock was carved into a pair of praying hands. Funny how she'd never noticed that before. It was from behind the carving that the crying came.

Peeping cautiously over the top, she was surprised to see Darren, head in his hands, sobbing his heart out. Kerry sighed inwardly. *What now?*

Moving round, she knelt down and put her hand on his shoulder. Darren jumped and looked up fearfully, his face dirty and tear-stained. He relaxed when he saw it was Kerry.

'What's the matter, Darren?' she said softly.

He shook his head and started to cry even harder. Kerry couldn't ever remember seeing him so upset. Out of the whole family, Darren seemed to just plod on, even more so than Robbie. So whatever this was about, it had to be pretty serious. She felt her pulse race in panic – she couldn't take much more in the way of family crises.

'Come on, Darren,' she urged. 'I can't help yer if yer won't tell me what's up.'

'I . . . I can't,' he sobbed.

'Yes yer can. It's me. Yer can tell me anything yer want to, yer know that.'

'No.' He shook his head. 'Can't grass.'

Kerry sat down beside him, her back against the rock. 'Now that depends. Sometimes, whatever it is, yer've just got to tell somebody before yer burst wide open.'

'No.' Darren was adamant. 'Can't tell anybody, not even you.'

Kerry felt her patience, not good at the best of times, starting to fade.

If the little bugger doesn't open his fucking yap pretty soon, I'm gonna have to shake it out of him.

'Darren.' Her voice held a warning note that Darren knew well. He looked up at her, and his dark eyes looked so sad that Kerry's impatience melted. He looked like he held the key to the world's darkest secrets, and it was fast burning a hole in his hand.

She squeezed his shoulder, her voice gentle as she said, 'If something's bugging yer that much, our Darren, I need to know. Yer need to tell me what's wrong so I can help yer.' Her patience ran out. 'Now, for fuck's sake, spit it out.'

Darren started to sob again, but a second before Kerry's fuse really blew, he started to tell her what Stevie was up to, and that he was worried about Jilly, and that Kenny was determined to become one of the living dead.

When he had told her everything he wiped his nose with his sleeve, and went on. 'I want me mam, our Kerry. And I want our Claire. You and Robbie never tell me anything that's going on, yer leave me out of everything – unless it's *make some tea, Darren, or do this, Darren.* Yer both think I'm a little kid.'

Kerry mulled over what he'd said, then put her arms around him and cuddled him. 'Sorry, Darren, yer just might be right. But look, Mam's coming home tomorrow, and the coppers are doing everything they can to find our Claire.' She gritted her teeth, then went on. 'And as for Stevie boy. Just leave him to me. He's gonna get well and truly sorted, so don't yer fret about him for a minute longer.'

Rising, she held out her hand and helped him to his feet. Her voice when she spoke a moment later was very quiet and tipped with ice.

'Come on, Darren, we're going home.'

18

Claire opened her eyes and stared into nothing. A deep enveloping darkness, unlike anything she had ever known. Even in bed on the darkest winter night there was something to see – shadows, darker patches of blackness – but here . . .

Her first impulse was to scream, and her mouth actually opened before the thought was fully formed, but nothing came out. Her throat was bone dry and her mouth felt as if it was stuffed with cotton wool.

She took a mental inventory of her body.

Her arms were pressed tightly against her sides.

It felt like she was lying on cool silk.

In fact, everywhere her naked body touched was cool and silky.

And then she remembered.

The silk was the lining of a coffin.

A coffin that she was lying in.

Her chest tightened. She couldn't breathe properly. She sobbed, terrified.

She started to cough, a panic reaction.

Her whole body felt on fire with pain. She started to choke, then panicked even more. What if she was sick?

Her heart started to race fast enough to burst right

open. Sweat popped out on her brow, and ran down to mix with the tears that coursed down her face.

Was she in the ground somewhere?

Why?

Why would they go to all that bother and then bury her?

Alive?

She screamed then. A scream of pure terror.

Where were the other girls?

Why me?

Please, Mam. Please help me.

A coffin. The words stretched across her mind, then snapped back to appear in mile-high proportions.

Total panic took over. She started banging with her heels, faster and faster. Thrashing her head from side to side, she managed with manic strength to raise her arms at her elbows and start banging on the coffin lid.

But, exhausted and near-starved, she had little endurance. Quite soon she was reduced to a pathetic miaowing, and a feeble scratching.

She sounded like a kitten that had been stuffed into a sack and thrown into a ditch.

Jade heard Claire from the corner of the room where she was crouched. They were in Robinson's Funeral Parlour. Soft red carpets covered the floor, and the walls were draped in red velvet.

At the far end, four coffins stood side by side. Three of them had their lids up, but the fourth one, the one that held Claire, was tightly closed.

The heavily drugged girls had spent the entire night in the coffins which had been used to transport them. The same coffins which would be cleaned of the smell of panic and of urine and used next week for real burials. Robinson had been in on the deal for the last five years, and only did funerals the first three days of the week.

Jade knew the terror that Claire was going through, she'd experienced it herself only a few minutes earlier, but she could shout no words of comfort to Claire because she was heavily gagged.

Jade looked at Donna, who had curled up into the foetal position and was snoring gently. Her eyes moved on to Tracy and she feared for the younger girl's mind. She sat less than a yard away from Jade, knees pulled up to her chin, head flopping. Now and then her whole body would shake as if she were the rag doll of a spoilt giant child. Not once had she lifted her head since Laughing Man, after copping a good feel of her naked breasts, had deposited her none too gently on the floor, as though she were nothing more than a sack of coal.

Jade struggled with the rope that bound her, even though her left wrist was swelling by the minute. She feared it was broken, because she had received the same treatment as Tracy and when she'd been dropped on the floor she had landed on it heavily.

She was getting nowhere fast, and deep down inside she knew she'd end up exactly where these two creeps wanted her to.

Would she give up though? No way. Broken wrist or not. Let the bastards do what they wanted, if she could get free she'd have a go at the pair of them. What did it matter now if the bastards marked her so badly they had to kill her?

She felt a sudden sting in her right wrist and realised the constant rubbing had drawn blood. What the hell. Somebody had to come soon, for God's sake. It's been nearly four days, or was it five?

But me dad won't give up. And surely the police were looking. She squeezed her eyes shut to stop the tears, and bit her lip. She blinked when she tasted blood, but the tears stopped.

Turning her head slightly, Jade looked at her jailers. They were playing cards. They must be able to hear Claire's screams.

How fucking cruel can they be?

The kid must be going mental in there.

She grunted as loudly as she could to attract their attention.

She got it.

Laughing Man, who had lost heavily to his friend, suddenly jumped up and ran across the room. He slapped her viciously across her face and her head snapped sideways and hit the wall.

'Shut the fuck up, yer stupid fuck. How many fucking times do I have to tell yer, bitch? We can easily get rid of yer the same way we got rid of the first one.' He laughed. 'Only she wasn't the first, was she?'

He raised his hand to strike again. Despite herself, Jade flinched, but she never once dropped her eyes from his.

'Leave her.' The other man had come over and he grabbed Laughing Man's arm. 'No marks, remember?'

Laughing Man pulled his arm free. 'I don't know what yer problem is with this one. She's that fucking black, nobody will see a fucking mark on her.'

'Just leave her alone, OK? Tomorrow we should be free of them. Paid and on our way. Come on, let's get the last one out.'

Laughing Man grumbled, but followed his friend over to Claire's coffin. 'Aye,' he said, as they positioned themselves at either side of the lid. 'What the fuck did they have to go and change the collection time for? Holding the fucking bitches this long is nowt but dangerous. Especially with two trouble-makers in the fucking pack.'

They started to unscrew the lid. 'At least this bitch should have calmed down now,' he continued. 'But this is definitely the worst fucking bunch we've ever had. I mean, yer expect trouble now and then, but three in the same batch and we're still stuck with two of them. Fucking stupid set-up if yer ask me.'

'Yeah, well no one's asking you,' the other man snapped. 'We've done it this way for long enough, and if you hadn't lost the fucking plot a few days ago we would have had all fucking five.'

'Yer know they like fucking virgins the best.'

'They still would have paid us something for her.'

As they lifted the lid, Claire, eyes bulging, sprang up. Before they could grab her, she was out of the coffin and screaming her head off.

'Fucking hell. Get a hold of the bitch, will yer?' Laughing Man shouted. 'She's screaming loud enough to have the fucking army down on us. For fuck's sake, come here, bitch.'

Run Claire, run. Jade was willing her on. *Please, Claire, run.*

But Claire, senses still numbed from the drugs they'd injected her with, managed only three steps before she slid to the floor, folding in on herself.

Grabbing an arm each, the men dragged her across the floor and dumped her beside the other three girls, where Laughing Man, grumbling to himself all the time, slapped tape over her mouth while the other man tied her up.

Sneering at her, Laughing Man lifted his boot to kick her, but his friend shook his head warningly. Knowing that he was no match for him, Laughing Man stamped his foot on the floor over and over again, venting his rage on the hundred-year-old wood.

'Fucking bitch! I've got a good mind to kick yer right in yer fucking kisser,' he snarled, showing tobacco-stained teeth. Claire cowered, trying to make herself less of a target for his huge steel-capped boots.

His friend shouted him away two, three times, but he just stood there, his eyes burning, boring holes into her. She could see he was itching to disobey the other man, who seemed to be the boss. Then he grinned at her and, laughing again, said, 'It doesn't matter, bitch, you'll soon be dead anyhow. Let the fuckers who are gonna pay for yer have that pleasure. I know exactly what's gonna happen to yer.' His laughter became more hysterical by the minute.

'Yer can't even begin to guess.' The fear in Claire's eyes was goading him on. 'But I'll let yer find out for yerself . . . Bitch.' He turned and walked over to the card table.

'I'm telling yer,' he said to his friend, as he sat down and picked up his hand of cards, 'I've got a real bad feel about this. For two pins I'd piss off right now and leave this lot to rot.'

'Aye, happen yer might, but when would yer stop running? Cos you know he'll find yer, wherever yer go. Remember Jack Holland? And he was supposed to be one of The Man's best mates. I for one want to be buried with me head still attached to me fucking neck. OK?'

Laughing Man spat on the carpet. 'All right then. But what the fuck did the stupid bastards change the arrangements for? Tell me that. They always pick them up at twelve o'clock on the third day. For Christ's sake, it's worked for fucking years. Now we've got yet another day in this fucking crap heap. And,' he looked suspiciously around him, 'how many fucking dead bodies have been through here, eh? Tell me that.' Without waiting for his friend to tell him, he went on. 'Fucking hundreds, I'll bet. In fact it's probably fucking thousands. The place looks like it's been here since the fucking year dot. Gives me the fucking creeps this place does.'

The other man shrugged and, picking his cards up, began to play.

Claire looked at Jade, then at the other two girls. Tracy, despite all the commotion, hadn't moved, and Donna looked like she was fast following Tracy into never-never land.

Sighing, Claire looked back at Jade and read in her eyes that they were both thinking the same thing.

Claire guessed they were in a funeral parlour. She'd racked her brains to figure out why she was in this predicament – ransom was out of the question, who'd kidnap anybody off the Seahills, for Christ's sake?

But now, thinking over what the two men had said, she realised with a cold shock that the nightmare they were currently living was only the beginning. From here she would be sold on to . . . God knows who. And God knows where. She might never get home.

And her beloved Brad had been the first link in the chain.

The chain to where, though? Some kind of slavery.

She felt the weight of the yoke that millions before her had felt.

The word was foul. Disgusting and degrading.

And if they put a higher price on virginity, then there was no doubt what kind of slavery was going on here. She shuddered.

What the hell did she know about sex?

Brad had been her first real boyfriend, and all they had ever done was hold hands and kiss, which had been pretty exciting and had made her feel all grown up.

But now, the very last thing she felt was all grown up.

She wanted to be home, safe in her own bed, listening to Kerry snore.

So what happens now?

She shied away from the answer. But, deep down inside, she already knew.

Why had she let herself be fooled like that?

He had been so nice to her. She looked again at her companions in misery, and a tear ran down her face.

I bet he was nice to them an' all.

19

Emma and Suzy sat at opposite ends of the kitchen table finishing the chips. Every now and then Suzy paused and sighed, but Emma just munched on.

The boys were in the sitting room, discussing the carry-on next door.

'I reckon they'll throw the bloody key away,' Cal said.

'Aye, me an' all,' Mickey agreed. 'I mean, like, there was no need to top the poor sod, was there?'

They were interrupted by Kerry bounding through the door with Darren in tow. All three boys looked up at her and Robbie's heart sank. He could tell by her face that there was gonna be trouble.

'That bastard, Stevie,' she exploded, 'is only trying to flog drugs to our Darren. And when the kid did the right thing, the bastard threatened him.'

Darren stood behind Kerry, with his head down. Robbie jumped up off the settee and, taking hold of Darren's chin, he tipped his face up.

'This true?'

Darren swallowed hard, then slowly nodded.

'Tell him all of it,' Kerry urged. 'Go on.'

Darren was hesitant at first, but once he started the whole story came pouring out.

Robbie's usually calm face flushed with anger. 'So, the bastard's threatening yer, is he? And the creep's trying to fund his own addiction by getting you and the rest of the kids hooked? Well, we'll just have to see about that, won't we.'

There was silence for a moment, then Mickey said, 'He hangs out at the Blue Lion now. I've seen him there meself when I've passed. I think he might be working there or something.'

'It'll be the something. Cos in that dump, anything goes. I never liked him, yer know. Even when he was a little kid the bastard was a creep.'

'Was Fartin' with him?' Mickey asked.

'He was at first, but,' Darren shrugged, 'I haven't seen him since.'

'Right, I've heard enough.' Robbie yanked his denim jacket off the back of the settee. 'And I've had enough. I'm gonna stop that bastard right now.'

'What yer gonna do, Robbie?' Kerry asked, as Robbie shrugged into his jacket.

'You stay with the kids. I'm gonna sort him once and for all.'

Then he was gone out the door and halfway up the street before the others even had time to blink.

'Jesus,' Mickey said, before breaking into a run himself. As he ran out the door he shouted over his shoulder, 'God help us, Kerry, cos he's turning into you!'

Kerry opened her mouth to reply, but she was beaten by Cal, who shrugged, and said, 'Guess I'd better be following them.' And she was left standing at the front door, staring up the street.

'Fuck this for a lark,' she muttered. Then, at the top of her lungs, 'Sandra!'

Clayton looked up from the puncture he'd been mending in his front garden. 'I think she's gone to the hospital, Kerry, to see yer mam.'

Kerry groaned aloud with frustration. Then, brain ticking over and her eyes lingering on Clayton, she said, ever so sweetly, 'Clay.'

Clayton looked wary. 'What, Kerry?'

'Do me a favour, mate?'

He rose, bike pump in hand. 'Oh, aye, and what favour would that be, like?'

'Watch the brats for a few minutes. It's really important, Clay, honestly.'

Clayton harboured a steadily growing crush on Kerry and he wasn't about to miss this chance of getting into her good books.

'Yeah, no prob. I'll be right over.'

'Yes!' Kerry punched the air, shouted to Emma and Suzy to behave, and disappeared around the corner at an alarming rate.

She passed Cal and Mickey halfway up the Burnside. Both of them had stopped for a breather and Mickey was bent in half with a stitch.

'Jesus, Cal,' he said, after a moment, 'check her out. How the hell can she run that bloody fast? It's not natural, if yer ask me.'

'Beats me. But Robbie must be pretty fast an' all, cos we ain't even seen his dust. Come on, or else we'll miss the action.' And the pair of them started to run again.

Kerry turned into Newbottle Street, Houghton's

main shopping centre, just as Robbie reached the Blue Lion door.

It was locked. He paused a moment to get his breath back, then began pounding with both fists on the blue-painted door.

'We're shut,' he heard Jason Smith shout from the inside.

'Open the bastard door now, before I tear it off its fucking hinges, yer fat creep.'

Jason's voice, when he finally answered, sounded surprised.

'Who the fuck's that? Yer cheeky bastard.'

'Open the door and find out.' Robbie kicked the door to get the message over.

Smith opened the door, just an inch, and tried to peek out. That was all Robbie needed, and he pushed the door wider.

'How, lad. What the fuck do yer think yer doing? I've told yer already. Do I have to spell it out for yer? We are not fucking open yet . . . Now fuck off, Lumsdon.'

Robbie stood his ground, keeping one hand firmly on the door, and snapped, 'Where's Stevie?'

'I haven't a clue who the fuck yer on about. Now how many times do I have to tell yer? Thick or what, Lumsdon?'

Kerry got there just in time to hear this exchange; she knew she should be scared, she'd heard about the woman who ran this place, but nobody – it didn't matter who the fuck it was – was gonna get Darren on drugs.

'Liar,' she said, stepping out from behind Robbie.

'Ohh, the fucking Lumsdons out in force, are we?'

'Where is he?' Robbie demanded again.

'I've already told yer. I haven't got a fucking clue who yer on about. Now fuck off before I squash yer.'

A fourth voice from behind Kerry said, 'And just what the hell's going on here?'

Kerry and Robbie spun round, Smith looked between them, and cringed, while Mrs Archer somehow managed to glare at all three of them.

'I want Stevie.' Robbie demanded again. 'And I know the ugly prick's in there. So wheel the bastard out.'

Mrs Archer looked Robbie up and down and then turned her attention to Kerry. 'Mr Smith has already told the pair of you that there is no one by that name here.'

Kerry shrugged. 'Like I fucking believe that creep.'

'Who are you calling a creep?' Smith objected, but everyone ignored him.

'And just who might you be, child?' Mrs Archer asked sarcastically.

'First off, Mrs, I am not a child, and the name is Kerry Lumsdon. This is me brother Robbie. And,' she stepped closer to Mrs Archer, 'the reason why we are here, is that Stevie, who *does* hang around here, has been trying to force drugs on our kid brother. OK?'

Mrs Archer's heart positively shrivelled when the girl in front of her said her name, but she never missed a beat as she went on, 'Well, I'm afraid you've got the wrong pub. He certainly isn't here. But I'll have a word with the bouncers over at the night club, and see if he hangs about there.'

She nodded, then with a forced smile, carried on. 'I know the boy personally, and if he's anywhere about, I'm certain I'll be able to contact you. After all, the last thing we want is for the young of Houghton to be contaminated with drugs.' The corners of her mouth turned upwards in a parody of a smile.

'They're being contaminated all right,' Robbie got in, before Kerry had a chance to. 'Our Darren doesn't lie.'

'Oh, in my experience all small boys are liars.' She pushed past them and stepped into the pub. 'So if you'll excuse me . . . Close the door, Mr Smith.'

Quickly Robbie stuck his foot in the door. 'You just tell the bastard from me: if he goes anywhere near our brother again, I'll have him, right?'

Mrs Archer stepped back out of the pub and stood very close to Kerry, so close she practically loomed over her. 'I do not take kindly to threats.'

Kerry knew she should be frightened again, but her stubborn streak came bursting out as she said, 'No, and neither do we, Mrs. So up yours!'

Mrs Archer snarled as she stepped back in the pub. 'Close the door, Smith.' Jason slammed it and Robbie pulled his foot out just in time to stop it being squashed.

Cal and Mickey finally panted to a stop behind them. 'Couldn't find him, eh?' Cal asked Robbie as Kerry glared at the door.

'She reckons she doesn't know him,' Robbie answered.

'She's telling a whole pack of porkies,' Mickey managed between gulps of air.

'Hang on a minute!' Kerry started to beat on the door with her fists.

'What now?' Mrs Archer screamed.

Kerry opened the letter box. 'Yer wouldn't by any chance know of a creep called Brad, would yer, Mrs Skelotor?'

'If yer don't leave right now, yer cheeky bastard, I'll have the coppers after yer.'

'Yeah, OK. Bye, Mrs Skelotor.'

Something that sounded remarkably like a heavy bar stool hit the door and made it shudder. Grinning, they started to move away when another sound stopped them. Kerry, Robbie and Cal, turned to see Mickey, his face bright red, making the most amazing choking noises.

'You all right, Mickey?' Robbie went to pat his back.

Mickey tried to nod, and managed a few deep breaths before saying, 'Mrs Skelotor . . . Fucking A.' He collapsed laughing against the wall, as Robbie and Cal joined in.

'Well,' Kerry said, unaware of the very serious enemy she had just made, and unable to keep a straight face herself, 'did yer ever in yer whole life see a more ugly fucker than her?' And soon she was laughing as loudly as the other three.

After they had calmed down and started for home, Robbie asked, 'Kerry, what made yer think she might know this Brad person?'

Kerry shrugged. 'I honestly don't know . . . just a

hunch, I suppose. But it did seem to get a rise out of her.'

'Aye, it did an' all. I'll tell yer something else, I bet that shit Stevie is in there with them.'

'Got to be. So what now?' she asked, frustrated at their lack of progress.

'Don't fret. I'll catch the bastard. He'll never threaten our Darren again, and that's a fact.'

'Do yer think we should tell the coppers that Stevie's selling drugs to the kids? I mean, as far as I'm concerned, grassing a drug dealer doesn't count.'

Robbie thought for a moment.

'Aye, yer right. The bastards are nothing but scum. He knows what happens to kids, they freak each other out, and end up totally skitzed. And if they're lucky and haven't slit their wrists, they end up in the nut house for months. Look at Petey, three years and he's still not right.'

They all nodded, thinking of Petey Mellows, a friend who was so far gone he hardly recognised any of his old mates when he scuttled past them the odd time he came out of the house. Petey, who had been by far the brightest of them all and the last kid in the world anyone ever thought would get hooked.

Inside the Blue Lion, Jason Smith, who unlike Kerry knew exactly what sort of foe Mrs Archer was, did his level best to stop his whole body from quivering. Mrs Archer was having fits.

She didn't know what scared her the most, people asking for Stevie, or the same people asking about Brad.

And that cheeky black-haired madam was Kerry Lumsdon her fucking self.

'Get that fucker Stevie in here now,' she screamed at Jason Smith. 'And I don't give a flying fuck what state the bastard's in either. He can be climbing the walls for all I care. Just get the bastard in here right fucking now.'

Smith hurried to do her bidding, wondering if it was time for him to do a runner. Cos she seemed awful edgy of late.

She watched him wobble away, then looked at the clock. *Oh Christ. Ten minutes till opening time. The fucking alkies will be banging on the door any time now.* And she bustled around making sure everything was just the way she liked it.

Smith helped Stevie into the bar. Apart from a serious case of the shakes, he wasn't too bad yet.

'What?' Eyes protruding, he glared at Mrs Archer.

She swung a neat roundhouse and caught him square on his left ear. 'What the fuck yer doing messing around with the Lumsdons for? Yer thick twat.'

He shrugged, not really feeling the punch. 'Nobody told me they were special. Anyhow, I haven't been near any of them, so what's the fucking big deal?'

'Yer have, yer moron. He was one of the kids yer tried to flog gear to up at the school.'

'Oh.' The penny finally dropped. The little shit *was* bitch-girl Kerry's brother, touch of the tar brush or not.

'Fucking oh? Is that it?'

'Aye. What the fuck do yer want me to say? I

307

didn't know who he was. The little bastard didn't actually have a fucking sign round his neck saying, *fuck off I'm a Lumsdon.*'

'Cut the fucking cockiness out, and believe me yer'll know who he is when his brother catches up with yer.'

'Robbie? He's nowt but a wimp.' Now Stevie was really confused.

'Didn't act much like a wimp to me. Or didn't yer know the old saying that the quiet ones are mostly the worst? Anyhow, it makes no difference now, it's over. Out yer go. Go on, fuck off.'

'What?'

'You heard.'

'But . . . I . . . I don't . . .'

Mrs Archer tapped her fingers on the bar. 'How many fucking times do I have to say it, thicko?'

But Stevie just looked at her, as if she was the one out of her head. 'Yer have to give me another go, Mrs.' His voice rose higher as panic began to set in. 'I don't think me ma will let me back in the house.'

'And? Like that's my problem, eh? I have to concern meself with the troubles of a useless junkie? I don't think so. Yer had yer chance and yer blew it.'

Stevie's shaking was now only partly due to the lack of drugs in his system, and his mother not letting him in the house was only part of the problem. He had a feeling he wouldn't even make it that far, knowing what he did. Boneface would probably kill him herself.

He was ready to beg. He knew it and she knew

it. 'Give me another chance, Mrs Archer. Please. I promise I won't fuck up no more. And I will get clean. Look.' He held out his hands, which were shaking more and more by the minute. 'Look I've had nowt today, just like yer said.'

She smiled at him. To Stevie it seemed like her smile just kept right on stretching, wider and wider, as though she was doing it in slow motion and time was stretching with it.

Finally she said, as if from a very long way away, 'One more chance, and you better fucking believe it, mate, because it's the only one yer ever gonna get. Smith,' she barked, turning her anger on to her side-kick. 'Phone Ally, tell him to get his arse in gear. I want him here like yesterday.'

Smith almost ran to the phone.

'You,' she poked Stevie in his cheek and twisted her finger round, 'will do everything Ally tells yer to do. The Lumsdon girl, who you seem to despise so much, has to be kept an eye on. I need to know everything she does, says or whatever. Got that?'

'Yes, yes, whatever yer say . . . Who's Ally?'

'A friend, of sorts. Yer would have met him this weekend anyhow. He's what yer might call our chief collector.'

Stevie looked dim for a moment, then it sank in. He nodded. It stood to reason they would be in the protection racket as well. Christ, they must have the whole of Houghton and God knows where else sown up tighter than a miser's purse.

'He's on his way, Mrs Archer,' Smith shouted from the far end of the bar.

She nodded, never once taking her eyes off Stevie, who was now so agitated he was practically hopping from foot to foot. She sneered at him then glanced at her watch, and tutting to herself she went to the door. Stevie sagged against the bar, pleased to be out of the glare of her piercing eyes. His head hurt from trying to think, and all he really wanted to do was lie down in a dark corner. Any dark corner.

'Where the fuck are those stupid moron barmaids?' Mrs Archer grumbled as she opened the door and looked up the street. 'The fucking tarts are late again tonight.'

Smith nodded his agreement even though she wasn't looking at him. When she was in a mood like this, he would agree to anything she said, no matter what it was.

'You talking about us, Mrs Archer?' Julie Miller asked, as she sauntered in with Sharon May close behind her. They might as well have been twins, although one was a natural redhead and the other a mousey brown underneath the coal-black hair dye. Both wore short black skirts with the same low-cut white tops, and each had a red rose tattooed on their right over-developed breast. The pair of them made more money after hours in Mrs Archer's spare room, after she'd taken her cut of course, than they could earn in a month at a normal job.

'And who the fuck else would I be talking about?' she snarled. 'Yer do know, of course, that there is an earlier bus from Hetton, don't yer? Course yer do, they run all fucking day.'

Julie shrugged, while Sharon, always content to

sit back and let Julie do the talking, even in a three-some, stared at a spot on the wall above Mrs Archer's head. She cracked her chewing gum and in the silence of the bar it sounded like a gunshot. Stevie screamed and cleared the floor by nearly a foot.

'Smith,' Mrs Archer shouted, causing Stevie to cringe, 'get him in there.' She pointed to the back room, then swung back to the girls. 'You two, get to work now. And, Sharon,' Sharon, jaws working furiously, looked wide-eyed at her.

'Yes, Mrs Archer?'

'Crack that fucking shit in yer mouth once more, and I'll fucking crack you.'

She walked to the door that led upstairs and, hand on the handle, turned. 'Also, if I see any more of that fucking pink lipstick yer both so fucking fond of on any more of the glasses in the morning, I'll have yer guts for garters and the pair of yer will be outta here. And I mean shit hot . . . Got it?'

They both nodded, dumbly following her every movement with their eyes until the door closed behind her.

Once upstairs, she locked the door, kicked her shoes off and flopped on to her black leather settee.

Anyone entering the room could be forgiven for thinking they were in the living space of a rich eight-eenth-century Chinese merchant. However, on closer inspection it all screamed cheap copy. Apart, that is, from the large decorated Chinese knife with the wicked-looking blade that hung in pride of place, above the fire.

Everything else was fake. She could afford the real

thing, but that would be letting on just how much she was really worth. She grinned to herself as her last bank statement sprang into her mind.

Enough for the Swiss plastic surgeon who had promised to change her face for ever, and more than enough to replace the junk with the real. Especially with the new gear on the way in.

Standing, she limped over to her desk. Taking the key from a chain around her neck, she opened the roll-top lid. Inside was a large brown envelope. Carefully she shook the contents on to the palm of her left hand, and with her fingernail she moved the brightly coloured tattoos around. Bart Simpson grinned up at her. Tweety Pie smiled shyly, and Sylvester licked his lips. These were only a few of the kids' favourite characters portrayed on the tattoos, which when applied to the skin in the traditional way, sent a dose of LSD right into the bloodstream. The tattoos would hit the streets tomorrow, and this venture was all hers. The Man knew nothing about it. She practically slavered when she thought how much money this lot would bring her way. And, if she had to run before then, they would go with her to sell when she was all healed up and holding a new identity.

Really, seeing as things were already getting a little hairy, she should go now. All her instincts told her that things were collapsing, and she should get out. But then again . . . no, she couldn't resist. She needed her cut from the last batch of girls just to pay for that extra bit of fun. The Man wasn't getting her share – after all, he mostly sat on his arse and left the traffick business to her.

Gloating, she put the tattoos away. Wouldn't do for anyone to see them yet. She moved from the desk to the fireplace, standing in front of the huge mirror. She stretched her arms above her head and moved from side to side, admiring her trim figure. 'Not bad,' she said to her reflection. 'Not bad at all.' She took another long look, then went into the kitchen to make a pot of tea. Chinese, of course. With the kettle on, she began watering the plants on the window sill.

She paused, watering can in mid air, when Kerry Lumsdon slid into her mind.

What the fuck's so special about the bitch and her family of fucking weasels? Whatever it is, the bitch is one cocky little bastard.

A sudden loud knock on the door caused her to spill some water. *Damn*, she thought, as she grabbed a tea towel and mopped it up. That's got to be Ally. He might know something about the little cow.

She opened the door. It was Ally, all six foot six of him. His grandfather had come from Pakistan in the early fifties and, being third generation, Ally spoke perfect English. He was immaculately dressed in a dark grey suit and white shirt, and she noted that his passion for cartoon character ties had waned none. She smirked to herself as Tweety Pie stared out at her from Ally's tie. 'Come on in.'

He sat down on the settee and she sat on a matching chair facing him. 'Right. For reasons only known to him, The Man wants this stupid bitch of a school kid watched. Her name's Kerry Lumsdon. Heard of her, have yer?'

313

'She got a bro called Robbie?'

'She certainly has.'

'I've been watching him for years. Remember when Reagan's shop got burned down?'

She nodded.

'The reason Reagan got burned out is because he set the kid on working there, Saturday mornings. He got a warning but ignored it – Reagan always was a pain in the arse, thought he didn't need protection. Well he needed it that night.'

'Is that why he got his leg broken an' all?'

Ally nodded.

'Hmm. Any idea what The Man's got against this family then?'

He shrugged. 'Haven't got a clue. And I don't really want one. It's The Man's business, and he pays me wages.'

Mrs Archer read the signs, and decided to back off.

'Aye, I guess yer right. Curiosity does kill the cat in this fucking town. OK then, seeing as you've already been watching the brother, stands to reason you'll know a fair bit about the sister.'

Ally shrugged. 'Apart from being a good-looking chick, the only thing I can vouch for is her being one hell of a runner. That's about it.'

Ally's information, scant as it was, only served to whet her curiosity all the more. For her own safety, she needed to know more about this kid – The Man was interested in her for some reason, and as far as she knew he wasn't into having it off with kids, so she would dig. Knowledge was safety in her game.

She decided that when Ally left she would phone him, not that she was supposed to – he always phoned her, and then very rarely. He'd probably go ballistic, but he'd thank her for letting him know that the Lumsdons had actually been at her door, and that they'd asked her about Brad. That would take the heat off her and put it on the stupid blond fuck.

20

Lorraine, dressed in her blonde bimbo outfit, locked the door behind her and strutted over to the unmarked police car. It was Luke's night off so it was Carter who sat behind the wheel and his mouth dropped open when he realised the tart he'd watched walking towards him was his boss.

He had been told to dress casually and Lorraine looked critically at his grey slacks and lemon sweat-shirt before muttering, 'You'll do.' As she fastened her seat belt she added, 'Remember we aren't together, you're there solely to watch my back.' He nodded.

'And Carter.'

'Yes boss?'

'Close yer mouth.'

Carter blushed. 'But, boss, you've even changed the colour of yer eyes.'

'Just drive, Carter.'

They were on the A9, heading towards Bolden where they would turn off for the dog track, when Lorraine said, 'That new gay bar, Lotus Lips or some such stupid name. It's around here somewhere, isn't it?'

'Just off the roundabout, past McDonald's, and the cinema.'

'OK, stop there for five.'

A few minutes later, they came to a stop outside a large pink building with pairs of six-foot-high red lips dotted liberally over the walls. They sat for a short while, watching several Elvis lookalikes enter the club.

'Must be Elvis night, eh?' Carter said. The look he received from Lorraine made him wish wholeheartedly he hadn't bothered to comment.

'A good policeman, Carter, would have already noticed the posters on the walls proclaiming that very fact. A good policeman might also have read about the event in the local paper.'

Carter felt like sinking into his seat. His face flushed scarlet; when his boss was prickly, she cut right to the bone. And my God, she'd been damn prickly of late.

'Right, you wait here.' Lorraine got out of the car and went to the entrance.

Her way was barred by a large golden-brown arm, whose owner obviously worked out daily. 'Sorry, love, but I don't think you quite belong in here.'

She followed the length of the arm with her eyes, then raised her head to gaze into a pair nearly as brown as the false lenses she was wearing. In a steely voice she said, 'If yer don't move yer fucking arm, I'll snap the bastard in half.'

Momentarily surprised, the bouncer stepped back. He weighed her up, noticed how she held herself, then with a slight smile said, 'Yer mean it, don't yer, love?'

'Yer better believe it.'

'OK, OK.' He shrugged. 'Your choice, love. No need to be nasty, now is there?'

Lorraine gave no quarter. 'You tell me.'

She moved forward, and he stepped quickly aside. She walked on without looking back at him and entered the bar.

It was indeed Elvis night. Ninety per cent of the men had come in costume, some so good you could be forgiven for thinking the King himself was alive and kicking and living in the North East of England. The rest were women – or damn good copies.

There was a huge dance floor, easily the size of a football pitch, and the backdrop to the stage was a waterfall. A couple of hundred people danced to the booming sound of 'Wooden Heart'.

Lorraine looked around, her sharp eyes missing no one. Every Elvis was dissected. She spotted dope or worse passed several times under tables, and made a mental note to have the place raided sometime soon. She was on her second circuit when her eyes skidded back to a couple sitting at a bar in the right-hand corner of the stage. The bar had a straw roof and they were sipping drinks with coloured umbrellas on sticks stuck in them. It wasn't the Elvis who had caught her attention, but his companion. There was something all too familiar about her. The hair, shaped in a bob and gypsy black, was definitely a wig. But it wasn't just the wig; most of the people here – herself included – had wigs on. It was something about the way she held her drink, something in the body language.

Lorraine walked slowly around the edge of the

dance floor, keeping the couple in sight. The closer she got, the more certain she became.

Then she was behind them. She slid into a seat and waited.

Finally the man wearing the Elvis costume went to the bar for a refill. In a split second she was on her feet round the table and facing her husband.

'John,' she said quietly and then, so huskily it was almost a whisper, 'why?'

John was too shocked to speak. He started to his feet, looking frantically around for an escape route, but Lorraine was quicker. The blow was powerful enough to knock him back over his chair and send him skidding across the floor.

Stepping over him, Lorraine stood with her hands on her hips, glaring down. The wig had slipped and hung halfway over his left eye lending him a comical air, but Lorraine wasn't laughing. She'd thought of a hundred things she would say when she caught up with him. But now, seeing him like this, and real-ising what a pathetic person he was, she shook her head sadly. She stood looking at him a moment longer then, with head held high, turned and walked away.

The bouncer with the tanned arms had stood and watched the entire scene. Lorraine gave him a look when she passed, inviting him to say something, but he wasn't fool enough to rise to the bait.

She climbed into the car next to Carter. 'Get me outta here. I feel like I've just spent ten minutes in the fucking Twilight Zone.'

Determined not to do anything wrong, which,

when she was in this mood, above all meant asking stupid questions, Carter started the car and headed for their original destination. He noticed a collection of Elvises staring and pointing at the car through his mirror, and although his curiosity was burning at an all-time high, he kept his mouth shut.

Five minutes later, Carter dropped Lorraine off at the entrance to the dog track, then went to park the car. There was a queue to get in, and Lorraine tapped her fingers impatiently against the wall while examining all the faces that queued with her. She listened to snatches of conversation; most were complaints about the recent price rise to get in the place. She tuned out those in front of her and, on the pretence of looking for someone, gave the same scrutiny to everyone in the queue behind her.

Nothing. The line began to move and a few minutes later she was in the hall. She chose a table at random and sat down with her back to the wall. She pretended to study the race card but the print was a complete blur, she just couldn't get her mind off the confrontation with John. She trembled inside – one minute regretting attacking him, the next wishing she'd done more. *Like broke his fucking legs, or maybe his neck.*

No, she told herself, she had done the right thing, no way could she have left it up in the air. He deserved what he got – and more.

One thing's for certain, if I've as much as caught a cold off the bastard, I will fucking kill him.

If anyone asked Lorraine how she felt right now, she'd be hard pressed to describe it. Weird was the only word that came to mind. It seemed as though she had one foot in the here and now, and the other one trailing a week behind. Of course if someone did ask she would give the standard response: *I'm fine, thank you.* How many times a day is that sentence uttered? And how many times is it nothing but a whopping lie . . .

Forcing her mind back to the job in hand she looked round the crowded hall – it was time to get on with the night's work. Four young lives depended on her keeping it together and she couldn't let emotion get in the way. She picked up the race card and ringed dog number three, just a regular punter on a night out.

On her way to place her bet she spotted Carter at one of the other windows but ignored him. She glanced around: still no sign of the elusive Brad.

Where the fuck is the bastard?

She was banking on a gambler like Brad not being able to keep away from his passion for very long. Being addicted to gambling was like being addicted to drugs – one way or another, you just had to have the buzz.

He'd got to show tonight. Time was fast running out for Claire and the others.

She checked her mobile phone, but no messages yet. For God's sake, come on. They must surely have traced his grandmother by now, how difficult could an old biddie be to find?

As she dropped her phone into her bag she noticed a thick-set burly man watching her closely, but giving no sign that she knew she was being given the once-over, she reached the window and placed her bet.

'Ten pounds to win, please, on number three. Dead cert that dog. Definitely on form tonight.'

Fifteen minutes later she watched Carter make his way to the pay-out window. Now what had made him pick dog number six?

Lucky bastard.

Mark jumped off the bus at Newbottle. He felt a little bit silly for turning up so soon but, for a reason he couldn't explain, he needed to see Kerry. He just couldn't seem to get her out of his mind. He'd thought it best not to turn up by car – and in any case, his dad seemed so preoccupied at the moment, he didn't really want to bother him.

Following Robbie's instructions he crossed the road, headed past the school and the fields, and on down to the Seahills. Kerry's house was not hard to find; the streets were well sign-posted, and all the doors were numbered. He walked up the path and knocked on the door. It was opened by a small boy who stared at him for a moment, then demanded, 'What do yer want?'

'Is, er, is Kerry in?'

'No.'

The door was just about to be closed in his face when Mark heard his name shouted from behind him. He swung round to see Kerry, Robbie and another boy coming up the path.

'Sorry, Mark,' Kerry glared at Darren. 'He's not usually so cheeky, are you, Darren?'

Darren shrugged and went back into the house, this time leaving the door open.

'Hi, Mark,' Robbie said, as he stepped past him, 'come on in.'

Mark nodded and waited till the others filed past him, then followed them into the house. He noticed Kerry trying to tidy up by shoving some clothes underneath the cushions on the settee. Two little girls were watching the television with an older boy.

'Thanks, Clay,' Kerry said. 'I owe yer one.'

'No prob, Kerry.' He stood to go. 'See yer later then.'

They all said goodbye to Clayton, then swung their attention to Mark, who was standing rather awkwardly behind the settee because all the seats had been claimed. There was a moment of silence then a loud sniff from Emma prompted Mark to say, 'I just thought I'd pay a visit, like. See if yer sister had turned up.'

'Well she hasn't.' Darren nearly spat at him.

Robbie gently cuffed Darren's ear. 'Move, Darren, and give Mark a seat.'

'Tell him to move,' Darren pointed at Mickey. 'This is my house not his.'

'Move it, kid. Mickey's a guest. And remember we've just been sorting your business out, and Mickey was there to help.'

Grumbling to himself, Darren got up and sat on the floor. A Bart Simpson re-run was on and Suzy was giggling as she watched Marge getting herself kidnapped by a motor-cycle gang. *The Simpsons* usually kept them quiet, and Robbie had often wished they had a video player. Endless Bart might make the house more peaceful.

Darren glanced at the television, then with a heavy frown on his face turned back to Robbie. 'So what about Kenny then?'

'It's sorted,' Robbie said. 'After the Blue Lion we saw his sister an' I'm willing to bet he'll be wearing a black eye tomorrow an' all.'

'Why, isn't that just great! And who do yer think he's gonna blame for that, eh?'

'His sister won't tell him who told her.'

'Do yer think Kenny's daft, or what?'

'Darren, I told yer, it's sorted, OK? Everything's sorted. Nowt more to worry about, except keeping well away from the bastards.'

Darren sighed, the weight of the world on his eleven-year-old shoulders.

Emma turned her attention away from Bart for a moment and looked Mark up and down. She sniffed and wiped her nose on her sleeve, before saying in a high-pitched whine, 'You our Kerry's boyfriend, then?'

'Emma!' Kerry shouted, her face burning. She threw a cushion at her sister who immediately threw it back, only for it to land on Darren. He in turn chucked it at Mickey, who promptly tossed it back to Kerry. Mark was unused to large families with their everyday squabbles. He tried not to show how uncomfortable he felt, though he knew his face was as red as Kerry's.

Seeing his embarrassment, Robbie quickly intervened. 'Come on, you lot, settle down. Feels like those chips were an age ago, does anyone fancy a pizza?' He was greeted with a chorus of yeses, and demands for various toppings.

Mark hastily pulled his mobile phone out. 'I'll get it. What's the number?'

Sharing grins, they all looked at him and Mark wondered what he'd said wrong.

'Couldn't really tell yer the number, like, cos one of us usually goes an fetches them.'

'Oh.' Mark put his phone back in his pocket.

'I know the number,' Mickey said. He gave it to Mark while the rest argued about what toppings they wanted. Mark ended up ordering three to please everyone.

'So,' Mark said two hours later, as he and Kerry reached the top of Coaly Lane, 'will you come for the day tomorrow? You can bring your bathing costume – we've got an indoor pool.'

Fucking hell, Kerry thought to herself. *What sort of fucking house has he got? A bastard mansion?*

She sighed inwardly before saying, 'I don't know, Mark. It's sort of awkward like.'

'How?'

'Why, yer know. You come from up there, and I come from here.' She shrugged.

Mark was perplexed. 'So?'

'*So*, he says. It's a whole world's difference, Mark. If yer can't see that, then you're blind. Jesus, yer must have felt as if yer was slumming tonight all right.'

'Of course not!' He stopped and turned to her. 'What makes you think that?'

'For fuck's sake, Mark, yer even paid for the supper. Didn't yer get it? There never would have

325

been any pizza. It's a joke Robbie cracks now and then to distract them. He does toast for the kids, and they pretend it's fucking pizza. Like sitting in the garden amongst the fucking rubbish and pretending we're in the Costa del whatever. We're good at pretending, us Lumsdons, we've had years of fucking practice.'

'Oh.'

Lost for words, Mark started to walk on to the bus stop, then spun round to face her. 'Look, it really doesn't matter that my family has money and yours doesn't. We've always been rich. Money isn't every-thing.'

'Oh for fuck's sake! How is it that people who have money always say that? You'll never hear it coming out of the gobs of people who have nowt, that's for sure.'

Mark's shoulders slumped. At the sight of his downcast face Kerry's anger started to melt and she said gently, 'OK, OK. I'll come. But just until two. Me mam comes out of hospital tomorrow, and I want to be home to welcome her back.'

Mark's face lit up. 'Mint! I'll meet you off the bus at ten, if that's OK. Honest, we'll have a hell of a day. Tell me what kind of food you like and I'll get the cook to make it for lunch.'

Kerry was momentarily stunned. *Fucking lunch. What have I fucking let meself in for here? And a frigging cook, for God's sake.*

'Anything yer like, I'm not fussy. As long as it's English. I'm not keen on foreign muck.' *Not that I've tried much, like.* She was about to voice the thought when Mark's bus arrived.

'Great.' He was smiling all over his face. Then he stepped forward and gave her a quick peck on her cheek.

Kerry was lost for words. She couldn't even return his goodbye, and was still standing there five minutes after the bus had gone with her fingers pressed against her cheek. Finally she tore her hand away and, smiling, headed for home.

She totalled up his pluses and decided she liked pretty much everything about him, especially the way he talked. She'd noticed that this had changed dramatically since she'd met him, and guessed rightly that he broadened his accent when he was with the lads in order to fit in.

Lorraine was about to go. She was tired, down fifty pounds, and fed up to her back teeth of seeing Carter at the winners' window.

Catching his eye, she gave him the signal for home. Then had to stop herself from doing a double take, for standing right behind him was the man they were looking for.

Carter, unaware of this, gave her a barely perceptible nod, only to become confused when a moment later she shook her head. Although he wanted to, he stopped himself from spinning round, instinctively knowing that it would be the wrong thing to do.

A moment later she was beside him, smiling up at him as if he were a long-lost lover. Then moving quickly, she grabbed hold of Brad just above his elbow. Her fingers sank into the soft flesh, immediately numbing his lower arm.

'What the fuck?' he managed to say through gritted teeth whilst trying to push her off with his free arm. Finally getting the message, Carter spun round and grabbed Brad's wrist, pinning it up behind his back.

Two burly men, one bald, the other with short cropped brown hair, who were obviously Brad's minders, were beside them in seconds.

'Back off,' Lorraine hissed at them, 'he's mine.'

Baldy laughed. 'Surely yer not that desperate that yer have to kidnap them off the street?'

'Get the bitch off me!' Brad winced at the pain in his arms. Lorraine knew exactly where to apply the pressure.

The other man stepped back, and his eyes narrowed as he weighed the situation up. Then, looking at Baldy, he shook his head. 'Leave it, man.'

'What?'

Ignoring him, the man looked at Brad. He held up both of his hands. 'I did warn yer to stay low for a while, son.' Turning he walked away and out of the corner of his mouth said to Baldy, 'Come on.'

Looking at Brad, Baldy shrugged, then followed his friend. As soon as they were out of earshot he asked, 'What do yer know that I don't?'

'She's a fucking copper. And not yer normal run-of-the-mill kind, either. She'll have yer balls for breakfast given half the chance. And that bitch kisses no fucker's arse. It's cos of her me brother's banged up for six years. She's a fucking ferret – once she has yer by the short and curlies, that's it.'

'How come I've never seen her around then? A looker like that. Yer don't forget.'

'Trust me, you'll have seen her all right. Yer just wouldn't have known it.'

Baldy shrugged. 'I know one thing though, The fucking Man's not gonna like this one little bit.'

It was nearly two o'clock when Lorraine let herself into her mother's cottage where she was staying for a while, unable to face the deserted rooms at home. Mavis was curled up on the settee.

'Mam.' Lorraine shook her gently. 'Mam, it's me.'

Mavis slowly opened one eye. 'I wasn't asleep, yer know. How are yer, pet?'

'Coping.' She nearly added, *only just*, but she knew her mother was as worried as she was.

'I'll put the kettle on, love.' Mavis swung her legs off the settee, rubbed her eyes then, tying the belt around her lemon bathrobe, padded into the kitchen.

A short time later they were both warming their hands around their mugs and Lorraine started to tell Mavis everything that had happened that night.

Mavis nearly choked when Lorraine described what had happened at the gay club. 'Jesus Christ,' she spluttered, wiping tea off her chin. 'Elvis bloody Presley! Now I have heard it all.'

Leaning forward she patted Lorraine's knee. 'Yer did the right thing, love. Don't yer ever fret on that score. A good clout is just what the arsehole needed.' Then she burst out laughing. 'Sorry, pet, but I can just picture it. I wish I'd been there.'

Lorraine tried hard, but Mavis's laughter had always been infectious. She grinned, then said, 'Yeah, well I suppose I do feel a wee bit better.'

'Just try to put it all behind yer. OK, pet?'

'Mebbe after the test results next week . . . until then, I guess I'll be pretty strung out.'

Mavis nodded. 'Stands to reason, love.' Her heart ached for her only child, and she prayed with every fibre of her being that she would test clean. But for now she knew the best thing to do was to try and keep her mind off it. A person could easily go insane just thinking about it.

'So, what's happened with this Brad creep?'

'Nothing yet. He won't talk. We've spent half the night on him and he hasn't said a word, so we've left him in his cell for a couple of hours to think on it. One of the lads will swear to all and sundry that he phoned his lawyer a thousand times and got no answer.'

'Good, let the bastard sweat. So now what?'

'We start again tomorrow. I'll find out one way or another what he's done with those girls. And they're bringing his flaming witch of a grandmother in an' all. They finally traced the old bitch to a house in Jarrow, visiting with three of her daughters. One of them is Brad's mother, but apparently all three seem reluctant to claim parentage.'

'Sound like a whole bunch of creeps to me.'

Lorraine yawned. 'Yeah, me too.' Rising, she kissed her mother's cheek. 'I'm off to bed, Mam. See yer tomorrow.'

Mavis kissed her back and watched her leave the room. Then with a deep sigh she collected the cups and took them into the kitchen.

* * *

Going cold turkey is a very noisy process. Twenty years ago, a copper on the beat would have heard the screams coming from the Blue Lion. His investigation of the unearthly din would have thrown a hundred doors wide open. As it was, the two policemen heard nothing but the heavy pattering of rain on the metal roof of the patrol car as they drove past.

Mrs Archer had been listening to the ear-splitting din for nearly two hours, and knew that it could go on all night. Her bedroom was above the back room where Stevie was going through his own private hell. She sat on the edge of her pink-satin covered bed, surrounded by her mock luxuries, and placed her hands over her ears. Stevie's pain was the least of her worries.

'Let the stupid bastard climb the fucking walls,' she muttered. When she'd phoned The Man with news of Kerry's visit he'd gone berserk, and whilst fingering Brad had taken a little of the heat off her, it wasn't enough. His ranting and raving had all but drowned out Stevie's agonies below.

The ungrateful bastard had seemed to forget that he owed her, big time. No way would he have that big fancy house, plus his millions, if she hadn't dealt with a few problems for him. But the bastard wasn't remembering that now, was he? No, he seemed to blame her for the whole pack of cards starting to tumble. *And when The Man is blaming yer, yer don't hang about an' try an' reason with him. Just what is it about that frigging kid that's winding him up so badly?*

She well and truly had the wind up and her stomach, usually cast iron, was churning.

She knew she had but one option, and that was to get out while she still could. The Man was furious, and the next mistake would be her last – that is if she hadn't run out of time already. She made her decision, and her hand trembled as she reached for the phone.

Saturday

21

Three times Kerry rose to leave the bus on the way to South Shields, and three times she sat back down. But now she was here and Mark was standing at the bus stop waiting for her. There was no going back.

She stepped off the bus and Mark grinned at her. 'I knew you'd come.' He nearly fell over in his eagerness to take her hand. Then he hurried her over the road to the waiting car. He'd badgered Jake to take him to meet Kerry, because Jake was a pushover compared to his father. He knew Jake wouldn't grass on him either.

Jesus Christ, Kerry thought, mouth agog. *Is this the grandest fucking car in England, or what?*

She didn't let go of Mark's hand, even when she was slipping into the back seat of the Rolls-Royce. She breathed in the deep-scented leather.

Fucking unbelievable.

Mark chattered all the way to his house, hardly leaving a gap for Kerry to get a word in. When they got there and Mark finally fell silent, she was far too stunned by the spectacle in front of her to say anything at all.

The Rolls-Royce had come to a stop outside a pair of black wrought-iron gates that were tipped with gold. Twin stone unicorns stood guard on either side. The driver spoke into a phone, and a moment later the gates slowly opened, then after they'd entered the long driveway, closed just as slowly behind them. Somehow, Kerry didn't quite like that.

The driveway was surrounded by rolling lawns and the house itself was enormous. She just managed to stop herself from blurting out, 'Wow', as she thought, *Not just a mansion, it's a super-duper fucking mansion.*

The driver opened the door and smiled down at her, but she didn't like the look of him at all. His smile reminded her of a poisonous snake she'd seen on the telly once.

'Come on!' Mark was giddy to have her here, and almost dragged her out of the car and up the six wide steps to the door.

It took a lot to faze Kerry, but the grandeur of the house with its imposing entrance was certainly getting there, and suddenly she just wanted to go home. She felt as if once she stepped over this magnificent threshold, she'd be swallowed up for ever.

She let go of Mark's hand for the first time since meeting him at the bus stop. He turned, a puzzled look on his face.

'What's wrong?'

Shaking her head, she began to back away.

'Please, Kerry, there's nothing to be frightened of. Come on in.'

Kerry was torn between obeying her instinct which told her to turn and run rather than enter the house, and the knowledge that her feelings were completely irrational. She had a sudden longing for home, but Mark was practically begging her to stay. If she refused to go in, Mark would think she was a total bloody idiot. And that was the last thing she wanted. She needed Mark to like her: she liked him more than any boy she'd ever met.

Aye, more than like, if I'm honest.

And Mark seemed to like her too – if she ran now she might never see him again.

Mark looked at her and held out his hand once more.

OK, if I'm gonna go in, I better do it now. It's only a house, for God's sake. Since when have I ever been frightened of anything, never mind a daft feeling about a house?

Taking a deep breath, and pasting a smile that was more like a grimace on her face, she climbed the steps and walked hand-in-hand with Mark through the massive doorway.

Half an hour later he had shown her round most of his home, and each room had been grander than the one before. The whole place seemed more like a big hotel than an actual house. The stainless-steel kitchen was huge, definitely not the kind where you'd sit with your mates and have a cuppa. Mark had told her that his father did a lot of entertaining, and Kerry knew enough to know that that wasn't the sort he meant. His dad had also been all around the world and on at least three African safaris. Kerry knew without doubt that she was right out of her league.

*　　*　　*

Ten o'clock, and Brad sat in the interview room, practically foaming at the mouth. He'd been sitting on the hard seat since seven.

Three fucking hours, and not a mouthful of food or drink had passed his way – the bastards hadn't even let him have a tab. So far, four different coppers had taken turns sitting in the room. Every half hour or so they changed places, and each time they came back smelling of coffee or cigarettes.

He could have sworn the ginger one who'd been grilling him half the night had sat outside and gobbled a plate of bacon and eggs, the greedy fuck. The smell had just wafted right in. Bastards, he was fucking starving.

What a tale he would have for his lawyer, *when the lazy twat finally gets here, that is.*

He wondered briefly if The Man was teaching him a lesson but, with the arrogance of the young and foolish, he shrugged the thought away and concentrated on just how fucking long he was going to have to stay.

And where the fuck is the slapper?

Fancy a good-looking chick like her being a copper. And what a fucking copper, an' all. She doesn't give a fuck what she says, or does.

Why aye, wait till me lawyer sees the fucking bruises on me legs, he'll have the fucking bitch carted off to the fucking nut house where she belongs.

And me arm, Brad rubbed his elbow. *Fucking bastard, it still doesn't feel right. Police brutality, that's what it fucking well is. I'll demand compensation, then the bitch will get what she deserves. Who the fuck does the cheeky blonde bastard think she is?*

She needs a sorting all right. If I ever catch her by herself, God fucking help her. One dark fucking night, that's all I need.

Hands clenched into fists, he ground his teeth together.

The ginger copper with more freckles than a dalmatian had spots, grinned.

And you an' all, yer fucking bastard. I'll be having you. He smirked at Carter. *Believe me, Ginger, you and the bitch will regret the day youse messed with me.*

Deeply frustrated, he grabbed hold of the chair arms. *Where the fuck is she?*

The person responsible for Brad's growing anger was in the incident room going over the missing-heads case with the team.

Lorraine wore a grey skirt-suit with a white blouse, her hair pulled into a severe bun at the back of her head. She twirled a pair of brown horn-rimmed glasses in her hand, her face pale and drawn from lack of sleep. She looked a million miles from the dolly bird who had arrested Brad last night, and kept him simmering between interrogations ever since.

'Really,' she said, as she closed her folder and looked at the assembled officers, 'we aren't that much further forward, are we.'

Her officers knew it was a statement and not a question. They also knew that for the last few days Lorraine had been almost impossible to approach, and that this was totally out of character for the boss. Speculation was rife, but few believed that she, of all people, would allow anything personal to interfere with her work.

They sat waiting for her lead and she soon gave it. 'Luke, what did Mrs Holland have to say about her missing son? Any clues there?'

Luke shrugged. 'Not really, boss. She started to cry when I explained everything, but five minutes later she was going on about how much she enjoyed her fish and chips. One little thing though, when she was eating, she asked where Dean Nesbitt was.'

Lorraine frowned as Luke went on.

'I haven't thought about Dean in years – he was a bit older than me. He hung around Jack quite a lot, but was pretty friendless once Jack vanished. He was rumoured to have gone South, looking for work, but I'm wondering if he could be one of our bodies, with him being a friend of Jack's an' all, and going missing around the same time.'

'It's gonna be tough. The trail is far too old. But get on that Dean Nesbitt lead, it could be just what we're looking for.'

Leaning over the table Lorraine opened a drawer and took out a pencil. As she started to chew the end, Sara Jacobs spoke up.

'Boss, Scottie says the youngest body is that of a sixteen-year-old youth, murdered not that long after the one we've identified as Jack Holland.'

Lorraine put the pencil down. 'If it is Nesbitt we'd at least have the names of two of them.' Luke nodded.

'The rest of yer, keep on digging.'

Thinking she was finished, they started to leave the incident room but froze when Lorraine added loudly, 'By the way, anybody who thinks I've forgotten about our little leak has got another think coming. The press are still fucking camping outside, and one of you lot is to blame. Anyone gonna admit it yet? Cos I tell yer, I'm sure as hell gonna get to the bottom of it, and when I do yer'll be fucking toast. Understand?'

Some of the team shook their heads, whilst others simply shrugged, and muttered amongst themselves. When no one would meet her eyes, she walked out, resisting the urge to slam the door. Realistically the chances of finding out who the leak was were very small, but a couple of lectures might scare whoever it was into keeping their mouth shut in the future.

Entering the interview room, Lorraine looked at the back of Brad's head and grimaced. Moving round the table, she sat down next to Carter and gave Brad a cold stare.

Glaring back at her he shouted, 'About bloody time an' all. I've got a list of complaints about this place that's as long as me friggin' arm. For starters, yer have a mad woman out there, arresting people for no reason at all. She's the one that should be friggin' well arrested. Arrested, and put in a fucking strait-jacket, if yer ask me—'

'How's yer arm?' Lorraine cut in.

'What?' He peered closely at her.

'The arm. How is it? I didn't hurt yer too much when yer were resisting arrest, did I?'

'I don't fucking believe it!' He jumped up,

knocking the chair over, but Carter reacted just as quickly. Righting the chair with one hand, he grabbed Brad with the other and pulled him back down on to the seat.

'Temper, temper,' Lorraine chided.

'I'm gonna have you, yer blonde bitch.' He waved his finger at her. 'And as for you,' he swung round to Carter, 'I'll get rid of yer freckles for yer. There'll be no fucking skin left on yer face when I'm finished, yer ginger bastard.'

Lorraine yawned and looked at Carter. 'Is it me, or something about the room that makes people come out with the most outrageous threats? Must be the job, eh Carter?'

'I'd say that, boss.'

'Oh, it's fucking Laurel and fucking Hardy, is it?'

Lorraine banged her fist on the table and said in a steely voice, 'Enough. Now then, Brad, or whoever you are today, it's time for you to start talking. And the first thing I wanna know is, have yer ever dealt in drugs?'

'Is this what it's about?'

Lorraine did not miss the look of relief that swept across his face, nor the smug tone of his voice as he said with conviction, 'Never.'

'Flesh, then?'

'What?' He looked at her as if he were being confronted by a gorgon. As Lorraine looked at him, watched his sudden realisation that the game was up, she felt a flicker of satisfaction. Then he started to scream. 'Where's me fucking lawyer? I want me fucking lawyer now, yer bitch.'

'Where's the fucking girls, arsehole?' Lorraine shouted just as loudly, banging her fist on the table again, so angrily that even Carter cringed.

Kerry and Mark were sitting by the pool. They had been swimming and splashing around for over an hour, and Kerry's earlier misgivings had disappeared for the moment. She loved the pool, which had a roof that opened in the summer and real palm trees growing in huge tubs scattered around it. She had never seen anything so luxurious in her whole life and couldn't imagine living somewhere where you could just swim every day.

'So,' Mark said, putting his can of diet coke on the wicker table. 'Hungry?'

Hungry? Kerry thought. *I'm bloody starving.* She'd been praying for the last half hour, to any God willing to listen, that he'd mention food soon.

'Now that yer asking . . .'

'Good. Should we eat here, or in the dining room?'

'Anywhere. I'm not fussy.'

Just starving to death. Please make it quick, before I really show meself up and start chewing on the friggin' table leg.

Smiling, Mark stood to press a button on the wall. He spoke into the grille, then turned back to Kerry. 'Burger, chips and salad all right?'

'Yeah, that's cool.'

And if it doesn't come soon, I'll be eating your leg as well as the table's.

A few minutes later, Jake arrived with a brimming trolley. The smell of the home-made burgers made

343

Kerry's mouth water, so much so that she was frightened to speak in case she drooled down her front.

Finally finished, and so full she could hardly move, she wiped her mouth with her napkin before smiling at Mark. 'I have never in me whole life tasted burgers like them.' She felt almost relaxed despite her extraordinary surroundings, but just then the clock on the wall above the pool caught her eye.

Jesus, where has all the time gone?

'God, sorry Mark, I'd really better get goin' now. If I don't go pretty soon, Mam will be home before me.'

'It's OK. We can use the car and be back at yours in no time.'

'I'm not going home in that! I'll be the talk of the bloody place.'

Mark laughed. 'That's silly, what are they going to say?'

'You'd be surprised.' She thought for a moment, then said with a small smile, 'I suppose yer could drop me off at Newbottle and I can run down the bank.'

'Don't you ever walk, Kerry?'

'Not if I can help it.' Her voice sounded happier than it had in days. For a short time her worries over her mother and sister had been on hold, and she was thankful to Mark for that small reprieve.

'I'll get dressed,' she said as she picked up her towel.

'OK, see you in the lounge. Remember, it's first right, then second left when you come out.'

Kerry dressed in a hurry, hoping to be as quick as

Mark, but when she came back into the pool area he was already gone.

Shit. Was it first left or first right?

She stood under the clock looking around. To her dismay, there was a door on either side of her.

Typical.

She chose the door on the left. It led into a long panelled passageway that seemed to go on for ever. When she reached a door that, apart from having a handle, looked like it was masquerading as part of the wall, she knew she'd taken a wrong turn.

Thinking that it had to lead somewhere, she was reaching for the handle when she heard a man's deep voice through the panelled door. Hand in midair, she hesitated. She couldn't make out exactly what was being said, but the voice was harsh and had a sarcastic edge. Backing away, she turned and retraced her steps.

This time she tried taking the other door and after a couple of twists and turns, and heaving a sigh of relief, she found the lounge at last.

Cos this is one damn creepy house.

Opening the door, she walked in to find Mark playing games on the television. He looked up and smiled, then went back to zapping the monsters on the screen.

The room fairly took Kerry's breath away. It was fabulous, there was no other word for it, although the pink-and-grey colour scheme was a bit pasty for her liking. For Kerry, bright colours were the order of the day. But to her taste or not, it dripped money.

She noticed some photographs in ornate silver

frames on a small onyx table. Trailing a fingertip along the back of the five-seater pink settee, she reached the table and picked one of them up.

A dark-haired three-year-old boy smiled out at her. Kerry smiled back. Mark, who she was starting to fancy like mad, hadn't changed much. Putting it back, she picked up the next one. This was a family picture, a man, a woman and Mark, who was probably a year younger than in the first photo. The man, obviously Mark's dad, looked familiar, but she couldn't place him. No doubt it would come.

I wonder why Mark hasn't said what his dad does, she thought idly before taking a closer look at the woman who she assumed was his mum.

'Jesus!' In her shock, Kerry dropped the photograph, shattering the glass and sending tiny sparkling shards everywhere.

Mark dropped his control pad and hurried to Kerry's side, leaving the monsters on the screen to take their chance and gobble up everything in sight.

'Have you hurt yourself, Kerry?' Mark asked anxiously, as he grabbed her hand. 'Good,' he said, relieved when he saw it was free from blood. Bending down, he picked the frame up and it was only when he looked back up that he saw Kerry's shocked face.

Her colour had drained away, and for a moment it was as though he was looking at another black-and-white print.

'Kerry.' Gently, he shook her arm. 'Are you all right, Kerry?'

After a moment she focused on him, then violently pushed him away with both hands.

In total Kerry fashion, she held nothing back, blurting out, 'What the fuck's me mam doing on a photo with you and yer dad?'

22

Claire stretched as best she could. Her muscles were
giving her hell, she ached in places she hadn't even
known she had, and the scab forming on her knee
had burst open.

The quiet man had untied them, taken their gags
off and warned them: one sound, and they'd seen
the last of any more food.

Wow, fucking wow, Claire had thought at the time.
*No more cornflakes. How fucking hysterical can yer
get?*

But they had kept quiet, all four of them, huddled
in the corner like lost lambs in a black mountain storm.
She and Jade had risked a few whispers once their
jailers had fallen asleep, and Claire had asked herself
over and over what Kerry would have done in Claire's
shoes. Each time she got the same answer: *she wouldn't
have been so fucking stupid in the first place.*

Once, in the night, she had been woken out of a
fitful sleep by the sound of drunken party-goers
passing by. She had opened her mouth to scream for
help, but Jade had kicked her, nodding furiously at
the two men who had also been woken by the noise
and who were staring threateningly their way. Whilst
it had been very dark in the funeral parlour, a beam

of light from the street lamp had found a chink in the curtains and had glinted off Laughing Man's eyes, giving him the look of some feral nocturnal creature. Claire had shivered, and Jade had whispered in her ear that by the time whoever it was out there gathered their wits about them, they would all probably be dead.

But the long night was at last over, and Claire watched as Laughing Man nudged the door open and came back into the room carrying a tray with four bowls on it.

'Not again,' she moaned softly.

She saw Tracy's leg move and turned her attention from Laughing Man to the girl. She'd had to be force fed yesterday, and she hadn't spoken a word since. Donna wasn't in much better shape.

Claire spent most of her time trying to provoke Tracy into communicating in some way, desperate that she shouldn't give up. She'd tried gently kicking her and knocking her with her shoulders, but nothing seemed to work. Tracy was completely out of it. Jade had tried the same tactics, but with the same result, or rather lack of result. She'd even stared for ages at Tracy's head, as if trying telepathy as a way of getting through to her, but Tracy stayed oblivious, sunk in a world of her own.

When Laughing Man suddenly began to spoon cornflakes into Claire's mouth, she realised that she'd been out of it herself. She tried as hard as she could, but the milk was warm and definitely on the turn. She had always hated warm milk and, without warning, she vomited the lot right back into his lap.

'Yer stupid cow!' he screamed, as he jumped back and knocked the other bowls over. Milk and cornflakes splashed all over the floor, covering his shoes and sending him further into a rage. He ran at the coffins propped against the wall and started punching and kicking them. 'Stupid, stupid little pig! I'm gonna fucking kill yer!'

Claire struggled to her feet. She did the only thing she could, she did what Kerry would do if she had been stupid enough to have been taken captive.

She was running out of the door and climbing the stairs before he, in his rage, had even noticed she'd moved. It was the door slamming shut behind her that gave her away.

Ally had followed Kerry's bus that morning and had been very surprised to see the Rolls-Royce pick her up. He'd driven past the gates and parked the car in front of another very impressive house. *Millionaires' row*, he'd thought, looking about him.

Wouldn't mind a bit of that.

Walking back up the lane, he'd hidden behind a large tree where he had a good view of the entire area and was certain that he wouldn't be seen.

After a couple of hours he grew restless and, deciding that waiting in the car would be a lot more comfortable, he started back. He turned the corner just in time to see his beloved car being towed away.

'Hey!' he yelled, waving his arms in the air as he chased after it, but the pick-up truck kept on going. 'Damn.'

Out of breath, he stopped in the middle of the road and looked about. Spotting an old man mowing the lawn of one of the houses, Ally walked over to him.

'Who phoned the fucking pick-up truck?' he demanded, his thumb pointing over his shoulder in the direction his car had gone.

The old boy shrugged, and kept on mowing the lawn.

'How, yer ignorant old twat. I asked yer a civil fucking question. Are yer daft or what?'

The old man stopped, straightened up, and gave Ally a withering look. 'Resorting to foul language like that will never get you an answer, you ignorant young man.'

'Aw, fuck you!' Ally stomped off along the street.

Back behind the tree he took his mobile out and phoned for one of his brothers to come and pick him up, but just as he was putting the phone away, Kerry burst out of the unicorn-guarded gates. He watched dumbfounded as she raced along the street; she was out of sight before he'd barely had time to blink.

'Jesus Fucking Christ,' he muttered, shaking his head. 'Not a hope in hell's chance of catching that. I wonder what the fuck's spooked her?'

Running faster than she'd ever run before and dodging round anyone who got in her way – apart from the few she actually tried to go through – Kerry melted the pavement all the way to the bus stop. She could see one goal only, and that was home.

A bus was waiting at the terminus and as she ran up she heard it starting to rev its engine. Running alongside as it began to move, she banged on the doors. The bus stopped, the doors opened, and the driver glared down at her.

'Have you any idea how dangerous what you just did is?'

Ignoring him, Kerry jumped on to the platform, and put a one-pound coin and a fifty pence in the tray.

'Newbottle, please.'

Giving her the change, the driver grumbled, 'Couldn't care less, you kids, could yer? Never a please nor a thank you.'

'Just drive the friggin' bus, will yer? The last thing I want's a lecture. And if you'd took the time to listen, I did say please. OK?'

'Right. I don't have to put up with that. Off yer go.'

'What?'

'Yer heard right. Off.'

Looking at the anger in his eyes, and faced with the prospect of a long walk home, Kerry calmed down, realising that she'd probably gone way over the top again. 'Look, mister, I'm sorry, really I am. But I just want to go home. Please, I need to get home.'

The bus driver had teenage daughters of his own and he well knew their mood swings but still, there was no need for blatant cheek. He was about to order her off again when he noticed how bright her eyes were with unshed tears, and although he didn't want to know her problems, real or imaginary, he relented and told her to sit down and shut up.

Kerry sighed. 'Thank you,' she said, pocketing her change and moving down the nearly empty bus.

*The world's full of fucking arseholes, and I have
to meet every one of them.*

Then she felt guilty, she knew it had been her fault
and not the driver's. If her mam had heard her, she
would have murdered her.

Sitting on the back seat, she looked out the
window.

*I hope she's in when I get home. There is no way
she's gonna get away with not telling me the truth now.*

That was her in the photo all right. But Mark was
nearly the same age as Robbie.

How could that be?

Jason Smith didn't know what to do. On the one
hand he had Stevie locked in the back room, alternately cursing him, then begging for gear. On the
other hand, he had the disappearance of Mrs Archer.

Yawning, he glared at the door which barred
Stevie's way. It seemed like the little shit had at last
fallen asleep. He moved the chair which had served
as his bed for the past night and put it in front of
one of the tables. Sometime during the night Mrs
Archer had left, and though he would swear that he
hadn't once shut his eyes, he must have.

Where was she?

He couldn't understand it at all.

He'd let Lily in and she was screaming at him
already to put a new barrel on. It seemed that everyone
screamed at him, and yet he was the only one who
ever did anything around here.

He went down to the cellar and connected a new
barrel. Really the pumps could do with a damn good

clean out, but that would have to wait until the boss woman came back.

Anyhow, after a few halfs, the regulars won't know. Half of them are wankers.

Sighing heavily, he heaved his bulk back up the cellar stairs.

'Where the fuck's the bony bastard at?' he muttered to himself when he reached the bar.

'What?' Davie Wilson, father of six little Wilsons who terrorised the Seahills, asked, sticking his chin forward.

'Nowt. Nowt.'

Jason was wary of Davie, as were most people: the man was a walking mountain. His sons ranged in yearly order from three-years-old to eight-years-old, and all six were streetwise.

'You sure? Cos if yer need me help, you've only got to ask.'

'No, yer all right Davie. Thanks, though.' Jason flung the thanks over his shoulder as he escaped into the yard to feed Jess, who was happily sunning herself in the first real sunshine they'd had in weeks.

He patted Jess's head. 'That's the last thing I need, old girl, Davie Wilson's help. His help, whatever it is, always has a price.'

Jess thumped the concrete yard with her tail, then jumped up and licked his hand as he scooped a tin of dog food into her bowl. He patted her head again. Somehow, Jess always made him feel better.

Inside, Lily placed Davie's fresh pint in front of him. 'Take no notice of him, Davie love, he's a right ungrateful bastard.'

Davie nodded his agreement. Picking his pint up he swallowed two thirds in one gulp before saying, 'Where's the two Hetton slappers then? I thought they worked Saturdays.'

'Something happened to one of their grandas, don't know which one, like. Cos, I can't hardly tell them apart anyhow.'

Jason finished feeding Jess then whispered in her ear, 'I bet the big bastard was sick when he saw it was Lily in today, cos we all know what he's here for and it's not the beer.'

He sniggered, then went to the back gate. Opening it, he looked out as if expecting Mrs Archer to suddenly materialise in the back lane, but it was empty. Grumbling away to himself, he made to shut the gate when a hand appeared and stopped him. He guessed by the colour of the hand that it was Ally.

'Where is she?' Ally demanded. 'I've been ringing her for over a friggin' hour.'

'Search me. I've been here all night babysitting that fucking idiot Stevie. I never even heard her go out. Mind, that bastard was kicking up such a racket, the fucking army could have marched in and out. She didn't come down at her usual time, and I've had to do everything meself.'

'Have yer knocked upstairs?'

'Why aye, man. Do yer think I'm daft, or what? She never answered first thing so I've been up a few times, 'case she was poorly or something.'

'She could have had a heart attack. Yer should have gone in.'

Jason gave him a scornful look. 'Would you have?'

Ally didn't even have to think on that one. 'No. She's as healthy as a horse anyhow.'

Jason couldn't help himself. 'She looks like one an' all.'

They both sniggered, then Jason asked, 'What do yer want her for, like?'

'It's that Lumsdon bitch. I followed her to South Shields. She went into this huge fucking mansion – actually, now I think about it, it might even have been a palace.'

'Oh aye, Prince Charlie moved up here. I don't think so.'

'Well anyhow, a couple of hours later, she hares it outta there like all the fucking demons in hell was after her.'

Jason's face was even more scornful as he looked Ally up and down. 'Don't tell me yer tried to catch her?'

'Do I look fucking daft, or what? I've seen the bitch run before.'

Jason shrugged. 'So, what do yer want me to tell her, if and when Archer shows up?'

'Tell her to ring me mobile, right away. OK?'

'Aye.'

Ally closed the gate behind him just as Lily popped her head round the back door. 'Yer mother's on the phone, Jason.'

Jason grunted his thanks as he hurried in. His mother only phoned when she had a right juicy bit of gossip.

Jason put the phone to his ear while Lily, Davie and Davie's friend Nick who had just joined them watched. After a few minutes Jason said, 'Never.' Then 'Never', again. Three pairs of ears pricked up.

Wiping the bar with her cloth, Lily moved in his direction. He saw her coming, knew what she was after, and turned his back on her. Looking at Davie and Nick, Lily pulled a face. A moment later Jason put the phone down and unlocked the back room, firmly closing the door behind him.

He glowered at Stevie. This piece of crap in front of him had done the one thing he'd had the nerve to refuse Mrs Archer, and that was to sell drugs to bairns. Now, according to Dolly, one of them might be dead.

Stevie was huddled in the corner, staring into space. Even from here Jason could see the sweat oozing out of him. Walking over, Jason kicked Stevie's shin. He moaned, and opened one eye.

'What yer do that for, yer fat freak?' He rubbed his shin, which had been hurting already. Both his legs felt as though they were on fire, part of his withdrawal which he knew would get worse, much worse. Just now his left leg, the one that Jason had kicked, felt as though it had spontaneously combusted and was burning merrily away.

'I'll tell yer what's the matter, shit-head. One of them kids is in hospital on a fucking life-support system. The word is, she might not make it.'

'That's not my fault. The stupid little twat shouldn't have held her hand out, should she?'

'Oh, yer heartless bastard,' Jason kicked him again. 'Do yer want to know something? I fucking hate yer.'

Stevie was clutching both legs in agony now. 'What

for?' He couldn't think of anything he'd ever done for Jason to hate him.

'Are yer for fucking real, or what?'

Stevie still stared perplexedly at him.

'Oh for fuck's sake.'

Jason walked back to the door, he didn't trust himself not to do damage if he was near him. 'Get yerself cleaned up, yer fucking stink.'

'Fuck off. You're not the boss and yer can't keep telling me what to do. I'm fucking sick of it. OK?'

'Aye, why. Yer'll be fucking sicker still if one of them kids blabs.'

Stevie, already grey-looking, went paler still. 'Fucking hell.'

He stood up, but finding himself none too steady on his feet flopped back down again.

'What am I gonna do if one of the little bastards talks?'

'About five years. That's if yer still alive. Cos this kid's got three big brothers, and one of them's a psycho without the aid of fucking drugs.'

'Fucking hell. I can't go to no prison. Where is she? Three big brothers, did yer say? Where the fuck's the Archer freak? She'll have to help me. Get me away . . . where the fuck is she?'

'God only knows.'

Claire managed the stairs out of sheer will-power and raging adrenalin. She opened the first door she came to. The room was dark, and the window was boarded up. Faint light peeped through the cracks, and after a moment she could see.

She was in some sort of storage room and when the vague shadows in the room took shape she realised that it was where they stored coffins.

What to do? Oh God.

Her whole body was trembling.

Where to run?

Help, please help.

These thoughts were running so quickly through her head that it didn't occur to her to shout out loud for help.

Terrified, she looked around again, then noticed there was a space between the coffins lined up against the walls.

Squeeze into there.

Squeeze into there.

He won't find me there.

She took a step forward but very nearly tumbled; her hair had been caught up behind her and she shook her head, frantically trying to get free. Reaching back, she felt for whatever was trapping her, and screamed desperately as her hand met other fingers firmly entangled in her hair.

Then she was yanked backwards, and Laughing Man was breathing heavily in her ear.

'Go on then, scream, bitch,' he muttered as he shook her. 'Give us an excuse. Fuck how much yer worth. Go on – I fucking dare yer.'

Claire froze. He spun her round to face him and grinned madly at her, before letting go of her hair and grabbing her upper arm. She was dragged out of the room and down the stairs in moments.

He hauled her across the floor and threw her

amongst her friends, towering over them as they cowered together. For a moment he stood there and simply laughed.

When he suddenly stopped, the silence was more threatening than the noise he'd been making. Goosebumps broke out all over Claire's body, and she shook uncontrollably.

She was surely dead now.

He began to leisurely unbuckle his belt. Claire could feel Jade's heart beating faster and faster against her shoulder, and her own heart raced as, oh-so-slowly, almost as though he were relishing the act, he pulled his belt through the loops on his jeans. When it was free, he folded it in half and slapped the air in front of him. The loud crack it made caused Claire and Jade, the only two who were really aware what was going on, to whimper.

He moved towards them, laughing once more.

Darren sat on the stairs with his head in his hands, and refused to tell Suzy for the seventy-first time that her new red shoes were class.

Suzy sighed, looked at the shoes with love, then skipped up to her bedroom.

When Emma appeared, dragging her right foot and sniffling for England, Darren jumped up. 'Yer needn't put an act on, cos it's my turn and yer getting nowt till I get some footie boots. OK?' He went outside, slamming the door behind him.

Without an audience, Emma shrugged and walked perfectly well up the stairs.

Darren decided to visit Kenny and with his hands

in his pockets he trudged up the bank towards Newbottle. He was halfway there when he saw Kenny running down towards him.

He waited and as Kenny got closer, Darren realised that the black smudge of muck across his eye wasn't dirt at all, but a hell of a shiner.

'I'm sorry,' Darren said, as Kenny reached him.

But Kenny shrugged his apology off; he had more interesting news. 'Have yer heard about Jilly Belmont?'

'What about her?'

'She might be dead!'

'No! No way! What happened, she have an accident?'

Kenny shook his head and the light dawned on Darren. 'I bet it was one of those Es she got off Stevie.'

'Aye. So they reckon. And if your Robbie hadn't told me sister, it might have been me. And when she found out about Jilly, I got another clout this morning, an' all.'

'Is Jilly really dead?'

Darren could see her on his side in last year's snowball fights. She'd worn a bright yellow puffa jacket. And Jilly's snowballs landed exactly where she wanted them to.

Kenny shrugged. 'Don't know, might be. I hope she's not though, she's all right for a girl. She's in hospital fixed up to some machine, that's what they say, like.'

'Kenny, man, we've gotta do something. I'm gonna tell her brothers who the bastard is what gave it to her. Are yer coming?'

'You must be joking! Snitch on Stevie? We'll be bloody dead, man. Besides, me sis says I've got to keep out of it. Keep me gob shut.'

Darren felt the first stirrings of real fear. He was just a kid, how could he fight drug Barons, or Lords, or whatever they were, all on his own? Knowing his luck, Stevie's dad was probably Mafia.

Would the Mafia bother Kerry?

Would Aliens bother Kerry?

Shit, now he was rambling.

He had to tell Jilly's brothers. She was his friend. And what's more, he would also tell the black copper what was going on. He'd know what to do.

Mind made up, he took off back down to the Seahills.

Kenny watched Darren go and hesitated. He chewed on a nail trying to make up his mind then, as if pulled by an invisible rubber band, he started to follow.

Lacking Kerry's long-distance running techniques, Darren was out of breath when he reached Jilly's house. Holding on to a stitch in his side, he leaned on the gate for a moment before going up the path.

He had already been seen though, and before he reached the door it opened. Jilly's youngest brother, Carl, stood looking down at him. He was well over six feet and for a moment Darren felt scared.

'If yer asking about our Jilly, Darren Lumsdon, she's still holding on. But we appreciate yer concern, an' all. And I'll tell her when she comes round.'

'I . . . I . . . I know who gave her the drugs,'

Darren blurted out. He spoke so quickly that it all sounded like one word.

'What did yer say?' Carl asked suspiciously.

'He knows who gave her the drugs,' Kenny piped up from behind Darren, 'and – and so do I.'

Darren swung round and smiled at Kenny. Relief that he didn't stand alone swept over him as fast as an incoming tide.

'I guess the pair of yer better come in then. Our Beefy'll not want to be missing this, no way.' Stepping back, Carl ushered them into the house and gave his older brother a quick rundown on what the boys had to tell them.

Scowling, Beefy rose out of his chair and the boys found themselves looking up, and then up some more. Darren figured that if Beefy didn't sit back down again, he and Kenny would both end up with stiff necks. If Carl was tall, this guy was a giant, from the tip of his huge feet to his massive shiny bald head. He'd been nicknamed Beefy as a kid, and Darren reckoned that even his family would be hard pushed to remember his real name.

'Your sister still running next week?' Beefy suddenly asked Darren, causing both boys to jump.

'Aye, she is that,' Darren quickly replied.

'Right, lads.' Carl was impatient to get on. 'We want the full story, and nowt second hand. We want to know what youse two have seen for yerselves.'

With back-up from Kenny, Darren told them everything he knew.

'OK, lads, yer done good,' Carl said, on the way

out. 'We won't be forgetting this. If ever yer need us, yer know where we are.'

'What we gonna do if Stevie finds out it's us that grassed him?' Kenny asked as they walked back down the pathway.

Darren shrugged. 'Our Kerry says grassing on drug dealers doesn't count as grassing, cos drug dealers are a pile of shite.'

'Aye,' Kenny replied, rubbing his black eye, 'and I'll bet yer something else an all,' he said with conviction. 'That Stevie can't no way punch as hard as me sister.'

'Aye, yer right. Fuck Stevie Shite.'

23

Mavis placed a bowl of home-made tomato soup in front of Lorraine.

'Get that down yer, pet. I swear if I didn't feed yer, yer wouldn't feed yerself. Food's fuel. Even the boss has got to take time to eat, for Christ's sake.'

Lorraine smiled as she dipped her spoon in the soup, 'Tell that to Clark.'

'I will an' all, the next time I see him.'

'Mam, don't you dare.' Lorraine waved her spoon at Mavis.

Mavis shrugged. 'I might, I might not.'

Lorraine gave her one of her looks. She wasn't sure she was up for banter with her mother right now. Despite her relief at nabbing Brad the previous evening, the bastard was still refusing to talk. She'd left Carter to deal with the lawyer they'd finally had to let him call, and to try to keep wearing down the little prick. She was convinced Brad was the one who'd been last seen with the girls, and by God, she was going to prove it. If only they could start to make some kind of headway on the buried bodies she might feel happier.

She'd only called in at Mavis's for a change of clothes on her way to see the Lumsdons – she felt sure the mother knew more than she was letting on. Might have known that her own mother wouldn't let her go without forcing some food down her.

'So,' Mavis said a moment later around a mouthful of soup, 'anything happening?'

'Not a lot. I think between the headless corpses and the girl in the river, Scottie is nigh on near to cracking up.'

Mavis waved her free hand in the air, dismissing Scottie. 'Scottie cracked up years ago, pet. But surely someone's missing that poor dead girl?'

'Mam, there are hundreds that go missing each year. Worldwide, it'll be in the thousands. And there are tons of reasons why dozens of them don't get reported.'

Mavis frowned. 'Surely not that many.'

Lorraine swallowed some more soup, before saying, 'Sad, isn't it?'

'And are yer trying to tell me that all of them as go missing are murdered? No, it can't be, cos we would never be able to sleep safe in our beds.'

'I'm not saying they're all murdered, Mam, you'd be surprised at just how many missing people don't want to be found. An' then there's the poor kids whose folk have given them away or traded them for whatever reason. They're not likely to turn round and run down the nick to report them gone, are they?'

Mavis shook her head, she'd been down this road before with Lorraine but she still found it acutely depressing. 'I still don't believe that a mother could actually sell her own bairns.'

'Like I've told yer, if that mother is addicted to crack, she'll sell anything. Besides, it's nowt new, selling kids has been going on for thousands of years, all over the flaming planet.'

'Yer don't think that poor girl's mother sold her, do yer?'

'Mam, at this stage we can't know anything for definite. But – an' I hate to say this – I've a feeling that she's linked in to our missing girls, even though there's no real proof that she's owt to do with them.'

'You and yer feelings.'

But Mavis couldn't help but remember how often her daughter's feelings, hunches, or however you wanted to describe them, came true. Except in the case of what'sisname. By God, Lorraine's feelings had failed her miserably there.

As Lorraine and Mavis talked, Vanessa Lumsdon stepped out of Trevor's car. Sandra tried to slip him a couple of quid, but he was having none of it.

Since his mother died, three years ago, Trevor had lived alone in the house he had grown up in. He was forty-two years old, and had never had a date in his life. Blond, and of average build and height, he could have been considered handsome were it not for the livid birthmark that covered half his face. Painfully shy around strangers, he managed to get on well with his neighbours and not one of them suspected just how much he fancied Vanessa.

Carrying Vanessa's small battered suitcase, he followed them both up the path.

'Fancy a cuppa, Trevor?' Sandra asked him.

'No – no thank you.' Trevor put the suitcase on the step, and began to back away. He said goodbye to both women before quickly making his way over to his own house.

They watched his hasty retreat, then looked at each other. Vanessa shrugged as Sandra reached for the door knob but, before she could turn it, the door was thrown open and Robbie stood smiling at them.

'Kettle's already boiled.'

Sandra picked up the case and handed it to Robbie. 'Come on, Vanessa, I'll make the tea, cos I'm not drinking the gnat's piss yer son calls tea.'

Robbie laughed as he took his mother's arm and helped her into the sitting room. When he had her on the settee in front of a well-banked fire, he sat on one of the chairs. 'Now, yer sure yer all right, Mam?'

'Why aye, lad. Pleased to be home.' Vanessa lit a cigarette then sat back and relaxed. Looking around the room she felt as if she'd been away for a year or more and for a moment she almost believed things were normal, that the past was still well and truly buried in the past. And that Claire was safe and sound, and not missing for almost a week.

'Where's our Kerry and the bairns?'

'Kerry went to see a friend. She'll be back any minute. Darren nipped out, said he'd only be a few minutes. And Cal's got Suzy and Emma up the park.'

'Hi, Mrs Lumsdon.' Mickey spoke up from the shadows in the back corner where Vanessa hadn't noticed him.

'I was wondering where you were,' Vanessa smiled.

She liked Mickey and he was around so often that he almost felt like one of her own.

She sighed, and Robbie jumped up from his seat. Draping himself protectively over the arm of the settee, he said, 'Are yer certain yer all right, Mam?'

She patted his arm. 'I'm fine, son. It's good to be home. I only wish . . .' Through her own misty eyes she saw the pain in Robbie's. 'Never mind, pet, we'll get sorted soon. I have to believe that.'

Sandra bustled through with the teas. 'Did yer forget about me, Sandra?' Mickey exaggerated a hurt tone.

'I didn't know yer were there, creep. Get off yer fat arse and make yer own.'

Mickey laughed. 'That's cool, I can do that.'

Sandra was about to come back at him when there was a knock at the door. Robbie went to answer it and found Dolly Smith on the doorstep, a big smile on her face and her arms laden with pies.

Although a born gossip, Dolly was never malicious, and she was truly pleased to see Vanessa home at last. 'I just popped along to see if yer mam was all right.'

Robbie translated this to mean, *I just had to find out what was going on before anybody else.*

'Oh,' she said, as if she'd only just remembered the pies, 'and I baked these for yer all.'

'Come on in, Dolly,' Robbie said, stepping back. Dolly's corned beef and potato pies were legendary and as far as he was concerned she could rabbit on all day for a slice of one.

A few minutes later, settled on the chair Robbie

had vacated to answer the door and armed with a cup of tea and a slice of her own pie, Dolly said, 'Have yer heard about these bodies that's turned up? Shocking, isn't it? An' all of them with no heads.' As usual, she didn't wait for anyone to answer, but rattled straight on. 'And as usual I bet the coppers haven't got a clue, when everybody remembers that old Mrs Holland's son Jack was born with six toes. It was the talk of the place at the time. Some of the oldies said it was a sign of the devil. But Jack wasn't a bad lad, not really, just a bit wild.'

Vanessa's face had turned chalk white at the mention of Jack Holland, but Dolly was too busy tucking in to one of her own pies to notice. She was oblivious to Sandra's warning frown and babbled on for a further ten minutes, extolling the virtues and the faults of the British police force. Just when it seemed as though she'd never get off the subject, she suddenly changed tack and started in on Jilly Belmont.

'What?' Vanessa interrupted her. The bodies had been the talk of the hospital, and she'd cringed every time they were mentioned. She now knew for sure who two of them were, and the memories that had surfaced were torturing her. But this was the first she'd heard about Jilly.

'Is the bairn all right?'

'Well, according to Mr Skillings, they took her off the machines about an hour ago.'

'And?' Sandra demanded.

Dolly shrugged. 'From what Mr Skillings says – and he should know because he was sitting with old Mrs Belmont when they phoned her—'

'For fuck's sake, Dolly, what the hell did he say?' Sandra was trying hard not to throttle Dolly.

'Oh, yes. He says she's gonna be fine.'

Neither Vanessa nor Sandra noticed the look of relief on Robbie's face, and neither dreamed for a moment that as soon as Dolly had mentioned Jilly, he'd thought about yesterday's incident between Darren and Stevie.

Dolly was still prattling on twenty minutes and another cup of tea later. She'd covered the lad next door, Siân Wilkes's shorter-than-short skirts, and was about to offer her services to Sandra for the Residents' Association they had talked about getting under way, when Kerry burst into the house with all the force of a small tornado.

Carter sat across from Brad. In every break in the interrogation Brad returned to whinging about his bruised shins and the absence of his solicitor although, unknown to him, an angry lawyer had actually been sitting outside for the last two hours, whining just as constantly about seeing his client.

Time was moving on and Carter knew they had to break him soon.

'Hungry?' Carter asked, just to change the subject.

'Yer know I'm fucking hungry, yer ginger twat. And I'm gonna sue the fucking socks off yer when I get out of here. Where's me fucking lawyer?'

'I don't think yer can sue somebody when the cooker's broken, can yer?'

'Fucking liar. Yer can bring food in from outside.'

'Oh, far too busy for that. Yer see we have to find

some very young girls, and they're our first priority. Anything could be happening to them. There's some very nasty people out there.'

'Taking the piss, copper, or what? It's me basic human right to be fed.'

'Yer heard the boss. While yer in her nick, yer have no rights. Anyhow, she'll be back to see yer in no time an' you can try telling her that. Sergeant Daniels is just setting up an identity parade, and she won't want to miss that.'

'A what?' Brad's colour drained so fast that he looked like an albino.

'Yer heard me, yer little toe-rag. There's at least three witnesses what saw the bloke who was with the girls before they went missing. And they all reckon they'd know him again anywhere.'

Brad sank his head in his hands. What the fuck should he do? Keep bluffing it out and trust to his luck in a parade? Or try to cut a deal while he still could, and make out that he'd been forced to take part?

A prison sentence from the coppers, or a lifetime sentence from The Man?

Fuck, fuck, fuck.

Carter's boss was at that moment pulling up outside the Lumsdons'; had she been five minutes earlier, she would have witnessed Sandra forcibly removing Dolly in the sweetest of ways.

She heard shouting as she walked up the path and reckoned it would be pointless to knock – there was so much noise coming from inside, there was no chance of being heard – so, opening the door,

Lorraine followed the noise to the sitting room.

The neighbour, Sandra, was standing in the far corner, next to a runaway rubber plant with her hands over her ears. Robbie was stood beside the window with his jaw practically unhinged. Another boy, who she took to be his friend, was in much the same state in the other corner. And Vanessa was sobbing her heart out on the settee with Kerry, hands on hips, standing over her.

'Tell me!' Kerry was screaming at her mother. 'Yer have to tell me who he is! Who is he?' Tears of frustration dripped steadily down Kerry's face as she harangued her mother.

'I can't tell yer, Kerry. Not for the life of me. He'll kill us all,' Vanessa sobbed.

Lorraine's mind spiralled into overdrive as she stepped into the room.

'Well, if it isn't Mrs Robo Cop,' Kerry snarled. 'Who told yer to come in then?' She'd worked herself into such a fury she couldn't think straight.

Ignoring Kerry – she realised the angry teenager was just lashing out – Lorraine said hello to each of them in turn. Vanessa gripped the arm of the settee and looked up at Lorraine with fear in her eyes.

'No, sorry, no news,' Lorraine rushed to reassure her. 'I just called in to see how yer are, Vanessa.'

'Fine, I'm fine,' Vanessa managed, wiping her eyes.

'No yer not, Mam,' Kerry said. 'She's never been fine for years, have yer, Mam?' Without waiting for her mother to answer, Kerry swung back to Lorraine. 'Explain this. What's me mam's picture doing in a strange man's house?'

'Kerry, leave Mam alone,' Robbie interrupted. 'She's just got out of friggin' hospital, let alone airing our business in front of all of Houghton.'

'It's all right, Robbie,' Vanessa said. 'I'll deal with it. It isn't me, Kerry. For the umpteenth time, will yer just listen? I swear, Kerry, I'm gonna clobber yer one in a minute.'

'Mam,' Kerry got on her knees and looked up at her mother's face, 'something funny's going on, and you've got to tell me what. You know what it is, Sandra knows what it is. Hell's flames, everybody but me probably knows. But things have changed now, see.' Her voice rose to a shout again. 'For God's sake, Mam, have you another kid an' a husband we don't know about? Cos it looks to me like I might be falling in love with me own bastard brother!' She shook her head, eyes wild and staring at Vanessa. 'Why's there a picture of you an' this lad an' his dad, holding hands an' all lovey-dovey?'

Vanessa sighed heavily. 'How many times do I have to tell yer? It. Is. Not. Me. All right?'

'For fuck's sake.'

'Now that's enough, girl.' Sandra moved from the corner to try and break things up. 'What do yer think yer doing, browbeating yer mother like that? And I've told yer before, cut the fucking lingo out. With a copper here an' all.'

Vanessa sighed again, then asked, 'Where did yer meet Mark?'

Kerry was thrown for a moment, but only a moment. 'So yer do know him!'

Rocking back on her heels, she gave Robbie an *I*

told you so look. Robbie gaped from one to the other in disbelief.

Knowing she had to answer her daughter, and very aware of Lorraine who was listening with keen interest, Vanessa said, 'The woman in the photo is me cousin Suzanne. We were dead ringers. She died. Cancer. OK? Are yer happy now?'

Reaching out, she gripped Kerry's fingers and stared deeply into her eyes as she desperately tried to convey that what came next was for family ears only.

Kerry got the message at once, and backed off quickly. 'Oh, that Suzanne, the one our Suzy's called after?'

Feeling weak with relief, Vanessa answered, 'Aye, Kerry, that Suzanne.'

'Oh well. That explains it then.' Kerry looked at Lorraine, willing to wait until the family were on their own again, but only till then. 'Cup of tea, Robo Cop?' Despite her obvious distress she smiled awkwardly, and Lorraine realised she meant the nickname as a compliment. She couldn't help but like the kid's cheek, and accepted the remark in the spirit it was given. She well knew the bond between mother and daughter, and knew too that she'd just witnessed a very strong one in action. Whilst she'd very much have liked to find out what all this fuss was about – and in particular who was going to kill who, or whether that was just an expression – she knew that little more was likely to be said in her presence. Whilst Kerry's trust wasn't easily won, she was pretty certain she'd made a breakthrough with the kid, and

375

she decided she'd call back later when things had calmed down. *Aye, an' when the kid'll have ferreted out the truth, no doubt.*

'Sorry, can't stay. I only called in for a minute as I was passing.'

Vanessa smiled at Lorraine. The policewoman had visited her a couple of times late at night in the hospital and, much to her surprise, she'd found herself liking the woman. But not enough to trust her with what she knew. No way.

'Thanks,' she said, 'an' sorry about—'

'Shhh now. Think nothing of it. By God, you should see me an' my mam when we go at it. I'll call back later when it's quieter, OK?' Lorraine saw herself out, and felt the silence following her.

Kerry managed to restrain herself for all of five seconds after hearing the door close. Tea-makings thrown to one side, she stormed straight back into the sitting room and, sitting down next to her mother, demanded – albeit in a gentler tone – to know the truth.

Vanessa was hesitant at first. She'd kept it all hidden for so long and had prayed that this day would never come.

But now it had. It was right here in her face and, what's worse, in circumstances right out of her worst nightmare.

How on earth had the pair of them met in the first place?

And just how deeply is Kerry involved with Mark?

For God's sake. What a bloody mess.

She could feel Kerry becoming edgy and, with a

376

sigh felt by everyone in the room, Vanessa launched into her tale.

'My cousin Suzanne was married to Mark's father.'

'So,' Kerry butted in, 'that means Mark's only me half cousin.' Her voice rose with happy excitement. 'That's all right then, isn't it? Isn't it, Mam? I mean, we're not even full cousins. I'm sure that's all right.' Clapping her hands, she smiled at everyone in the room.

Vanessa, unable to bear her daughter's happiness, shook her head. 'Wait, Kerry, there's a hell of a lot more.'

Taking a deep breath and faltering every once in a while, Vanessa carried on and finally told the story she'd kept close to her chest for all these years.

'Suzanne was never very strong. Even before she had cancer, when him, with all his money, couldn't help her one bit.' She took another breath.

'Richard Kingston was an only child and his folks were that rich, we couldn't even begin to imagine. His mother died when he was nine. Or maybe ten. But don't feel sorry for him, he doesn't want, nor does he need – and he certainly doesn't deserve – anybody's pity. I met Richard's father once, and believe me I was pleased never to meet him again. I know Suzanne didn't like him. But however big a bastard his old man was, it's not enough to explain the son. Anyhow, I didn't know when I met him just what sort of business he was into, and neither did Suzanne, cos believe you me, she'd never have married into it. The whole family's been crooked for years – you name it, they're in it – and if yer had any idea of the big knobs they've got in their pockets, yer wouldn't believe it.' She paused a moment, remembering.

'Anyhow, the old man died, and not long after that our Suzanne went too. And Richard . . .' She hesitated, her face blushing. 'I feel crap telling yer all this, but it's why it all happened. Well Richard . . . well, he, er, he thought he could have me as a kind of substitute Suzanne.'

There was stunned silence for a moment, then Robbie blurted out, 'The creep! The fucking dirty creep.'

Vanessa smiled sadly at her eldest son although her heart was breaking and she dreaded telling the rest.

'Now I know this is gonna sound corny, but Big Robbie and me really loved—'

'Mam,' Kerry interrupted, 'this does sound corny.'

'Aye why,' Vanessa hesitated, hating what had to come next, especially as Kerry was haring down the wrong track, 'I was only gonna say that Big Robbie an' me had a good thing together, but anyway . . . once or twice after Suzanne died I visited the house, to check things were OK. Mark and Robbie were toddlers together and had always got on well, and I felt that sorry for the poor kid without his mother. All this was when I thought Richard Kingston was all right. He once offered Big Robbie a job, but he refused it and wouldn't say why, although I can guess now what the bastard was trying to put him up to. Anycase, it soon became obvious which way the wind was blowing, so of course I stopped going. But then it began to get frightening. He started sending presents, really expensive ones – the sort Big Robbie could never afford in a month of Sundays.' Little Robbie made to ask a question, but Vanessa carried on.

'I sent them all back. But he even, believe it or not, booked a holiday in America, just for me, him, and the two kids. Of course I refused to go, and he didn't like that one little bit. He was used to having it all his own way, see, and it was round about then that I began to realise just how many people were frightened of him. Anyhow, then Big Robbie lost his job and the debts began to pile up.' Vanessa took a very deep breath. 'And well, unknown to us, Richard Kingston bought the debts, then demanded me in payment.'

'Right, that's it. I've heard enough,' Robbie shouted. 'I'm gonna kill the bastard! Kerry, get yer coat on. I want to know where the fucking freak lives.'

Vanessa grabbed hold of his arm. 'Please, son, sit down, or I won't tell yer the rest of it. But you've gotta promise me yer won't do anything daft. Yer no match for that man and the kind of people he knows. None of us are.'

'How can I promise yer that, Mam? After what the bastard's done, how can I?'

Robbie was close to tears, but Vanessa's spilled over first. She sobbed for a few moments, then managed to get control of herself. 'Because yer have to, Robbie. Because he'll kill the lot of us if yer once go near him.'

'Who does he think he is,' Kerry burst out, unable to keep quiet any longer, 'the fucking Mafia?'

'The Mafia doesn't worry this man, pet. Believe me, he's beyond them. He can – and will – have us murdered in our beds, and that's the truth.'

'Well, it just keeps on getting more and more weird, if yer ask me. What did yer cousin get involved with the likes of him for? She must have been a right stupid bitch. At the end of the day it's because of her that we're in this state now.'

'Suzanne would die all over again if she knew what had happened. She was kept away from the seedy side of his business – we both were. But there's a lot more.'

'For fuck's sake. How much more can there be? Jesus Christ.'

'There'll be no more if I hear that kind of language out of yer mouth again!' Vanessa glared at Kerry, as she licked her dry lips.

'Sorry, Mam.'

Vanessa's eyes lingered on Kerry, before moving on to Robbie. She wondered if they could take the whole truth. She knew though that if she didn't tell them everything, they might be tempted to go digging on their own. She looked back at Kerry. *Might's the wrong word. This one will, for sure.*

'What I'm gonna tell yer now, must *never* leave these four walls.' She looked at Sandra, then at Mickey.

Sandra nodded and Vanessa thought how grateful she was to have her as a friend. If there was a God somewhere, he had sent Sandra for her to lean on.

Mickey shuffled his feet. 'If yer want me to go, Mrs Lumsdon, that's cool. And I promise I'll never tell anybody what I already heard.'

'I know yer won't, Mickey. That's why yer here. Now sit down somewhere and stop fidgeting, will yer?' Mickey sat.

Vanessa sighed, still weighing the pros and cons but also taking time out to search for words that wouldn't hurt. There were none.

She decided that the only way was the straight-forward truth. She would have to pick up the pieces later. She went for it.

'Robbie. When we couldn't pay the debt, and to get back at me for defying him, Richard Kingston had your father murdered. I'm sorry, son, but there is no kind way of putting it.'

Robbie stood up and began pacing backwards and forwards, his face frozen with shock.

The floodgates had opened and Vanessa went on. 'I'm pretty certain that one of the bodies is his. And I know for a fact that one of them is Jack Holland, who refused to kill you.'

Robbie found his voice, but it was full of aston-ishment as he blurted out, 'Kill me? Yer mean Mark's dad was gonna have me murdered? He was like some sort of uncle, and he was gonna have me murdered?'

'Now yer have an idea of what sort of person he is, and what we're dealing with here.'

Kerry stared at her mother. The look on her face would have been no different if Vanessa had suddenly announced that she was a rich heiress and that she'd chosen poverty as a way of life.

'So', Kerry said, after a moment's deliberation, 'are we talking about my dad an' all? Are you saying that I've gone an' fallen for someone whose dad had my dad killed?'

'Pet, I know I've always let you believe that Robbie's dad was yer dad. But I'm sorry, he wasn't.'

'Well who the bastard hell was, then?'

Vanessa was silent for a minute; if she ever needed a drink, now was the time. And if she got through the next half an hour without one, she'd be teetotal for the rest of her life.

'Well?' Kerry said impatiently.

'Richard Kingston.'

'What?' Kerry screamed.

Vanessa burst into tears and covered her face with her hands.

'Please, Kerry, please don't hate me. He raped me the night they came for Big Robbie. There was nothing I could do, nothing at all. He would have murdered Robbie with his own lily-white hands if I'd tried to stop him, though I fought for all I was worth.'

For a moment there was a silence so heavy you could almost feel it. Then Kerry screamed, an unearthly cry like nothing they'd ever heard before. At the top of her lungs she began yelling, 'No! No!' over and over again. She ran into the kitchen and picked up everything she saw and began smashing it against the walls. Cups, plates, kettle, saucepans – in the red haze that surrounded her, nothing was sacred. When the kitchen was all but demolished she did the only thing she could. She ran.

In the shocked silence she left behind, a sob exploded into the room. Vanessa looked over at Sandra who was crying quiet tears. The sob had come from Mickey who sat with his head in his hands, his slim shoulders heaving.

'Why didn't yer tell the coppers, Mam?' Robbie pleaded. 'Why didn't yer just tell the coppers?'

Vanessa sighed. 'Because you and me would never have seen daylight again. If I hadn't sworn on your very life. He said he would make me life hell and the bastard's been true to his word. But it's water under the bridge now. It all happened years ago. And nowt good ever comes of raking old muck up. I wish to God you'd none of you ever had to find out.'

Standing up, she went over to her son and took his hand. 'I had to think of you, Robbie. Yer were so little. Yer had to have a chance. That's all I thought of, Robbie, you.'

Darren and Kenny had gone straight from the two Belmont brothers to the police station where they'd hesitatingly asked for the black copper. It turned out that there were at least half a dozen black policeman at the station, but through a process of elimination they'd managed to make it understood just who they wanted to see.

The desk sergeant had tried to bully them into telling him what they wanted him for, but they'd steadfastly refused to speak until Luke arrived back from collecting Katy and the other witnesses for the parade.

Seeing the two small boys in reception, Luke

imagined it was going to be a tale of playground bullying or a stolen football, but within minutes he realised the seriousness of the story they had to tell and radioed for Lorraine.

By the time Lorraine arrived back at the station, Luke had put out a warrant for Stevie, and only half an hour later they'd pulled together a raid on the Blue Lion where he was known to hang out.

As the three police cars screamed to a halt outside the pub they little realised they had an onlooker, for a forlorn Kerry sat at the top of Table Rock and gazed miserably down at the scene below. She had run herself into the ground and now sat, flanks heaving and yet unable to stop sobbing even to draw breath. The sight of Stevie and Jason being driven away distracted her for a moment and she whispered, 'Good fucking riddance,' between her tears, before slumping back down with head on her knees.

She didn't know what to do, or what to say.

Or even what to think.

It was one thing to be told that your father was not the man yer thought, but someone else entirely.

Then, in the next breath, to have it dumped on yer that the same man was a gangster, worse even than the Mafia.

And then to top it all, yer told that he'd murdered the man yer thought was yer dad. And that he'd raped yer mother.

Me dad's a murderer. An' me mam never wanted me. No wonder she fucking hates me – must remind her every day of what that bastard did.

The whole business was a fucking nightmare.

And Mark, the very first boy she'd ever fancied, what about him? She moaned softly, then yelled to the wind, 'He's me fucking brother! For Christ's sake! And we've both got a murdering bastard for a father.'

She punched the grass over and over as hot angry tears coursed down her face. She knew in her heart of hearts that Vanessa didn't really hate her, but her world had fallen apart and her thoughts raced around as she desperately tried to make sense of it all.

No wonder our Robbie couldn't get a job, poor bastard. I bet that evil sod's been ruling all our lives an' we never even knew it.

As she cursed the man who had ruined her mother's life and who she simply couldn't bear to think of as her father, she thought back to the black and white photograph she'd seen at Mark's that morning. Something else was nagging away at her, something more than Suzanne's resemblance to her mother. She worried and worried, picturing the family group and Richard Kingston's arm around his wife and child. And then it came to her, she knew she'd half recognised Kingston in the picture.

That's the bastard what was watching me run. The fucking creep.

Kerry took some deep breaths to try to calm herself. Standing up, and looking towards the Seahills she thought, *Talk about fucking family secrets, this one's got to be the secret of the century.*

Slowly she set off for home. Although her heart was quieter, it was heavy with remorse.

I've fucked up big time again.

There's nearly nowt left of the kitchen, and none of this was really me mam's fault.

It's all that fucking madman's fault.

An' our Claire's still missing, an' God knows what's happened to her.

Kerry couldn't stop the tears starting up again. For the life of her she could think of no way to make everything come straight.

24

Claire and Jade were both seriously worried for Tracy. Her breathing sounded strange, and the cut above her right eye was still bleeding. Donna was doing her usual low moan, and seemed scarcely to have taken in what had gone on.

When Laughing Man had freaked out, Claire had lunged to the right and Jade to the left. Donna, through luck more than anything else, had also got off lightly. But Tracy, lost in her own little world where none of this was happening, had taken the full brunt of the assault.

Over and over he'd lashed out. Each time the thick black leather belt landed, Tracy's body had jerked like a wooden puppet whose strings were being pulled by an epileptic puppeteer.

The last lash had been so furious, and given with such force, that the belt had snapped out of his hand and the buckle had caught Tracy's face.

If the other man hadn't come back at that moment, Claire knew he would have picked the belt right back up and carried on with the beating until Tracy was dead. Then he would have started on the rest of them. She had never in her entire life seen anyone in such a rage. If she wasn't already terrified by the situation they were in, what he'd done to Tracy would probably have frightened her to death.

And now, along with the horror, came the guilt. If she hadn't tried to do a runner, Tracy wouldn't be in the state she was in now. Thank God the other man had managed to calm the maniac down: at least she was still alive.

She watched as the quiet man lit a spliff up, took a long draw, then handed it over. Laughing Man, still muttering angrily, took it before retreating to the far corner. But Claire could tell that his fire was far from out by the tense way he held himself, and the way he stamped his feet when he walked.

His anger was only smouldering and she knew it could flare up again at any time. She tried to curl up tighter to lessen the chances of being his next victim, and she saw the other man put a finger to his lips in a warning gesture. He then looked back at Tracy and stared at her for a minute, as if he were calculating her loss in sterling. Shrugging, he took his coat off and threw it over her quiet, still body.

When he turned and walked back to his friend, Claire risked a peek at Donna. She'd noticed earlier that Donna was starting to get the same hopeless look in her eyes that Tracy had worn for days, as if all hope was gone, and there was nothing left to do but shut down.

Claire feared she was right.

Quietly, she struggled to sit up, biting her lip to trap the groan that threatened to escape as every joint and muscle in her body screamed its pain.

Resting her aching head in her hands she thought over what she'd learned today.

They were to be sold at midnight. She'd gleaned that much when the quiet man had been arguing with his freaky friend.

Who the hell to – or even where to – was anybody's guess. And the thought terrified her. Midnight.

Would she still be sane by then?

Had others before her experienced the same horror? What had happened to them?

Claire's body began to tremble, and it felt as if her mind was doing the same.

She would never see her family again.

Never have to be the first one up in the morning to get to the bathroom before one of the others claimed it.

Never sit on dark nights, when there was no money left to put the electric on, and eat crisps whilst listening to the stories she used to think were so boring. Darren's bloodthirsty alien tales, Suzy's garbled ramblings about fairies, and Emma's constant Three Little Pigs.

And then it would be her turn to hold the story-stick. So what if Kerry used to pretend to yawn her head off. She'd give anything to be back there right now, she'd even promise never to row with her sister again.

She started to cry then. Silent, pointless tears, as she realised that her *nevers* were countless, and that her *might bes* didn't exist any more.

She flopped down like a discarded rag doll, and curled up into a ball. She knew, way down deep, that she was going the same way as the girls who huddled beside her.

During the last five days she had gone through every human emotion possible.

But now – now there was no hope left. Nothing.

Back at the station, Lorraine had broken Stevie in less than five minutes. A wrap of heroin was all it had taken. Just the sight of it had him babbling like a five-year-old, home from his first day at school and anxious to tell every minute of it to Mam.

He'd screamed when Lorraine dropped it on the floor. And again when she'd used her heel to grind it into the carpet. Flinging himself after it, he twisted his body like a world-class contortionist as he tried to lick the carpet.

Shaking his head in disgust, Luke picked him up and put him back on the chair.

'So,' Lorraine said, 'yer selling the kids drugs, are yer?'

'It's not me. It's Mrs Archer. She threatened to kill me if I didn't do it. It's her yer want. Her and that Brad. And Jason Smith's nicking outta the bandits.'

He'd added this in a desperate attempt to deflect attention away from himself but he needn't have worried, at the mention of Brad both Lorraine and Luke exchanged a glance. If Stevie knew Brad, then it could mean they were on the home straight.

'Tell me more,' Lorraine demanded. 'Who's this Brad, and what do yer know about him?'

Stevie's eyes took on a cunning look. 'What's it worth?'

Lorraine was up out of her chair and had him by the throat in seconds. Shaking him, she yelled in his face, 'What's it fucking worth? Four kids' lives could depend on you, yer little bastard, an' if you think I've time to play your games, you're fucking dreaming, lad.'

Stevie shook, he was no match for Lorraine and minutes later it was all over. In an attempt to save his own skin, he'd sung like the proverbial bird. He'd not only fingered Mrs Archer for the drug dealing, but also told them everything he'd overheard about the sordid trade in human flesh, and where it was due to take place. A disgusted Lorraine ordered him to be charged and taken back down to his cell.

Just seconds after a snivelling Stevie was led away, Carter burst into the room, a huge grin on his face. 'Boss,' he said, before she had a chance to ask him what he wanted, 'Katy Jacks has positively identified Brad.'

Lorraine punched the air in her excitement and spun round to face Luke.

'Yer know what, Luke? We're finally fucking there. I just hope to God we're in time.'

Darren arrived home from the police station to find Kerry on her hands and knees in the kitchen, picking up a mound of broken crockery.

'What's happened here, Kerry? A spaceship landed on the place?'

'I'll give yer spaceship, yer muppet. Piss off.'

Darren didn't have to be told twice – Kerry was obviously in one of her moods.

'Hi, Mam,' he yelled, as he bounded into the sitting room. Seeing Emma and Suzy cuddled up to Vanessa, he flung himself amongst them.

Vanessa ruffled Darren's hair. 'Hi yerself, son. High five.' They slapped hands in mid air.

A second later Sandra walked in holding a carrier bag. 'Here, Robbie,' she passed the bag over, 'there's some odd cups and plates that I was gonna throw out. A couple of them's chipped, but they'll do the trick till yer get some new ones.' She didn't add, *whenever that might be*, though she guessed rightly that Vanessa was thinking along the same lines.

'Sandra, yer never throw anything out,' Vanessa accused her, with a warm smile on her face. And Sandra noticed how much younger and fresher her friend looked, now that her secret was told.

'So,' she shrugged, 'I was gonna do a car-boot sale. I can easily save up some more stuff.'

'Want some pie, kids?' Robbie asked. 'Now that we've got some plates to put it on, like.'

'What sort of pie?' Emma asked suspiciously.

'From Dolly.'

'Yeah!' all three of them shouted.

'Is the lass back yet?' Sandra all but whispered.

Vanessa nodded, and pointed to the kitchen. Darren didn't miss the exchange, but at that moment his curiosity was held at bay by two facts. The first, that his mam was finally home. The second, that he was about to have some of the best pie in the world.

When Robbie came back from the kitchen, Vanessa

took the opportunity to disengage herself from the younger ones and went through.

When she walked in Kerry dropped the bag of broken crockery and flung herself into her mother's arms.

'I'm sorry, Mam,' she sobbed, 'but it's just too much. How can he be allowed to get away with it? What he's done is horrible.'

'I know, I know, pet. But believe me it happens. Some people do get away with murder and, the sad thing is, there's very little we can do about it. We don't stand a chance with the likes of him.'

'But I still don't understand.'

'Fear, pet. Fear and money. That's what the world runs on. Who's gonna stand up and shop the likes of him when he can reach just about anywhere? It's not like me and Sandra having a blazing row that we sort out ourselves, then forget about. Not him, pet. He forgets nothing.' She shook her head sadly.

'Suzanne told me once, when the blinkers had started to come off and before either of us realised just how bad he was, that he kept a book full of people's names. It went way back to when he was a kid – one or two were even old teachers of his that had upset him in some way.'

'That's sick.'

'True. But at the start he was always so charming in front of me and Suzanne. The only thing I ever remember them having words over was his safari trips. Our Suzanne loved animals and couldn't bear to see him hunt them, let alone have them stuffed and mounted and kept about the place.'

'Aye, an' I don't blame her. I'd've felt the same an' all. He's sick, Mam, really sick.'

Vanessa nodded. 'Just remember, people like him manage to keep themselves above the law. They get others to do their dirty work while they live in their own world, what the likes of us can only dream about. People like him, they take what they want, when they want it.'

'But he didn't get you, Mam, yer stood up to him.'

'Yeah, and look at the price I paid. He won in the end.'

'No he didn't. That's the point, can't yer see? You didn't give him anything, Mam. He stole it.'

Vanessa looked at Kerry strangely for a moment as she thought over what she had just said. Then, shaking her head, she smiled. 'Out of the mouths of babes.'

'What?'

'An old saying, pet. Come here.'

She held out her arms and Kerry threw herself into them. Still cuddling her mother she asked, 'Mam, do yer think The Man could be behind our Claire being missing?'

'No, love, that's all in the past. Just put him out of yer head.'

'I bet yer one thing though, Mam, Robo Cop woman wouldn't be frightened of the likes of that broken brain.'

'Kerry,' Vanessa panicked at where Kerry's mind was taking her and she had a sudden yen to reach for a bottle, any bottle. Taking a few deep breaths, and firmly putting her mind on the problems at hand, she resisted the urge and said, 'Yer must promise me, Kerry, that yer won't ever tell her. Raking up what happened won't do any of us any good. Promise me.'

'OK, I won't.'

If Vanessa was slightly suspicious of how easily Kerry had capitulated, she kept it to herself, not wanting to lose the closeness she had just gained.

Lorraine and Luke came to a stop up the street from the funeral parlour. Luke counted the unmarked police cars and reported, 'All here, boss.'

'Good. Would yer look at that. Who would have thought it, eh? A fucking funeral parlour. God knows what state those poor lasses are in. Be prepared, Luke, we could find anything.'

Lorraine opened her door and stepped out, giving the signal for the dozen armed police surrounding the building to move.

Claire had been dreaming of home – freezing cold nights and fighting over the quilt, before giving in and cuddling up to her sisters. Fighting Darren for the last slice of toast, only to have it snatched out of her hands and quickly devoured by Emma. Their once-a-year trip to Seaburn Beach became mixed up in her mind with blackberry picking, Emma's whole face stained purple. And Kerry running round the track, her feet banging harder and harder on the ground. *Bang. Bang.* She stirred and softly moaned as Kerry's feet grew bigger and bigger, and banged the ground all the harder.

She opened her eyes. It was dark, very dark, and

the noise was overwhelming. Drained of energy, she slowly pulled herself into a sitting position, too weak even to feel the pain.

She'd thought days ago that her heart was about as low as it could go, but now she realised it had one more floor.

She rubbed her eyes but even that took some doing, and with a deep sigh she dropped her arms back down. This was the end of the line and she knew she just couldn't fight any more.

They've come for me.

She sobbed helplessly. It wasn't fair, it just wasn't fair. She'd done nothing to deserve this.

'Please, please I just want to go home,' she murmured, as her soft sobs began to sound like a lost three-year-old's. Then there was another loud bang, and for a brief moment the room lit up.

Claire gasped. It looked as though right in front of her Laughing Man was being pulled to the ground and handcuffed, but it couldn't possibly be true.

She shook her head and gave one last sob before curling back in on herself as her mind, as starved of energy as her body, discounted what she'd just seen and tried instead to convince her that she must be dead. Then the most beautiful of angels, blonde hair cascading over her shoulders, bent down and smiled at her.

Claire could see the pity in the angel's eyes as she leaned over her, and she reached up with her hand to touch the lovely face. 'Thank you,' she said, just before she closed her eyes.

25

'Mam.'

'What, Darren?' Vanessa looked up from the newspaper she was reading to try to take her mind off things, especially the constant longing for just a tiny tipple.

'Them two coppers is coming up the path.'

Vanessa frowned. 'This late? Let them in, son, there's a good lad.' She crossed her fingers as she whispered the same words that many a parent missing a child has said over and over again. 'Please, God. Please let it be good news. Let them have found me bairn safe and well.'

She knew deep down inside that if Claire was hurt or, God forbid, dead, it would be the end of her. She could take no more.

A moment later, Lorraine and Luke were in the doorway and smiling round at all the anxious faces.

Vanessa, heart bouncing off her ribs like a brick on a pendulum, and finding it increasingly hard to breathe, slowly rose from her chair. She took a step towards Lorraine.

Lorraine stepped further into the room, her smile growing wider by the second. Then she nodded.

'Oh!' Overcome with emotion, Vanessa brought

her hand to her mouth. Her legs wobbled, and Luke moved quickly past Lorraine just in time to catch her. Gently he helped her back into her chair.

'She's gonna be all right, Vanessa,' Lorraine said. 'She's in the hospital and I've come to fetch yer to go an' see her.'

'Me an' all!' A chorus of Lumsdons, who had similarly been holding their breath. Suddenly the din was overwhelming, as they all jumped up and started dancing around. Lorraine covered her ears as Suzy ran to her and flung her arms around her waist.

Grinning, Mickey tried the same thing and with a smile Lorraine warningly wagged her finger at him.

Luke stayed behind to wait for Kerry who had gone to see her trainer. Vanessa might think that her daughter was going to let the past stay buried, but Kerry was determined to keep digging away. She couldn't rid herself of the sight of Richard Kingston watching her at the race track, and was convinced that Stan knew more than he'd let on.

Luke looked forward to telling Kerry that her sister was safe; passing on good news was something that didn't happen too often in this job. While he waited for her to show, he sat on the step and watched the tiny world of the Seahills revolve around him. The squad cars carrying the Lumsdons, Sandra and Mickey had barely cleared the street before he saw Josh Anderly bouncing off each garden wall as he made his way home from another session. Anderly lived round the corner with his five sons who ranged in age from six to seventeen.

Although the man was drunk practically every day of his life, Luke felt sorry for him. It hadn't always been this way. Maria, his wife, had been killed four years ago in a hit-and-run, and they still hadn't found the bastard. It seemed the only way Anderly could cope was looking at the world through the bottom of a glass.

Thankfully he was on the whole a placid drunk. Luke had only once seen him lose control, and that was over a year ago when he'd come to collect his fourteen-year-old, Chris, from a three-hour stint at the station. The lad had been caught shoplifting in Woolworths, and they hadn't even left the nick before it blew up. Anderly had moved so quickly that neither Luke nor Chris had seen the fist, until it landed fair and square on the boy's jaw. His spell in custody had been followed by another three hours in casualty, but only a week later Chris had got himself a paper-round and found some new friends. He had never been in trouble since.

Luke grinned as Anderly fell sideways through an open gate. It took him a few minutes to pick himself up, all the while heaping curse after curse on the hapless gate. Then he was bouncing back along the street, happy as Larry.

Sunday would be a different day though. On Sunday mornings the whole family visited Maria's grave. From eleven o'clock onwards the station was besieged with phone calls demanding to know if the useless bastard coppers had found his wife's murderer yet.

Dolly Smith, head down and walking faster than

she'd done in years, was the next to make an appearance. No doubt on her way to the station to bail out her son Jason.

She had no need to worry, her precious little boy had managed to keep his nose clean. They had nothing to hold him on unless Mrs Archer turned up and pressed charges against him for pilfering from the bandits, and somehow neither Luke nor Lorraine thought that would happen.

All they had a chance of pinning on him was illegal dog-fighting, and even if they made that stick – and if the case ever came to court – at most he'd get a year's probation, or community service.

Stevie though, even at his tender age, was definitely looking at a number of years. And Brad and his accomplices should, in a fair world, get for ever. That would be in a fair world though, in a place where the guilty were treated as such, and not in this world where more and more often the victim paid the main price, and where life sentences rarely meant life.

The head honcho, however, looked like he would escape once more. No one would name him; they all claimed they did their business solely through Mrs Archer who, frustratingly, had completely disappeared. Warrants had been issued and there were checks in place at airports and ferry terminals, but Luke wasn't convinced that they'd find her. Although – and he smiled at the memory of it – Lorraine had personally vowed never to rest until she was caught, claiming that once she'd got her she'd literally shake out of her who was masterminding the whole bloody set-up. He knew that Lorraine thought it was the same gang boss who'd got away all those years ago, and Luke was inclined to agree with her.

Lorraine. Her name conjured up her vision. Luke was madly in love with her, and had been since the first day he'd met her. *Not that she'd look twice at me. Why should she, when she's married to that handsome rat of a husband?*

Luke knew that something was troubling Lorraine deeply, and it hurt that she hadn't confided in him. They had been through a lot together over the years, and he couldn't believe that she didn't know that she could have his shoulder any time and that he'd keep it quiet. He could only think that she didn't trust him enough, and that made him sick to his heart.

Sighing, he looked back up from the clump of weeds he'd been staring at, and saw Mr Skillings talking to two of Jilly Belmont's brothers. The younger one was making threatening gestures, though it was obvious they were not aimed at Mr Skillings, but describing in graphic detail just what was gonna happen to the drug-dealing bastard who'd put his sister in hospital, when he found him.

Thank God the kid was gonna be all right. And God help Stevie, if this brother ever got his hands on him.

Ten minutes later, his thoughts back on his boss and softly humming the Eagles' hit 'Hotel California', he saw Kerry enter the top of the street. For once she wasn't running, and Luke noted how deep in thought she seemed to be.

*   *   *

Kerry had badgered her trainer mercilessly. But Stan had been adamant that he didn't know the man in the posh car who'd visited the track a few days ago.

No, he definitely hadn't been before.

No, he hadn't said anything else.

'In a pig's eye,' Kerry muttered, as she opened the gate and walked up the path, totally oblivious to everything around her.

He had definitely been the man in the picture with Mark and Suzanne. Stan Bloody Lying Mayfield could deny it till he was blue in the face. *That's the bastard all right. I knew there was something fishy about the twat.*

'Hello, Kerry.'

Kerry jumped. The last thing she'd been expecting was to find a copper parked on her doorstep. 'Christ, yer nearly give me a heart attack.' Then she saw a hint of gold as Luke smiled. Her heart quickened and she held her breath for a moment, before bursting out with a victorious shout, 'You've found her!'

Luke nodded. 'Yup. She's safe and well, and I've been waiting bloody ages for you to show.'

'Where is she?' Kerry couldn't stop herself skipping from foot to foot, all thoughts of The Man shelved for the moment.

'She's in the hospital.' He held his hand up when her face dropped. 'It's all right, just for a day or two. She's going to be fine.'

Kerry was finding it hard not to grab this fantastic man and simply hug him to death. 'Have Mam and the others gone already?'

'A good half hour ago.'

'Ha'way,' she yelled, turning and running back down the path, 'get a move on! There's no time to mess about.'

Smiling, Luke followed her to his car.

Darren finally managed to push everyone out of the way and grab hold of Claire's hand. He knew he had a stupid grin on his face that no way could he wipe off, but it felt so good to see her. He felt over the moon – and then some.

'Hi, Darren.' Claire smiled weakly at him, feeling every bit as chuffed to see him as he was to see her. During the last hour her heart had soared from the basement to the penthouse.

'Hi yerself, sis,' was all he could think to say, gripping her hand so tightly it threatened to cut all circulation off.

'So how are the other girls, pet?' Vanessa asked, gently smoothing Claire's hair down, scarcely able to believe that her daughter had been given back to her.

'They say Jade's gonna be all right, same as me. And Donna probably will be too, after she's had a chance to rest. But they won't tell me anything about Tracy.' She grabbed her mother's hand. 'I'm really worried about her, Mam. Can yer find out what's going on?'

Entering the room in time to hear Claire's last question, Lorraine said quietly, 'She's very sick, Claire. The poor kid had a hell of a beating. And it seems she's locked in on herself, probably doesn't

403

even know she's been rescued. But later on tonight they're gonna move Jade in here with you, and they want the pair of you to visit with Tracy to try to help bring her back from wherever she's hiding.'

Claire didn't say anything, but she sank back in the bed and her eyes filled with tears. Despite her joy at seeing her family, she was still incredibly fragile, and whilst the doctors had confirmed that her physical condition was amazingly good in the circumstances, they'd warned that it might take a long time for the mental scars to heal.

'It's all right, pet.' Vanessa cradled Claire's head. 'You're safe now.'

'I know, Mam, it's just like, oh – I really love you all. And I, I thought they were gonna take me away, and that I'd never see you all again.' Huge racking sobs threatened to choke her as she held on tight to her mother.

Emma sniffed, before saying, 'Do yer reckon yer love me enough to give me yer pocket money for the rest of the year?'

'Me too!' Suzy piped up.

This made them all smile, including Claire, who replied, 'Not that much.'

The smiles turned to laughter, which Kerry heard as she came down the corridor. She grinned at Luke. 'That sounds good, man.'

Luke nodded his agreement as they walked into Claire's room. He looked at Lorraine but she was already saying her goodbyes and refused to meet his eyes as she left the room.

Kerry stood for a moment, taking in the sight of

her sister, safe and relatively unharmed. She shook her head before saying, 'Jesus, kiddo, for a while I thought I was never gonna see yer stupid moany face again.'

'Yeah, same here,' Claire said, then yawned her head off. 'That soup was delicious, but now I feel blown out.'

'Cardboard would taste delicious after a diet of flaming cornflakes!' Vanessa patted Claire's hand.

'Cornflakes?' Kerry said.

'That's about it.' Claire's eyes were beginning to droop. She yawned again and a moment later she was fast asleep.

Mark packed his suitcase, his mood swinging from sadness to anger then back again. He'd not slept a wink last night, and his eyes felt as though they were full of sand.

Why had Kerry run off like that?

Why had she insisted it was her mother in the photograph with his dad?

He'd asked himself the same questions over and over again, and he still hadn't found any answers.

His dad had gone ballistic when he'd seen the broken frame. And when he'd told him what Kerry had said, he'd behaved really strangely, demanding to know Kerry's full name. Instead of answering Mark's questions he'd quizzed him for almost an hour – how did he know Kerry, where had they met, and why had he brought her to the house. Something weird was going on but his dad, as usual, was shutting him right out of it.

Grim-faced, he turned back to his packing. Dad

had said enough for a month. He'd also said the skiing holiday had been a long-planned surprise for his good work at school. Mark just didn't believe him, coming so quickly on the back of their row it had to be a ruse to get him away from Kerry.

Why?

What has Kerry ever done to Dad?

And why did Kerry freak out and insist that my mam was hers?

He chewed his lip as he knelt on the suitcase to close it, then sitting back on his chair he stared at the case, as if it was going to open its zipped jaws and tell him just what the fuck was going down.

He punched the silent suitcase just as the dinner gong went. Standing up, he kicked his bed for good measure, then slouched out of the room and made his way downstairs. He swore to himself that this time he wasn't going to back down, no way. He wasn't still a kid to be pushed around, and he certainly wasn't going to just take off without first speaking to Kerry.

Facing his father over the table, Mark swallowed a Brussels sprout whole before taking a deep breath and rushing the words out. 'Dad, I want to go out for a couple of hours. Gotta see some friends. They'll be wondering where I am if I'm not gonna be seeing them for a while.'

'No,' came back the very firm answer.

'But, Dad—'

'I said *no.*'

Mark heard his father's knife hit the plate and their eyes locked over the table.

His father wiped his mouth with the cream silk

napkin, and looked at Mark with a cold anger in his eyes.

'Go to your room. I will not have my own son questioning my orders.'

So it's orders now, is it? Mark thought, but simply said, 'No.'

'Don't you dare say no to me, lad. I'm your father and you'll show me the respect that's due to me.'

Here we go. The lecture. By and large, Mark was allowed to do more or less what he wanted, just so long as he kept out of his father's way and brought no trouble to the door. But now and then the pair clashed head on and it looked as though this was going to turn into one of those rows. It was at times like this that Mark longed for the mother he'd never known – maybe she'd have been on his side and able to calm his dad's sudden and frightening anger when it arose. *Well, she's dead, mate. You're on your own, and for once – fuck the lecture.*

'Dad,' Mark said firmly, though quaking inside, 'I don't care what you say, I *am* going out. And I'll tell you another thing, I'm not going on this skiing holiday. No way.'

'Who do you think you're talking to, boy!' Richard Kingston's voice rose as he banged his fist on the table hard enough to make their supper spill over the cream damask tablecloth. 'You will do as I say.'

Mark was frightened but defiant, 'No.'

Kingston practically ran round the table. He back-handed his son and his ring, a heavy sovereign, drew blood from Mark's bottom lip.

The sight of blood seemed to send Kingston over

the edge and unleashed the anger he'd barely suppressed all evening. Screaming with rage, he seized Mark by the arm and dragged him to his feet, his chair falling to the ground with an angry clatter.

'Dad . . . Dad . . .' Mark shouted, too shocked to resist. 'What are you—'

'You will not disobey me!' Kingston bellowed, jerking Mark towards him so that their faces were just centimetres apart. 'Do you understand me?'

All Mark's senses screamed at him to surrender, and for a moment he nearly did, but then something within him refused. 'No,' he yelled. 'It's you who don't understand. You can't just order me around. I'm not one of your belongings, one of your staff, and you can't just send me away. I'm not a little kid any more.' He fought and kicked out at his father, determined to break free. But his untrained jabs and punches were useless against the bigger, stronger, angrier man. And, faced with his father's cold, steely fury, he felt himself go limp.

A horrifying silence, more sinister than the argument that preceded it, descended on father and son. 'You're wrong, you know, Mark,' said Kingston. 'You do belong to me.' And he dragged him bodily into the nearby study. Pinning him down by the throat he reached round the desk and as Mark watched in shock and astonishment, the bookcase slid open to reveal a door and a flight of steps.

'Dad, no!' Mark screamed as his father forced him to the entrance and flung him down the stairs, but Kingston wasn't listening. He seemed totally crazed – almost possessed.

Mark fell heavily, landing on his side and feeling an agonising pain in his ribs. For a moment he lay stunned, but then realised that the bookcase was being rolled back into place, leaving him in the pitch dark in a windowless room which he hadn't even known existed.

Mark's childhood fear of the dark had never really left him, and he began to panic.

'Dad! Dad!'

Breathing heavily through the pain in his ribs, he slowly dragged himself back up the steps. Although sweat broke out all over his body, he tried to contain his fear and began knocking quietly on the panelled wood.

'Dad, please, Dad. I'm sorry. I didn't mean to cheek you. Don't leave me here, Dad. Dad . . . Dad, *please*.'

There was no answer.

His knocking increased in tempo as his voice rose steadily higher, '*Dad!*' But Mark was wasting his breath for his father had already left the room.

Deaf to his son's pleas, Kingston had stormed upstairs to his bedroom where, in a fuming rage, he paced back and forth. 'This *will* be sorted,' he muttered through clenched teeth. 'No one, least of all the bitch I spawned, will take my son away from me. I should have put an end to this years ago, and got rid of the lot of them. She will not have my son.' Spit flew from his mouth as he paced and cursed.

What Richard Kingston failed to realise was that his daughter had far more grit than his poor son would ever possess, and that her will was just as strong as his own.

One Week Later

26

Race day at last, and the North East had woken up to a day better suited to Florida. Some runners preferred the cold, even a little light rain, but Kerry wasn't bothered, she'd run in a heatwave or a snow storm if she had to. Hands on her hips, she breathed deeply from the top of Table Rock. She'd been out for a gentle jog, just enough to loosen up and get her engine revving.

Claire had been home for four days and things seemed almost back to normal. So much so that Kerry had found herself having a blazing row with her sister that morning – over something trivial, as usual. There were times, though, when Claire drifted off to somewhere else and was hard to reach. The doctor had warned them that this might happen, but had also said that these silent moments should eventually fade away.

Shaking her head, Kerry turned from the sight of Houghton's early-morning shoppers. Whilst she'd been running, her thoughts had spun from Claire to Mark to The Man and back again. In fact, she'd done little but think about the whole mess all week. Her determination to get to the bottom of it all and to see Richard Kingston punished hadn't wavered, but she still didn't know if she could deal with knowing that Mark was her half-brother, and The Man her dad. She knew that for today she just had to try to forget about them and concentrate, but it was one thing to know it and quite another actually to do it.

'Pull yerself together, girl,' she said aloud then, sighing, headed for home.

She slowed down to a brisk walk when she entered her street but stopped dead when she saw Sandra with Darren, Emma and her own three boys, throwing mud balls that Suzy was happily mixing. Their target: the pop van. It passed Kerry covered in mud, its furious driver shouting abuse that no one could hear.

Sandra stood victorious in the middle of the road, proudly giving the departing van the finger.

'Feel better now?' Kerry said, when she reached her.

Grinning, Sandra replied, 'You bet yer life I do! An' I bet the next time the wanker comes down this street, he'll be going a hell of a lot slower.'

Mr Skillings passed. 'Nice one, Sandra. And,' he smiled at Kerry, 'good luck for today, young Kerry. You just make sure yer show them all the road home.'

'Thanks, Mr Skillings, I will.'

Kerry looked at Sandra. 'Nearly everybody's wished me luck, even people I hardly know, people that live at the other side of Houghton.'

Sandra shrugged. 'Why look so puzzled? Most of them have known yer all of yer life. Of course they're gonna be rooting for yer.' She jumped as a well-aimed mud ball hit the back of her neck. 'Yer little

414

bastards!' Laughing, she ran at the kids who scattered in all directions.

Grinning, Kerry moved towards home, where, she told herself, there had just better be plenty of hot water for a good long soak.

Feeling about as substantial as a wraith, Mavis drifted around the kitchen. She picked things up, then put them down again, without a clue as to why she'd ever picked them up in the first place. She had to do something – anything – to take her mind off the clock ticking its way towards ten, when the phone would ring and they would know Lorraine's test results.

She'd resisted the urge to make a full breakfast, knowing that neither of them would be able to eat it – Mavis's stomach actually heaved at the thought of putting anything substantial in it. She decided to take Lorraine a glass of fruit juice; at least it was something.

That took all of one minute to prepare. She knocked softly on the bedroom door but Lorraine immediately called out for her to come in.

Fool for thinking she'd still be asleep, on today of all days.

She walked into the bedroom with a wide smile. 'Here, Lorry pet, I've brought fruit juice. A good thing to start the day with, eh?' Moving over to the window, Mavis opened the blinds. 'Look, pet, it's a lovely day. Just the sort of day for getting really good news.'

'Is it?' came the grumpy reply from somewhere under the covers.

Mavis knew the sound of misery when she heard it. She went over to the bed and gently shook Lorraine's arm.

'I know it's gonna be good news, pet. Trust me, I have a feeling for these things – yer know that. And it was great how Jenny managed to get the results back so fast. It proves what I always say, it's not what yer know but who yer know.'

Scowling, Lorraine surfaced. 'Yeah, well I just wish for one minute, Mam, that I could have your faith.'

Mavis put her arm round Lorraine's shoulders and squeezed her. 'Come on, out of bed with yer. The garden needs weeding.' Pleased that she'd come up with something to occupy them, Mavis beamed at Lorraine before making her way out of the bedroom and in the general direction of the garden shed.

Lorraine watched her go. 'The garden needs weeding,' she muttered in disbelief. 'Well, Mam, on me first day off in over a month, that puts a whole new perspective on things, that surely does.'

Shaking her head, she flung the covers back and swallowed the juice in one gulp. After a quick shower she dressed in blue jeans and a white T-shirt and went down to the kitchen. Mavis, back from the shed, had already put on dark blue overalls and flowery garden gloves.

Lorraine sighed. 'Yer do know, don't yer, Mam, that no amount of bulb planting, weeding or whatever, will make the phone call go away?'

'But that's not the plan, Lorry pet. The plan is to make the phone call come quicker. Now follow me.'

Not quite believing what she was doing, and

unable to find a reason to refuse, Lorraine followed her mother into the garden.

An hour later she was finding the dandelions to be just as obstinate as the wall of silence around The Man. They'd found only one loose brick, and Luke was busy chipping away at it for all he was worth. A creep pulled in for questioning about an unrelated incident had mentioned that he used to work as a driver for a rich bloke called Richard Kingston, and that this Kingston had fingers in every pie in Sunderland and Newcastle.

Knowing he was trying to deflect attention away from himself and the burglary charge they had him on, Lorraine didn't place too much faith in his story. But on the other hand, this Kingston guy just might – under pressure – provide another link in the chain. Neither Brad nor the two men who had been holding the girls were talking, and whilst they were hard pressed to shut Stevie up, he didn't know who worked at the top. Maybe Kingston could be persuaded to name a few names if he was connected to the underworld. Yes, it was an outside chance, but she was going to pursue it and Luke was busy trying to track him down.

She sighed when she thought of the poor girls. She'd interviewed them with as much delicacy as she could, but they knew very little.

The Archer woman though, well that bitch was for the high jump when Lorraine caught up with her. They'd ransacked the Blue Lion and the ornate Chinese knife they'd found on Archer's wall was definitely the one used to separate the heads from the bodies. It was still with forensics in the hope they could prove that it was Mrs Archer herself who wielded it, but what was certain, was that the girls' abduction and the buried bodies were connected in some way, and that all roads led back to The Man.

It's just finding the bastard. He's the one running the whole bloody show. Aye, an' finding Mrs Archer would help an' all.

Gritting her teeth, she gave an extra strong pull on another dandelion root and had nearly wrestled it out of the ground when her phone rang. Dropping the weed and snatching her glove off, she pulled the phone from her pocket, all thoughts of gangland bosses swept from her mind. She felt sick with dread. Her heart beating faster than it ever had in her life, she put the phone to her ear.

Watching her, Mavis forgot to breathe. *Please,* she silently begged. Lorraine's face was giving nothing away as she listened intently to the voice on the other end of the phone and Mavis had to fight the urge to go over and strangle the news out of her. Suddenly Lorraine started to smile, and it was enough for Mavis. Dropping her garden shears, she all but hopped, skipped and jumped over the lawn. 'Yes! Yes!' she yelled, over and over. Reaching Lorraine she grabbed her round the waist and tried to dance her around the garden. 'Thank you, God,' she cried. 'Thank you, God.'

Lorraine, giddy and scarcely able to take it in, simply clung to her mother, tears coursing down her cheeks.

When Luke arrived a few minutes later, he found

them both out of breath and collapsed in a heap in the middle of the grass. 'Some sort of ancient family ceremony?' he asked, smiling at both of them.

'Never mind, Luke,' Mavis said. 'It's just a fine piece of news we've been waiting for.'

Harry arrived as Luke was helping them both up and guessed by their wide smiles that the news had been what they had all been praying for. 'Time for that bottle of champagne you've been storing away, eh Mavis?'

'I'll get it, Mam!' Lorraine ran towards the house. When she reached the door she turned back to find all three of them watching her. 'Yer can tell Luke, Mam, now that it's all over. I know we can trust him to keep his gob shut.' She laughed at the look on Luke's face then ran on into the kitchen, still reeling with the knowledge that she was really – thank God – OK.

After a light lunch, Kerry went upstairs to collect her kit. To her amazement there was a brand-new navy-blue Nike tracksuit, new red running shorts and a white vest on her bed.

Unable to quite believe her eyes, she picked the clothes up and pressed them to her. She'd never even dared to dream of such fine gear.

I must have took a wrong turn up the stairs and entered one of Darren's parallel worlds. This is not for real.

Tears pricked the back of her eyes.

By rights it's Darren's turn, he so wants them football boots.

Then the tears spilled over. 'Everyone's so kind and I'm such a bitch,' she muttered, as she buried her face in the kit. The smell of newness set her off again.

She decided then and there that she was going to try as hard as she could to be a better person. *For God's sake, the whole place has wished me luck.*

'Only one thing to do now,' she wiped the tears away with the back of her hand, 'gotta win.'

A moment later, Claire, wearing her first real smile since she'd come home, burst into the room. 'It's all right, everybody, she hasn't even tried it on yet.'

The rest of the clan soon filled the small room. Everyone was smiling and wanting to touch Kerry. Darren pushed to the front and, holding up a pair of second-hand football boots, told her, 'From the car boot, sis, but I don't mind, not really, not if yer win. At least I can play proper footie now.'

Vanessa looked around her family, unable to remember when she'd last seen them all looking so happy. She felt a twinge of guilt, knowing that because of her love of the bottle she'd probably missed many other special moments. But that was over now, everything was at last going to be all right. Suddenly she was so proud that her heart actually hurt.

'Kerry's gonna win for all of us. She's gonna show the whole world that us Lumsdons are worth something. Isn't that right, Kerry?'

'Yer can bet on that, Mam.' Kerry grinned, and gave Robbie a high five.

Mark lay alone in the darkness, trying yet again to make some kind of sense of it all. He'd long since lost count of the days and hours passing and couldn't have said whether he'd been down there a week or a month. He was a pitiful sight, black with dirt, save for the white runnels his tears had made on his cheeks.

When he'd first realised that his father wasn't coming back to get him, he'd still thought that his punishment was going to be to stay down there for just a night. His father had blown up at him before, but it had always passed after a few hours and although this was the worst he'd been, Mark was sure he'd eventually calm down.

He'd tried to make himself comfortable on a chair he'd found after groping around in the dead black room, telling himself that he was way too old to get freaked by the dark. He'd actually slept for a while and woken thinking he'd dreamed it, but no, he was trapped in a pitch-black room, with no chance of any way out. He thought it must have been at least Sunday evening when he'd heard the door moving, at which point he felt giddy with relief. But it had been Jake, not his father, and ignoring Mark's pleas he'd simply shoved a bucket, some water and some food into the room. Since then he'd been back less and less regularly and although Mark had tried his best to persuade him to let him out – and even fought him – it was as though the man was deaf, dumb and blind. Now the room stank and Mark, half-starved and becoming more and more desperate, had started to believe that his father had left him here for ever.

What have I done that's terrible enough to warrant this?

When he thought about it, he'd been frightened of his dad for as long as he could remember. It wasn't the first time he'd thought his father was mad. He'd heard things he wasn't supposed to, heard the way he talked to people as if they were nothing. Heard him threaten more than one man who turned up at the house late at night.

Oh Mam, I wish you'd lived. You'd never have let this happen.

Thoughts of his mother took him back to thoughts of Kerry, who'd surely – hopefully – be missing him. Though the way she'd taken off when she saw the photo might mean that she never wanted to see him again. He sighed, she'd probably already forgotten him. Everyone had forgotten him.

I'm never gonna get out.

Then he wondered, for probably the hundredth time, just what was in this room that he'd never known existed. In the early days he'd groped around it, hoping that he'd find a way out. But all he'd found had been empty boxes, what he thought was high shelving, and a musty old blanket that he'd had to use to try to keep warm.

Wrapping it back around him he turned over, trying to ignore the pain in his still-aching ribs and the soreness in his throat from all the shouting.

It's so unfair. What have I done?

'Please come, Dad, I'm sorry. I'll do whatever you say,' he murmured, before drifting into an uneasy sleep.

27

Cal was the first to arrive at the track. Because of the recent flooding at Durham, the venue had been changed to Gateshead International Stadium, meaning a longer journey in the minibus. He had three of his old ladies from the home in tow. Betty, at least four stone overweight, looked like a huge pink jelly in her eighties-style shell-suit, of which she had one in every colour of the rainbow. Painfully thin Flo, in black leggings and black polo neck jumper, and with as much junk jewellery on her body as she had wrinkles on her face, could have been taken for an old beatnik. Whilst Jane, with a pink bow on her wide-brimmed straw hat to match the pink flowers on her silk dress, was dressed, as always, like a demure lady.

Betty and Flo had done nothing but squabble all the way here. Jane – better known as Lady Jane behind her back because of her aloof ways and her insistence that she had royal ancestors – had watched the pair of them with disdain.

The bus was scheduled to pick them back up at six, but listening to them now, Cal was beginning to wish he'd said three.

'Hot dogs, girls?' he asked, after he'd seated them

– and after he'd apologised to the man in front who'd had his hat knocked off by Betty's stomach as she squeezed past him.

'Oh aye,' Betty and Flo said in unison.

'No onions for me, please, they give me terrible wind,' Jane said, looking at Cal reproachfully, as if he harboured some secret plan to deliberately upset her digestion. Cal tried to keep the grin off his face as he left them and went for the hot dogs.

Betty and Flo watched him with adoring eyes like two mother hens until he was out of sight. Then with military precision, they both turned to Jane. Flo, who was sitting next to her, elbowed her in the ribs.

'Don't you go picking on him! It's not his fault onions give yer wind, is it now?'

'But I only said—'

'Yeah,' Betty glowered at her, 'well yer oughta know, Madam Fucking Muck, with all yer high and mighty ways, that there's ways of only saying. OK?'

'That's right,' Flo added, 'and if yer don't stop picking on the bairn, I'll snap yer fucking neck, right.'

It was the first time in the four years since they'd met that Betty and Flo had been in agreement about anything.

Flo wagged her finger in Jane's face. 'At least the canny bairn takes us out for a breath of air now and then, which is a damn sight more than yer royal fucking relations ever do, isn't it?'

Moving over in case another nudge was coming her way, Jane nodded as she fished around in her handbag for a tissue.

A few silent minutes later, Cal was back with the hot dogs and Lorraine, Luke and Mavis in tow. Jane took hers with the largest smile Cal had ever seen her give anyone, and with a very enthusiastic thank you to follow.

Mavis said hello to the women as she passed along the row. She knew Betty and Flo quite well as they both attended the pottery class she gave once a fortnight at the home. Surprisingly, Betty with her thick pork-sausage fingers was one of her best students, while Flo, usually the neater of the two, was a pathetically hopeless case. Jane never put in an appearance; getting one's hands into what was basically mud was beneath her.

They had all sat back down when the Lumsdons and friends arrived. Everybody said hello again, and Cal asked Robbie where Kerry was.

'She's down below in the changing rooms.'

'Did yer expect her to start from here, Cal?' Mickey grinned at him.

Cal cuffed Mickey's ear in reply. 'Why aye, man, she's that damn good, I expected her to start from the middle of Sunderland.'

They all laughed, then settled down as the mascot race got under way. The crowd was in stitches when the Newcastle magpie fell after three steps, and roared with delight as Sunderland's black cat crossed the finishing line first.

In the changing rooms Kerry calmly dressed and did her running shoes up before going outside to where Stan sat on the bench, nervously chewing his nails.

Next to Kerry's calmness, he was a bundle of nerves.

'Chill out, mate, I'm gonna win.' She sat down beside him.

'I know that, I just can't help it. I get this way before every race. Nice threads, by the way.'

'Mint, eh?' She looked at him. 'I still don't know why yer wouldn't let me enter the smaller races, yer know I would have won them an' all.'

He grinned. 'I want to see the shock on all their faces when a newcomer wins the big one.'

Kerry laughed. 'You're right devious, you are.'

They talked some more, then it was time.

Kerry walked over to the starting block; she was in lane three, and quite happy about it. She never cared where she started, she always clocked the same time whether on the inside lane or the outside, or even right in the middle. It made no difference to her.

She looked up to where she knew her family were sitting. This race was for them, and to show the whole fucking world that the Lumsdons were taking no more shit. There was no reason for her to look across to where, unknown to Kerry, her father sat, staring fixedly at her.

The gun went, and she was off. Kerry took the lead from the beginning and even had time to grin to herself as she cut in across the lanes – already she was ten yards clear.

At the end of the first circuit she was half the length of the track in the lead, and barely breathing hard. She knew there was only one girl who would come even remotely close, and that was the girl from

Silksworth. Keeping her lead, she settled down. All she could hear was the sound of her feet pounding the track, almost in time with the steady beating of her heart as she ate up metre after metre.

Then the last lap was coming up and, as she'd suspected, the Silksworth girl broke away from the pack in a bid to catch her. *No way. This is mine.* Kerry's head went back and she widened her stride as the finishing line came in sight.

This was everything she lived for: her dream moment, and nothing was going to stop her. Her heartbeat quickened with the sheer delight she was feeling. She – Kerry Lumsdon – was going to cross that line way out in front and at last be what she longed to be. The best.

With ten strides to go, she almost felt like stopping and jumping up and down on the spot with sheer exhilaration, but she shot forward with a new burst of energy, and a heart filled to the brink with excitement.

The whole stadium rose as Kerry hurtled down the track. Vanessa was sobbing her heart out and Sandra put her arm round her friend as she rubbed her own tears out the way. The kids were going completely crazy, and Darren felt as though his mind was stuck in a loop. 'Yes! Yes! Yes!' he kept on shouting. 'Yes! Yes! Yes!'

Betty managed to knock the man's hat off again when she got up to help Flo stand on her seat so she could see above the crowd. Flo did her own version of the Mexican wave, bobbing up and down in sheer joy.

Then Kerry, wearing a grin wide enough to split her face in half, crossed the finishing line.

The first sign that something was wrong was when, two steps over the line, Kerry stumbled before folding in on herself like a limp rag doll. Luke, who was closest to the scene unfolding below, blanched when he saw the red pool forming round her body.

As they realised that something had happened to the bright new star they had just watched break every record in the book, the crowd fell silent. Vanessa, Luke, Sandra and Lorraine pushed their way through and hurried down the steps. Vanessa got to her daughter the same time as the St John Ambulance men, who only just managed to stop her from grabbing Kerry and pulling her on to her lap. She was still struggling with them when the others caught up.

When Cal arrived after dropping his ladies off at the home, the hospital waiting room was full to overcrowding. Looking around, he nodded at Luke who had Suzy on one knee and Emma on the other. Darren had begun pacing the small room over an hour ago and was still at it. Robbie sat with his head in his hands with Sandra's arm around him, and Mickey was trying to comfort Claire who seemed at risk of going into shock. There were a lot of police around as well – talking quietly in corners, muttering into radios; not surprisingly, they were all over the shooting of a young girl in such a public way.

Cal noticed that Vanessa and Lorraine were both missing, and he guessed rightly that they were at

Kerry's side. Vanessa had been uncertain about letting Lorraine wait with her, but Lorraine was determined to interview Kerry as soon as possible. Carter and a few of the men were already questioning everyone in the stand where the shot had come from.

An hour later and nothing much had changed in the room, save for the return of Vanessa and Lorraine. Kerry was undergoing delicate surgery to remove the bullet lodged in her shoulder and it seemed to those waiting that the operation had been going on for ever.

The room was quiet. There was nothing left to say to one another – it had all been said, over and over, until each word held too much desperation and way too much pain. They all looked up when at last the doctor, wearing a very grim expression, entered the room. Before he had a chance to speak Darren started to scream, pushing everyone out of his way as he ran from the room. His harrowing cry was catching and Vanessa started to sob. Claire, looking absolutely terrified, was edging towards the door after Darren, and the rest all wore expressions of fright and bewilderment.

The doctor quickly held his hand up. 'It's all right, please calm yourselves.'

'She's all right?' Vanessa managed with a gulp.

'Yes, Mrs Lumsdon. It was slightly more compli-cated than expected, but Kerry is now out of surgery and back in intensive care. We managed to success-fully remove the bullet, but she has lost a great deal of blood. She hasn't yet regained consciousness—'

'What?' Vanessa jumped up.

The doctor held his hand up and continued, 'But that's not giving us too much cause for concern right now – it's still very early. Her vital signs are good, but as I say, she has lost a lot of blood and it will take her body some time to recover.' He paused for a moment and looked round. 'If she hasn't woken naturally in the next couple of hours then it would start to worry us—'

'She'll come through,' Vanessa interrupted, 'yer don't know our Kerry.'

Every head in the room nodded agreement.

'Stubborn, is she?'

'For England,' Sandra answered, as she rose and put her arm around Vanessa's waist.

The doctor looked around again, and for the first time since coming into the room, he smiled. 'Well that will make a big difference to the speed of her recovery.'

'Will she . . . ?' Vanessa hesitated. She looked help-lessly at her family and friends, trying to find the right words for what she wanted to ask, for what she really wanted to know. 'Will she be all right for her running, Doctor? Cos that would just destroy her . . .'

He shook his head. 'There's no way of knowing that yet. It's far too early. The wound itself will heal leaving only a small scar, but it's impossible to tell how much nerve damage has been done.' At the sight of their faces he became more encouraging. 'But she's young, and she's very healthy, and with the aid of physiotherapy the odds are good that she'll regain full use of her arm.'

He smiled kindly at Vanessa. 'What she'll need

most is the love and support of her family, and it looks to me as though she'll get plenty of that.'

Lorraine had watched Vanessa while the doctor was talking and seen fear, relief and now resignation chase across the poor woman's face.

She stood and walked over to the window and looked out at the view of congested traffic below.

Could it possibly be just a ghastly coincidence that such horrendous things could happen to two of Vanessa's daughters so close together? And why did she seem so resigned? If it were Lorraine she'd be screaming and ranting, and demanding that the police find the culprit.

And talking of the culprit, *just what sort of fucking creep gets his kicks shooting a sixteen-year-old after she's just won a race, for Christ's sake?*

Could it be the opposition?

Yeah, like rival trainers take it into their heads to go round shooting kids that are better runners.

Lorraine shook her head at the daft route her thoughts were taking her.

No way, this is something deeper, something that goes way back, I'm sure of it.

Hadn't she overheard the row at the house over a week ago? What was it Vanessa had said? *I can't tell yer, he'll kill us all.* Terrifying words to say to a child. There was something going on with this family.

Aye, an' I'm gonna make sure I find out just what it is.

She left the waiting room and walked down the corridor to the intensive-care ward. Opening the door quietly, she went over to Kerry's bed.

431

Poor kid. Kerry's face looked whiter than any face should ever look.

'I'll get the bastards responsible for this, girl,' she murmured, so low that the hum of the machines in the darkened room covered her voice. 'Don't fret, Kerry, you just get better, eh? And I promise, the bastard will suffer. I don't care how fucking big he is, or who I have to take down to get to him.'

Sunday

28

Mrs Archer sat in her cousin Jill's house in New Silksworth, barely able to contain her rage. She hated her family so had long ago severed any connection with them, and she particularly hated her cousin Jill. Jill had always been pretty – chocolate box pretty, with her fluffy blonde hair and big baby-blue eyes. It was enough to make a person sick just to look at her. Plus the dippy bitch had been married to the same man for the last ten years and had half a dozen scruffy brats to prove it.

A whole fucking week she'd had to hide out here. A week in hell. She'd known when she made the phone call it was going to be bad, but she hadn't guessed how bad. Screaming kids and fucking stinking nappies.

And it had cost her two hundred.

Fucking greedy bitch.

That's fucking family for yer.

No fucking wonder she'd stayed away this long.

She looked slyly around. The kids were eating cereal as if there was no tomorrow, and a full gallon of milk sloshed about on the table.

Bastards.

Jill was standing at the sink, and her husband, fat Ollie, had his arms around her.

Dirty twat, she'll be pregnant again in no time.

It never occurred to Mrs Archer that Jill and Ollie were still very much in love and had planned their large family. In fact, the love that surrounded Jill, Ollie, and the kids washed completely over her. It was an emotion she simply didn't recognise.

Look at him, slavering bastard. They're all the same, given half the chance he'll be playing away.

She thanked God silently that in another half an hour she'd be well rid of them.

Aye, an' with a bit of luck, I'll never have to set eyes on the fuckers again.

She nibbled on a slice of dry toast, then warded off a well-aimed spoon with her arm. She glared at the kid responsible, a five-year-old Ollie, just as pug ugly as his dad. The boy shivered.

Giving the kid an unseen shove, Mrs Archer stood up. 'I'll just be getting me things, then,' she told them, 'me lift won't be long.'

'Thank God,' she said to Ally twenty minutes later as she climbed into the car. 'Hurry up, in case the bastards think I haven't paid them enough.'

Jill and her family were standing at the door, and waved as the car left. Mrs Archer waved back. After all, one never knew when they might be needed again.

Stupid fuckers.

'You've got me money, I hope,' she demanded, as Ally drove out of the street.

He pointed to the back seat with his thumb and, glancing back, she saw a dark green holdall. 'Good.' She smiled.

This early on a Sunday morning the roads were

quiet and they would be in plenty of time to pick up the London train. Mrs Archer sat back and thought of the conclusions she'd come to during her week of hiding. One thing, she wished to God she'd got out from Kingston before now. She could have left quietly and calmly in her own sweet time instead of running scared and having to hide away with those grinning idiots for a week. And she wouldn't have to be paying Ally a fucking fortune to go behind Kingston's back, neither. But once in London she should be home free. She'd be out of this damned country like a shot.

Aye, an' out of that damn bastard's reach an' all.

She might have done some vicious things in her time, things that people who knew nowt about it would call evil, but at least she had a motive and a fat bank balance to prove it.

But Kingston could kill on a whim, just for the fucking sake of it.

And now the bastard was after her.

They reached Doxford International Business Park five minutes later and she turned from thoughts of her past to thoughts of her future, and the small private plane waiting for her at the other end. But when Ally passed the Durham turning and headed towards Houghton, that future suddenly seemed a whole lot less certain and she felt the poison tip of a huge spear enter her heart.

'Where the fuck yer going?'

Ally ignored her.

She punched his arm. 'Where the fuck are yer taking me, yer bastard Judas?'

Still he said nothing.

Real panic set in then and she tried the car door, wildly thinking of jumping, but it was locked.

'Stop! Stop now.'

'Can't do that,' Ally said.

Somewhere in the back of her fear-fogged mind she registered the fact that this was the first time that Ally had actually spoken since he'd collected her.

'How much is he paying yer?' She'd double it, even if it meant no plastic surgery and keeping this face for the rest of her fucking life. 'How much?' she demanded to know.

'Nowt.'

'Nowt!' She was outraged. 'I told yer I'd give yer five thousand and yer selling me down the river for nowt?'

'For me own life, if yer have to know. Now shut the fuck up, cos he says if yer any bother I'm to smash yer teeth in.'

'Aye, an' just try it, buddy.'

Ally laughed. But it was a nervous laugh. He was still frightened of Mrs Archer and knew just how she'd earned her money – and her nickname.

Mrs Archer's mind was boiling over with possibilities but if she knew one thing, it was that she could not afford to reach wherever this car was heading. She lunged at Ally, clawing the side of his face, wishing to God she had her knife to use, and not just her nails.

Ally screamed with pain, and nearly lost control as he swerved to avoid two bikers, but he managed to swerve back and stay on the road. He left the dual carriageway at Vardy's Garage and headed for Newbottle, using one hand to fend off Mrs Archer who by now was trying to pull out every hair of his head by the roots. Suddenly she stopped and, changing tactics, went for his face again. This time her finger dug straight into his eye. She yanked hard, and the skin tore.

Screaming in agony and half-blinded, Ally let go of the wheel and punched out at her. The car spun across the road, smashed through the fence, and bucked violently.

Lacking a seat belt Ally went straight through the windscreen, whilst Mrs Archer went sideways, smacking her head against the door. The car travelled on for a few yards, then slowly came to a halt, bogged down in the field. For a few minutes silence descended, but then a stunned Mrs Archer groaned, and her eyes flickered open. Seeing the huge hole in the windscreen she took in what had happened to Ally, and with the muscles in her right shoulder painfully throbbing, she pulled herself upright and peered out. There was nothing in front of her but the empty field. She loosened her seat belt and turned round for the holdall, her grip on it tightening when she spotted Ally.

He was lying face down in the soil. She didn't know if he was alive or dead, and she cared even less. She tried the car door again – thank God the crash seemed to have tripped the lock. Quickly pulling the holdall into the front, and clutching it to her chest like a newborn, she scrambled out of the car. She took a few deep breaths to settle herself as she scanned the area around her.

The poison-tipped spear returned, twice as deadly, when she saw Richard Kingston's car coming along the High Lane.

'Oh Jesus!' Turning, she started to run in the direction of the woods.

She'd gone maybe two hundred yards when she heard footsteps following her. She ran harder, but the soil was damp and heavy from the recent rains and it dragged her down as if each tiny particle was determined to keep her in the field. The weight of the holdall wasn't helping any, but no way was she going to let go of it.

She made it to the very edge of the woods where the birds were just beginning to sing again; if only she could get in there and hide amongst the trees she might stand a chance. But it was not to be. The nearest tree was less than a yard away when they caught up with her. Two big burly men – men she'd never seen before – had outstripped her and one ran in front, while the other grabbed her from behind. She fought them as best she could, but her speciality was with the knife, and mostly when her prey was already disabled – most often by the likes of the two who had now brought her down.

Each holding an arm, they dragged her screaming and kicking back over the field, to where Richard Kingston was casually leaning on his car with a sarcastic smirk on his thin lips.

She tossed her head and struggled to fling the heavies' arms off her, but it was only when Kingston nodded that, like well-trained soldiers, they finally let her go.

Clutching her holdall to her chest she stood there and faced him defiantly, earning herself a crashing fist right in her mouth. She gasped with the pain, but refused to cry out as she spat blood and fragments of her front teeth on to the ground.

'Did you really think you could escape? No one gets away from me. You should know that.'

Her mouth felt like hell, a mangled mess of screaming nerve ends, but she raised her head once more and stared him out. If she was gonna die it wouldn't be willingly, but if he was expecting her to beg then the bastard was in for one fucking big shock.

'Had a good week hiding out at your cousin's house in Silksworth?'

That threw her and, seeing her startled expression, Kingston laughed.

'Stupid, silly, ugly woman. Did you really think you could escape *me*?'

While he had her off-guard, he lunged and snatched the holdall out of her hands.

'No . . .' she managed, at great cost to her swollen mouth, as she frantically scrambled to get it back.

He pushed her and she fell back, landing heavily. But she still stared sullenly at him as she lay there. He laughed again.

'I'll say this, bitch, I've seen bigger men with less guts.'

She turned her head and spat blood and snot at his feet.

He nodded grudgingly. 'Really, I should kill you right now. But no, I've decided to be kind.'

That had her scalp prickling. Richard Kingston

had never been kind in his life, and if he was starting at this late stage, then it meant ill for someone.

Aye, an' who's the likely candidate, lying here on their arse?

He gestured with his head for the two men to get into the car, and when they were out of sight he threw the holdall at her. Eyes wide with surprise, she caught it, ignoring the flare of pain as the zipper hit her mouth.

'You're a stupid bitch to think you could cross me, but you've been a good servant. You needed a lesson and now you've had it. But I'll tell you this: only your silence will stop your cousin and her family going up in flames.' He stood for a second, then turned and walked away.

Filled with elation, Mrs Archer watched him go. At that precise moment she practically adored him, and my God, she'd do anything he asked. She'd keep quiet all right. But not on account of fat Ollie and her bastard cousin. Wasn't her own neck just as much on the line?

Giddy with relief, she desperately needed to see her money. Just to hold it. Just to feel it. Barely able to control her excitement and with all pain forgotten for the moment, she unzipped the holdall, laughing out loud as she opened it. But a moment later she was screaming with rage. Bundles of newspaper scraps cut into the shape of twenty-pound notes lined the inside of the holdall, and from the midst of them Jack Holland's mummified face stared out.

She was still screaming as the patrol car called to

the site of the accident pulled up, and two uniformed policemen slowly got out.

Vanessa stood outside the corner store where she'd gone for cigarettes. After making her purchase she had stared so longingly at the bottles of whisky, vodka and other spirits behind the counter, that the assistant had coughed nervously to hurry her along. God she so wanted a drink, she could nigh on taste it.

Turning to Sandra, who had stayed overnight at the hospital with her, she smiled wanly and opened the cigarette packet to offer her one. When they had both lit up Sandra blew several smoke rings thoughtfully, before saying, 'Another milestone, Vanny.'

Vanessa nodded, knowing that her friend meant the booze. 'Come on, we better be getting back, cos if I know our Kerry she's probably awake and screaming for breakfast.'

Kerry had come round briefly the previous evening but had seemed to recognise no one and had soon drifted back into unconsciousness. But her breathing had been regular and her colour good, and the doctors were cautiously optimistic. The police were desperate to talk to her, but although she was improving steadily she wouldn't be telling anyone anything yet.

'Why aye, no one can keep our Kerry down.' Sandra was nodding her head in agreement as they set off. But Vanessa's shoulders were still slumped as they crossed the road and entered the hospital grounds.

To get to the intensive-care ward they had to pass maternity where they watched a young man, looking much the worse for wear, celebrate the birth of his daughter with anyone and everyone who passed by. Vanessa couldn't help remembering the lonely time she'd had when Kerry was born. Ten hours of solid agony with no one's hand to hold and at the end of it all, a screaming red-faced baby.

The kid had looked angry the very minute she'd drawn breath. Then Sandra had arrived – God bless Sandra. Turning up with a bunch of flowers and Little Robbie clinging on to her skirt.

Throughout her pregnancy Vanessa had thought about getting rid of the child she was carrying; the last thing she'd wanted to look at every day of her life had been a reminder of her husband's murderer. And a reminder of her own brutal rape. For nine long months she'd mostly wished the baby inside of her dead. That was when the drinking had really started – bottle after bottle of gin, but the old wives' tale had never worked, at least not on her.

Later, when she'd been left alone with her new baby, nothing had changed. She'd hated her, hated her heart-shaped face and the mop of black hair. She'd thought about adoption but Robbie had already fallen head-over-heels for his little sister, and at the end of the day it had been easier to go home with the baby than without her. Far easier to foster the lie that the child was wanted, than to face all the whispering tongues. The easy route had also been to pass her off as Robbie's full sister, although by the time the others came along, she couldn't have cared less what anybody thought. Each new baby had put food on the table for the rest, and for a time she'd been able to rest up.

But back when there'd only been Robbie and Kerry, she'd slowly – and it was slowly – let the helpless baby steal into her heart. Through the drink and the pain she'd known deep down that she couldn't let her own flesh and blood go. And God knew, the kid had loved her big brother. Even as a tot she'd been the one who'd comforted Robbie through his nightmares, while his mam had been in bed with any Tom, Dick or Harry who would pay.

That fierce and angry baby was nearly a woman now.

And I adore the ground the kid walks on.

Deep in her heart Vanessa knew that Kingston was the reason her daughter was lying in the hospital. Knew too, that Sandra thought the same.

But knowing something was one thing, and doing something about it, quite another. And what could she do?

Sandra would say it was time to talk to the police and tell them everything, but was that really going to keep the rest of the Lumsdons safe?

At the end of the day, I'm damned if I do and damned if I don't.

Vanessa sighed as she pushed the ward door open and missed the concerned look Sandra gave her.

They entered the intensive-care ward to smiles all round and Vanessa's heart skipped. *Please,* she silently begged, *let those smiles be for me and me bairn.*

'Is she . . . is she awake?' she asked the head nurse falteringly.

'She sure is. Five minutes ago, and demanding to know when she can get out of bed. And where the hell's the trophy she won.'

'That's my Kerry!' Vanessa shouted, as she ran to her daughter's room with Sandra by her side.

Robbie had fed the kids, then sent them up to the play park with Darren in charge. Cal and Mickey had spent the night and none of them had had much sleep, fully expecting Cal's mobile to ring at any time.

'No news is good news,' Dolly Smith had told them, when she'd called in on her way to the shop ten minutes ago.

Mickey was making the rest of them bacon sarnies whilst Claire, who'd refused to go with the others, sat staring into space. The smell of burned bacon wafted into the sitting room to where Robbie and Cal watched TV, and moments later Mickey followed, with a plate piled high in his hand. 'They're a bit crispy, guys.'

'Crispy!' Cal said, picking black bits off the bacon.

Mickey shrugged. 'Best way to have it. Claire, fancy a bite?'

He practically shoved the sandwiches under her nose to get her attention and gradually she came back from wherever she'd been and helped herself.

When Cal's phone rang it startled everybody, and Mickey nearly dropped the plate.

'Sorry, I can't hear yer properly, can yer speak up? It's a bad line.'

The three of them were staring at him as though by their combined efforts they could force him to say what they wanted to hear.

Cal rang off and let out a huge whoop of pleasure. 'She's awake, and she's talking, and she wants to come home.'

Robbie started to cry. 'I can't believe it, man,' he managed past a huge lump in his throat. 'I just can't believe it. Things is finally starting to go right.' He beamed at Claire who gave a huge sigh, then looked out the window.

Mickey started wolfing down the sandwiches. 'That's fantastic news, mate,' he said, spraying breadcrumbs all over. 'Knew she'd be all right – our Kerry's a winner, don't forget.'

The boys were still laughing and horsing around when Claire's quiet voice stopped them. 'What if he does it again?'

'What?' Robbie asked, staring at her.

'What if he does it again? The man who shot our Kerry. What if he does it again? When he finds out she's not dead.'

'But that's not gonna happen . . .' Robbie felt his world falling apart again, '. . . it can't. And it won't cos . . . cos the coppers will stop him.'

'How do yer know that for sure, Robbie?'

'Cos I just cleaned me fucking crystal ball, Claire. I'm telling yer, whoever he is he'll not touch her again.' Robbie stormed out of the room but a moment later he was back and shrugging into his jacket. 'Claire's right,' he said to Cal and Mickey. 'We've all been kidding ourselves. I'm gonna see our Kerry's Robo Cop. Fuck what Mam says.'

'Way to go, Robbie,' Mickey said, realising that the family couldn't go on like this. 'Want me to come?'

'No, mate. You just stay here with our Claire and watch out for the little'uns.'

Cal and Mickey watched Robbie stride down the street from the window. Mickey, who knew the Lumsdons' secret, felt proud of his friend, but Cal was completely in the dark. 'What's he gonna tell the police, then?' he asked, but Mickey ignored him.

'Come on, man, we need to see to Claire, she's nigh on back in never-never land.'

'She is that. I think she's getting worse. Them's the first real words she's said since Kerry got it.'

'Yer can't blame her after everything that's happened. But don't worry,' Mickey added with utmost confidence, 'she'll make it. There's no one and no thing as can keep the Lumsdons down.'

Lorraine rested her chin on her hands and stared at Mrs Archer who stubbornly stared back. She'd been in the interview room for two hours and the dreadful woman had not said a word, not even to confirm her name. For God's sake, she hadn't even asked for a lawyer.

One good thing, there was no way she was getting out of here. Even without the drug dealing and the evidence of the knife at the Blue Lion, good God, the woman had been found in charge of a human head.

She looked at Luke. 'How many years do yer

automatically get for being in the possession of human body parts?'

Luke came right back with a convincing, 'Fifteen years, boss.'

'Did yer hear that? Fifteen years, Mrs Archer, and that's just for being in possession of. Cos to my mind, even though we've not proved it yet, you were the one who sawed the bugger off.'

Is anything gonna stir this bastard up? Time to play an ace.

Lorraine banged her hands on her desk. 'What the fuck are yer doing with Jack Holland's head in a fucking holdall?'

At last a fucking reaction, even if I've only made the bitch blink.

'Aye, we know who it is, Mrs Archer. Luke here identified him the minute he saw him. And in remarkably good nick compared to the rest of his body – where've you been keeping it, you evil old witch?'

Mrs Archer regained control of herself and simply gazed at Lorraine.

Lorraine shook her head and stood up. 'Something else I know,' she leaned over Mrs Archer, 'you're gonna be doing some long lonely time, cos I can't see anybody wanting to be mates with yer, yer know. Not with that mug anyhow.'

This brought another reaction and Lorraine heard what she could only describe as a snarl before Mrs Archer spoke just two words.

'Fuck off.'

'Oh wow. Take her away, Luke. I can't stand to

look at her any longer. It's enough to give anybody chronic diarrhoea.'

Mrs Archer rose out of her chair and, with a shrug of indifference, followed Luke to the door.

When she was gone Lorraine snapped half a dozen pencils, then decided to grab a coffee. When they'd got the word that a patrol car had found Mrs Archer in a field with a mummified human head the whole station had been practically ecstatic – they could all see the case coming to an end. But, and she kicked the chair that the damned woman had been sitting in, really they were no fucking further forward. If she couldn't get the bitch to talk they only had the monkey and not the organ-grinder.

Aye, an' a fucking ugly monkey at that.

Robbie was at the end of his patience. He'd sat in this room so long, he swore to himself that he had corns on his arse. A small black-haired copper woman had put him in here saying that Detective Inspector Hunt was busy and would find time to see him later.

'She didn't say how much later,' Robbie grumbled to himself.

He decided enough was enough; if she didn't want to hear what he had to say, then to hell with her.

He opened the door into the passage and practically bumped into Lorraine as she came out of the door facing him. Both of them looked surprised.

'Robbie! What are yer doing here?'

'Waiting for you.'

Bit by bit, and with constant interruptions by way of Lorraine's questions, the whole story came out.

He cried a bit when he got to his dad being killed and Lorraine let him pause long enough to find his hanky. But when he finally got to the name Richard Kingston, her patience vanished and she almost pinned him to the chair.

'I don't fucking believe this, Robbie, it took yer sister getting shot to make yer come here? Why the fuck didn't you or yer mam tell me about this Kingston before?'

Tears filled Robbie's eyes again as he looked at the policewoman.

'Cos if yer don't get him for this – an' I mean pin him down good and proper and for ever – then me and me whole family are gonna be dead.'

Lorraine stood slightly back as Luke pounded on Kingston's door half an hour later.

And what a door an' all, Lorraine thought, as they waited for him to answer. She nodded for Luke to hammer again but before he had a chance the door opened.

'Yes?' Richard Kingston asked, looking them both up and down.

'We need to have a word, Mr Kingston,' Lorraine said.

'Sorry, the tradesmen's entrance is at the back.'

He went to shut the door, but Luke pressed his hand against it and prevented him from closing it.

Lorraine flashed her badge. 'As yer can see, Mr Kingston, we ain't no tradesmen. Now we can talk here, or we can talk at the station. Either way, we will talk.'

Kingston let go of the door and gestured with his hand for them to follow him. They walked down a beautiful panelled hallway and entered a room on the right. He sat down at the desk and nodded for Lorraine to sit opposite him. There was only the one chair meaning Luke had to stand, but Lorraine was very aware of the fact that Kingston was acting as though Luke simply didn't exist. She'd also noticed the trophies from his safaris displayed around the walls.

What sort of ego am I dealing with here? she thought, as she stared at him, noting that he didn't seem the least bit worried by having police turn up at his house.

'OK, Mr Kingston, we'll cut straight to the point. We're here about Vanessa Lumsdon.'

He shrugged. 'Who?'

'Yer know fine well who. Your dead wife's cousin.'

'Oh,' he said after a moment, during which he appeared to be thinking although the ploy didn't fool Lorraine for a minute. '*That* Vanessa Lumsdon. I had actually forgotten all about the woman. Now I don't think that's a crime, my dear.'

'No. But murder is. And so is kidnapping. My dear.'

He smirked. 'Really? Are you accusing me of either or both? I must warn you—'

'Yer must warn me! I think yer've got yer wires crossed, Mr Kingston. I'm the copper here, not you. Me and me friend here.'

She saw his eyes flicker. He looked at Luke like he was dirt.

A racist with an ego as big as a mountain – I've got your card marked, mate.

'Ah, so he's your friend, is he?' It was said with the utmost sarcasm and laced with a thousand meanings.

That was it – Lorraine had had enough. *The smarmy bastard.* She jumped up and leaned over his desk.

'Look, Kingston, I fucking know yer've got something to do with all this bad luck the Lumsdons are on the wrong end of.' She wagged her finger in his face, practically touching his moustache. 'Don't, I warn yer, get too fucking clever. Cos I'm gonna have yer. Yer nowt but a bully boy and, get this, creep, yer don't frighten me one little bit.'

She saw the change come over his face but whether it was fear or not, she couldn't quite tell. Probably this prick had never feared anybody in his life, but she knew she was certainly getting under his skin.

His voice crackled with anger as he snapped, 'I don't know where you were brought up, but it was obviously not as a lady.'

'You wouldn't know a lady if she slapped yer in the face and sang the national anthem on the top of Penshaw Monument.'

That brought a flush of anger to his face. 'If you'll excuse me, I think I will just phone my lawyer. There is no reason why I should be subjected to this.'

He made to stand up but Lorraine, still on her feet, pressed her hands on his shoulders forcing him down. The look on his face was comical as she said, 'Phone from here, creep.'

Kingston picked the phone up, his knuckles white as he clenched it in his hand. 'I warn you,' he told Lorraine, 'that he will inform Superintendent Clark at once.'

'Know him an' all, do yer?'

'Know who?'

'Fucking Santa Claus, who the fuck do yer think?'

'I refuse to say any more until my lawyer gets here.'

'Why aye, tell him to make it quick then.'

He dialled the number, and it was obvious by his face that he wished her dead.

The next fifteen minutes were spent in silence under the steady gaze of the dead wildlife. Kingston calmly read a book that was on the desk.

I'll give the bastard top marks, Lorraine thought, as she examined her nails, *he's certainly cool.*

Then Luke's mobile invaded the mock peace of the panelled room. He went outside to take the call.

A few minutes later he was back. 'Boss . . .' He gestured with his head.

Lorraine stood. 'Won't be long, arsehole,' she threw over her shoulder as she left the room. She could practically feel a dozen daggers penetrating her back.

She looked at Luke and said, 'I just know you've got something to tell me that I don't want to hear.'

'We can't touch him, boss.'

'Fuck off.' She angrily slapped the panelling with her hand. 'Who the fuck is he? For God's sake, don't tell me he's got Clark in his pocket?'

'Not Clark, this has come from the top. Unless

454

we have water-tight evidence instead of hearsay, he walks. Now.'

'Luke, I can't just leave it. I promised Robbie – you know we're leaving the Lumsdons as exposed as fuck to whatever this maniac decides to do to them?'

But even as she argued with Luke, Lorraine knew there wasn't a thing she could do. If she ignored the phone message and took him in, he'd be back out in minutes.

Aye, then I'll be the one banged up, and what good's that gonna do the Lumsdons?

She didn't even go back and tell Kingston, but just turned and headed for the door. Luke followed her. Since he'd walked into Mavis's garden and caught them celebrating the good news she had been much more relaxed. So much so, that he'd been trying to pluck up the courage to ask her out. He'd thought today might be the right time, but not now. Judging by the look on her face she was more strung out than ever. In fact, he thought, the way she was looking she might just burst a blood vessel or two.

Mark had crawled to the top step where he sat, his chin resting on his knees. He had heard voices in the study and dragged himself up there ready to bang and shout for help, but he'd quickly realised that his father was being interviewed by the police. He didn't know whether it was loyalty or sheer cowardice, but he'd stayed quiet, clutching the stinking blanket and only able to make out one word in three.

It was starting to get really cold and he rubbed

his arms as he imagined his father coming to open the door after the coppers had gone, only to find him frozen to death.

He shivered again, only this time it wasn't with the cold. Perhaps his father did mean for him to die. Perhaps he was never going to forgive him.

'Please, Dad. I'm sorry, please let me out,' he whimpered, then remembering his earlier resolution, bit into his hand.

I am not gonna cry no more.

No way.

Sighing, he rested his head against the wall.

He had to believe that his father was going to release him – he couldn't leave him here for ever. It must have been days and days now, and even if he'd told the school that his son had gone skiing, they'd want to know when he didn't come back. And Kerry, surely Kerry wouldn't forget him altogether. She did like him – he knew she did – and surely she'd come back.

At that, he couldn't stop the tears coming and, crying, he crawled back down the steps to the chair. Huddling the blanket around him like some kind of security blanket he moaned softly through his snivels.

'What did I do wrong? Just what did I do?'

Monday

Monday

29

Kerry woke, stretched, then let her arms flop down by her sides, causing the sheet to stretch tightly across her chest. Apart from a burning in her shoulder, she was feeling much better.

Her foot went into a cramp and she looked down the length of her body. Her eyes rested on her foot, then were dragged back up when her mind caught up with the picture of a pair of very slight bumps in the region of her chest. Staring, she used her good arm to pull the sheet tighter.

Very slowly, as if any sudden movement might cause the bumps to disappear as magically as they had arrived, she moved her hand up her side. When it was poised over the bumps, she hesitated a moment.

What if me mind's seeing things?

Do boobs grow over night?

Nah.

Our Claire's did.

Biting her lip in anticipation, she gently touched the bumps.

Still there.

'Yes!' she shouted. 'Yes! Yes! Yes! Boobs, tits, breasts.'

She was that pleased with herself, and so engrossed in her new body shape, that she failed to notice the teenage boy standing outside her door with his mouth hanging open.

The boy, recovering from appendicitis, had been on the wander to relieve his boredom. When he'd passed Kerry's room he'd heard her shout. He was so transfixed by what was going on in front of him that he failed to hear Cal and Mickey coming along the corridor until they stood toe to toe with him.

Cal glanced quickly into Kerry's room then back at the boy. 'Yer dirty little bastard.'

The boy flushed blood red. He swallowed hard as he tried to explain. 'I wasn't doing anything wrong, honest. I've been for a walk. She . . .' He gestured towards Kerry who was still oblivious to what was going on outside her door. 'For fuck's sake, give us a break, will yer?'

'I'll give yer a break, yer creep,' Mickey said, as he pushed him, 'I'll break yer scrawny neck.'

They watched as the boy, heroically protesting his innocence, went to his own room.

As Cal and Mickey went into Kerry's room she looked up and gave them both a glorious smile. It was obvious to them that she hadn't seen her peeping Tom and Cal gave Mickey a slight shake of his head, which Mickey understood at once.

Kerry sat up. 'Come to take me home, guys?'

'Not yet, wonder girl,' Cal replied. He blushed as he handed her a bunch of red and white carnations. Holding the flowers had been the only reason he'd kept his hands off the boy.

'I chipped in an' all,' Mickey piped up, as he helped himself to a tangerine from the bowl of mixed fruit on her bedside cabinet.

'Thanks,' Kerry muttered, looking at the flowers as if they were going to bite her, and feeling every bit as embarrassed as Cal, especially now. Now that she was turning into a woman right in front of them.

Shit! Can they see them?

Hastily she pulled the covers up to her neck.

'Cold?' Cal asked.

'Aye. Er, where's me mam and our Robbie?'

'Yer mam's not feeling too well, so seeing as yer might be getting out tomorrow, Robbie's stopped at home with her.'

The colour drained out of Kerry's face. 'She's not—'

Mickey hurried to reassure her. 'No, Kerry. She's not. She's not drinking again. It really is just a headache.'

He shifted uncomfortably. Whilst Robbie hadn't told Vanessa that he'd been to the police, he'd felt badly about it. And when he'd found out that Richard Kingston hadn't been arrested, he'd felt even worse. Mickey had tried to tell him that he hadn't placed his entire family in jeopardy – they were *already* in danger, for Christ's sake – but Robbie was feeling both guilty and scared.

For the next half hour the boys managed to keep Kerry entertained, Mickey hiding his worry for his friend. When Cal said it was time to go home, Mickey had scarcely unfolded his lanky legs from underneath him, before Kerry had thrown the bed covers off.

'Cool, that's just where I'm going.'

'What?' Cal said, thinking how cute she looked in her pink pyjamas, even with her arm in a sling, completely oblivious to the fact that Mickey had swallowed a tangerine pip from his third piece of fruit and was beginning to choke.

'Yer heard. I'm all better and I'm coming home. I'll die of fucking boredom if I'm in here a minute longer.'

'But yer can't,' Mickey said between coughs, 'you've still got yer bandages on.'

'Zip it, Mickey, and watch.'

And watch they had to, as Kerry trotted to the door and began yelling down the corridor for a nurse.

Robbie was looking out the window as the street-lights flickered on. Vanessa had gone upstairs to nurse her headache and Robbie, all alone for the moment, had been endlessly churning things over in his mind. The sheer injustice of everything was really weighing him down.

He couldn't believe that Lorraine had failed to keep her promise to him and that Richard Kingston was still on the loose. And if that wasn't worry enough, there was Claire still scarcely uttering a word, and his mam sick with a headache.

An' now bloody Darren to think on an' all.

Darren had run in at least three hours ago and grabbed a couple of crumpets. Dripping melted butter all over the place, he'd slung his football boots over his shoulder and, yelling to the world that he would be back before dark, scurried back out.

Well it was past that now. Robbie peered up the street. No sign of the little brat. Feeling hungry, despite his nervousness, he went into the kitchen and toasted more crumpets. He'd got six packs today, all half-price because they were a day past their sell-by date, and already they were nearly all gone.

Thank God Dolly had taken the girls up to hers for a while. She'd just bought a second-hand video and Emma, not shy at the best of times, had blatantly asked if they could watch the cartoon tapes that had come with it.

He buttered the crumpets and went back to his post by the window.

Full dark now, where the hell is the little git?

A movement to his right caught his eye and by squashing his face sideways against the window he could make out the steps. It was Jess, wagging her tail as Claire stroked her.

Claire was smiling, but instead of soothing him it made him angry. Angry because Claire should always be smiling – at her age she should never drift off to wherever it was she went to. Angry because the police were useless lying bastards. And doubly angry because he had one sister in the hospital and her bastard dad had murdered his.

His hand clenched around the crumpet, making the butter run through his fingers. Choking back tears of anger and frustration, Robbie dropped it in the bin.

Bastard. Bastard.

He was in the bathroom washing when he heard

the door bang. 'About time, brat,' he muttered into the towel as he dried his face.

He hurried downstairs to read the riot act, only to find Cal and Mickey, and still no sign of Darren.

'Oh, it's youse two.'

'Sorry to disappoint yer.' Mickey grinned at him. 'Was it Britney Spears yer were expecting?'

Cal grinned, then moved back to the door. 'I've got to get straight on to work. I thought yer better know that Kerry's on the warpath.'

'Oh God. That's all I need.'

'Aye,' Mickey put in. 'What a job we had to get her to stay. It took Dr Happy Face and a seventeen-stone nurse to convince her. But I think it's really because she went all dizzy. She'd be able to give that mud-wrestler the slip any time.'

'Anyhow,' Cal said as he opened the door, 'they've said she can come home tomorrow after one. I told her you'd sort it and be there to pick her up then.'

'Thanks. Didn't see our Darren about, did yer?'

'No,' Cal said, 'but if I see him on me way home, I'll tell the little sprout to get his arse in gear.'

Claire had wandered in from outside using the back door. 'When's our Kerry coming home?' She looked at Robbie.

'Soon, Claire. It's Darren I'm looking for now.'

Mickey, always fascinated by Claire, smiled and gave her a little wave, and was thrilled when she smiled back before going upstairs.

'Did yer see that, Robbie?' He followed Robbie into the kitchen like an eager puppy. 'Did yer see?

She smiled, and before that she spoke a whole sentence. I think she's coming back.'

'Good.'

'Good, is that all—'

Before Mickey could say any more, Robbie turned on him.

'Fuck off, will yer, Mickey! I've got more to fucking worry about than our Claire. Yer heard the doctor, she was coming back anyway.'

Mickey didn't know how to take the huff, it wasn't in his nature. Neither was it in Robbie's to be nasty. He knew that other things were bothering his friend.

'What's the matter now?'

Robbie sighed. 'The whole lot of them are doing me fucking head in. And now our Darren. I told the little rat to be in before dark.'

Mickey tutted. 'Ha'way, man. Give the kid a break here. He's not a toddler yer know.'

'This time of night is when the local vampires come out with their tempting little sweeties. Stevie getting banged up isn't the end of it, yer know. I spotted that lot on the corner last night. I didn't know half of them, but I knew what they were after all right. More fucking converts.'

Mickey digested this statement for a moment then asked, 'Yer mean like cults?'

Robbie stared at him, shook his head then reached for his jacket before saying, 'Aye, Mickey, only that lot worship drugs, and the more converts they get, the more they line their pockets.'

'Why, man, yer know Darren's said no once – he's not gonna suddenly take up with them?'

'Mebbe he did tell on them last time, but he's only a kid. Besides,' he lowered his voice before going on, 'that bastard Kingston's still free as a bird out there – remember?'

'I know, I know. Where are yer going now?'

'To look for our rat.'

'Ha'way then, I'll come with yer.'

They were halfway up the street when Mickey, who had the night vision of a fox, spotted Darren coming towards them. Mickey pointed him out and although he was still some distance away, both could see that there was something wrong.

'Oh God!' Robbie started to run. Anxiously, Mickey followed.

'What's the matter, Darren?' Robbie was shouting when they were still ten yards away. 'What's the matter?'

Darren's face was void of expression as if he'd had an enormous shock to his system or, Robbie thought, gritting his teeth, as if he was drugged up to the fucking eyeballs.

'I'll kill the bastards! I'll fucking kill them.'

Reaching Darren, Robbie gripped hold of his brother's shoulders and shook him. 'What the fuck's going on, Darren?'

Darren grinned at him, his face a picture of pure ecstasy.

'Oh, fuck,' Robbie was nearly screaming, 'what have yer taken, Darren? Who give yer it? Tell me now, kid, cos I'm gonna kill the bastard!' Each word had been punctuated with a shake, but it failed to wipe the smile off Darren's face.

'The man . . .' Darren laughed.

'What?' Robbie yelled.

Before Darren could say anything else, a thousand different emotions rocketed through Robbie's heart and head. All he could see was his family lined up and waiting to die one by one. His blood burned with the need to protect them and his grip tightened.

'Robbie! You're hurting!' Darren wriggled as hard as he could, but Robbie's grip became more fierce by the moment.

'Robbie, mate.' Mickey pulled on Robbie's arm. He could feel the strength in his friend's muscles, and feared for what might happen.

Darren's legs started to go and Mickey looked from Robbie's red-veined face to Darren's deathly white one, then faced with no other choice, he stepped back and launched a right hook to Robbie's jaw.

Robbie's head snapped back. He glared at Mickey, blinked a few times, then suddenly seemed to come to his senses. A look of fear came into his eyes and quickly he let go of Darren.

'What did yer do that for?' Darren blinked away tears of pain as he sniffed. 'Yer gonna have me on the bench before me first game.'

'First game?' Robbie repeated, looking confused.

'Aye, the man came to see me tonight. The man from the Academy.' Darren rubbed his shoulder. 'What'll he say when he sees these bruises in the changing rooms though?'

Mickey jumped up and down with delight, what was really going on, finally dawning. 'Yer've been given trials for Sunderland Academy!'

'Aye.' Darren's grin nearly split his face in half. 'The man says I'm a natural.'

'But yer looked so spaced out, yer little rat,' Robbie said. 'And when yer said The Man . . . Jesus God.'

'I was dreaming, Robbie. Me in the red and white. Playing up front for Sunderland. Me, scoring goals past the best of 'em.'

He jumped up and tried to punch the stars.

'Me, Robbie, yer very own brother. He only went and said I'm the best he's seen in years. What yer crying for, Robbie?'

Mickey, who had been totally engrossed in Darren, swung his head round to see tears coursing down Robbie's cheeks. Quickly he put his arm around his friend, feeling his chest heaving with pent-up sobs. He led him over to the wall. 'Here, mate, sit down.'

Robbie sat. He had been so relieved that the tears had just come and now was all right that they wouldn't stop. He knew that if anything had happened to Darren, that would have been the end – there was only so much a person could cope with. Each day had become harder than the day before, until each morning he dreaded getting out of bed.

Mickey took his friend's tears in his stride, but Darren was both worried and embarrassed to see his big brother crying like a baby. Agitated, he tried as hard as he could to keep his own tears in check.

After a while Robbie's sobs stopped and, reaching out, he grabbed Darren and hugged him. 'I thought he'd got you as well, yer little rat.'

'Well he hasn't,' Mickey said, 'and he never will.

This kid's gonna play for Sunderland, and fuck The Man.'

All three of them grinned as Robbie squeezed Mickey's arm in gratitude. Pleased with himself, and on a roll, Mickey went on. 'Do yer realise just how lucky yer are, Robbie?'

Robbie looked at Mickey as if he wasn't real. Lucky was the very last thing he felt, but this he had to hear – and by God it better be good.

'So how do yer work that one out, mate?'

'Well, first off, Claire disappeared. But she's back and she's gonna be all right. Second, Kerry got shot. But she's gonna be all right too. Well actually I'd say she was all right already, judging by the way she was eyeing that big fat mama nurse up. Third, yer mam's off the booze – and that's cool, innit? Fourth, I think yer just had one of them nervy breakdowns, not that I blame yer mind. But, yer gonna be all right, aren't yer? So, I reckon things is gonna be canny good from now on. What do yer say?'

Robbie shook his head in amazement. *Where the fuck does he get it from?* But he had to agree, by Mickey's logic things looked like they might be canny good from now on.

He wiped his eyes and blew his nose, then smiled at Mickey. Together they demanded a word-by-word account from Darren about exactly what the man from the Academy had said. Then, feeling better than he had in weeks, Robbie led his brother and his friend home.

As the trio came to the top of the street they were so intent on talking about Darren's forthcoming trial that the car parked up at the kerb passed unnoticed. Neither did the boys see the man inside it, staring so intensely as they wandered by.

But inside an unmarked police car one person saw him. And she vowed again that she'd keep after him for as long as it took.

Tuesday

Tuesday

30

Kerry pushed the breakfast tray away, and got out of bed. As she'd chewed the nearly indigestible toast she'd made her mind up. She would sign herself out and go see the man responsible for the mess her family was in. She could not bring herself to call him Father, or Dad, or whatever. She hated him, and what's more, she just knew that he was the reason she'd ended up in here.

Lying in bed these past days she'd thought it through again and again. He was the only person with a reason to want her hurt.

An' even if it wasn't him, it's still time the bastard answered a few questions. He owes me that much, at least.

A small red-headed nurse came in to change her dressings. Kerry bided her time and when the nurse had finished and left the room, she put on her clothes. It was an effort given her injured shoulder, but she bit down on her lip each time the pain hit her, determination driving her on.

She found enough loose change in her jacket pocket to take the bus to South Shields; if necessary, she would walk home.

At the desk the nurse kicked up a fuss but Kerry

had made her mind up. After wasting another five minutes arguing the pros and cons, she had her sign some forms, and Kerry was on her way.

An hour later she was stepping off the bus. She retraced the journey she had made over a week ago, caution, together with pain from her arm, making it a good deal slower than it had been then. Finally she stood outside the gates looking up at the stone unicorns.

'Yeah, very impressive,' she muttered as, shrugging, she tried the gates. They were locked. There was a three-foot wall topped with a metal fence, the kind with thick bars spaced four inches apart. A doddle for someone as fit as Kerry, even with an arm in a sling.

It took her all of five seconds and feeling only slightly nervous, although she didn't show it, she walked up the main path expecting at any moment to be stopped. Reaching the main doors without seeing anybody, she knocked four times at one minute intervals. No one came.

Kerry looked around, then tried the handle. It turned easily.

She hesitated, wondering what to do, then thought, *What the hell*.

Opening the door wide, she entered, calling out 'Hello' to anybody there to hear her. She fancied she heard an echo and shouted again, but no one replied.

She walked down the hallway passing three open doors, and looked in each of them after politely knocking, but they were empty. She thought she smelled cigar smoke in the last one, but couldn't be quite sure whether it was fresh, or whether the room was the only one used for smoking in.

Really, this is one creepy house.

Reaching the end of the hallway, she turned left towards the pool house. Maybe they were having a morning swim. She felt excited for a moment at the prospect of seeing Mark, then firmly put thoughts of him out of her mind.

No way.

She had to forget about that kind of thing now. She was here for one reason only, and Mark was not it. She didn't blame him for his father – for *their* father – but she was still having a hard time adjusting to thinking about the boy she'd fancied as her brother.

As she turned into the panelled corridor she thought she heard a muffled banging noise coming from the room where she'd heard the angry voice the last time she'd been here.

Scarcely aware that she was tip-toeing, she moved along until she was outside the door. She put her ear to the smooth wood.

Nothing.

Shrugging, she turned back in the direction of the pool room. She'd gone three steps when she heard the noise again. With a puzzled expression on her face, she walked back to the door and knocked. Almost at once the muffled banging started up again.

Slowly she opened the door, but stepped back immediately at the sight of a huge lion's head snarling at her from the wall. Her eyes moved round the room taking in animal after animal.

Shaking her head in disgust she stepped right into the room. In here the banging was much louder. She traced it to the far wall, and as she crossed the room, felt as if all the dead animals were staring accusingly at her.

She reached the wall and knocked loudly, and was rewarded with an instant reply. Putting an ear to the panelling she was about to knock again when a familiar voice cried out for help.

'Mark?' Kerry was astonished.

'Kerry, is that you? Let me out, Kerry. Quickly, please let me out.'

Kerry looked around the wall. 'There's no handle. What yer doing in there?'

'Please, Kerry, you have to get me out of here! There's a door behind the bookcase; it's some kind of hidden switch.'

Kerry pulled a face. 'I knew the place was creepy the first time I set eyes on the dump,' she muttered, as she started pressing sections of the wall.

'Who locked yer in there?' Mark didn't answer, but Kerry knew already. It was his dad. It was *their* dad. The thought made her grind her teeth together.

'Please hurry!' The urgency in his voice spurred Kerry on, but nothing was happening.

'Are yer sure the switch is on the wall?'

Silence for a moment, then Mark, whose voice, although muffled, was starting to sound frantic, said, 'Try the desk. Look for anything that resembles a button or whatever.'

Kerry searched the top of the desk. Panic spreads quicker than a forest fire and as she pushed papers

476

around scattering most of them on to the floor, she could hear her own heart pounding. There was no bastard button – what was she meant to do to get him out of there?

Desperately she tried the handles on the drawers then, just as panic threatened to overtake her, the third one down did it. With a slight hum the bookcase swung open.

She could see it was pitch black down there and turned on the desk lamp, angling its head towards the doorway, but as she did so Mark let out an unearthly scream. Wondering what was wrong, she made to go through the opening but Mark shouted, 'Don't come in, Kerry, stay outside, for God's sake!'

He stumbled through the doorway, holding his arms out to stop her going down the steps.

'Yes, Kerry, Mark's right. You do not want to be going in there.'

Kerry froze at the sound of the deep voice behind her and she felt a horrible tingle at the base of her spine. She spun round knowing, even though she had never heard his voice properly, just who it would be.

Richard Kingston stood in the study doorway, a cruel smile playing on his thin lips.

Lorraine was sitting at her desk, steadily working her way through the record of Kingston's telephone calls for the last six months, which she'd forced a weary Clark to allow her to have seized. She was bored out of her skull, and desperately tired. Last night she'd followed Kingston for hours but nothing had come of it. In fact, she was certain the bastard knew she was there and, after leaving the Lumsdons' street, had driven up and down the county half the night just to spite her.

She was also more than peeved with Mrs Archer, who was still refusing to say anything. Luke and Carter were with the damned woman now, but Lorraine didn't rate their chances very high. Mrs Archer's driver, the man who'd gone through the windscreen, had died at three o'clock this morning, so whatever he knew was well and truly lost.

The selfish bastard could have hung on a bit longer.

She chewed on a pencil, her mind wandering from Mrs Archer to Kerry Lumsdon to Richard Kingston, and then back again.

She sighed heavily, before muttering, 'Damn the whole bloody thing.' Throwing the sheet she'd been looking at down on the table, she wearily picked the next one up. As she scanned down the page, something caught at her subconscious. She looked again, more carefully this time. Wasn't that number familiar? Wasn't it . . . she cross-checked, holding her breath. If she was right . . . Yes. Halfway down was a call from the Blue Lion to Kingston. And they'd stayed on the line for a good half hour.

'Yes!' She made a fist. 'Got yer, yer bastard!'

Quickly she was off her chair and hurtling down the corridor. She banged open the interview-room door. 'Get yer coat on, Luke. We've got the bastard.'

Mrs Archer's nostrils flared as if she could smell Richard Kingston from here. Slowly she turned her head and looked at Lorraine. Lorraine met her gaze with one just as steely, and it was Mrs Archer who looked away first.

Kerry gathered all her courage. Shoulders back, and head high, she faced her father. She could see Mark in him, but very little of herself, *thank Christ*.

So this is him?

She felt nothing.

No sudden rush of emotion like she'd always imagined. Just the same empty dad place that had always been there. And somehow, although the space was rightly his, Kerry knew that this man would never fill it.

He, on the other hand, must have felt something, since his eyes glittered briefly with a grudging admiration as he took in her stance.

'Dad!' Mark said shakily, blinded by the light he hadn't seen in over a week.

Kingston's eyes moved to his son.

'What did you . . . What did you do it for? How could you do something like that?' Competing emotions flickered across his face – fear, anger, betrayal, confusion – but Kingston just watched him coldly.

Kerry, not knowing of the horrors hidden in the underground room, and not realising just how dangerous Kingston was, thought Mark was talking about being locked up. 'It's cos the bastard's mad, Mark. Mad as a fucking hatter. He's nearly ruined all our lives.' She turned to Kingston. 'Yer turned me mam into a drunk, didn't yer? Just cos she wouldn't have nowt to do with yer. Yer nowt but a fucking dirty creep.'

'Kerry, no—' Mark reached out to stop her, desperate to prevent another explosion. Desperate to make sure he never again ended up in that grotesque room, but it was too late.

'Enough,' Kingston shouted, and with a chill Mark recognised the glitter in his eyes. 'You may be my daughter, but by God, girl, you've a foul mouth on you. You know nothing of what went on – do you hear me? Nothing.'

Mark looked aghast. 'Daughter?'

Kerry turned to Mark, and remembered how much he didn't know – how much of his father's life was a mystery to him. 'Yes, Mark, I'm his child. Just like you.'

'But . . . but we can't be. We can't be brother and sister!'

'We are. The woman I saw in that photo? It's my mother's cousin. Your mother. And when she died, your bastard father raped my mother.'

Mark took a step back, confusion blurring his vision, and Kerry turned back to Kingston.

'But rape doesn't give you the right to call me daughter. How dare yer! Yer haven't wanted to know me since I was born. Till yer started to hang around the track like a fucking creep. And I'll talk any fucking way I want, thank you very much. You haven't earned the right to say otherwise.'

Mark's face was as white as a baker's hand dipped in flour. 'Kerry, please, don't say anything else. You don't know what he's like, he's—'

He yelled out in pain as his father slapped him viciously across his face, bursting his lip. 'Shut the fuck up, boy. Just shut it.'

'Oh, yer useless bastard. Leave him alone!' yelled Kerry as she moved to comfort Mark, but Kingston stepped in her way. Towering over her, he said, 'He is my son and he will do as I say. And do you know what, *Daughter*? So will you.'

'I fucking will not. You're fucking insane. I mean,' she risked a guess, 'you fucking shot me!'

Suddenly Kingston's tone changed, and he laughed. 'Don't be ridiculous, Kerry, of course I didn't shoot you.'

'You fucking bastard. I know you did. You—'

'I didn't shoot you,' he repeated firmly. 'I don't dirty my hands with that sort of shit.' He smiled. 'But I did have you shot. And I was there of course – wouldn't have missed your big race for the world.'

Kerry stared at him, mouth open. She'd known deep down he'd been behind her shooting, but had never guessed he'd admit to it. 'Right,' she said, trying to pull herself together despite the shock. 'Me an' Mark are getting out of here an' we never want to see you again.'

'You're not leaving,' he replied, his tone cold again.

'Fuck you,' was her only answer, but it seemed to push him over the edge.

'Shut up!' he shouted in her face, spittle flying all over her hair.

'Oh, you—' But that was as far as she got. Kingston slapped Kerry every bit as hard as he'd slapped Mark. The blow knocked her backwards and she dropped heavily to the floor, striking her head against the chair as she fell.

Momentarily stunned, Kerry could do nothing as he grabbed hold of her neck. With his other hand he grabbed Mark, then wrestled them both towards the still-open door to the underground room. Handicapped by her shoulder and bleeding from the mouth, Kerry struggled for all she was worth, but she was feeling dazed now. Muddled. The pain in her head was confusing her. Kingston was winning and she knew she didn't stand a chance.

'You little bitch, I'll teach you!' Kingston shouted. 'Do you think for a moment you're a match for me?'

And in that moment Kerry felt herself begin to give up. She'd fought so hard to find Claire, she'd fought so hard to keep her family together, but she didn't know if she had the strength to fight any longer. She was so exhausted. She was in such pain. Kingston was so much bigger and stronger than her. Maybe the only thing left was just to give in and—

'Stop right there.' Suddenly, from behind them, came a voice Kerry knew and had prayed for.

'About time an' all, Robo Cop,' she murmured past her sore lips, more pleased to hear the older woman's voice than she could quite believe.

'Let go of her now,' Lorraine said, as Luke circled the room.

'I have every right to chastise my children. And how I do it has nothing to do with you.' His hands tightened on both of their necks.

Lorraine knew instinctively that the man in front of her was capable of anything, including snapping both Mark's and Kerry's necks. Her gut feeling was that he had to be taken out, and fast.

Luke was behind Kingston now and as he glanced down the stairwell into the hidden room he gasped loudly. Lorraine had no idea what he'd seen, but she did know that throughout all the time they had worked together, she'd never seen such a look of pure horror on his face.

When he moved, he was fast and he was brutal. Grabbing hold of the doorframe with both hands to support himself, Luke kicked Kingston hard in the back. The older man fell to his knees, but still kept his grip on Kerry and Mark. Kerry started to cough and Kingston shook her.

'Fuck off,' Kerry managed to say, though Lorraine could see the effort it took to defy the man squeezing her neck.

Luke moved his foot back to kick again, and Lorraine matched his timing, launching a roundhouse kick to his jaw which landed just as Luke's foot again struck his back. Kingston screamed once then, eyes bulging, his head fell forward and he crumpled to the floor.

Kerry and Mark managed to roll free from under him, and Mark crawled immediately to the corner where he alternately vomited and sobbed. Rubbing her neck, Kerry stood up and watched Luke handcuff the unconscious Kingston. Lorraine made a move to put her arm round her, but she shrugged it off and went over to Mark.

As she turned round, she saw Lorraine make her way to the doorway. There was still just enough light from the lamp to make out the contents of the room below. When Kerry saw her father's handiwork her scream was neverending: six heads sat on high shelves grinning out at her.

Epilogue

Epilogue

Lorraine finished typing her report for Clark. She laid it to one side then, rising from her chair, went to look out the window.

Court was in session and the usual crowd of misfits mingled around outside. She fancied she could smell the smoke coming from their endless cigarettes. Mrs Archer was up this morning, with not a chance of bail before it went to Crown Court, but Lorraine wouldn't relax until she was locked away under the harshest sentence possible. When you looked back at what she'd done – her varied career as a hired assassin, head of a protection racket, a drug dealer intent on seducing younger and younger children with her lethal cartoon character pills – nothing the judge could inflict on her was too severe.

And as for Kingston . . . she still couldn't believe he'd had his own daughter shot, just because of the friendship that had started to blossom when she met Mark, but Kingston wasn't a man she wanted to understand. Psychotic bastard. Lorraine felt herself tense with a freezing anger as she thought back to his hearing. Having escaped Colin Stone and the whole North East police force for two decades, he'd evaded justice again, declared insane and not fit to stand. That's what a fortune spent on lawyers did for you. *Although at least the bastard's locked up where he can't do any more harm.* A wry smile flickered across Lorraine's face: she rather suspected that Kingston had no idea how horrific the institution he'd been sent to would turn out to be. She'd lay money on seeing him back in court in a few years, desperate for a good old-fashioned prison.

She'd almost been surprised to see Kerry and Mark at the hearing, but not quite. They were both tough kids, and after what they'd been through she could understand why they had to see it through to the end. She'd picked up on the attraction between them from something Robbie had accidentally let slip, but seeing them in court had reassured her that things had settled down. Mark, suddenly all alone in the world except for the Scottish aunt he'd been packed off to live with, could do with a sister; and Lorraine suspected that, coming from as big a family as she did, Kerry might enjoy having a brother who belonged to her alone. As they stood side by side, watching the father who tried to kill them put in the fucking performance of a lifetime, they'd looked remarkably self-possessed. Dignified, almost. Survivors, those two. They'd be OK.

As for the rest of the Lumsdons, they seemed good. Vanessa was doing well, staying off the bottle, and was faithfully attending AA meetings. Claire and Kerry had both been marked by everything they'd gone through – apparently Claire still woke up screaming at night, but she was learning to deal with it, and just last week Lorraine had finally seen in her eyes the naughty, excited young girl who'd skived off school all those weeks ago to meet her new boyfriend. She'd be OK too.

And the others? Jade and the other Newcastle girls were all now fit and well; Scottie had been given custody of the heads and had already matched three of them, and things were returning to normal. Whatever that meant.

Lorraine couldn't help but smile as she watched Ada Johnston go up the court steps, back on yet another shoplifting charge. But it faded fast as she saw Luke's car pulling up outside.

One thorn left.

How the hell can I go on working so close to him?

Was it love?

Lorraine made a decision.

If it was love, then love could just go and do a running jump, she'd had enough of it to last her a lifetime. Perhaps her hormone levels were simply scrambled because of all the stress of the last few weeks. Whatever, the whole business was starting to become damn ludicrous; she kept finding herself thinking of him when she ought to have her mind on her work.

She sighed, chewing the end of a pencil.

She was back thinking of Mark when the idea came. Simple. The Strathclyde police were looking for an exchange – some poncey new government policy to do with sharing ideas and investigative techniques – and now she had her candidate. She would arrange an exchange and send Luke to Scotland.

Over the border, he would be out of her hair. She could get on with her life.

Lorraine nodded to herself as the smile returned. Case closed.

Coming soon, Sheila Quigley's
next thrilling bestseller

BAD MOON RISING

A young woman walks home by herself, the tapping of her high heels the only sound. At two o'clock in the morning, it's cold, the streets are deserted, and she thinks she's all alone. Waiting for her, sleeping soundly in his bed, is her baby son. When he wakes the next morning his mother still isn't back. She's never coming back. Because the streets weren't as deserted as she'd thought.

Three women are dead, and Detective Inspector Lorraine Hunt is searching for a serial killer. In Houghton-le-Spring it's Feast week, a time when all hell is let loose as the fair comes to town, and a frenzy of celebration and decadence provides a temporary distraction from the grim realities of everyday life. It's not a good time to be searching for a stranger. It's not a good time to be a woman alone . . .

Read on for an exclusive extract . . .

Prologue

The little boy watches the other children playing. They are in the park and it is a bright sunny day with only the faintest hint of a far-off cloud. Mother said earlier that it might, or might not, rain by teatime and he puzzles over what this contradiction really means.

He longs to join in the game the others are playing: Mother is talking to another lady about things he doesn't understand and it is really dull. Every now and again they laugh and Mother's face goes a funny red colour and then she glances at him, frowns, and shoos him away. 'Go and play, now. This isn't for your ears. Go and play.'

He doesn't know what isn't for his ears, only that it has something to do with that thing called sex. He doesn't know what sex is either, only that it makes Mother go red and funny and then she doesn't want him around. And he wants to play, he really does. Only they won't let him. The big girl called Jessie whose mam is talking to Mother called him a little freak and a mammy's boy. And then her brother Simon started calling him names too and made all the others join in.

And Mother won't listen.

He sidles up to her, his arm resting on her knee. Jessie and Simon's mam, who has the same skinny lips that her children have, stands up and calls to her children before saying goodbye to Mother and walking away. Jessie pulls a face at him behind her mam's back and he quickly looks at Mother's face, but she is looking away.

Then Mother takes hold of his hand and he feels happy until she starts speaking in that cross voice she sometimes has.

'Really,' she says, tugging hard on the hand she holds and hurting him, 'you've got to start mixing with the other children.'

'But Mother –'

'What did I tell you? You're to call me mam, like the other kids do, at least when we're out.'

'Mm – mam. Sorry, mam.'

She relents then, as she always does, and bends down to cuddle him to her chest. He is truly content then: he doesn't really want the other kids with their silly games, he never has. He just wants Mother. Or mam.

Smiling, he puts his free hand in his pocket and rubs the red button which fell off Mother's cardigan between his finger and thumb. The button will go in his box with all the other things. He already has a special place for it. Yes, it will look nice next to the piece of black hair he picked up from the floor when Mother had her hair cut by Jessie's mam.

1

The girl's long dark ponytail swishes from side to side as she struts along the Broadway. Her white high heels make a loud tapping noise in the deserted street, scattering the tiny night creatures that infest every human habitation.

Scantily clad, in a short red top and even shorter black skirt, she shivers as she crosses the road and heads towards St Michael and All Angels church. The church has towered over Houghton-le-Spring since the thirteenth century, but there is evidence of an even earlier church on the site. On a moonless night like tonight it harbours many dark corners.

It's two o'clock in the morning. It's early October and winter's chill has arrived with a vengeance. There's frost on the ground but something special in the air because Houghton Feast is just a week away, and for many the celebrations have started early.

The girl stumbles slightly, having left the night club with more than one vodka under her belt, but she rights herself, and starts to walk a bit faster. She'd had two or three offers of an escort from the local studs but had announced to all her intention of going home alone. Proclaiming loudly that she'd had enough of men. *Bastards, the fucking lot of them.*

She loves Houghton Feast though. As her nan tells her every year, it's been celebrated in Houghton since the middle ages, and was established as a feast of dedication to the church. By custom it takes place on the nearest Friday to October tenth, when the lights are switched on by the Mayor of Sunderland and the locals are treated to a Tattoo, complete with bagpipes, after which the fairground opens. On the Monday, after a weekend of celebrations, a huge ox is roasted in the rectory field which lies between the rectory and the police station.

But there's more to it than that: the feast, the Tattoo and the fair may be the official story but everyone knows Feast time is a chance to let go, to go wild, to let off steam. It's like a get-out-of-jail-free card letting you off the hook for things you've wanted to do but not dared all year round. For most of this week and at the oddest hours imaginable, the fairground travellers have been pulling onto the field and the excitement is building. She can almost taste it.

Feeling a sudden cold breeze she rubs her bare arms, but the vodka is a good insulator and will keep her warm enough, for the moment. She heads for the almshouses that lie directly behind the church just as a huge truck with rearing wild-eyed carousel horses painted on the side hurtles through the Broadway. A minute earlier and the driver would have hit her. The horses would have ended up on their heads with blood on their hooves. Shivering, she walks faster still.

To the right of the almshouses, the stone steps will

lead her to the bridge over the dual carriageway, then on up to Hall Lane where she lives with her two-year-old son Dillon. Dillon will be fast asleep – just as well, because the babysitter is probably stoned out of her mind. She grumbles to herself about the fiver she'll have to hand over for having Dillon minded, especially since she hates that cheeky twat Simone.

Fancy fucking name for a cheap tart. But she'd been the only one available on short notice and after five days and nights cooped up with Dillon, she'd been desperate to get out.

Winter nips at her exposed shoulders, breathing down the nape of her neck, and she wraps her arms around her body. The cold air should be sobering her up but instead it seems to have the opposite effect and in a fit of vodka-fuelled animation she starts to sing, her voice – poor even when she's sober – sounding remarkably like that of the black cat which streaks across the path behind her.

The cat is not the only warm-blooded body behind her tonight, but she hears nothing above her wailing and the rhythmic tap of her shoes. When the fingers creep round her throat, she's still singing . . . but only for a moment.

Too late, realisation pierces the alcoholic fog. The hard rough fingers tighten their grip, digging with relentless cruelty into the soft delicate flesh.

She's struggling now. Fighting for her life.

The heel of her left shoe snaps, her ankle turns but her brain, struggling for oxygen, does not register the pain.

The cat sits on the fallen gravestone of some

eighteenth-century industrialist beside the path, watching with the disinterested air cats save for humans, as she grows weaker and weaker and slides quietly to the ground, his hands still at her throat in a deadly embrace.

She manages one quiet, pathetic little cry into the dark as the cat, unconcerned, turns tail to hunt the mice foraging for food in the almshouses' bin.

So easy she slips into death, and how peaceful she looks. The last thing she sees in her mind's eye is the smiling face of her infant son.

Déjà Dead

Kathy Reichs

The Number One Bestseller

The bones of a woman are discovered in the grounds of an abandoned monastery. The case is given to Dr Temperance Brennan of the Laboratoire de Médecine Légale in Montreal: 'too decomposed for standard autopsy. Request anthropological expertise. My case.' Brennan becomes convinced that a serial killer is at work, despite the deep cynicism of Detective Claudel who heads the investigation. Dr Brennan's forensic expertise and contacts at Quantico finally convince him otherwise, but only after the body count has grown and the lives of those closest to her are more than just endangered.

'Better than Patricia Cornwell'
Express on Sunday

'A guaranteed sleep-deterrent. Genuinely thrilling'
Literary Review

arrow books

Grave Secrets

Kathy Reichs

The bones of a child no more than two years old are uncovered when mass graves are excavated.

Twenty-three women and children are said to lie where forensic anthropologist Dr Temperance Brennan is searching for remains, in what is one of the most heartbreaking cases of her career.

And when a skeleton is found in a septic tank at the back of a run down hotel, only someone with Tempe's expertise can deduce who the victim was and how they died.

But her path is blocked: it appears that some people would prefer that Guatemala's 'disappeared' stayed buried. And others seem to want the missing girls kept the same way . . .

'Reichs has proved that she is now up there with the best'
The Times

'A chilling, atmospheric thriller'
Sunday Express

arrow books

ALSO AVAILABLE IN ARROW

Blindsighted

Karin Slaughter

The sleepy town of Heartsdale, Georgia, is jolted into panic when Sara Linton, paediatrician and medical examiner, finds Sibyl Adams dead in the local diner. As well as being viciously raped, Sibyl has been cut: two deep knife wounds form a lethal cross over her stomach. But it's only once Sara starts to perform the post-mortem that the full extent of the killer's brutality becomes clear.

Police chief Jeffrey Tolliver – Sara's ex-husband – is in charge of the investigation, and when a second victim is found, cruci-fied, only a few days later, both Jeffrey and Sara have to face the fact that Sibyl's murder wasn't a one-off attack. What they're dealing with is a seasoned sexual predator. A violent serial killer . . .

'Don't read this alone. Don't read this after dark.
But do read it.'
Daily Mirror

'Unsparing, exciting, genuinely alarming . . . a formidable debut'
Literary Review

arrow books

A Faint Cold Fear

Karin Slaughter

Sara Linton, medical examiner in the small town of Heartsdale, is called out to an apparent suicide on the local college campus. The mutilated body provides little in the way of clues – and the college authorities are keen to avoid a scandal – but for Sara and police chief Jeffrey Tolliver, things don't add up.

Two more suspicious suicides follow, and a young woman is brutally attacked. For Sara, the violence strikes far too close to home. And as Jeffrey pursues the sadistic killer, he discovers that ex-police detective Lena Adams, now a security guard on campus, may be in possession of crucial information. But, bruised and angered by her expulsion from the force, Lena seems to be barely capable of protecting herself, let alone saving the next victim . . .

'A great read . . . crime fiction at its finest'
Michael Connelly

'Fast-paced and unsettling . . . A compelling and fluid read'
Daily Telegraph

arrow books

Order further Arrow titles
from your local bookshop, or have them delivered direct to your door by Bookpost

☐ **Déjà Dead** Kathy Reichs	0099255189	£6.99
☐ **Grave Secrets** Kathy Reichs	0099307308	£6.99
☐ **Blindsighted** Karin Slaughter	0099421771	£6.99
☐ **A Faint Cold Fear** Karin Slaughter	0099445328	£6.99

Free post and packing
Overseas customers allow £2 per paperback

Phone: 01624 677237

Post: Random House Books
c/o Bookpost, PO Box 29, Douglas, Isle of Man IM99 1BQ

Fax: 01624 670923

email: bookshop@enterprise.net

Cheques (payable to Bookpost) and credit cards accepted

Prices and availability subject to change without notice.
Allow 28 days for delivery.
When placing your order, please state if you do not wish to receive
any additional information.

www.randomhouse.co.uk/arrowbooks

arrow books